Billionaires Galore!

LEANNE BANKS

First published in Great Britain 2013
by Mills & Boon, an imprint of Harlequin (UK) Limited,
Eton House, 18-24 Paradise Road, Richmond, Surrey TW9 1SR

BILLIONAIRES GALORE! © by Harlequin Enterprises II B.V./S.à.r.l 2013

Bedded by the Billionaire, *Billionaire's Marriage Bargain* and *Billionaire Extraordinaire* were published in Great Britain by Harlequin (UK) Limited.

Bedded by the Billionaire © Leanne Banks 2008
Billionaire's Marriage Bargain © Leanne Banks 2008
Billionaire Extraordinaire © Leanne Banks 2009

ISBN: 978 0 263 90552 6
ebook ISBN: 978 1 472 00125 2

05-0513

Harlequin (UK) policy is to use papers that are natural, renewable and recyclable products and made from wood grown in sustainable forests. The logging and manufacturing processes conform to the legal environmental regulations of the country of origin.

Printed and bound in Spain
by Blackprint CPI, Barcelona

Leanne Banks is a *New York Times* and *USA TODAY* bestselling author who is surprised every time she realizes how many books she has written. Leanne loves chocolate, the beach and new adventures. To name a few, Leanne has ridden on an elephant, stood on an ostrich egg (no, it didn't break), gone parasailing and indoor skydiving. Leanne loves writing romance because she believes in the power and magic of love. She lives in Virginia with her family and her four-and-a-half-pound Pomeranian named Bijou.

Special thanks to Cindy Gerard, Rhonda Pollero and all my wonderful, supportive writing friends and the great Melissa Jeglinski, who continues to make my work better! This book is dedicated to the comeback kid in all of us.

One

"I understand you're pregnant with my brother's child."

Lilli McCall instinctively put her hand over her swollen belly and studied Maximillian De Luca. She'd reluctantly allowed him and his associate into her small suburban Las Vegas apartment. Heaven knew, she'd had several unwelcome visitors since Tony De Luca had died two weeks ago.

She'd spotted the family resemblance between Tony and Max through the peephole of her door—the natural tanned complexion, similar bone structure. Only this man wasn't as pretty as Tony. Tony had been full of easy smiles and charm, and ultimately lies. This man's face was so hard she wondered if it would break into pieces if he smiled.

Tony had told her about his brother, Max. He'd frequently complained that his brother was cutthroat, even with his own family. He'd called him the man of steel, a steel mind and a steel heart.

Lilli had detached herself from Tony for good reasons. She wanted nothing to do with him, his friends or his family.

"Miss McCall?" Max prompted.

Taking a quick breath, she gave a slow nod, willing herself not to be intimidated by the tall man. "Yes, we got involved after my mother died, but things didn't work out between us," she said in a voice she knew was stilted, but she couldn't smooth it for the life of her.

"The details aren't necessary. As you know, my brother died in an automobile accident. He had no will and no provision for children, so—"

"I didn't expect anything from him," she interjected.

He paused, his gaze flickering over her in a considering way again. "Really," he said in a doubtful voice.

His tone jabbed at her. "Really," she said. "Tony was kind to me after my mother died, but it became clear to me that I didn't belong in his world."

"Why is that?"

"I—" She hesitated, her chest tightening as she remembered the fateful night that had made her break up with him for good. "We had different values. I wanted the baby brought up in a different environment."

His gaze fell to her pregnant belly. "You came to that decision a little late, didn't you?"

In more ways than he could know, she thought. "Yes, but I can focus on the baby or on my failures. Focusing on my failures isn't going to help me. So," she said, more than ready for him to leave, "since I wasn't expecting anything from Tony, you don't need to—"

"That's where we disagree," he said and nodded toward the man standing behind him. "Jim, could you give me the paperwork? Lilli, this is Jim Gregory. You may recognize him as someone who has knocked on your door a few times recently."

Lilli tore her gaze away from Max long enough to look at the older man and recognized him. "I apologize," she said. "I live by myself, so I'm not really comfortable opening the door to men I don't know."

"I understand," Jim said and she thought she saw a hint of compassion in the older man's eyes. "Here it is, Max," he said, producing some papers from a manila envelope, along with a pen.

Max took the papers and pen and handed them to Lilli. "It's a simple document. In exchange for one million dollars now and another million dollars if and when the child reaches the age of twenty-five, you agree to give up any rights to my brother's inheritance. If you should die or fail to raise the child in a responsible manner, you agree to relinquish custody of the child to a suitable guardian of my choice."

Lilli felt her jaw drop to the floor.

"It's all there," Max said. "Let me know if you have any questions."

Lilli stared blankly at the paper and felt her hands begin to shake with anger. Shoving the papers back at him, she stepped backward. "Are you nuts?"

"Should have known," Max said to Jim. "I told you she would want more money."

Stunned, Lilli continued to stare at him. "So you *are*

nuts," she said. "You didn't hear me earlier, did you? I didn't expect anything from Tony. I don't now. And I certainly don't expect anything from you. And if you think for one second that I would let someone I've never met choose who raises my child, you're totally crazy."

"That clause is just to protect the child in the event of your death or in case you develop any dangerous habits." He placed the agreement on top of her mother's marble-top table. "Read it. Sleep on it. I'll negotiate the amount within reason."

She snatched it up to give it back to him again.

He shook his head and held up his hand. "The drama is unnecessary. It costs a lot to raise a child. It will be difficult since you're doing it alone. Think about your child's needs. Do you really want to give up everything this money can buy for your child?" He paused while her heart pounded in her chest five beats. "I'll be in touch."

As soon as the two men left her apartment, Lilli flipped the dead bolt in place. Incensed and insulted, she paced into the den. Her pulse was racing in her ears, her nails digging into her palms as she clenched her hands together. Who in hell did he think he was, coming into her home and talking to her that way?

Granted, there were a few things that didn't put her in the best light, such as the fact that she'd even gotten involved with Tony in the first place, and the fact that she was unwed and pregnant. But everyone made mistakes. The solution was owning up to them and making the best of whatever choices have been made.

Although she hadn't intended to get pregnant by Tony, Lilli was determined to be the best mother she could be. Even with all the uncertainty and responsibility she was facing, from the moment she'd learned she was carrying a life inside her, she'd felt a little less lonely.

Lilli walked into the nursery she had begun to decorate and took a deep calming breath. She'd given the walls a fresh coat of paint and hung a puffy Noah's Ark wall hanging with removable animals. The crib was solid maple, and she'd already attached a mobile with friendly colorful butterflies and birds. With her next paycheck, she planned to buy soft crib sheets and blankets in blue for her little guy.

Pressing her hand to her belly again, she thought of Max De Luca. She'd never met a man like him. Arrogant, insulting, charm-free. At least to her. She couldn't deny, though, that in different circumstances he would have fascinated her. But lions had always fascinated her, too, and she knew better than to get into a den with one of them.

"That went well," Jim said in a wry voice as Max led the way to the black Ferrari.

Loosening his tie a fraction of an inch, Max unlocked the car and slid behind the steering wheel. Max preferred being in the driver's seat. It gave him the illusion of control. He slid into the leather seat. "Damn Tony for this," he said, even though his grief was still fresh. "He was going to be a father, for God's sake. You would think he could have at least provided for his child."

"You've been cleaning up his messes a long time," Jim said as Max sped out of the apartment complex. "Just curious. Did you have to be a total ass to her?"

Max had known Jim since he was a child and that was the only reason he allowed the older man to talk to him so bluntly. "She surprised me," he said, shifting into fourth as he turned onto the interstate. "I was expecting one of those showgirls he went through like cheap wine."

"I told you she's a pediatric dental hygienist."

"I figured that was her day job. She had to have another angle." He shook his head. "She looked almost wholesome. I mean, aside from the bump, she had a nice body as far as I could tell. Did you notice she was wearing bunny slippers?"

Jim laughed. "Hard to miss them."

"She wasn't wearing a speck of makeup. Her hair color didn't look like it came out of a bottle. She looked soft," he said, still trying to come to grips with his impression of Lilli McCall. "Real. Not Tony's type at all."

"She must have been his type for a while."

Max felt his chest tighten in a strange way. How had Tony lucked into her? A woman like that shouldn't have been abandoned. Not if his first instincts about her were correct. "Yeah. He got lucky."

Lilli was that irresistible combination of soft and sexy that every man craved. It was all too easy to wonder how that mouth of hers would feel all over a man's body.

He felt himself grow warm at the thought and shook his head. He'd never been attracted to one of his brother's women. Turning the AC on high, he directed the vent at his face.

"I really ticked her off with my offer," he said, his lips twitching in amusement. She'd looked as if she would have gladly ripped out his vocal cords. He'd found her reaction surprising and oddly attractive.

That didn't change the fact that everyone had their

price. Even a blond woman with pink cheeks, bee-stung lips and blue eyes that lit up like sparklers when she was angry. "She'll take the money," he said to Jim, shifting gear. "They all eventually do."

Max would clean up this mess. He had a lot of practice. Left to deal with his father's disastrous personal and financial choices, Max had worked nonstop during the past ten years to rebuild the family name and wealth.

His investments had delivered triple returns. The merger of Megalos Resorts with De Luca Inc. to form Megalos-De Luca Enterprises had sent the shares of his stock in the company skyrocketing. Determined to keep talent in the merged company, the new board paid the top performers eight-figure salaries.

Max's father may have been kicked off the board of the family company, but Max was determined that the next CEO would be a De Luca. Nothing would stop him. Especially not a feisty little blonde who happened to be carrying a De Luca baby in her belly.

The following evening, as she left the dental practice where she worked, Lilli winced as she flexed her fingers. Three-year-old Timmy Johnson just couldn't resist chewing on her index finger. Although she wore rubber gloves, they didn't always protect her from a chewing child.

She worked late three nights a week for two reasons. One, she earned a little more money working after five and two, she didn't really have anything else to do in the evenings. It wasn't as if she were a party animal. She'd left that brief period of her life way in the past.

Pulling her keys from her purse, she walked toward

her trusty four-year-old blue Toyota Corolla. Just as she neared her car, two men stepped in front of her. They both appeared to be in their twenties and they looked so much alike they could have been brothers.

"Lilli McCall?" one of them said.

The one man looked vaguely familiar, although she couldn't recall his name. One of Tony's friends? She tensed. "Why do you ask?" She backed away.

Both men took a step toward her. "We're hoping you can help us."

She bit her lip and took another step back. "I—uh." She cleared her throat. "How could I possibly help you?"

"We're here about Tony," one of the men said with a shrug. "He left some unpaid debts. We knew you two were close and we were hoping you could help us."

She shook her head. "I broke up with Tony a long time ago."

"Not before he knocked you up," the other guy cracked. "That baby's gotta be worth something to the De Luca family. Tony must have left you something."

"He didn't," she said, even though her throat was squeezing tight with fear. "Look at my car. It's four years old. I'm working as a dental hygienist. Do I look like someone who is loaded?"

The men frowned.

"Maybe you're hiding it."

Frustrated and afraid, she shook her head. "I'm not. Just leave me alone."

"It would be a lot easier to leave you alone if we got our money." One of the men pulled a card out of his pocket and walked toward her.

She wanted to run, but her feet seemed to grow roots into the pavement. The man pressed his card into her hand. "Call me if you find something. We'll check back in case you forget."

Her heart racing, she watched the two men leave and felt sick to her stomach. How much longer would they harass her? And how many more of Tony's so-called business acquaintances were going to show up at her door?

Taking a deep breath, she walked quickly to her car and got inside. Maybe she should move out of town. That could be expensive, though, and she'd like to keep the few friends she'd made over the last couple of months. The idea of being surrounded by strangers after she had her baby unsettled her.

She mulled over a dozen different options as she drove through a fast-food restaurant and ordered a milk shake. After she got home, she sipped on it and changed into a tank top that covered her pregnant belly and a pair of terry cloth shorts. Then to drown out her disturbing thoughts, she turned on the television to watch a rerun of her favorite medical drama.

Five minutes later, her doorbell sounded. She sighed, hoping it was her best friend Dee, off early from her second job as an aerobics instructor. The doorbell rang again before she could reach it. She looked through the peephole, but her porch light wasn't on. She could only make out the shadow of a man.

Fed up, she pounded on her side of the door. "Go away! I don't have Tony's money. I—"

"Miss McCall," a male voice cut in.

Lilli immediately recognized that voice. Mr. Steel, she'd named him. She bit her lip.

"Lilli," Max De Luca said again. "Can I come in?"

She glanced down at her outfit. It was far from swimsuit bare, but she knew she'd feel more comfortable wearing something else. Armor would work. "I'm not really dressed for visitors."

"This won't take long," he insisted.

Swallowing a groan, she opened the door. "I don't think we have anything else to—"

Max walked past her. He was dressed in a black suit that probably cost more than her car. Meeting him again, she could see why Tony had resented his older brother. Max was taller, his shoulders were broader, and he oozed enough confidence for a dozen men. Lilli suspected he was the type who would command any situation no matter how he was dressed. Despite the hard edges of his face, there was something sensual about the shape of his mouth. His thick black eyelashes gave his dark eyes a sexual cast.

If he were inclined, she would bet he could reduce a woman to melted butter with just a look. There was nothing boyish about him. He was all man and he would want a woman as tough and confident as he, a raving beauty. Lilli knew she would never make the cut.

Max stared at her, his dark eyes flashing. "Why do you keep talking about my brother and his money?"

She met his hot, hard gaze. "Since Tony died, some of his business acquaintances have been asking me to pay off his loans."

He frowned. "You? Why you?" His expression turned cynical. "Were you involved in some of his business dealings?"

"Absolutely not. I told you I stopped seeing Tony

over six months ago because I realized we didn't share the same values." She remembered that terrible last night and closed her eyes, trying to push it from her mind. "We were only together for about four months."

"Long enough for you to get pregnant," he said.

Offended by his tone, she glared at him. "Just in case you weren't paying attention in your high school biology class, it doesn't take four months to get pregnant. It takes one time. One slip." She shook her head. "Listen, I didn't ask you to show up at my home, insult me, offer me a big check and threaten to take my baby away if you don't approve of how I'm raising him."

"Him," he said. "So it's a boy."

"Yes," she said and felt her baby move inside her. Cradling her belly, she watched as Max's gaze raked over her from head to toe. After lingering on her breasts and legs, his eyes moved back up to her mouth. The intensity in his eyes made her feel as if she'd stayed out in the sun too long.

He finally lifted his gaze to hers. "How many men have come asking for money?"

"Five or six," she said. "They usually come in pairs. I stopped answering if I don't recognize who's ringing the doorbell."

"So this has happened, what three, four times?"

She bit her lip. "More like seven or eight," she admitted. "And two men showed up in the parking lot of my office after work tonight."

He paused one moment then nodded. "You shouldn't stay here by yourself any longer. You can come and stay at my house. I have ten bedrooms with staff and security."

Stunned, she stared at him. "Whoa, that's kind of

fast. Don't you think they'll stop coming around when they realize I really don't have anything to give them?"

"But you do," Max said. "You have a De Luca growing in your belly. Did any of them give you contact information?"

"One of the guys tonight gave me his card."

"Please get it for me," he said in a voice that was so polite and so calm it made her uneasy.

"Okay," she said and went into her bedroom to retrieve the card from her purse. She gave it to Max.

"I'll have Jim find out about this guy by morning." Max looked at her intently. "You got involved with a De Luca. We're a powerful family and there are people who resent us. There are people who want to hurt us. If you really care about the safety of your baby, then you need to come home with me."

She immediately shook her head. "I just met you. Why in the world would I leave my apartment to go to your home?"

"Because you'll be safe there," he said, impatience threading his voice. "Do you really trust that door against someone determined to get inside?"

Her mouth went dry at the image of an intruder, but she refused to be intimidated. "You're deliberately trying to scare me."

"No, I'm not," he said. "I'm merely protecting you and my nephew."

His words rocked her. He seemed to take the responsibility for granted, where Tony had been just the opposite. She shook her head. Could two brothers be so different? "How do I know you're not like him?" she had to ask.

His eyebrow creased in displeasure. "Like who? Tony?" He gave a harsh laugh. "I'm nothing like my brother. Or my father, for that matter."

She wondered what that meant, but from his expression, she suspected there was a world of history in his statement. A world she wasn't sure she wanted to know. She felt his shimmering impatience, but she resisted the pressure. "The only thing I know about you is what Tony told me."

Max gave a slow nod. "And that was?"

She bit her lip, reluctant to repeat the insults. "I'm not sure it's a good idea for me to—"

"Okay, then let me guess. Tony said I was heartless and unforgiving, straitlaced, boring, power-hungry and greedy."

She winced at his accuracy. "I'm not sure he used those words. He did refer to you as a man with a steel heart and steel mind. And he said you were ruthless."

"Ruthless," he said with a nod. "That was the other word I forgot. Not that far off the mark. I can be ruthless and I guard my heart and mind. I'm not distracted and I won't be tricked or deceived. But tell me, if I were completely cold and ruthless, why would I give a damn about you and your baby's safety?"

Good point, she thought, but the man still made her nervous.

"What do your instincts tell you about me?" he demanded.

She bit her lip again, and felt a flash of disappointment in herself. "My instincts got a little off-kilter after my mother died. I'm not sure how much I can trust them."

His expression was enigmatic. "Then you have a choice to make. You can either trust your door to those thugs who have been showing up and who aren't going away. Or you can trust me."

Two

"Dee," Lilli said. "This situation is crazy."

Max paused just inside the open sliding-glass door that led out to the patio, and watched Lilli as she paced and talked on her cell phone. After just one night in his home, she looked rattled and nervous. He couldn't remember a time when he'd had to work so hard to get a woman to stay overnight at his place, and this one hadn't even slept in his bed.

"Oh, it has to be temporary," she said. "It has to be."

He turned to walk away.

"It's clear that I don't belong here and I'm sure Max De Luca would be thrilled if I could disappear from the earth."

He stopped at the mention of his name, curious despite himself. Turning around, he watched her wavy hair bounce against her shoulders and her silver hoop earrings reflect the late-afternoon sunlight. She was wearing shorts that revealed her long, shapely legs, and he noticed her toenails were painted a vibrant pink. A silver chain wrapped around her ankle. She was an odd mix of feminine and practical. He didn't know why, but he'd liked the combination of strength and vulnerability he'd witnessed in her last night. She'd been determined not to be a pushover, but she'd also revealed her regret over her involvement with Tony. Although Max could name a million reasons, he wondered what had made Lilli decide to break up with his brother.

"How would I describe Max? Tony always called him a man of steel, but he didn't mean it as a compliment." She laughed. "Yes, he's disgustingly good-looking and completely lacking in charm." She sighed. "Maybe I just bring that out in him. Anyway, I can't imagine staying here. I can't imagine a baby living here, spitting up on carpets that probably cost twice what my car does. And speaking of my car, you would get a good laugh at how ridiculous it looks in the garage next to a Ferrari."

Max felt a twitch of humor at her colorful descriptions. Crossing his arms over his chest, he decided to listen to the rest of the conversation. She was providing him with more amusement than he'd had in a while.

"His wife? I don't even know if he has one. This house is huge. Maybe she hides in a different wing. Or maybe he keeps her chained to his bed to take care of his every *need and pleasure,*" she said in an exaggerated voice. "Come to think of it, he's not wearing a ring and he doesn't really strike me as the kind to pin himself down to just one woman. Not that it's any of my business," she added. "I would move to the other side of the world except I hate the idea of going to a new place with a baby and not knowing anyone."

The honest desperation in her voice slid past his cynicism.

"I know I should be more brave about this. Maybe it's just hormones. And what happened when I was with Tony doesn't help."

Besides the obvious, what exactly had happened between Lilli and his brother? Max wondered, and he decided to make his presence known. Clearing his throat, he pushed the sliding-glass door farther open.

Giving a jerk of surprise, Lilli turned to look at him. "Uh, yeah I should go now. Dinner next Tuesday with the girls. I wouldn't miss it. Bye, Dee." She turned off the phone and lifted her chin defensively. "I, uh, didn't see you."

He nodded. "Was your room okay last night?"

"It's beautiful, of course," she said. "Your entire house is beautiful."

"The parts of it you've seen," he said, recalling what she'd said about his bedroom. He could practically see her mind whirling, wondering how much he'd heard. "It was too late for me to give you the complete tour last night. I should do that tonight."

"Oh, you don't have to—"

"I insist. The rumors about the dungeon are all false," he joked and watched her eyes widen. Swallowing a chuckle, he continued to meet her gaze. "And your bed? Did it work for you? Too soft? Too hard?" Last night the image of her in bed had bothered him. He'd wondered what kind of nightclothes she wore, if she ever slept naked.

"Oh, no. It was very nice, thank you." She cleared her throat. "I've been thinking about my living arrangements and—"

"So have I," he interjected. "If you're free for dinner, we can discuss it then."

She worked her mouth in surprise then shrugged. "I'm free."

"Okay, then we can eat on the terrace." He glanced at his watch. "Will you be hungry in an hour?"

"Sure," she said. "How do you dress for dinner?"

He allowed himself a leisurely gaze down her body. He wondered why she made something inside him itch. "Casual is fine. It will be just you and me."

Despite Max's insistence that dinner would be casual, Lilli changed from shorts into a periwinkle cotton baby-doll dress she hadn't worn in a while.

To bolster her confidence, she stepped into a pair of sandals with heels. She suspected she would need every bit of confidence she could muster when she told Max that she was returning to her apartment.

She walked downstairs through a hallway of marble and a living area that looked as if it had been taken out of a high-end decorator magazine. The sliding-glass door was open and Max stood, holding a glass of red wine, in front of a warming stove. With his back to her, she couldn't miss the V-shape of his broad shoulders and his narrow waist.

She felt a strange dip in her stomach at the sight of him and grabbed an extra breath. He must have heard her because he turned to face her. He was dressed in slacks and a white open-neck shirt that contrasted with his tanned skin. Moving beside a small table already set with plates and platters with sterling covers, he pulled out a chair for her.

"The chef prepared orange juice and seltzer for you. Is that okay?"

"Very nice," she said, surprised he'd known about the no-alcohol-during-pregnancy rule because he didn't seem to have any children of his own.

"My chef has prepared one of his specialties. He's excellent, so you should enjoy it."

A woman dressed in a uniform appeared from the sliding-glass doors. "May I serve you now, Mr. De Luca?" she asked.

"Yes, thank you, Ada," he said. "Lilli, this is my assistant housekeeper. She assists my chief housekeeper, Myrtle. Ada usually covers the 6:00 p.m. to 6:00 a.m. shift, so if you need anything after hours, feel free to ring her."

He had an assistant housekeeper? Lilli took another gulp of her drink, feeling more out of place than ever. "It's nice to meet you, Ada."

"My pleasure," Ada said with a smile and proceeded to serve the meal.

As soon as Ada left, Max turned to her and lifted his glass. "To a good meal and a meeting of the minds."

His gaze dipped to her décolletage and she felt a shocking awareness of him as a man. A strong, sexual man. Pushing the feeling aside, she took a deep breath and gave a determined smile. "It was very generous of you to invite me to stay here last night and tonight. I've given it some thought and I believe it will be best for me to move back to my apartment."

He shook his head. "I'm sorry. I can't allow that."

She blinked. "Allow?"

"I have some information that makes the choice clear, but I intended to tell you after our meal. I suspect you're concerned about staying here. You're probably afraid this setup isn't conducive for a baby."

She nodded. "Yes."

"Please go ahead and eat."

Lilli wanted to protest, but politeness compelled her to force down a forkful of the beef dish. The delicious taste momentarily distracted her and she took another bite. "Oh, you were right about your chef. This is amazing."

"You'll find I'm often right," he said. "I learned at an early age not to allow emotion to determine my choices."

"Why?" she asked, taking another bite.

"I watched my father spend half his fortune trying to keep his mistress happy."

She heard cynicism creep into his tone again, and for the first time understood why. "I'm assuming his mistress wasn't your mother," she ventured.

"She wasn't. She was Tony's mother."

"Oh," she said again, remembering something Tony had told her. "But I thought Tony's parents were dead."

"They are both dead. Died in a boating accident."

She set down her fork. "I'm so sorry."

He shrugged. "It was ironic because the boat was called Franco's Folly. My father's name was Franco. He spent a good part of his life chasing after things that eventually ruined him. Something I refuse to do. But that's a different subject." He took a sip of wine. "Jim did some research on the man who gave you his card yesterday. Trust me, he's bad news. You may as well be a sitting duck if you move back to your apartment without protection."

"Protection?" she echoed, appalled. "That's got to be an exaggeration. The man was a little pushy, but he backed off when I told him to. I'll just have to be very firm—"

"Lilli," Max interjected in a quiet, ultracalm voice that immediately got her attention. "It turns out he's involved with the local mafia. They're not above kidnapping or murder to collect on a debt."

Lilli froze, her appetite fleeing. "Oh, my God."

Nausea rose inside her and she turned from the table, automatically turning away. Terror coursed through her. How could she protect her child?

She felt Max just behind her. His body heat warmed her back. "You won't need to worry if you stay here. No one would dare hurt you as long as everyone knows you're in my care."

"Maybe I should go ahead and move out of town. I didn't want to do that, but—"

"You're too vulnerable for that right now," he said.

She turned to look at him. "What do you mean, too vulnerable?"

"Physically, for one thing. It's not like you'd be able to beat off an attacker."

"But if I moved away, I wouldn't have to beat off anyone."

He shook his head. "They're watching you too closely. Maybe later, but not now."

"Oh, God, I feel so stupid," she said, fighting back tears. "How did I let this get so out of control?"

"It could be worse," he said. "You can set up a nursery here. I'll cover the cost. We'll make the necessary adjustments in the house. Your life will be just like it was before, with a few perks."

"Just like before," she said, laughing with gallows humor. *As if anything could ever be like before.* "There's no way I could allow you to cover the cost of the nursery. It wouldn't be right. And I can't imagine living here. It's just so—"

"So what?"

"Perfect. This isn't at all what I pictured for my child."

"Why wouldn't my home be appropriate? I'm a blood relative. How is it right for your child not to know his uncle?"

Oh, Lord. She hadn't even thought of it that way. Her heart splintered. Her father had left before her third birthday and since her mother's relatives had lived on the other coast, she'd never had an opportunity to meet them, let alone enjoy any sort of family bond.

She shook her head. "I'd never considered any of this. Once I broke off with Tony, I knew it would be just me and the baby. I didn't think Tony's family would want to be involved, and frankly I didn't want anything to do with anyone bearing the name De Luca."

Max narrowed his eyes. "Tony and I are not the same man."

"I'm beginning to see that," she said. "I need to think about this."

"Finish your dinner," he said, cupping her arm with his strong hand. "We can discuss this more later."

Lilli's stomach jumped. She wasn't sure if it was a result of Max's hand on her bare arm or the terrible

news he'd just delivered. She looked into his eyes and
had the sense that this man could turn her world upside
down in ways she'd never imagined. She stepped backward, needing air, needing to think. "I'm sorry, but I
can't eat right now. Please excuse me. I need to go
upstairs."

Max watched Lilli as she fled the patio through the
door. With each passing moment, he felt more drawn to
her, but for the life of him, he couldn't explain why.

Her immediate rejection of his offer to pay to furnish
the nursery had caught him off guard. He was so accustomed to covering expenses for a multitude of people
that he rarely gave it a second thought.

Women had always been more than happy to accept
his generosity. In fact, on a couple of occasions, his com-
panions had tried to take advantage of him. One woman
had even gotten herself pregnant by another man and
tried to make Max take responsibility for the child.

Lilli was the exact opposite. Unless it was all an act,
which it could be, he thought, his natural cynicism
rising inside him. Still, Lilli didn't strike him as a
woman adept at hiding her emotions or motives.

He suspected she didn't want him to know that she was
attracted to him, but he had seen it in her eyes. The attraction was reluctant, but strong, the same as it was for
him.

In other circumstances, he would want her for himself.
And he wouldn't just *want* her. He would take her.

Lilli paced her bedroom for two hours. With her
head feeling as if it were going to split into a million

pieces, she lay down and surprised herself by falling asleep. When she awakened at eleven-thirty, her stomach was growling like a mountain lion.

"Sorry, sweetie," she murmured, rubbing her stomach. The idea of that dinner going to waste nearly made her sob. Max had told her to call Ada, the housekeeper, if she needed anything, including a snack, but Lilli couldn't imagine imposing at this hour.

Dressed in a tank top and shorts, she quietly crept downstairs to the kitchen. She opened the refrigerator and peered inside. She found the leftovers and turned around.

"I'm glad you got back your appetite," Max said, startling her so much she almost dropped the container she was holding. Swearing under her breath, she managed to save the dish. Her heart racing, she backed away and closed the refrigerator door.

"I didn't think you would be down—" She broke off when she saw that he was shirtless, his pajama pants riding low on his waist. His chest was a work of art. Her mouth went dry.

"I heard a noise," he said casually, as if he didn't know that seeing him half-naked took her breath away.

She needed to keep it that way, she told herself and locked her gaze on his forehead. "I was hungry. I can just grab an apple and go back upstairs."

He moved closer to her and pulled the dish from her hands. "Why would you eat an apple when you can have this?" He put the dish in the microwave and started to warm it up.

Lilli tried very hard not to allow her gaze to dip across his naked shoulders, but she didn't quite succeed.

When the plate was hot, he directed her to a seat at the table.

Twenty minutes later, she'd polished off a reasonable portion of beef, bread and a brownie he'd insisted she eat.

She leaned back in her chair and stretched her legs. "That was delicious. Thanks."

His gaze enigmatic, he gave a slight smile. "You're welcome. Not bad for Mr. Steel."

Lilli blinked, then realized there was only one way he could have known she'd called him that. Her cheeks heated with embarrassment. "How long were you listening to my phone conversation?" she accused.

"It wasn't premeditated," he said. "I was going to tell you about the report I got from Jim, but you were so absorbed in your conversation that you didn't notice me."

Lilli closed her eyes, wishing she could hide. "Great."

"And no, I don't have a wife or mistress tied to my bed. I haven't found it necessary to tie women up to keep them in my bed."

She opened her eyes. "I didn't mean it the way—"

He waved his hand. "We may as well get this on the table. I know you're attracted to me," he said without a millimeter of arrogance.

She opened her mouth to deny it, but her throat closed around the lie.

"I'm flattered that you think I'm hot," he said. "But it's probably a good idea that you also think I'm cold because, for some reason, I find you attractive."

Lilli gaped at him, sure he was mocking her. "No."

"Yes," he said.

"But I'm pregnant," she blurted out. "And not with your baby."

"Your pregnancy doesn't conceal your other assets. It doesn't conceal your fire." His gaze traveled to her breasts and lower to her legs, then all the way back up to her mouth, making her feel as if a hot wind had blown over her. He gave a short laugh as if the joke was on him. "Don't worry. I'll get over it. You may have seduced one De Luca, but I'm not as easily impressed as my brother."

She felt as if he'd slapped her. "I haven't been trying to impress you," she told him. "Besides, your brother did the seducing, not me."

"It doesn't sound like you fought him."

"I didn't," she told him, but there'd been a time he'd taken advantage of her. "My mother died one week before I met Tony and I freely admit I was a mess." She met and held his gaze for a long, fierce moment. "And besides the fact that you're hot, what makes you think I would want to go round two with anyone with the last name De Luca?" She stood and whirled away.

He snagged her wrist, pulling her against him when she stumbled. Her hand fell against his chest and she felt his heart against her palm, his heat all over her.

"Hold on to that thought," he said. "You're going to need it. But just so you know, if you ever went to bed with me, you would never think of it as round two."

Looking into his hard, sensual gaze, Lilli felt a shiver run through her. Somehow, deep inside her, deeper than her bones, she knew that again he wasn't bragging. He was just telling the truth.

Three

Lilli awakened to the sound of the Bose alarm clock on the elegant bedside table. The strains of classical music lulled her into consciousness. Rolling to her side, she pulled the pillow over her head.

Just a couple more minutes. This bed was divine. It felt so wonderful she hated to leave it. Much better than her lumpy mattress back at her apartment.

She stiffened at the thought and immediately sat up in bed. Frowning, she told herself not to get used to this level of luxury. Sometime, more likely sooner than later, she would be living in a place where she was both the chief housekeeper and assistant housekeeper. There would be no Bose stereo systems and the closest she would get to a gourmet meal prepared by a chef would be a frozen dinner.

Rising from the bed, she padded across the luxury carpet to the large shower in the connecting bathroom. She would need to get up earlier since her commute to work was longer from Max's home. The very thought of him made something inside flutter and flip.

Hunger, she told herself. It had to be hunger or the baby. After she donned her colorful scrubs, she headed downstairs and was surprised to see Max pacing and speaking into a cell phone via a Bluetooth in his ear. He wore running shorts and a tank top that showed off his muscular legs and arms. Everything about him oozed strength. "Tell Alex we're limiting our domestic expansion until we see what happens with the dollar."

He saw her and lifted a hand. "Yes, I know Alex still resents that I was promoted over him. We each serve an important purpose. I provide the balance. He provides the fireworks. Tell him I said to think global. I'm working from home this morning. I'll be in the office this afternoon and will get an update then. Thanks. Bye."

He immediately turned to Lilli. "Good morning. Did you rest well?"

She nodded. "Yes, thank you."

"We have fresh-squeezed orange juice and the cook will be happy to prepare anything you like."

She shook her head. "I need to get on the road if I'm going to make it to work in time."

He frowned. "You can't skip breakfast. What about the baby?"

"I'll grab something at work. We always have fruit and bagels in the workroom," she said.

He shot her a disapproving glance. "That's not good nutrition."

"I don't think my baby is suffering. I'm taking my prenatal vitamins." He moved toward her and she struggled with the urge to flee. She was doing her best to keep her gaze fixed on his eyebrows. She refused to look into his eyes, or at his mouth, or at that stubborn chin or at those shoulders. Or lower. Feeling a flush of heat, she stepped backward. "Better go. See you la—"

"Your things from your apartment should be here by the time you return," he said.

Lilli stopped abruptly and blinked. "Excuse me?"

"I arranged for someone to pack your belongings and bring them here. Duplications like most of your furniture, dishes and linens will be put in storage. All the baby items will be moved into the nursery."

Trying to catch up with him, she shook her head in confusion. "Where is the nursery?"

"Across the hall from your bedroom," he said. "A decorator will be calling you later today so you can tell her what you would like done to it."

She shook her head again. "Did I ever actually say that I was going to stay here?"

He lifted a dark eyebrow. "There was another choice?"

She sighed, hating him for being right. "Well, you could have given me a little time to adjust to the idea. There's no reason I couldn't pack my own stuff and—"

His eyes widened in horror. "Moving in your condition?"

She sighed. "I'm very healthy. Women have been getting pregnant and delivering babies for years. In ancient times, it wasn't unusual for a woman to be working in the fields one minute, having her baby the next, then back at work immediately."

"I won't have you in the fields, period," he said in a dry tone. "In terms of the speed of the movers, there was no need to wait. We both agree, even if you don't want to admit it, that you belong here until we figure out a safe place for you and the baby. And that will be months from now."

She made a face at his imperious tone. Lord help her, he sounded like an emperor.

"In the meantime, I've asked my personal attorney to draw up some documents regarding custody of the child in case something should happen to you."

Lilli felt a chill. "I already told you I'm not signing those papers. If signing those papers is part of the bargain for me staying here, then I'm leaving."

"I never said that."

"No, but even you admitted that you could be ruthless. I'm not signing my child over to Ruthless Mr. Steel," she said, mentally drawing a line and daring him to cross over it.

"Yet," he said.

"I won't be manipulated over this," she warned him.

"Manipulation is for sissies," he said with a scoff.

"Then what do you call what you do?" she asked. "Bullying?"

"Reason and logic prevail among rational human beings."

Lilli knew she wasn't totally rational about this subject. It was too close to her heart. She took a shallow breath and met his gaze. "I don't want you to intimidate me about this," she said in a quiet voice.

He studied her for a moment, his gaze more curious than threatening. "Okay. Are you open to gentle persuasion?"

"Not if it involves any power plays," she said.

He nodded, stepping closer. "Deal. By the way, I'm hosting a casual business gathering Friday night. It's just a barbecue. Feel free to drop in and fill up a plate."

His closeness made her feel as if he'd set off a dozen mini electrical charges inside her. He lifted his hand to a stray strand of her hair. "Your hair reminds me of your personality."

He looped the strand around one of his fingers and she felt her heart accelerate. "How is that?"

His mouth stretched into a sexy grin. "It's the color of an angel's hair, but the curl shows it's rebellious."

Looking into his eyes, she felt as if she were sinking into a place where she was aware of only him. He was the most dynamic man she'd ever met in her life. She felt totally fascinated and totally out of her league.

Grasping on to that thought, she took a shallow breath and stepped back. It was a move totally motivated by survival. Max De Luca was a powerful force, too powerful for her.

The strand of her hair stretched taut between them. Max hadn't released her. She lifted her hand to unravel her hair from his finger, brushing his skin. "I should go. I don't want to be late," she said and fled out the door, feeling as if she'd been burned.

Max arrived home after going several rounds with Alex Megalos, Director of Domestic Operation and Expansion for Megalos-De Luca Enterprises. Alex had been Max's rival for his current position as Director of Worldwide Operation and Expansion.

Talented and aggressive, Alex was always trying to focus resources and energy in his area. Max, however, was forced to continually remind Alex that he had to consider the big picture.

Alex provided a lot of energy, but he also caused more than his share of heartburn. Suffering from a burning sensation in his gut even now, Max just wanted a quiet peaceful evening and an opportunity to wind down. He headed for the bar downstairs and poured himself a glass of red wine.

Sitting in the darkness of the den, he took a sip and savored the stillness of the moment.

A crashing sound followed by a scream shattered the quiet. Alarm shot through him. Immediately jumping to his feet, he raced upstairs. That had been Lilli's scream. What had happened?

Rounding the corner, he found her on the floor of the nursery surrounded by scattered pieces of a crib and tools.

"What in hell are you doing?"

Dressed in shorts that revealed her long legs, her hair straying from the ponytail in back, she glanced up at him with a scowl. "Trying to put this crib back together. Your moving guys took it apart."

He frowned, entering the room. "They should have put it back together." He reached into his pocket for his cell phone. "I'll get my driver up here immediately. He's excellent, extremely mechanical. He'll put it together in no time."

Scrambling to her feet, she put her hands over his to prevent him from dialing. "No. No."

"Why not?"

"Besides the fact that it's not his job to put together cribs and it's almost ten o'clock," she said, "I want to do it myself."

He stared at her for a long moment. "Why?"

"Because I just do. I put this crib together after I bought it. I should be able to do it now."

"Why is it so important that you be the one to assemble it? The baby isn't going to know."

She lifted her chin. "Someday he will. Someday he will know that his mother loved him so much and was so excited that he was coming that she put her time and energy and money into making a nice place for him."

Her heartfelt determination tugged at something inside him. "That never would have occurred to me. I'm certain my mother didn't assemble my crib. I had a string of nannies and was shipped off to boarding school before my parents divorced."

"My mother could sew and knit and she made blankets and caps and booties for me. I'm going to use some of them on my little one."

"But not anything pink," he said.

She smiled and laughed. "Nothing pink. I have a few white and yellow things. After my father left, it was just my mom and me." She bit her lip. "I wish she was still around. I have a feeling I'm going to have a lot of questions."

"I'm sure you'll do an excellent job and when he goes to boarding school—"

Lilli gaped at him. "I'm not sending my child to boarding school."

"There's no need to automatically reject the idea. A

young man can get an excellent education and important connections at an elite boarding school."

"And they end up with warm, affectionate family
ties just like you," she said.

He opened his mouth then closed it. "Mr. Steel
haunts me again." He shook his head. "There's no need
to discuss boarding school. That's years away."

"Never," she corrected.

He loosened his tie and unfastened the top couple of
buttons of his shirt. "Let me help you put this crib
together. Where are the instructions?"

Lilli winced. "That's the problem. I threw them away
after I put it together the first time."

He couldn't swallow a chuckle at her stymied expression. "Okay, then we'll just look it up on Google."

"Google it?" she echoed. "I never thought of that."

"So I'm good for something," he said in a wry voice.
"My laptop is in my quarters. Come on. I still haven't
given you that tour. From the way you act toward me, I
wonder if you still think I have a woman tied to my bed."

Her face bloomed with color and she groaned.
"When are you going to stop teasing me about that?"

"When you stop calling me Mr. Steel," he said and
led her to another wing of the house.

When Max opened the door to his suite, all Lilli
could do was stare. Lush carpet covered the floor, cush-
ioning every footstep. A gas fireplace featuring a stone
mantel provided instant warmth. On either side, stone
shelves held books, electronic items and a full bar. A
large bed covered with luxury linens provided the cen-
terpiece, but what captured her attention was the

dramatic arched window that showed the starry sky in all its glory.

"I have shades to cover them if it's too bright," he said.

"How can you bear to do that? It's so beautiful," she said.

"Thank you. I like it. I also have a flat-screen television that comes down from over that wall." He walked through one door and motioned for her to follow. "Personal gym and lap pool."

Lilli blinked at all the equipment. "But you already have a pool."

"That one is for being lazy. This one is for exercise." He glanced her. "You can use it anytime you like. It's okay to swim during pregnancy, isn't it?"

She nodded. "Yes."

He led her to another room, which held a desk, sofa and more electronic equipment. He turned on his laptop. "There's another office suite downstairs, but I tend to accomplish more up here. Would you like some juice or sparkling water?"

She shook her head. "No. I'm fine. All you need to live in here are a kitchen and washer and dryer."

His lips twitched. "There's a galley kitchen across the hall. Laundry chute in my closet."

Tugging off his tie, he released another shirt button. Lilli was struck by the sight of his tanned fingers against the white shirt. He truly was an amazing male. She wondered how many women had shared his bed. No chains needed for him.

She cleared her throat and tried to move her mind in a different direction as he tapped on the keyboard. "Just curious, but do you even know *how* to do laundry?"

He glanced at her and gave a cryptic smile. "Yes, I know how. We were required to learn in boarding school, along with basic mechanics, financial management, survival skills and cooking."

"You can cook?" she said in disbelief.

"I make a damn good omelet, can broil a steak with the best of them and I was recognized for making the best grilled cheese sandwich in my class."

She couldn't stifle a laugh from his defense of his culinary abilities. "Nothing chocolate in your repertoire?"

He shot her a level glance. "I buy only the best." He looked at the screen. "Here we are. Instructions for assembling your crib."

She joined him to look at the screen, surprised at how fast he'd found the instructions. "How did you know what kind?"

"I looked at the brand and model before I left the nursery." He hit the print button and seconds later, they returned to the nursery armed with instructions.

An hour later, they proclaimed victory as Lilli put in the final screw. "We did it," she said, punchy with excitement. She lifted her hand for a high five. "I hate to say it, but I couldn't have done it without you. Thanks."

"My pleasure," he said, his hair mussed from raking his fingers through it. She'd known he'd spent the entire time itching to do the work himself. He'd offered and insisted every five minutes, but she'd demurred. "If only everything were this easy," he said, offering his hand to help her up from the floor.

Her knees cramped from staying in one position too long, she wobbled as she stood. Strong arms wrapped around her and pulled her against his warm body.

Bracing herself on his arms, she was immediately distracted by the sensation of him, smooth skin over hard muscle. Her breasts pressed against his chest, her belly meshed with his and her thighs just barely touched his trousers.

"Are you okay?" he asked in a low voice.

Her heart pounding a mile a minute, she nodded and barely managed a whisper. "Yes. I guess I sat a little too long."

He slid his hand through her hair, surprising her with the sensual but tender gesture. "You stopped seeing my brother months ago. How is it that you don't have a man in your life now?"

She swallowed hard. "I'm pregnant."

"And no man has approached you?"

"No." She closed her eyes, trying not to sink into a helpless puddle on the floor. He felt so strong, so good. The intimate sound of his low voice both soothed her and wreaked havoc with her nervous system. "I didn't want a man in my life. I don't know if I ever will," she said, remembering how victimized she'd felt.

He gave a low laugh that caught her off guard. "You've got to be kidding."

She looked up at him, searching his face in the low lighting. "No. I'm not."

"Every woman has needs," he said.

"I don't," she told him, because it had seemed all her sexual needs had disappeared. "Not for a long time."

"How can you say that? You're attracted to me," he said and slid his fingertips from her hair to her throat.

"That doesn't mean I want to have sex with you," she said, but her skin was heating and her heart was racing.

"I could make you want to be with me," he said. "I could make you want it more than you ever have."

For a sliver of a moment, she believed him and the possibility sent her into turmoil. She had to shut this down once and for all. She took his hand and put it on her belly. "There will always be this between us," she said. "Always."

Max returned to his suite and poured himself a glass of red wine. There was something electric between him and Lilli. He could feel it in his skin and deeper in his gut. She was a little afraid of him, but still determined to hold her own. That attracted him even more. She was resolved to push him away, but she was fascinated by him. He could see it in the way she looked at him, hear it in her quick intake of breath and he felt it in her response to him.

The passion she tried to hide got to him more than any other woman's overt seduction had. He was still aroused from being so close to her.

Plowing his fingers through his hair, he walked to his office and pulled out another legal proposal from his attorney. After watching what had happened to his brother because his guardian had been permissive and irresponsible, Max couldn't stand the idea of another De Luca plunging down the same path.

He suspected Lilli would never sign a document giving him guardianship unless she became ill, and she might not even sign it under those conditions.

There were other options, though. Other ways to make sure this De Luca was raised properly. His attorney had outlined each of them. Some were more costly than others, and not just in terms of money. Rubbing his chin, he remembered when he'd got the news of his brother's death. The feeling of loss and despair had slammed into him like a concrete wall.

He would never let the same thing happen to another De Luca. Never.

JEANNIE WATT

Four

The next evening, after a full day at work, Lilli entered the De Luca house to the sound of jazz music, tinkling glasses and animated conversation. She'd noticed a few extra cars in the driveway, but she hadn't known what to expect once she got inside.

The scent of grilled food permeated the house, making her mouth water and her stomach growl. Then she remembered. This must be the barbecue gathering Max had mentioned the other day. All she wanted was a sandwich and she could fix that herself. Heading for the kitchen, she found two men and two women preparing food and placing it on serving trays.

A large bald man barked orders from one end of the large kitchen island. The man pinned her with his gaze as she approached the island. "No guests in the kitchen, *bella,*" he chided and pointed to himself. "Louie can't have you stealing secrets."

This was Max's fabulous chef. She hadn't had a chance to meet him yet because he seemed to cook and disappear.

"I'm not really a guest and I won't steal your secrets. I just want to make a peanut butter sandwich. It won't take a minute."

He gasped in horror. "Peanut butter sandwich, when you can eat this?"

"I need to make this quick," she said, more than ready for the solace and quiet of her room. She stepped behind the island. "I just want to take it to my room. Upstairs."

Louie's eyebrows shot upward. "Upstairs? You are a special friend of Mr. De Luca. Only the best—"

"No, no, I'm sure he doesn't think of me as a special friend."

"I don't know why not," a man said from behind her.

Lilli whipped her head around to look at a tall, muscular man with brown hair and luminescent green eyes. "Alex Megalos," he said with a smile as he stood on the other side of the kitchen island.

"Nice to meet you. Lilli McCall."

His eyes crinkled when he smiled. She liked that. She liked that he smiled at her instead of frowning. But she felt the need to disappear. She didn't want to call attention to herself. "I really should go," she said. "This is a business gathering."

"No reason we can't mix business and pleasure. Let's get you a drink. Come out on the patio."

Lilli shook her head again. "Thank you, but I—"

Max stepped into the kitchen and Lilli felt her heart take an extra beat. "When did the party move in here?"

"Max, you've been holding out on us. How did you lure this angel into your dark castle?"

Max met her gaze and she took a deep breath. A snap of electricity crackled between them. "Just lucky, I guess," he said.

"Well, if you need anyone to take her off your hands," Alex ventured.

Max shot him a sideways glance. "Always competing," he said, then turned to the chef. "Louie, the lady is hungry."

"We can't have that," Louie said and quickly put a plate together.

"Max, don't be so greedy. You've already got Kiki," Alex said. "Share her with the rest of us. She should join us tonight."

Lilli stared at Max in panic.

"If you would like—

"I wouldn't," she said. "Like," she added, gulping and shot Alex an apologetic look. "I'm a little tired. Thanks, though."

"I'm crushed," Alex said. "Maybe I could give you a call when you're rested."

Confusion rolled through her as she watched a beautiful brunette appear from behind him. "Max, sweetheart, you disappeared," the woman said.

He turned to the woman. "Kiki, I'll be back before you finish your next drink. I need to take care of a personal matter."

The woman looked at Lilli and lifted one of her perfectly arched eyebrows. "Is this the personal matter?" She narrowed her eyes.

"I—uh—need to go," Lilli said.

"No need to rush," Alex said.

"Exactly," Kiki said.

Lilli felt as if she were suddenly surrounded by vipers. There were too many competing agendas for her comfort. "All I wanted was a peanut butter sandwich," she murmured.

Kiki snickered. "How charming."

"Here's your plate, bella," Louie said.

"Bless you," she said. "Thank you. It looks delicious." She turned to Alex and Kiki. "It was nice to meet you. Have a lovely evening."

"I will," Kiki said and slid her hand around Max's well-developed bicep.

Lilli nodded, feeling an odd combination of emotions, most of which she didn't want to examine. "Good night," she said and stepped from behind the kitchen island.

Kiki's jaw dropped. Alex blinked.

They were looking at her pregnant belly.

"Want Lilli all to yourself for the rest of the evening?" Max asked, shooting Alex a sly grin. He winked at Lilli and his humor helped her get through the incredibly awkward moment.

"Uh…uh…" Alex seemed unable to pry his gaze from her belly. He cleared his throat and closed his eyes then forced his gaze upward. He exhaled and smiled. "Hell, I bet she would be more fun than you are. And trust me, Lilli, I'm a lot more fun than Max."

"Who is the lucky father?" Kiki asked in a strained voice.

Lilli glanced at Max. "Um, it's—"

He met her gaze. "That's between me and Lilli."

Kiki's face tightened with suspicion. "That's a little vague, darling," she said with an edge to her tone.

"Kiki, this is not the place for this discussion," he said. "Louie will be upset if we don't enjoy his meal. I'll talk to you later," he said, looking at Lilli.

"That's okay," she said, feeling her nerves jump in her stomach. "I'm hitting the sack early tonight. Very tired. Thank you again, Louie. G'night. Enjoy your evening," she said and scooted out of the room, thankful that Kiki wasn't armed. Otherwise, she was certain she would be so dead.

While Lilli ate, she watched a boring show on her flat-screen television. Afterward, she took a shower and went to bed, but didn't fall asleep. Pulling a book about newborn care from her nightstand, she added to the list of items she would need to purchase for the baby.

A knock sounded on her door and she tensed, but didn't answer. The knock sounded again and she held her breath.

"I know you're not asleep," Max said. "I heard you walking around three minutes ago."

Lilli frowned. She'd gotten a drink of water from the attached bathroom. Sighing, she rose from the bed and opened the door.

Max stepped inside and closed the door behind him. His gaze fell over her body, and he gave her a bottle of water and a cookie. "You've charmed my chef. Louie said you looked like you could use a cookie."

"Thank you," she said, appreciating his kindness. "But I'm sure it's because he thinks I'm a special friend of yours, even though I told him I'm not."

"It's safe to say we have a special relationship," he said. "A bond, in a way."

His tone made her stomach dip. "Speaking of special friends," she said. "Just curious, was there a particular reason you didn't tell Kiki the real father of my child?"

"Yes. For safety reasons, I've decided it's better not to comment on your relationship with Tony. There are too many people he owes."

"Oh," she said, remembering the threat and feeling a sinking sensation in her stomach. She sat down on the bed. "I keep trying to forget about that."

"Don't," he said, moving toward her. "You need to be on guard when you go out in public. People will try to take advantage of you if they know of your association with the De Lucas."

"I don't think my real friends would dream of taking advantage of me," she said and put the cookie and bottle of water on the nightstand. The soft glow of the bedside lamp intensified the intimacy of the moment. He was close enough that she could smell a hint of his cologne and masculine scent. She could almost feel him.

He gave a cynical smile. "People will always try to take advantage of you when you have money."

"You forget," she said. "I don't really have any money."

He sat down beside her on the bed and studied her. "That could change," he said.

Feeling his gaze on her, she looked at him. The expression on his face affected her in a strange way. "How?"

"There are options," he said.

"If this involves that crazy contract," she began.

"We won't discuss it at this late hour," he said. "Alex

asked me to give you his card. He couldn't stop talking about you."

"That didn't have anything to do with me," she said, her hair drooping over one of her eyes. "I could tell he was only interested because he liked the idea of taking something away that he thought was yours. Just a game."

"You're right that Alex is very competitive with me, but you underestimate your appeal," he said and lifted his hand to her hair.

Her heart fluttered. She could have pushed him away if she'd had the inclination, but she couldn't find it anywhere inside her. He slid his hand over her cheek and then down to her mouth, rubbing his thumb over her bottom lip.

Her skin tingled everywhere he touched. She swallowed hard. "Why are you touching me?"

"You don't like it?" he asked, his dark gaze meeting hers. "There are so many reasons you should be off-limits." He moved closer. "But I like the way your skin feels. I like the way you look at me when I touch you."

She inhaled a shallow breath and caught another draft of his spicy scent mixed with cologne. In some corner of her mind, it occurred to her that she'd never been this close to such a powerful man. He knew who he was and what he had to do, and he was the kind of man who would make whatever he wanted a reality.

For Lilli, it was like getting up close and personal with a wild tiger. At the same time, he was solid and strong and she knew he would never force a woman. He wouldn't need to. And to have him looking at her as his object of desire made her dizzy.

"There's something about you," he said, gently urging her mouth open so he could slide his thumb just inside to her tongue. "Wide blue eyes with secrets, a sweet smile." He glanced downward. "You make me curious."

Lilli was shocked at how quickly her body responded. She'd considered herself sexually dead, but she felt her skin heat and the tips of her breasts tighten against her white cotton gown.

He saw it, too. She knew it by the expression on his face.

"I shouldn't want you," he muttered and slid his hand around the back of her neck. "But dammit, I do." He lowered his mouth to hers and took her lips in a kiss that made her lose track of time and space.

His tongue slid over hers and she felt herself respond. It was all instinctual. Her heart pounded in her head and her blood pooled in secret, sensitive places. Every second that she felt his warmth, his touch, she was shocked by her immediate response to him. Something inside her could not push him away.

She felt him lower one of his hands to her breast. Air caught somewhere in her throat as he caressed her through her gown. He rubbed the palm of his hand over the side of her breast and she shivered, pressing up against him.

He gave a low groan of approval and drew his hand closer to her nipple, but not quite touching it. She felt the peak of it stiffen against her nightgown, aching for his touch.

Full of wanting, she held her breath.

He finally pushed the top of her gown down and slid his thumb over her nipple. She couldn't swallow a moan of relief with a twinge of frustration.

He pulled his mouth from hers and slid his lips over her skin, down her throat and collarbone. A riot of sensations shot through her. She wanted him everywhere at once.

His other hand slid over her back, massaging her, holding her in a solid embrace. The combination of security and caresses hit her physically and emotionally.

He looked up at her, dark desire in his eyes. Swearing under his breath, he shook his head.

Pulling back, he rose from the bed and prowled toward the window. Moonlight spilled over his profile as he raked his hand through his hair.

Lilli drank in a gulp of air, trying to clear her head. Shocked at herself, she tugged her gown back in place and tried to make sense of what had just happened. That night after she'd broken up with Tony, the night made doubly awful because she couldn't recall it, she'd changed. She'd known she would never be the same. She would never be able to let a man touch her again unless she trusted him.

Why should she trust Max? There was no good reason. But something inside her did. Either that or she was crazier than she'd thought she was.

"You're so responsive. I wonder…were you this responsive with my brother," he ventured in a low voice.

"I wasn't," she said, the words popping out before she could stop them.

He turned to look at her. "Why not?"

She bit her lip. "I can't explain it. It's just different."

He continued to hold her gaze. "Did you leave my brother before or after you found out you were pregnant?"

"Before." She looked away from him. "Something happened one night. I knew I couldn't stay."

"What was it?"

"I don't like talking about it," she said, twisting her fingers together. "I knew I had to get away from him and his—" her stomach clenched with nausea "—his world."

"And you weren't tempted to go back with him when you found out you were pregnant?"

She shook her head vehemently. "Oh, absolutely not. If I didn't belong in his world, there was no way a baby would."

"Did he ask you back?"

She nodded. "Several times. But I think he was relieved when I said no. Tony wasn't ready to be a father."

"What about the baby? What will you do about a father figure for him?"

"I'll deal with that later. Right now, I need to get through the pregnancy and delivery. My girlfriends have promised to help me through the scary first few months." She felt a sense of dread in the pit of her stomach. "Then I guess I'll have to move."

Feeling his gaze on her, she looked up at him, wondering what he was thinking, what judgments he was making. "You probably don't understand any of this. How I could end up with your brother and then pregnant with no husband? You would never get yourself into such a crazy situation because you don't let emotions make your decisions."

"You're completely correct."

"I'm also completely human. Are you?"

His mouth lifted in a half smile. "Unfortunately, yes. Human enough to want to finish what we started a few minutes ago." He moved toward her, and she felt her heart jump into her throat. "Don't worry. I won't. I may be human, but I'm not ruled by my hormones. Good night, Lilli."

Staring after him in surprise, she took a ragged breath. She felt totally off balance.

I'm human, but I'm not ruled by my hormones.

That was part of the reason she'd responded to him. She had a gut feeling that he had maintained control of himself. He wouldn't lose it unless he chose to do so. She'd never been around such a man but she could sense it about him and it made her feel secure at the same time that it knocked her sideways. She closed her eyes and pushed her hair from her face. She needed to stay on guard.

Five

Lilli's hands were shaking as she turned onto Max's street Saturday after working at the free dental clinic. She'd been so careful at work lately, always making sure to have someone walk her to her car. Afterward, she'd stopped to visit Devon Jones, one of the hospice workers who had helped her mother during her last days. Devon was now caring for his own father during the end stages of a long illness.

After she'd left, she'd noticed a black car in her rearview mirror. Even after making a few turns, the car remained behind her. She became so nervous that she'd taken some wrong turns and had got lost.

Glancing over her shoulder as she pulled into the driveway, she shook her head. Surely they wouldn't follow her all the way to Max's house. Biting her lip, she grabbed her purse and rushed into the house, leaning against the door as she closed it, and took a deep breath. She closed her eyes for a moment to calm herself. When she opened them, Max was five feet away from her, pinning her with a searching gaze.

"And you look like you've had some excitement," he said. "Anything you want to tell me?"

She tried to shrug, but shivered instead. Despite the way he'd left her feeling last night, she couldn't deny feeling ten times safer in his presence. "Not right now," she said and headed for the kitchen. "Water sounds good."

Her heart still racing, she took another deep breath and put her hand to her chest.

"Lilli," he said from behind her and she thought she heard a note of concern in his voice. Hallucinating, she told herself. "Are you okay?"

"I will be," she insisted, getting a glass and filling it with filtered water from the refrigerator.

He moved in front of her and studied her. "Where have you been?"

"Work, well, not really work," she corrected.

"Your office isn't open on Saturday," he said, his expression growing suspicious.

"That's right. But we volunteer for the free clinic downtown. I filled in for one of the other hygienists."

"Downtown? Where?" he asked, clearly not pleased.

She winced. She had expected he wouldn't approve of her driving downtown by herself, but no one had bothered her for days.

She told him the address and his mouth tightened. "Afterward, I stopped by to check on a hospice assistant who worked with my mother." She shook her head. "Poor Devon. His own father is dying now."

"Devon? What did this guy want? Did he ask you for anything?"

"No, but if he did, I would try to help him. He helped my mother and I during a very difficult time."

"This is what I warned you about. You need to be careful because people will come out of the woodwork playing on your sympathy and asking for *help*."

"That hasn't happened," she said, folding her arms over her chest.

"Then what happened to make you so upset? Did one of Tony's buddies show up?"

"Aside from getting lost, the only thing I can tell you is that someone in a black Mercedes followed me most of the way home."

He swore under his breath. "That's it. You're quitting."

She gaped at him. "Quitting?"

"It's the only rational thing to do. Each day that passes I learn more about how deeply Tony was in trouble. You can stay here until the baby is born and you're ready to move and say goodbye to your contacts here. I've told you before. You need to be on guard in every way. People will try to take advantage of you."

She shook her head. "I can't quit. I need the income for the baby. As you said, babies aren't cheap."

"Money won't be a concern after you sign the agreement."

She supposed she should have been intimidated by him and part of her was, but she refused to give in to it. "I'm not signing that stupid agreement and I'm not taking your money."

"You would turn down a good life for your child in exchange for pride."

She scowled at him. "That was low. The point is that I'm not giving control of my child to you or anyone else. I don't know you well enough. You may give the impression of being very responsible, but at the same time you're bitter, cynical and a workaholic. I want my butter bean to be happy. You may be loaded, but you don't seem very happy."

"Butter bean?" he repeated.

"Yes, butter bean. An affectionate nickname. Something you wouldn't understand."

Exasperation crossed his handsome face. "Most women would kill to have the equivalent of an extended vacation here, but you're fighting it every inch of the way. Have you always been this disagreeable?"

"I think you just bring it out in me," she said.

"Do you have a will?"

"Yes, I do," she said.

"Have you chosen a guardian for you child?"

She resisted the urge to squirm. "I'm working on it."

"Why don't you name me the guardian?" he demanded.

She bit her lip. "Because you don't smile enough." As soon as she blurted out her answer, she knew it sounded a little crazy. "I think kids need smiles and lots of hugs."

He moved toward her. "I think you trust me more than you admit."

Her heart flipped. Maybe she did. There was something so solid about him. "I trust you to be rational, but some decisions should be more emotional."

He lifted an eyebrow. "Are you saying your emotional decisions have turned out well?"

"Not all, obviously," she said. "But it was at least partly an emotional decision for me to take a leave of absence from work to take care of my mother during her last months. I wouldn't trade anything for the time I had with her, because I won't have a chance for that again."

A trace of sympathy softened his hard gaze.

"If you were my son's guardian, what would you do if you had to choose between attending an important business meeting or going to his T-ball game?" She shrugged. "I'm going to make a wild guess and say you'd choose the former because it would be the more rational decision."

"You make a good point, but most parents have to balance career and children's needs. There's no reason I couldn't learn to do the same thing."

She crossed her arms over her chest. "How would you do that?"

He looked surprised that she would question him. "Why do I feel as if I'm being interviewed for a position?"

She nodded. "Maybe you are," she said. "You've pretty much asked, no, demanded to be the baby's guardian in case of my death or path to self-destruction. If someone asked you to give them the most important job in the world, wouldn't you interview them? Probably conduct a background search. Ask for references."

He gave an incredulous laugh, his teeth gleaming brightly in contrast to his tanned skin. "I don't know whether to be offended or—" A cell phone rang and his smile fell. He pulled the phone from his pocket and checked the number. "Excuse me," he murmured. "Yes, Rena?" He paused and shook his head. "I've sent a donation for the event tonight, but won't be attending." He listened for a moment. "I'm sorry they'll be disappointed. Hopefully the money I sent will soothe some of their pain. Okay. Have a good day."

He turned off the phone and turned back to Lilli. "Sorry that was my cousin Rena. She thinks I'm a recluse and she's determined to get me more socially involved."

"But you don't want to," Lilli included.

"This will be a boring chicken dinner with a silent auction afterward. I get enough social involvement at work. And I'm not stingy with my donations."

"But maybe Rena thinks that more people would be more generous with their contributions if they actually saw you show up at the charitable functions sometimes. You would be a good example," she said.

"Maybe," he said, clearly not convinced. "Do you know how painful these things can be?"

"Probably not," she said. "But it's not like you're making a lifetime commitment."

He sighed and met her gaze. "Okay, I'll tell you what. I'll go to the fund-raiser for the children's wing of the hospital if you'll go with me."

"Me?" she said, shocked. "But I'm pregnant."

"Does that mean you're disabled?"

"No, but—" she shook her head "—why would you want me to go? You're bound to have a dozen other women on the line who would want to go with you."

"Meaning you wouldn't," he said in a dry, amused tone.

"I didn't say that," he said. "What about Kiki?"

"I didn't invite Kiki," he said. "I invited you."

Her heart sped up. She cleared her throat. "I don't have anything to wear."

"I can have someone take care of that within an hour."

He was shredding her protests more effectively than a paper shredder. She stared at him, her mind spinning.

"Think of it as an opportunity to continue your interview," he said, as if he weren't at all worried that he would meet and exceed her expectations.

Must be nice to have that kind of confidence, she thought. "This is crazy. I can't believe you want to take me to this kind of event. Aren't you concerned about the gossip?"

"With my father, his mistress and my brother, I've been dealing with gossip most of my life. This will be a cakewalk."

Lilli took a shower and as she was fixing her hair, a knock sounded on her door. She opened it to Max's housekeeper, Myrtle, who held a large box. "For you," the older woman with iron-gray hair said and carried the box to the bed.

"Already?" Lilli asked, glancing at the clock. When Max said an hour, he meant an hour. "Thank you very much, Myrtle," she said, opening the box and pushing aside layers of tissue paper. "Omigoodness, this is beautiful. Did you see it?" she asked the chief housekeeper. She held up the black gown with the fitted bodice and deep V-neck. Just under the bustline dotted with tiny embroidered pink flowers, the remainder of the dress fell in a swirl of silk.

The woman nodded. "It's beautiful. Perfect for you. Mr. De Luca is always very generous."

"Yes, he is, isn't he?" She looked in vain for a price tag, wishing she could reimburse him for the dress. "Do you think he would let me pay him—"

Before she even finished, Myrtle shook her head. "Never," she said.

Sighing, she met Myrtle's gaze. "I don't want to be on the long list of people who sponge off of him."

Myrtle gave a slight smile that softened her usual stern expression. "You will have a difficult time outgiving Mr. De Luca."

Lilli frowned thoughtfully. "How long have you worked for Mr. De Luca?"

"Six years. One of those years, my husband was ill and he allowed me extra time off with pay. I'll always be grateful to him for that."

"I don't know how to ask this, but does Mr. De Luca have any *real* friends?"

"Very few," Myrtle said. "He keeps very busy with his company and socializes very little. And there are his godchildren."

Lilli blinked. "Godchildren? I didn't know he was a godfather."

"With such wealth, he's a natural choice. I should go," she said. "You'll look beautiful in your dress. Mr. De Luca would want you to enjoy it."

"Just on more thing," Lilli said as the woman headed for the door. "When is Mr. De Luca's birthday?"

"Next month, the fifth," she said. "But he never celebrates it."

Lilli's mind immediately flew with possibilities. *He*

never celebrates it. Well, maybe this year should be different. And he was a godfather? Who would have guessed? Sheesh, she should talk to Myrtle more often.

She glanced at the clock again and felt a kick of nerves. She would think about that later. Now she needed to get ready for the charity dinner. She wanted the rest of her to measure up to that beautiful dress.

It occurred to Lilli that perhaps she could have used a team of hairstylists and consultants to get her up to snuff for this event. Instead she would need to rely on the cosmetic tips she'd gleaned from the last fashion magazine she'd read and that had been two or three months ago.

One hour and ten minutes later, Max checked his watch again and wondered if he should sit down and review some reports while he waited for Lilli. Just as he headed for his downstairs office, she appeared at the top of the stairs. He stared for a long moment as she descended the steps. Her blond hair flowing in loose spiral curls to her shoulders and fair skin made her look like an angel. The cut of her black halter dress dipped into a deep V that drew his gaze to her breasts, and the way the fabric bonded lovingly to her curves made him hard.

Her pregnancy was obvious. The dress made no attempt to hide it. He wondered why he was so attracted to this woman. It made no sense at all, especially knowing the baby she carried belonged to his dead brother.

He clenched his teeth and nodded. "You look lovely."

"Thank you," she said with a smile. "So do you."

His lips twitched. He chuckled. "Thanks." He extended his elbow. "Ready?"

"As ever," she murmured and slid her arm through his. "You can still back out if you want. I mean, unless you've changed your mind about having me tag along."

"Not a chance," he said, guiding her through the doorway. "You're not backing out, are you?"

She shot him a sideways glance. "Not a chance. It's not as if I'm ever going to see these people again."

"You never know," he said, escorting her to the luxury sedan parked out front. He opened the car door for her. "You may enjoy yourself."

"I just hope the food is good. If it's not, we can always stop for a cheeseburger with everything on the way home."

He just grinned and got into the car. Adjusting the sound system to play an operatic aria, he noticed Lilli began to fidget after a few minutes. "Problem?" he asked.

"No, no, not really," she said, pushing her hair behind her shoulder as she moved her foot in a staccato beat at odds with the aria. He heard the soft jangle of her anklet with every movement. It was difficult to keep his gaze from straying to her sexy legs.

"Are you sure there's nothing wrong?" he asked.

"Do you know what she's saying?" she asked, pointing toward the CD player.

"It's from a German opera by Mozart called *The Magic Flute*. I didn't study much German, but if I remember correctly, she's saying something along the lines of 'The vengeance of hell boils in my heart. Death and despair flame about me.'"

"Cheerful little ditty, huh," she said. "That's why I'm not crazy about opera. Someone is usually pissed off, plotting to kill someone or getting killed."

"True. But some are more upbeat than others. I'll

have to take you sometime," he said, amused at the image of sharing such an experience with Lilli. "Have you thought about what kind of music is good for the baby's development?"

She nodded vigorously. "I want him to enjoy a variety of music, so I play instrumental Mozart for him. Based on what you just told me about the translation to that aria, I think I'll skip most opera for a while. I've also already started him on the Baby Einstein series."

"You've done some research," he said and felt the weight of her gaze on him.

"You sound surprised."

"Maybe I was," he admitted. "Since this pregnancy was unplanned—"

"Doesn't mean I'm not going to be informed. I've signed up to take an infant care class in a couple of weeks, and I've been researching pediatricians. Since I've changed where I'm living, I may need to do some additional research."

"I can get you the best pediatrician in Las Vegas anytime you want," he said finally, determined that Lilli and his nephew would have no less. "What kind of preschool you want him to attend?"

"I'm leaning toward a Montessori school but they can be expensive, so I'll have to see."

"Money won't be an issue—"

"As long as I sign your agreement, which I won't," she said.

"Yet," he corrected, feeling a twist of impatience. He'd made sure he didn't do anything that would cause his character to be called into question. Not after his father. "You can change your mind after you know me better."

"Maybe," she conceded. "But I still don't like the idea of signing my butter bean over to anyone."

"It's the job of a parent to make sure the child is taken care of in the event of the parent's death."

"I know."

A swollen silence followed, and he sensed she was thinking about things that made her sad. His gut twisted. He couldn't explain it, but he didn't want Lilli sad, so he changed the subject. "You didn't say anything about sports. The De Lucas are naturally athletic, good with any competitive sports. I could teach him soccer, tennis, basketball."

"That's nice, but the important question is can you play peekaboo?"

Max blinked and glanced at her. From the glow of the dashboard, her eyes gleamed with a combination of innocence and sensuality. "Peekaboo?"

She nodded. "Yes, and how good are you at giving hugs and pats on the back? A kid needs hugs and pats on the back more than soccer."

Max digested her comments for a long moment. "You think I may not be affectionate enough."

"I didn't actually say that."

"But you thought it."

She opened her mouth then closed it. "I think a child needs someone who means safety and security, home. That person will love you whether you make the goal or not. That person will teach you how to take a bad day and make it better. I think a child needs compassion."

He pulled in front of the resort where the event was being hosted. "We'll continue this discussion later."

"Okay," she said and lifted her mouth in a sexy smile. "Are you ready for your grand entrance?"

He looked at her for a long moment, unable to tear his gaze away from her. With her sunbeam hair and eyes full of life, she literally sparkled. She took his breath away. "Sweetheart, they're not going to be looking at me," he said, and gave his keys to the valet.

Six

Lilli felt curious gazes fastened on her as she sat next to Max at the dinner table. Chandeliers lit the luxurious ballroom, warming the red carpet and creating a glow on faces belonging to the who's who of the Las Vegas elite. Walls lined with elegant mirrors reflected women outfitted in designer gowns swishing alongside men dressed in expertly tailored suits. Servers refilled her glass of water before she had an opportunity to make a request.

It was by far the most luxurious event she'd ever attended and she constantly reminded herself not to put her elbows on the table. She noticed many people made a point of stopping to speak to Max. Even the mistress of ceremonies introduced him and thanked him for donating the resort's grand ballroom for the night's festivities.

Just as Max picked up his fork to take a bite of coq

au vin, a man stopped and touched his shoulder. "Good to see you here, Max. And congrats on the success of your latest refurbishment project in your Luxotic resorts in the Caribbean. I understand they're often booked over a year in advance."

"Thank you," Max said. "It takes a team. Good to see you too, Robert."

The man walked away and Lilli leaned toward Max and whispered, "Would you like me to put a sign on the back of your chair telling people not to talk to you until you finish eating?"

His lips twitched. "There are only three words appropriate for that question."

"What?"

"I told you," he said and took a bite.

"True," she said. "But maybe people wouldn't feel it necessary to try to talk to you if you attended more of these. Think about it. If they know this is their only shot at actually speaking to the mighty Max De Luca, they've got to grab it. If, however, they know you'll show up at some other events, maybe they won't feel the need to speak to you every time they see you, which is almost never."

"You're saying the attraction to me is how rarely I appear. It has nothing to do with me or my position. If I showed up more often, I would be old news."

She realized he could take that as an insult. "I never used the word *old news*. I'm just saying maybe some of the attention could be spread out over several appearances instead of concentrated on just one."

"Spread the torture out over several evenings instead of getting it done in one."

She sighed and shook her head. "Maybe it wouldn't feel as much like torture if it was spread out." She glanced up and saw a familiar woman walking toward them. "Is that—"

"Max, what a surprise. You told me you weren't planning to come tonight," the woman said and Lilli recalled who she was. Kiki.

Lilli felt a nervous twitch at the back of her neck.

"Last-minute change of plans," Max said, rising to his feet. "Are you enjoying the event?"

Kiki shot Lilli a venomous glance. "Not as much as if I were with you," she said and touched his arm.

"Oh, I'm sure I would have bored you to tears. I'm doing the same to Lilli. Just ask her," he said, glancing down at Lilli with a devil's glint in his eyes.

"I'm sure *Lilli* would never call you boring," Kiki said. "No woman in her right mind would."

"Let's ask Lilli. Tell the truth," he said.

She searched his gaze, wondering why on earth he was putting her on the spot like this. "Kiki is right. I wouldn't have described you as boring."

"See?" Kiki said.

"But he can complain right up there with the best of them," she added.

Kiki's eyes narrowed in disapproval. Max stared at her in surprise and Lilli heard the clatter of sterling silver hit the floor beside her followed by the sound of nervous laughter from the woman sitting in the chair beside her.

Fighting a twinge of nervousness and regret, Lilli lifted her shoulders. "You told me to be honest."

"Yes, I did," he said, giving the distinct impression he wouldn't make the same request again.

Kiki cleared her throat. "I need a quick private word with you, Max. It's urgent. Do you mind?"

He shot a longing glance at his food and Lilli. "Oh, go," she urged him. "If you're not back soon, I'll ask the server to wrap it up to take home."

He bent down and whispered in her ear. "At this rate we may be stopping at Wendy's for me."

She smiled. "Drive-through is open until midnight."

He gave a rough chuckle and turned toward Kiki.

"He's so hot," the young woman beside her said. "How could you send him off with that beautiful woman? You must be confident of your relationship with him," she said in admiration.

Lilli turned to the pudgy young woman with the sweet face. "Max and I have an unusual relationship," she said wryly.

The woman nodded, glancing at Lilli's pregnant belly. "You don't have to tell me anything. I've heard him dodging questions the entire dinner. I know what it's like to be surrounded by people with hidden agendas. Oh, I'm sorry. I should have introduced myself. I'm Mallory James."

"I'm Lilli—"

"McCall," Mallory said, then blushed. "I overheard him introduce you several times. I'm not usually nosy, but since I'm here by myself tonight, and the two of you were more interesting than the almost-dead and completely deaf eighty-seven-year-old beside me...well..."

Lilli smiled. "I'm glad we at least provided a little entertainment. Nice to meet you, Mallory."

The other woman glanced past Lilli's shoulder. "Good grief, you're surrounded by them," she murmured.

"Lilli, you're looking delicious tonight," a male voice said just behind her.

Lilli turned around to meet Alex Megalos's friendly gaze. She couldn't help smiling as she shook her head. "Do you give lessons on flirting on the side?"

"No way. Gotta keep my edge. Where did Max go? Not wise to abandon a woman as beautiful as you."

"You're so right," she said. "I'm bracing myself for the stampede any minute."

Mallory cleared her throat loudly.

Lilli glanced back at the woman whose expression clearly said *please introduce me.* "Oh, Alex Megalos, have you met Mallory James? She's new to town. Alex works for Megalos-De Luca Enterprises."

Alex extended his hand to Mallory and lifted it to his lips. "Enchanted. Have I heard of your father?"

"Perhaps," Mallory said, stuttering. "James Investments and Wealth Management."

Alex nodded in recognition and gave a roguish smile, dipping his head toward hers. "Yes. I bet he keeps you under lock and key. I hear he's excellent. I'd love a chance to chat with him. Is he here tonight?"

"Not tonight," Mallory said and pulled out a card. "But I'd be happy to introduce you. Give me a call?" she asked, rising, bumping into a server carrying a tray of drinks.

"Oh, no." Lilli watched helplessly as the drinks tumbled, splattering Mallory's pink gown and at least one leg of Alex's pants.

The server's face froze. "I'm so sorry."

"Club soda," Lilli said, quickly standing. "Club soda works magic for stains. And we need more napkins," she called after the waiter as he left. She gave her napkin to Alex and blindly accepted one that someone else offered her.

She gave the other napkin to Mallory, meeting the horrified gaze of her new acquaintance. "Mallory, go ahead to the powder room. I'll bring the club soda, sweetheart. These servers move so quickly," she said.

As soon as Mallory was out of earshot, she turned to Alex. "Shame on you for causing all this trouble."

"Me?" Alex said in an incredulous voice, wiping his slacks.

"You're such a flirt. I'm sure you know what kind of effect you have on most women. You really should be more careful doling out those kisses and smiles."

Max appeared at her side and glanced at Alex. "Did someone finally decide to douse him?" he asked, half-joking.

Alex met Max's gaze and gave a heavy sigh. "No. it was the server. Dammit, Lilli can explain it to you," he said and left.

"He didn't hit on you again, did he?"

She shook her head. "He's a flirt. I introduced him to the woman beside me and he got her all flustered. She bumped into the server and there was a spill. Ah, here comes the club soda," she said, smiling at the server as he delivered the bottle and some extra napkins.

"I'm so sorry," he said.

"Accidents happen," she said then looked at Max. "I need to do a little emergency stain removal."

"Saving the day?" he said, his gaze glinting with something that looked like approval.

"That's a stretch, but I would hope someone would do the same for me in the same situation."

He lowered his head toward her. "I could kiss you right this very minute."

Lilli's heart slammed into her rib cage and she gaped at Max. "You—"

"You heard me," he said and his voice was so seductive she immediately felt hot and flustered. "Now go do your good deed."

Stepping backward, her gaze still trapped by his, she nearly stumbled. Max's hand shot out to steady her. "You're worse than Alex."

His eyes widened in outrage. "What the hell—"

She pulled away. "I need to do my good deed," she said and forced her gaze away from his so she could regain her equilibrium. *Men,* she thought and headed for the powder room.

As soon as she entered the luxurious room with a sitting area separate from the stalls, she looked for Mallory, but couldn't find her. Lilli walked into the connecting room filled with stalls and tentatively called, "Mallory?"

"I'm here," she said, covering her face as she exited one of the restrooms. "I can't believe I did that. I'm so embarrassed. I can't go back in there."

"Of course you can. It was just a little spill. They happen all the time," Lilli said, urging the young woman into the sitting area. "Come on. Let me work on your dress."

Mallory moaned. "Why did I have to make a server spill wine on the most amazing man I've ever met?"

"Alex can afford to be taken down a peg or two." She poured a little club soda on the worst spots.

"But not by me," Mallory said. "Do you think he'll run from me every time he sees me from now on?"

Lilli shook her head, dabbing at the dress. "Of course he won't. If nothing else, your meeting was memorable. He'll probably talk to dozens of people tonight, but not many—"

"None," Mallory corrected and gave a reluctant laugh. "None will have gotten his slacks wet." She smiled and met Lillie's gaze. "You've been very kind to me. Would you mind getting together with me sometime for lunch if I promise to try not to spill anything on you?"

Lilli laughed. "I'd love to," she said. "You know this is the same kind of thing that could have happened to me."

"I can't see it," Mallory said. "You look so graceful."

"Thank you, but it's true. Now it's time for us to get back to dinner. The auction should start soon."

Mallory sighed and stood. "Okay, let me put on a little more lipstick."

While Mallory took a couple extra minutes to primp, Lilli walked out into the hallway. She'd gone no more than three steps when she nearly ran into Kiki.

Lilli immediately backed away. "Oh, excuse me. How are you?"

Kiki narrowed her eyes. "I could be a lot better." She stared at Lilli for a long moment then cocked her head to the other less busy side of the hallway. "Do you have a moment? I'd like to talk with you."

"I probably should get back to—"

"Max," Kiki said, her beautiful face tightening with displeasure. "He can wait. This won't take long."

Lilli reluctantly followed Kiki.

"You probably don't know this, but Max and I have

a very close relationship. *Very* close," she emphasized. "In fact, no one would be surprised if we were to get married. We've been seeing each other for a couple of years."

Lilli nodded. "I see."

"A man like Max, well, a woman just has to accept that he may stray every now and then. It doesn't really mean anything. Men, especially powerful men, have women throwing themselves at them all the time."

Lilli wondered what this had to do with her.

"Now Max hasn't wanted to admit anything," Kiki continued with a determined smile that didn't reach her eyes. "I'm sure he doesn't want to hurt my feelings. But I'm not stupid. He obviously feels obligated toward you and I can understand why you would want to take advantage of the situation."

"Not really," Lilli said.

Kiki waved her hand. "You don't need to deny it. I can't imagine any woman in your position who wouldn't exploit the situation to her advantage."

Lilli felt a spurt of anger. "I'm—"

"Just hear me out," Kiki interjected. "What you need to understand is that you won't be able to hold him. Sure, he'll be a great father to the child, but Max is a special man and trust me, he requires special handling. I know he will provide financial support for your child. But you seem like an independent-minded woman, so I thought you might like some additional support of your own."

Confusion and wariness mixed inside her. "Additional support?"

Kiki lowered her voice. "Here's the deal. You leave

Max, never come back and don't get in my way and I'll give you fifty thousand dollars."

Lilli blinked at the woman in disbelief. "Are you serious?"

"Dead serious," Kiki said. "Max is very important to me."

Incredulous, Lilli shook her head. "I can't—"

"Sure you can. Think about it. Imagine getting all that money and a clean break to do what you want where you want." She paused a half beat. "If you make the move within a week, I might even throw in a bonus. You could buy yourself a little condo or house and be in charge of your own life. Trust me, if you stay with Max, he'll have an opinion about everything you say and do." She pressed a card into Lilli's hand. "Call me. I'll make it worth your while."

Lilli stared after the woman as she strode away. She couldn't believe what had just happened. The conversation ran through her mind again, but it was almost too much for her to comprehend.

"Hey, Lilli," Mallory said, moving her hand in front of Lilli's face. "Are you okay? You look a little sick. Should you sit down?"

Lilli shook her head to clear it. "No, I just—" She sighed and headed back to the table.

"Are you sure?" Mallory asked as she followed after her. "You look pale. Like you're sick or you just had a close encounter with an alien or something. Some people don't believe in that stuff, but I do."

Lilli shook her head at the irony. "That's a pretty good explanation," she said.

"What is?" Mallory asked.

"A close encounter with an alien," Lilli said, crumpling Kiki's card into a little wad and tossing it onto a passing waiter's empty tray.

Mallory nodded and whispered, "The place is full of aliens tonight, isn't it?"

Still shaken from her encounter with Kiki, but trying to get past it, Lilli returned with Mallory to the table just as dessert was being served. Max immediately stood and helped both Lilli and Mallory into their chairs while Lilli introduced Mallory.

After they all sat down, he turned to Lilli. "Everything okay?"

She gave a circular nod, but mustered a smile.

"You want to explain that remark about Alex?" he asked.

She felt her cheeks heat with embarrassment. "I was just commenting that it's not fair for him—or you—to use your—" she searched for an appropriate word "—appeal to put a woman off balance."

His lips twitched. "Are you admitting I put you off balance?"

She reached for her glass of water. "I'm not saying anything else. I offered my explanation."

"Sounds like you're pleading the fifth."

"How is Kiki?" she asked, changing the focus off herself.

Irritation crossed his face. "How is it that a woman can appear perfectly sane and rational at the beginning of a relationship then turn totally insane and irrational at the end?"

"It's all the man's fault," she said. "Men turn women

into raging lunatics. They hint, they promise, they mislead."

"I am always up-front in my relationships with women. I make it clear that I'm not interested in marriage and—"

"Why not?" she asked. "Why aren't you interested in marriage?"

"It needs to be the right woman at the right time. I've never found the right woman."

"Why not Kiki?" she asked, keeping her voice low.

"This isn't the best place for a private discussion, but I've never been serious about Kiki. She's a beautiful, intelligent woman, but not right for me in the long run. I told her that from the beginning."

Ouch, Lilli thought. That couldn't have gone over well. "Is there anything you did that might have led her to believe that you'd changed your mind and that you and her were getting close to a commitment?"

He narrowed his eyes. "Why are you asking these questions?"

She shrugged. "Just curious. She seems a little…"

"A little what?"

"I don't know. Maybe possessive."

"I made it clear tonight that we're through. Now, don't you want to eat some of this dessert? It's chocolate cake."

Lilli's stomach twisted. "I'd love to, but I'm full."

He studied her for a long moment. "Something's not right," he began.

"Ladies and gentleman," Ann Wingate, the mistress of ceremonies announced, saving Lilli from replying to Max. "It's now time for the Silent Auction. Please make your way to the display tables and loosen your purse strings. And remember, it's all for a good cause."

"You're sure you don't want your cake," Max said.

She shook her head. "Thanks, no. I'm curious what they've put up for auction."

He nodded and stood, pulling her chair back for her to rise. "Pick a couple things you like and make a bid on my behalf."

"Oh, I couldn't do that."

"Why not? It's for charity."

"Yes, but—" She broke off. "It wouldn't feel right."

He gave a heavy sigh. "Then pick out something I can donate to a good cause."

She liked that idea much better. "That could be fun."

With the exception of several interruptions, Max actually enjoyed himself during the next hour. Lilli's careful assessment of the items amused him. He noticed she spent an inordinate amount of time studying an expensive baby stroller before she dismissed it and moved along.

"Which should I buy to give away?" he asked, curious what her answer would be.

"The spa and makeover packages for the women's shelter downtown. The deluxe computer system for the homeless shelter."

"That's all?"

"I think they'll provide good bang for the buck."

"You didn't see anything you like? Jewelry? A luxury cruise?"

She shook her head and he continued. "Baby stroller."

She gave a start then shook her head again. "That thing costs almost as much as a car. Crazy expensive."

Max couldn't help wondering how long her attitude would last if she were exposed to luxury all the time. In his experience, women tended to easily grow accustomed to the finer things. She amused him at the same time that she attracted him. Her laughter affected him like a strong jolt of java and her determination not to brown-nose him startled him. He was surrounded by yes people and she didn't hesitate to tell him no. Even though she was pregnant, or perhaps partly because of it, she drew his attention the way no other woman had.

How could she possibly be so innocent and sexy at the same time? He couldn't believe his half brother's damn good luck in finding her. She couldn't be perfect, though, he reminded himself. No one was, and he'd never met a woman who didn't have the capacity for deceit and manipulation. Still, he wanted her. And he wasn't inclined to resist her.

Seven

"You absolutely shouldn't have gotten that baby stroller," Lilli said in a huffy voice. "It was insanely expensive."

"Butter bean will like it," Max said.

She threw him a sideways glance as he opened the door to the house for her. "He would have been just as happy with a less costly model."

"You don't know that," Max argued. "The cutting-edge aerodynamic design, which features an unparalleled smooth ride," he quoted from the manufacturer, "may make a huge difference."

"In that case, he'd better be flexible because my compact car gives a high five to every bump in the road."

He chuckled.

She turned to face him. "But seriously, I cannot accept the jewelry."

"It's just sterling silver."

"David Yurman's top-of-the-line." She shook her head. "I don't understand why you bought it for me. I told you I didn't want anything."

"I'm sure that was part of it," he said.

"You mean you gave me this just to be disagreeable?" she asked, her eyes rounding in surprise.

"It contributed, plus as the hostess kept saying, it's all for charity."

Her lips twitched. "You don't believe any of it. You don't believe the manufacturer's brag about the stroller and you think it's stupid to hold an auction to get donations."

"It's a lot easier to just guilt people into giving money through the mail," he said.

"But for some people, it's more fun to give it away at an auction."

He nodded. "Depends on the people."

She bit her lip and her expression changed. "Maybe." She paused. "I still don't understand why you got me the jewelry."

"The blue topaz reminded me of your eyes," he said.

He saw a hint of something deeper than desire flash through her eyes before she took a quick breath and looked away. "Oh."

His gut twisted with a surprising instinct to pull her against him and kiss her. Take her. He swore under his breath.

She cleared her throat. "Well, you shouldn't have, but it was very nice of you."

"I surprised you," he said. "You thought I was a selfish miser like Scrooge."

"I never thought you were like Scrooge." She paused and seemed to decide that she shouldn't elaborate.

He would love to know what she was really thinking.

"Thank you again. I should go up to bed," she said and paused. "I was wondering," she began and abruptly stopped.

"Wondering what?"

"It's really none of my business."

"I won't know if that's true until you ask the question."

"I was wondering," she ventured. "Do you have any godchildren?"

He narrowed his eyes. "Why do you ask? Did someone mention that to you tonight?"

"At the auction?" she said. "Of course not."

He tugged at his tie. "The truth is I have five godchildren."

Her eyes rounded. "Omigoodness. So many."

He waved his hand in a dismissive gesture. "I'm not expected to do any real parenting. I'm actually a co-godparent. The parents just want my financial management in case anything should happen to them. Along with the gifts and tuition," he added.

"Gifts and tuition?" she echoed, her brow furrowing in confusion.

"They're counting on me to provide a significant college fund."

"For five children?" she said. "Isn't that a bit much?"

"I've got it," he said. "But I've started dodging the opportunity to add any more godchildren."

"I can't blame you for that. My goodness, no wonder you're so cynical."

"No need for flattery," he said, chuckling at her assessment.

Her gaze softened. "But it is very generous of you to accept the responsibility."

"Financial responsibility," he corrected.

She gave a slow nod. "Whatever would you do if, for some unforeseen reason, you became the guardian of five children?"

"Boarding school," he said.

Her face fell. "Oh. That's why I'll never sign your agreement for butter bean."

"You don't really have anyone in mind to be the guardian for your child, do you?" he asked.

She looked away. "I really am working on it."

He touched her arm. "Lilli, tell me the truth."

She bit her lip. "The closest I have is my good friend Dee. She's loving and affectionate and adores children. But she's also a free spirit and loves to travel." She sighed and lifted her lips in a smile that didn't reach her eyes. "Maybe I should place a want ad."

"Never," he said.

"That's what I have to say about boarding school," she replied. The silence hung between them, thick with pent-up desire and emotion. It was so strong he could taste it.

"I should go to bed. Thank you again for an amazing evening. Good night," she said and turned to go upstairs.

He felt the same twitchy sensation he'd felt the first time he'd met her. It was the same feeling of intuition he had just before he made a successful business move. He'd never felt it about a woman, he thought, shaking his head. Loosening his tie, he picked up the weekend edition of one of his newspapers and sat down for a few minutes.

Restless, he decided to pour a glass of red wine. Taking it outside on the patio, he inhaled the scent of the flowers his gardener kept in meticulous condition year-round and listened to the soothing sound of the waterfall in the pool.

Max wondered what would have happened between him and Lilli if they'd met under different circumstances. If she'd never been involved with his brother and gotten pregnant. For just a moment, he indulged himself. He would have seduced her immediately. He would have talked her into quitting her job so she could travel with him at a moment's notice.

The image of her pale naked body available to him at all times made him hard. She was a passionate woman and he would want to learn all of her secrets. He would find out what made her moan, what made her sweat and what would make her come alive in his arms.

He would want to mark her as his with jewelry, but not marriage. Although he'd never invited a woman to live in his home, Lilli may very well have been the first.

Of course, he would have asked her to sign a financial agreement that would protect both her and him for the time when their relationship ended. Every good thing came to an end, Max knew that. He suspected she would have refused to sign the agreement, he thought with a twinge of humor, and he would have had the affair with her anyway.

He swallowed a drink of wine and ruthlessly cut off

his little mental fantasy. With the impending birth of his brother's child, there was far more at stake than Max's libido. Even though he was encouraged by how seriously Lilli was taking her maternal duties, he knew that attitude could change for a variety of reasons.

His own brother's guardian had started out well, but when Tony had hit his teens, the guardian had seemed to give up. She'd allowed Tony way too much freedom and Max was convinced the lack of parental influence had sent Tony down the road into trouble and eventually to his death.

Max refused to allow that to happen to another De Luca. If Lilli continued to refuse to sign an agreement with him, there were other ways. More drastic, more costly, but perhaps ultimately necessary.

Two days later, Lilli left work a little early because Max had invited her to join him for dinner at The Trillion Resort's rooftop restaurant. His assistant had made the arrangements with her, and she had no idea why he'd invited her. Since the auction, Max had worked such late hours she hadn't seen him at all.

She fussed over what to wear and finally chose a pair of maternity slacks and a silk top with varying colors of sea-blue that featured an Empire waist and fell nearly to her knees.

She wore the sterling jewelry Max had purchased for her at the auction and had gone a little more daring with her makeup by giving her eyes a smoky look.

Although she cursed herself for it, she wanted to look nice for Max. She rolled her eyes at the way she minimized her feelings. The truth was she wanted to make his head spin. It was only fair since the man could turn her upside down with just a glance.

Max's chauffeur drove her in one of the luxury sedans. As he pulled in front of the palatial resort, a valet rushed to her door to open it. "Good evening. Mr. De Luca's guest?"

She nodded in surprise as she accepted his assistance out of the car. "Yes, how did you—"

The young man smiled. "We know all of Mr. De Luca's vehicles."

"Oh," she said, nodding. "Thank you." She turned back to Max's chauffeur, Ricardo. "Thank you for the ride."

Ricardo smiled at her and waved. "My pleasure, Miss McCall. Enjoy your evening."

Lilli made her way to the glass elevators that whisked her up to the top level of the resort. Walking into the restaurant, she looked for Max. A man beside her said, "May I help…"

Her gaze collided with Max's across the room and she didn't hear anything else. He rose from the table where he sat, his gaze fixed on her.

The intensity with which he watched her made her feel as if she couldn't breathe. Her heart felt as if it were tripping over itself. Why did this man affect her on so many levels?

She walked to his table and he extended his hand, taking hers. "You look beautiful."

"Thank you," she whispered and took a shallow breath. "This is lovely."

"I thought you might enjoy a night out," he said and glanced down at the necklace she wore. He touched the pendant and his warm fingers brushed her bare skin. "I like the way my gift looks on you."

The hint of sensual possessiveness in his tone gave her a surprising, forbidden thrill. She was a liberated woman. For Pete's sake, what was wrong with her?

"Have a seat," he said before she could reply. "I already ordered orange juice and seltzer for you."

"Thank you." She sat down and felt the hum of anticipation and electricity wind a little tighter between them.

The waiter appeared at their table, offered suggestions and they placed their orders. Max was all charming conversation, pointing out different sights from the restaurant's breathtaking view as the sun slid lower on the horizon.

Tonight interruptions were kept to a minimum. Although Lilli felt plenty of gazes on her and Max, no one approached the table. The waitstaff were perfect, appearing to refill drinks, clear plates and provide nearly invisible but courteous service.

"I told the maître' d I wanted as few interruptions as possible tonight," Max said as if he'd read her mind.

She nodded. "I couldn't help comparing this experience to the auction."

"The auction was a free-for-all. Now you understand why I don't attend many," he said and lifted his hand. "Although I must say I enjoyed it much more because you were there."

"It was fun and I made a new friend," she said.

"Who?"

"Mallory James. She invited me to lunch on Saturday."

He nodded his head in approval. "Good. You'll be occupied."

Strange response, she thought. "Occupied for what?"

"I'm going out of town for three weeks."

Her heart sank. Crazy. She would have to think about that later. "Oh, wow. That's a long trip."

"Yes. I knew it was coming. We have several grand reopenings in different locations scheduled over the next few weeks and my presence is required at all of them."

"The bane of being the boss," she said, forcing a smile because, heaven help her, she would miss him.

"These arrangements were made before I knew you existed. I'll be out of the country," he said, clearly displeased. "I'm not comfortable leaving you at this stage."

His confession made her feel as if the sun came out from behind a cloud. "I've got six weeks until my due date. Everything's been perfect so far. There's no reason to think I'll have any problems."

"Still," he said. "It's best to be prepared for everything. Give me your cell phone."

She blinked. "Why?"

"So I can program in my contact numbers," he said.

"Oh, I can't imagine that I would need to call you while you're out of the country," she said.

He waved his fingers impatiently and she gave him her phone. "Of course, you'll be talking to me. I'll be checking in with you on a regular basis. For any immediate emergencies, you're to call my assistant, Grace. I've told her to be on twenty-four hour call."

"That's ridiculous. I wouldn't call your assistant. I've never even met her."

"If you're not comfortable, I can arrange a meeting."

Overwhelmed, Lilli shook her head. "No. That's not

necessary." She lowered her voice. "None of this is necessary. I'll be fine."

He met her gaze. "It's my job to make sure you stay that way."

"Why?" she demanded. "It's not as if you're my hus—" She broke off, horrified that the words had just popped out of her mouth.

Unable to tear her gaze from his, Lilli felt something snap and shimmer between them. A forbidden possibility neither of them would consider. What if Max *was* her husband? What if… Feeling as if the circuits in her head had scrambled and misfired, she looked away from him.

She took a mind-clearing breath. "That was stupid. This is about the baby. You feel responsible because you're the uncle. It's not about me."

He cleared his throat. "It's all connected. The baby, you, me. And since your delivery date is growing closer, you must make a decision about guardianship if something should happen to you."

She glanced back at him and watched him pull a manila envelope from his suit jacket pocket. "I've asked my attorney to come up with an agreement that should be more palatable for you. While I'm gone, I want you to look at this and take it to another attorney if that will make you more comfortable."

Her heart twisted. This entire meal had been a setup. Max wanted one thing and one thing alone from her. Control of her baby. Although she wanted to toss the agreement back at him, she felt forced to take the envelope for the sake of civility.

Max seemed to sense the change in her mood and signed for the check and escorted her from the dining room. She hated sharing the close space of the elevator, but getting into the Ferrari with him was far more excruciating. The darkness closed around them, creating a veil of intimacy.

Every time he shifted gears, her gaze strayed to his hand tightening around the knob. His long legs flexed as he accelerated and pushed in the clutch. Despite her hostility, she couldn't help noticing a commanding sensuality with the way he drove the luxury sports car. He would be a commanding, demanding lover, she knew, but he would also make sure his partner was satisfied. In fact, she suspected a woman might never be the same once she'd shared a bed with Max.

As soon as he pulled into the garage and came to a stop, she turned to unlock her door. The second after she hit the button, the automatic lock clicked again, effectively trapping her in the car with Max. Inhaling a shallow breath, she caught a draft of his masculine scent with just a hint of cologne.

Although she fought its effect on her, she couldn't deny feeling light-headed and entirely too aware of him as a man. "What do you want?" she asked without turning to look at him.

"You haven't had a chance to read my attorney's proposal, so you can't be upset about it. But you haven't said a word since we left the restaurant. Why?"

She stiffened her resolve against his gentle, reasonable voice. "You don't seem to understand. My baby is not for sale."

Three seconds of silence passed before she felt his hand on her arm. "Look at me. You can't really believe that I intend to buy your child."

She reluctantly faced him. "Why should I believe anything else? You've been trying to cram money down my throat since the first time I met you. In exchange for control of my child." She willed herself to keep her voice from wavering. "You said I should find this agreement more palatable. You don't seem to understand that it doesn't matter how much money you pile onto the agreement, I'm not giving up my baby to you."

He stared at her in shock. "Is that what you think? That the new agreement is about money? It isn't. It gives you far more rights than the previous one. Good God, do you really think I'm that much of an ogre?"

Glimpsing his sincerity, she bit her lip in confusion. "I didn't know what else to think. You invite me to a fabulous dinner where you act as if you're actually enjoying my company then slap me with a contract."

"Of course I enjoyed dinner with you. Otherwise, I could have left the contract with one of my staff to give to you. And I wanted you to have my contact numbers. This is my last night in town for a while. I wanted to spend it with you."

Her heart hammered against her rib cage and she shook her head. "You're confusing me. I don't know what you want from me," she said. "Other than to sign your agreement."

He looked into her eyes for a long moment then his gaze traveled to her lips and lingered. He lifted his gaze again to hers and she felt scorched by the desire she saw there.

"You want to know what I want from you?" he asked in a low voice. Then he lowered his head and took her mouth. He slid one of his hands under her jaw and cupped her face as if she were both precious and sensuous. The gesture undid her.

He devoured her mouth in dizzying kisses as he gently rubbed his hands down her neck, massaging her taut muscles.

His kiss turned her body into a bow of tension, eager for him. His massaging fingers gentled her, clouding her mind, making her willing to do whatever he wanted.

His mouth continued to take hers while his fingers drifted across her collarbone and lower to the tops of her breasts. She felt her nipples strain against the cups of her bra. Restlessness and need swelled inside her.

He paused a half beat then slid his fingertips beneath the top of her blouse, brushing them over her sensitized nipples. She gasped in pleasure at the sensation.

He pulled his hands from her breasts and placed them on her shoulders. He pulled his mouth a breath away from hers and it was all she could do to keep from asking him not to stop.

"I want you," he said against her mouth. "I want you in every way you can imagine and probably a few you can't. But now is not the time." He slid one of his hands through her hair. "Promise me that you'll take care of yourself while I'm away. No taking chances. And call me if you need me."

Lilli closed her eyes. She'd felt the power of his desire. What frightened her was the fact that her desire for him matched his. What frightened her even more was the very real possibility that she could need Max in ways *he* would never dream.

Eight

Two and a half weeks later, Lilli dragged herself from her little car up the steps from the mansion's garage. Her back and legs had been aching all day. She felt tired and cranky and, heaven help her, she missed Max. He called frequently, and every time, she felt the tension between them twist a little tighter.

She'd spent more than one night flirting with the forbidden fantasy of Max being the father of her child. Right now, though, all she wanted to focus on was getting a sandwich, taking a shower and going to bed.

Stepping into the foyer, she stopped and drank in a moment of peace and quiet then walked toward the kitchen.

"Surprise!" a chorus of voices called, startling her so much she dropped her water bottle and purse.

Her friends clapped in delight.

"We did it," her best friend Dee crowed. "We surprised you."

"Yes, you did." Lilli felt some of her weariness fade away and smiled. "How did you pull this off?"

"Because we're your brilliant friends, of course," Dee said. "And I think Mallory here has a magic wand. She knew how to deal with the staff, and just wait until you see the cake she brought."

"Cake?" Lilli echoed and gave Mallory a hug as the woman walked toward her. She'd enjoyed a few lunches with Mallory during the last two weeks and Lilli already had a soft spot for the woman. "You shouldn't have."

"It's nothing. I'm just glad to be a part of all this. Now come in and sit down. Let me get you some sherbet punch."

After Lilli opened the gifts for her and the baby, Mallory presented Lilli with a large sheet cake decorated with a baby in a blue buggy inscribed with frosted letters, "Happy Baby, Lilli!" The cake was lit with one candle.

"Make a wish and blow out the candle," Mallory said.

"But it's not my birthday."

"It's your first baby. You can add more candles when you have more babies."

Lilli looked at her in horror. "More?"

"Okay, let's just focus on one, then," Mallory quickly amended. "Make a wish and blow out the candle."

Lilli closed her eyes and wished for a safe and easy delivery and good health for her baby. Secretly, she wished for a father for her child. An image of the man she would choose appeared in her mind. She blinked, pushing aside the thought. Crazy and impossible, she thought. Must be the hormones.

Just after she opened the last gift, the room abruptly turned silent.

"Major hot guy alert," Dee whispered.

Lilli turned to see Max standing in the doorway, a wrapped package in his hand. "Max," she said, stunned. "I thought you were still traveling."

"I just got back thirty minutes ago. You didn't tell me you were having a baby shower," he said in a lightly chastising tone.

Lilli drank in the sight of him. Holding her breath, she wondered if he had looked forward to seeing her again as much as she had looked forward to having him back home. She wondered if he still wanted her the same way he had before.

Dee cleared her throat. "It was a surprise shower," she said to Max. "What's in the box?"

He gave a brief glance to Dee then moved toward Lilli. His gaze dipped to her belly.

"I've gotten bigger," she said, unable to keep herself from smiling.

He gave a half grin. "So you have. And still glowing." He gave her the small but beautifully wrapped box. "Myrtle left a message for me about the shower. I thought you could use this."

Her hands trembled and she wished they would stop. She hadn't seen Max in weeks and she would just like to sit down and talk with him. She managed to open the box and found a gift certificate inside. "One mother's helper of your choice from Personalized Nanny Services for one year."

Mallory nodded in approval. "PNS is the very best."

"A nanny?" Lilli said, staring at Max. "I hadn't planned—"

"Oh, no," Dee said. "You're not turning this one down. She loves it," Dee said to Max. "Perfect gift. Thank you very much." She turned back to Lilli. "If you get tired of having her around, you can send her over to my place. I would love for someone to make peanut butter and jelly sandwiches and chocolate chip cookies for me."

Several of the women moaned in agreement. "Will she do laundry? Will she grocery shop?"

Max met Lilli's gaze. "She'll do whatever Lilli wants her to do."

There was another group moan followed by a collective sigh.

"Can I see you privately for a moment?" he asked.

Lilli felt a combination kick from the baby and a flutter from her heart. "Sure," she said, rising from her seat.

"Ask him about Alex," Mallory whispered.

Tearing her gaze from Max, she glanced at Mallory. "Ask him what about Alex?"

"Where he hangs out after work. I introduced him to my father and haven't seen him since."

"From what Max says, that could be for the best. Alex is supposed to be a major player."

"I'd just like the opportunity to find out for myself," Mallory said.

"Okay. I'll see what I can do," she said, but her mind wasn't on Alex or Mallory. It was dominated by Max.

She followed him into the foyer, noticing subtle changes in his appearance. His hair was just a little longer, more wavy. When he turned to face her, she noticed his eyes looked a bit weary as he studied her.

"It's a nice surprise to see you," she said. "I had no idea you'd be back so soon."

"I'm glad I could make it. Are you okay? Any of Tony's friends hanging around?"

"I'm fine and I haven't seen any of Tony's friends in a long time."

"Good," he said and held her gaze. "I have another event I'm expected to attend tonight, but we need to talk sometime soon. Have you looked over the agreement I left with you?"

She felt a rush of disappointment. "Yes, I have."

"Good," he said again. His gaze seemed to say so much more, but Lilli wondered if she was imagining it. "I won't keep you from your friends."

She felt another twist of disappointment. That was it. No *I'm glad to see you, I want you...* Nothing. She stared, waiting, wanting.

"Good night," he said and turned toward the door.

Lilli continued to stare after him, starting to feel like a fool. Had she misunderstood? "Wait," she said.

He stopped just as he reached the door and turned around. "Yes?"

Her heart raced. Confused, she didn't know what to say. "I...uh..." She groped for something to say. "Mallory asked me to ask you about Alex."

"Alex Megalos?" he said with a frown, walking back toward her.

"Yes. I think she'd like to get to know him better. She

was wondering where he usually hangs out after work," she said, suddenly feeling like a middle schooler.

He shook his head. "I have no idea."

She gave a slow nod. "Okay" she said. "I'll tell her."

He shrugged. "I can probably find out something from my assistant."

"Thanks." She hesitated a half beat, hating the awkwardness between them. "Are you okay?"

"Yeah. Just tired and harassed. I've been on longer trips, but this one felt like it went on forever."

She nodded again. "Yeah, it did—" She broke off before she added *for me, too*. Feeling her cheeks heat from his knowing gaze, she cleared her throat. "Why do you think it felt so long?"

"I think you know," he said and moved closer to her.

"You want me to sign the agreement about the baby," she said in a husky voice.

"That's part of it." He lowered his head. He inhaled sharply and closed his eyes then stepped back. God help him, if he started kissing her, he wouldn't stop. Being away from her hadn't cleared his perspective or dampened his desire for her. And Max knew there wasn't a damn thing he could do about wanting her at the moment. He'd missed the sound of her laughter and knowing she would be there at home for the end of the day.

Maybe it was a good thing he had to attend the charity fund-raiser tonight after all. Being with Lilli was a constant reminder of what he couldn't have.

"I should go," he said in a low voice. "We can talk more on Friday. Tomorrow will be a busy day."

"Okay, thank you for the gift."

"You're welcome," he said and held her gaze for a long moment before he left.

The following evening, Lilli flipped through the newspaper as she put up her feet at the end of a long day. She glanced at the bad news on the front page, skipped the Sports section and stopped at the Life-style section. The front page featured photos of a charity function sponsored by Max's company. In one of the photos, Kiki stood next to Max, her arm looped through his. He didn't look as if he were suffering at all.

A surge of something dark twisted through her and when she realized what it was, she felt more stupid than ever. She was jealous. Maybe it was hormones. Oh Lord, she hoped so. Because if it were hormones then at some point, when her hormones straightened out again, the crazy longing would go away.

Restless after reading the article, she took a long bath and listened to soothing music. She sipped herbal tea to calm herself and tried not to think about that photo of Max with Kiki.

She slept horribly, unable to get comfortable. Giving up on sleep, she rose earlier than usual. When she got out of bed, she felt exhausted and noticed her abdomen tightening. As she prepared for work, the sensation didn't go away. Were these contractions?

Although she had a few weeks left before her due date she called her doctor's office. The doctor on call asked a few questions then, erring on the cautious side, instructed her to go to the hospital.

Lilli grabbed her purse and went downstairs. Max

stood poised to leave. He met her gaze. "Good morning. How are you?"

Lilli burst into tears.

Alarmed by her response, Max dropped his briefcase and immediately took her in her arms. "What is it? What's wrong?"

She choked back a sob. "I may be in labor. My doctor told me to go to the hospital. Max, this is happening too fast." Her blue eyes filled with tears of desperation. "I'm not ready."

"Of course you are," he said firmly even though his own gut was clenching in apprehension. "I'll drive you to the hospital and—"

"Are you sure that's what you want—?"

"Of course I'm sure," he said, appalled that she would expect anything less of him. "We'll take the town car." He ushered her to the garage. "I'll drive. You can sit in the backseat and stretch out."

His own heart hammering in his chest, Max helped her into the car and sped to the hospital. He shot a glance at Lilli in the rearview mirror and the expression of fear on her face tore at him. "You're going to be okay. The baby is going to be okay."

"Do you really believe that?"

He nodded. "Yes, I do." He had to believe it.

Pulling the car to a stop outside the emergency room door, he helped Lilli inside. An admission clerk took her information and Lilli was whisked away. Just before she disappeared behind the double doors, she looked back at Max. "Are you leaving?"

He shook his head. "I'll be right back after I park the car." Returning to the hospital, he was consumed with concern for Lilli and the baby. He would get the finest doctors in Las Vegas to care for her. He would do whatever it took to keep Lilli and the baby safe and healthy.

He strode toward the emergency room double doors, making a mental list. A woman stepped in front of him. "Excuse me, sir. You're not allowed inside unless you're a member of a patient's family."

Frustration ripped through him. He needed to take care of Lilli, but it wasn't his official duty or his official right. At that moment, he made a life-altering decision. He knew there would be no going back. But never again would he worry about being barred from taking care of Lilli or the baby. He would make her his wife. That way, taking care of her and the baby would always be his right. "I'm the baby's father," he told the woman, and she allowed him to pass.

Two and a half hours later, a mortified Lilli left the hospital with Max. "I'm so sorry," she said, shooting a wincing glance at him. His hair was ruffled from plowing his fingers through it and his tie hung loose from his collar. He was more gorgeous than ever and she felt like a lunatic. "I should have realized it was false labor."

"Like the doctor said, it's an easy mistake to make. This is your first pregnancy."

"Maybe," she said. "But now you've lost half a day of work because of my mistake."

"A half day of work is nothing to make sure you and the baby are safe," he said, his words barely softening the harsh sound of his voice as he drove them home. "Stop apologizing."

She bit her lip and looked out the window then back at him. "Are you sure you're not angry?"

"I'm not angry, but I am concerned. This underscores the need for you to provide for the baby if something, God forbid, should happen to you," he said and swore under his breath.

"I know," she said glumly. She knew she couldn't dodge it any longer. "I'm going to change my will today so that you'll be the baby's guardian."

He narrowed his eyes at her words. "That's a good start, but we may need to take that further."

Her chest tightened. He was talking about the agreement he wanted her to sign. Even though she understood the money in the agreement was designated for support, she still found it distasteful. "I don't want your money and I don't want to sign the agreement. It just feels totally wrong to me."

"I'm not talking about that agreement," he said, pulling the car into a bank parking lot and cutting the engine.

Lilli looked at him in surprise. "Then what?"

"I've been thinking. How do you feel about the baby's last name being De Luca?"

She frowned in confusion. "I thought I was going to try not to draw attention to the fact that Tony was his father. For safety's sake. That's the reason I'll be moving away."

"What if you didn't move away?" he asked, his gaze searching hers. "What if your last name became De Luca, too?"

More confused than ever, she shook her head. "How could that happen?"

"If you named me the father of—" he paused "—your child. And married me."

She gaped at him, feeling as if someone had turned the whole world upside down. "Married you? But you don't love me."

"Starting out in love isn't the best predictor of success in marriage."

Her head was whirling. "I don't understand. You don't want to get married. You're pretty cynical about marriage."

"I want to provide a good life for the baby. I feel responsible for him. For you," he said as if he didn't totally understand his own feelings.

"I don't think that's a good basis for a marriage."

"There's a lot worse," he said.

Her chest tightened. "I don't want to feel like a responsibility. Like a burden. And I don't want the baby to ever feel that way."

"It *wouldn't* be that way. I think you and I could make this work." He slid his hand under her jaw. "And there's the fact that I want you. And you want me," he said, his tone intimate.

"I wondered if maybe that had changed."

He slowly shook his head.

Her heart skipped over itself. "What about when that does change?"

"How do you know it will?" he asked, his dark eyes holding hers.

Lilli felt herself sinking into a delicious, forbidden pool of hope. "I don't know."

He caressed her jaw. "I think you know that you and I would be good together. In a lot of ways."

True. But that didn't mean they should get married. Lilli tore away her gaze to clear her head. If she put the baby's needs in front of hers, what would she do? She felt an immediate smack from her conscience. Who was she fooling? It wasn't as if being with Max De Luca would present a hardship for her. But this was a huge decision. Huge enough that she wanted to make it with a clear head.

"Could you give me some time to think this over?"

He met her gaze and nodded. "Sure." He paused a half beat. "Think about it. You'll realize it's best for everyone."

She felt a sliver of relief. She'd bought herself a little time.

"Do you have any questions you'd like to ask me?" he said, as if he sensed what was going on inside her.

She closed her eyes so she wouldn't be affected by his presence, but she still sensed him, still smelled the faintest scent of his sexy cologne. "If you raised the baby, would you blow bubbles with him?"

He didn't even pause. "Yes."

"Will you read him books at night? You can let the nanny do it every now and then, but you need to do it most nights."

"Yes," he said.

"Will you tell him he's wonderful?"

"Yes."

"Will you hold him when he cries?"

"Yes. And I'll hold you, too, Lilli, whether you're crying or not."

And Lilli felt her heart tumble a little farther away from good sense and sanity.

Nine

"**I** like it," Max said to Alex during a one-on-one meeting in his office. "At first glance, when you say West Virginia, I would think the local economy wouldn't be able to support this kind of luxury resort."

Alex tapped his pen on his outline. "Because it's close to Washington, D.C., there's great transportation access. D.C. residents will be rushing there every weekend."

"The sticking point with the board will be the mid-week challenge," Max said. "Who wants to go to West Virginia in the middle of the week?"

"We can hold meetings and conferences. Plus, if we do it right, this place will have a spa, golf course, special events and all kinds of luxury amenities that will draw people year-round."

"Like I said, I like it. You've got my—" His intercom

beeped, interrupting him. Surprised because he'd told his assistant no interruptions during his meeting, he picked up his phone. "Yes."

"I'm terribly sorry to interrupt you, Mr. De Luca, but security downstairs has called and they said a very pregnant woman insists on seeing you."

There was only one very pregnant woman in his life. Immediately concerned, he frowned. "Lilli," he said. "Is she okay?"

His assistant, Grace, made a sound between a cough and swallowed laughter. "She sounds quite healthy, sir. Just very determined to see you. Security was unsure what to do with her."

He nodded, feeling a twinge of amusement at the notion of the beefy guys downstairs trying to handle a demanding pregnant woman. "Send her up immediately."

Alex stood, lifting his eyebrow. "Does this mean our meeting is over?"

"For now," Max said. "Let's set up a time to discuss a strategy for approaching the board about this."

Alex extended his hand. "Sounds great." He gathered his report and headed for the office door. Just as he reached for it, the door flung open and Lilli burst inside. Her cheeks bright red, she carried a large rectangular plastic food container.

"Good grief," she said. "Do you train your security to suspect that every pregnant woman is a nut or did I just get lucky today?"

Max chuckled under his breath and moved toward her to take the container. "It won't happen again. Here, let me help—"

"No," Alex said and grabbed the container before

Max could. "Allow me and let me say you look gorgeous as ever."

Flirting again, Max thought with more than a pinch of irritation. Did the man ever stop?

"I look like a blond beach ball," she told Alex. "But thanks for the effort. Would you do me a favor and call a few of the assistants into the office?"

Max frowned. "What—"

"Sure," Alex said and set the container down on a table.

Lilli smiled nervously as she met Max's gaze. "This won't take but a few minutes. Then you can get back to whatever you were doing."

Max shook his head. "But what is *this?*"

She gnawed her lip. "Just a little something."

Her expression made him uneasy. *What the…*

Alex reappeared in the doorway with several members of the staff, their faces filled with curiosity. "Ready for service," Alex said.

"Thank you," Lilli said and went to the table where the plastic container sat. "I just need to borrow your voices for two minutes. Today is Max's birthday, so I was hoping you would join with me in singing 'Happy Birthday.'" She whipped off the top of the container to reveal a collection of frosted cupcakes decorated with sprinkles. "Sorry you can't blow out the candles," she said with a moue. "Security took my matches. Okay, let's go."

Max stood in stunned disbelief as she led the small group in song. Alex laughed the entire way through the tune.

When they finished, Lilli shot him a wary glance and a tentative smile. "Happy Birthday, Max."

Max met her gaze and felt his heart swell to at least twice its normal size. He hadn't celebrated his birthday in years. It was just another day to him. "How did you know?"

"That's a secret," she said. "But I didn't know your favorite kind of cupcake, so I made a variety. Vanilla with chocolate frosting, chocolate with chocolate frosting, chocolate with vanilla—"

Alex extended his hand into the container. "I'll take the chocolate with—"

Lilli lightly swatted his hand. "It's Max's birthday. He gets to choose first." She glanced at Max. "What kind do you want?"

I want Lilli with Lilli frosting, he thought and cleared his throat. "Chocolate and chocolate," he said and nodded toward the staff. "Go ahead, help yourself."

Each of his employees took their treats and wished him a happy birthday before they left. Alex lingered an extra moment. "For your information, my birthday is November 16 and I love cupcakes."

Max felt a surge of possessiveness. "Call a bakery," he growled.

Alex laughed and shook his head. "You're a damn lucky man, Max. Happy birthday," he said and left the office.

Closing the door, Max turned toward Lilli, who was sitting in a chair across from his desk, biting off the top of a chocolate cupcake. He walked to the chair across from hers and sat down. "What possessed you to do this?"

"You're not angry, are you?"

He shook his head. "Off guard. Surprised." And a

few other things he didn't want to name. "You didn't answer my question."

She licked her lips and he wished he could do it for her. "It occurred to me that you may not have celebrated your birthday very much when you were in boarding school. That was a bad habit to start at such a young age," she said in a chastising voice that made his lips twitch. "So I thought I should get you back on track."

"Why?"

She met his gaze and he saw a flash of deep emotion shimmer in her eyes. Max could identify things that held a high value and what he saw in her gaze was more precious than all the gems in the exclusive jewelry store down the street.

"I think you are an amazing man. So the day you were born should be celebrated."

Her simple explanation held no false flattery. He heard the sincerity in her voice, saw it on her face, and it was the most seductive thing anyone had ever said to him. Lilli, pregnant or not, made him hungry for more of her. Standing, he took her hand and pulled her close. "Marry me."

He saw the desire and fear collide in her gaze. "It's right," he said. "For all of us."

"How can you be so sure?" she whispered.

"Be honest, Lilli. Underneath it all, you want it, too."

She closed her eyes for a long moment and he could feel her heart hammering against him. She took a small shallow breath and opened her eyes. "Yes, I'll marry you."

Max made the arrangements so quickly Lilli barely had time to catch her breath, let alone her sanity. Three days before he'd scheduled a private wedding ceremony with a judge who was a friend, he and Lilli shared late-night conversation on the patio.

"I picked this up today. Let me know if you like it." He casually slid a box across the table toward her.

Curious, she opened the box. Shocked at the diamond ring winking back at her from the velvet fold of the box, she choked on the water she had just swallowed.

Max patted her on her back. "Are you okay?"

She coughed, tears coming to her eyes, then waved her hand. "Yes." She coughed again and shook her head. "I didn't expect an engagement ring."

"Of course I'd get you a ring."

She stared at the ring, almost afraid to touch it. "The stone is huge."

He was silent for a moment then laughed under his breath. "You're complaining about a large diamond?" he asked in disbelief. "That's a first."

"I'm not complaining," she quickly said. "I just didn't expect it. When I think about us getting married, I haven't thought about diamonds, or even rings."

"Then what have you been thinking?"

She bit her lip, reluctant to reveal the fact that she was wondering if it was such a smart thing to marry Max. She shrugged, not meeting his gaze. "More about how all three of us will adjust to family life." She hesitated. "Wondering how you and I will adjust to being married."

"I think we've demonstrated we won't have any problems," he said, sliding his hands over her neck, making her feel as if her collarbone was a sensual hot spot for the first time in her life. It amazed her that he could make her feel so sexy with just a touch.

She closed her eyes for a second. "In bed," she said in a voice that sounded small to her own ears.

His hands stilled. "What do you mean?"

"Well, it may be a rumor," she said, trying to keep a light tone, "but I hear married couples tend to spend a lot more time out of bed than in bed."

"Damn," he said. "So you may actually have to join me for dinner most nights and we'll have to do things together." He walked around her chair and bent down over her, meeting her gaze. "Sounds rough, but I think I can do it. What about you?"

She smiled reluctantly. "Probably," she said.

"But you're still bothered."

"You have to admit this isn't the typical romantic wedding. We don't even have a honeymoon planned. For that matter, how did you find out my ring size? I didn't know yours."

"While you were sleeping," he said and added, "in your bed. Say what you want, but sex between us will take away a lot of your doubts."

The notion filled her with a combination of anticipation and anxiety. Would she have any leftover reactions to that last experience with Tony? So far, Max seemed to push everything from her mind, but him.

"So try on the ring. Maybe you'll like it better on your finger," he said casually and plucked the ring from the box and slid it onto her hand.

It fit perfectly. It sparkled like a bright star. "It's beautiful," she said and wiggled her finger. "Does it come with a crane?"

* * *

Lilli woke up the next morning full of anticipation and hope. She was just two weeks from her delivery date, two weeks from when she would hold her baby in her arms. The excitement inside her seemed to build with each passing hour. And she was getting married in just two days.

Glancing at the diamond ring that felt heavy on her finger, she fought the slivers of trepidation that stabbed at her. She felt as if she were on the precipice of falling completely in love with Max. What if she spent a lifetime waiting for him to love her and he never did? What if he fell out of lust with her and left her? Or worse yet, what if he never allowed himself to love her, but stayed with her even though he was miserable?

Lilli shook off the thoughts. She had every reason to hope everything would work out well. The sun shining brightly outside seemed to invite her to take a short stroll along the driveway that led to Max's home and then down the block. The fresh air cleared her head and the sunshine gave her a boost of optimism.

Returning from the stroll, she spotted a car parked in the driveway. It was a Jaguar, so she knew it didn't belong to any of her friends. Mallory drove a BMW.

Curious, Lilli entered the house and overheard a woman talking with Ada, the assistant housekeeper. "I left some of my things here several months ago. I just want to pick them up."

Recognizing the woman's voice as Kiki, Lilli stiffened. She turned away to quietly climb the stairs. She didn't want a confrontation with the woman.

"Oh, look, the sweet mother-to-be. Don't run off. It's been too long. We should visit for a little bit," Kiki said.

Lilli reluctantly stopped and turned. "Hello, Kiki."

Looking as svelte and perfect as ever in a fashionable black-and-white sheath, Kiki moved past the house-keeper. "Omigoodness, you look like you're ready to go any minute. Positively glowing," she said. "Babies are pure magic, aren't they? They make the impossible seem possible. I mean, look at how your life has changed."

"I just want what's best for my baby," Lilli said.

"Of course you do," Kiki said. "I was surprised that I never heard back from you after we met at the charity auction. Did you lose my card?"

"Yes. I think I did," Lilli said.

"You seem like a smart woman. I thought you might take me up on my offer. But rumor has it you're placing your bets somewhere else."

Lilli and Max hadn't announced their decision to marry, so Lilli refused to confirm or deny any implica-tions. "I should go upstairs. I have a doctor's appoint-ment this afternoon."

"You can at least show me the nursery," the other woman said with a fake pout. "I'll go upstairs with you. I need to pick up a few things I left here."

Ada stepped forward. "I'm sorry, Miss Lane, but I'm not sure Mr. De Luca would be comfortable with you going through his private quarters. If you'll wait, I can call him."

Alarm shot across Kiki's face. "That's not neces-sary. I'll give him a call myself. It's just so awkward to ask a man to return lingerie," she whispered. "But it was

La Perla. One of my favorites," she said with a sigh. "One of his, too, as I recall. Oh, well. Lovely seeing you. You can still give me a call if you change your mind about anything, but don't wait too long."

Watching Kiki leave, Lilli told herself not to trust the woman. Kiki was clearly desperate and would do anything to get Max back. She shouldn't let the woman generate any doubts about her decision to marry Max. Her rebellious mind, though, hung on to Kiki's description of lingerie. She remembered the photo of Max and Kiki in the newspaper just recently. Perhaps she had underestimated their relationship.

Ten

Lilli's day went from bad to worse when Max presented her with a prenup agreement late that evening. With the exception of the clause that gave Max custody of the baby if they separated and she was determined to be an unsuitable influence, the prenup was very generous. Financially, anyway.

Lilli slept on the agreement, not wanting to overreact. The day before she was scheduled to marry Max, she rose and looked at her large diamond engagement ring and took it off. In a calm voice completely at odds with the turmoil raging inside her, she called Max and asked him to meet her at the house as soon as possible. He arrived an hour later.

"I'm not going to sign it the way it is," she told him and set the ring and the agreement on the patio table in front of him.

His mouth twisted as he glanced down at the ring and the unsigned agreement. "You want more?"

"No. I'm not going to leave the judgment of my ability to parent up to a court that could be bought or skewed by your influence.

He met her gaze. "It's not money?" He paused a half beat. "Are you sure this isn't about Kiki's offer?"

She couldn't hide her surprise.

He walked toward her, dressed in a suit that emphasized his height, power and attractiveness. "You didn't know that I knew? The housekeeper told me she came to visit. She seemed to imply she'd made some prior offer and I can only imagine it was meant as a buy off."

"Apparently she came by to collect some expensive lingerie she'd left," she said, refusing to give in to his effect on her.

"That was a lie. I've never invited Kiki to stay in my bedroom. Why didn't you tell me that she was trying to buy you off?"

Trying to digest the fact that Kiki's La Perla lingerie had never made it into Max's bedroom, she fought another wave of confusion. "I didn't know if you were still in love with her."

He lifted a dark eyebrow. "I've told you my opinion of romantic love. It doesn't last."

His words cut, but she didn't want to show it. "I didn't feel comfortable telling you. I felt like I should handle her on my own."

"Or maybe you were holding out for a better offer than I gave you in the prenup."

Lilli felt a spurt of anger. "If you really believe that, then we definitely shouldn't get married."

Max met her gaze. "What do you want?"

"Strike the clause about my being an unfit mother."

"Done," he said. "If Kiki contacts you again, you must tell me."

She paused a brief second. "I will," she said. "Are you sure you don't have some leftover feelings for her? She is more beautiful than I am," she impulsively blurted.

He stared at her in surprise. "I disagree."

Perhaps she should have felt affirmed. Instead her insecurities seemed to bubble up from deep inside her. "She knows how to operate in your crowd."

"She's manipulative as hell. Do you really think I want to be married to a woman like that?"

Lilli realized she needed to get her questions answered, or she would be victimized by her doubts forever. She took a deep breath and braced herself. "I think I need to know your stand on fidelity in our marriage. Since this isn't a love match, do you consider yourself free to have—" she forced the word from her tight throat "—affairs?"

His face turned to stone. "Absolutely not. Once we marry, you will be the only woman in my bed and I will be the only man in yours. I take my vows very seriously. If you can't make the same kind of commitment, then you'd better tell me, because I'll expect the same complete fidelity that I'll give."

His fierce response took her breath away. Perhaps she should have known. A man like Max wouldn't make a marital commitment easily and he would not only give, but expect to receive complete loyalty from his wife.

"I can't even imagine being unfaithful to you." What woman would want to?

His expression gentled a millimeter and he picked up the ring. "Then you won't need to take this off ever again," he said and slid the diamond on her finger. "I'm giving you and your baby my name and adopting him. Our marriage will work. I've decided it will," he said. "Understand?"

Even though there was no judge or minister present, at that very moment, she felt as if they were exchanging vows. He was making a promise he would keep and she was doing the same. "Yes, I understand."

The following day, Max arranged for the prenup to be changed. Lilli signed it and put on a cream-colored silk dress with a voluminous amount of material beneath the Empire waist that allowed for her advanced pregnancy. Her stomach jumped with butterflies. She told herself to put aside her fears, but in the back of her mind, although she feared that Max would take his commitments seriously, she knew he might never grow to love her.

A dull nagging ache in her back and those dancing butterflies continued to distract her, but she was determined to be as beautiful a bride for Max as possible. She clipped her hair back in a half up-do and added a fresh pink rose above the clip.

The ceremony was truly private with only the judge and Jim Gregory and Myrtle serving as witnesses. The weather was beautiful as usual and she and Max said their vows on the patio where they'd shared dinner the first night she'd stayed at his house. There was something right about that, something right in knowing they would share many more dinners on the very spot where they'd made lifelong promises to each other.

She told herself not to worry, but her hands were cold with nerves as Max held them.

"I pronounce you husband and wife," the judge said. "You may now kiss the bride."

Max drew her against him and slowly covered her mouth with his in a kiss that echoed the promises they'd just made.

Afterward, they shared a private lunch on the patio, just the two of them and toasted their marriage with sparkling water and orange juice.

"To us and our life together," he said.

She nodded. "To us." She took a long sip then another, her mind reeling with what she'd just done. She'd just married a man who cared for her, but didn't love her.

"You're very quiet."

She nodded again. "It's a big day. A lot to think about," she managed.

"You can relax now. We'll have more to think about after the baby is born. After your recovery."

He was talking about sex, she realized. There would be no night of passion tonight. One more way this day was odd. "The doctor told me that's usually four to six weeks," she said, feeling her cheeks heat.

He covered her hand with his and her heart took an extra beat. "Where would you like to honeymoon? We can go anywhere you like."

"I haven't even thought about it," she said.

He stroked the inside of her wrist. "You should. By the time we go on ours, we will have both earned it. Yes?"

Her chest tightened at the sight of his hand caressing hers. "I guess you're right."

"So tell me where you'd like to go," he said.

She fought a sudden shyness. "Somewhere with a beach?"

He nodded. "The company has resorts all over, but I also have access to some private spots. We would have staff, but no one else around to intrude."

"That sounds nice," she managed. "I wish it could be sooner."

He gave a rough chuckle. "You and me both, sweetheart." He sighed and lifted her hand to his lips. "The anticipation will either kill us or make the experience explosive."

"Or both," she said.

He laughed again. "We should eat."

Her stomach still doing dips and turns, Lilli picked at the meal. Her back was hurting like the dickens. She shifted uncomfortably in her chair.

"Is something bothering you?" he asked.

"I hate to complain, but may back hurts and—" She sighed. "I don't know. Maybe it's the excitement, but I don't feel very hungry at all." She felt a sudden telltale surge of liquid and stared at him startled.

"What is it?"

"I think I'm in labor. Real labor, this time," she added. "I think my water broke."

Her announcement galvanized Max into action. The wide-eyed expression of fear on her face clutched at his gut. He immediately told his driver to start the car and grabbed the suitcase Lilli had packed after her experience with false labor.

Hustling her into the backseat of the town car within three minutes, he slid in beside her and made the call to Lilli's doctor. He got the answering service since it was a Saturday. "Lilli McCall is going to the hospital right now. I don't care who is on call. I expect to see Dr. Roberts at the hospital. My name is Max De Luca. I'm her husband."

He disconnected his cell and turned to find Lilli staring at him. "That's not how on call works. If you deliver on a weekend, you don't necessarily get your specific doctor."

"Not my wife," Max said.

She blinked and shook her head. "I'm not used to the idea of being your wife."

"I'll help you," he said in a dry tone. "Do you need to lie down?"

She shook her head and winced. "I'm too uncomfortable to lie down. The contractions are much stronger than they were with the false labor." Fear glinted in her eyes. She bit her lip and reached for his hand. "Max, I'm going to have a baby. I want him to be okay."

He pulled her into his arms. "He will be."

Within two hours of arriving at the hospital, Max could tell that Lilli was suffering. Her body tensed in pain. With each contraction, she stared straight ahead and did the breathing she'd learned in her prepared childbirth classes.

Her fingernails dug into his hands during the height of the pains. The sight of her dealing with such pain horrified him. He'd never known modern childbirth was so barbaric. A newfound respect for Lilli grew inside him.

"I think I want an epidural," she announced breathlessly after what looked like an excruciating contraction.

Relieved, he immediately called the nurse and demanded the medication.

After what felt like forever, the obstetrician checked Lilli's progress and shook her head. "Too late for an epidural."

Outraged, Max stood. "What do you mean too late? She's in pain. She needs medication and she'll damn well have it."

The doctor shot him a long-suffering look. "Mr. De Luca, the baby is crowning. Your wife is ready to deliver."

His wife. His son. The knowledge hit him like a ton of bricks. Within thirty minutes and what had to be a thousand pushes, the baby, a small squalling mass of humanity, made his entrance into the world.

The baby cried. Lilli cried. Max swore. Seconds later, Lilli held her son, *their son,* in her arms. "You're here," she said to the baby, touching each of his tiny fingers and toes. "You're really here." She looked up at Max, her eyes filled with tears. "Look. We did it."

Max shook his head. "You did all the work. I didn't do anything."

"Yes, you did," she said. "You were here for me. For him. You watched over me. I want you to hold him."

Max gingerly took the baby in his arms and looked down into the infant's face. "Nice hat," he said of the tiny blue cap the nurse had placed on his head. "He's—" Max paused. "He's pink."

Lilli laughed. "That's a good thing. It means he's healthy."

Max gave a slow nod and studied the baby. "Little hands. Soft skin. What are we going to call you? There's got to be something better than butter bean." He glanced at Lilli. "Do you know what you're going to name him?"

Lilli felt something inside her quiver and shake. Watching Max hold her son made her bones shift.

The baby waved a hand toward Max and he looked surprised. "Hi there," he said in a low voice. "Looks like your mom did an excellent job."

Lilli bit her lip as she felt another stabbing urge to cry.

Max returned the baby to her arms. "He looks perfect."

"Thank you," she said, blinking against threatening tears. "I think I want to name him David."

He nodded. "Excellent choice. Solid. Not trendy or ambiguous. He won't have to beat anyone up on the playground to defend his name."

She took a careful breath and watched his face. "And for his middle name, I was thinking of Maximillian."

He stared at her for a long moment in silence.

The longer the silence lasted the more nervous Lilli felt. Even the baby squirmed in her arms. "If it's okay with you," she added. "If you don't want that, then—"

"No, I do. I'm just surprised. I wondered if you would name him after Tony."

"You have already been more of a father to him than your brother could have ever been."

The next month passed in a blur of bottles, diapers and middle-of-the-night interruptions. Lilli fell head over heels in love with her son, but when she showed the first sign of weariness, Max insisted she choose a mother's helper. Although she fought the idea at first, Lilli couldn't deny that getting a full night of rest made her feel like a new woman.

Since the baby had been born, Max continued to sleep in his room and she slept in hers. It seemed as though he was at work all the time. At first, she'd been too tired to focus on it, but now she was starting to get nervous. The more she thought about it, the more she realized he'd barely touched her during the last few weeks. Had his desire for her waned? Now that she was a mother, had she somehow become less sexy? The notion tortured her.

Unable to stand their polite distance any longer, she waited up for him one night. She sat in the dark, drinking her first glass of wine in ten months, rehearsing her conversation. She'd carefully chosen a silky camisole top and flowing blue skirt that made her feel feminine. She'd even put on a little makeup to perk up her features.

Sitting in the den, she turned on the lamp beside her and flipped through an architectural magazine. With only the soft glow from a lamp to keep her company, nine o'clock passed, then nine-thirty, then ten o'clock, but she was determined to wait for him.

It was close to ten-thirty when Max dragged himself through the door from the garage. He rubbed the back of his tense neck. These late hours were going to kill him.

But it wasn't as if he had any choice. He sure as hell couldn't hang around the house. Now that Lilli had delivered the baby, he had no visual reminder of why he couldn't take her to bed.

He would be an inconsiderate bastard to take her before she was fully recovered. That left him with the option of playing an exhausting game of keep-away. Sighing, he tugged his tie loose the rest of the way and unbuttoned the top few buttons on his shirt. Out of the corner of his eye, he noticed a light from the den. Curious, he walked into the room and found Lilli sleeping, her arms wrapped around a large throw pillow.

A stab of hunger twisted his gut. Lord help him, he was jealous of that damn pillow. He wanted her wrapped around him.

Her skirt had risen above her knees, revealing her shapely legs, and the material clung with sensual ease over her feminine curves. A strand of her hair had fallen over her cheek.

She was so inviting it was all he could do not to carry her up to his room right then. Instead, he tempted his self-control by lifting his fingers to touch that silky strand of hair and slide it away from her cheek.

Her lashes fluttered and she gradually opened her eyes. Her sexy, dazed expression lingered a few seconds before it cleared. "Hi," she said with a trace of self-consciousness and pushed herself up from the pillow. "I must have fallen asleep."

He nodded. "You're dressed up. Did you have plans?"

Her cheeks warmed with color and she pushed her hair from her face. "I was waiting up for you."

Surprise kicked through him and he sat down beside her. "Why? Is there a problem with David? Is the mother's helper still working out?"

"No problem with Maria. She's perfect. David is

perfect," she added and paused. "Although I would like you to spend a little more time with him."

He nodded. "I can do that. I just wanted to give the two of you time to get adjusted first."

She bit her lip and met his gaze. "Is that why you've also been avoiding me?"

"Caring for an infant is demanding, plus you need to recover from the birth."

She continued to look at him as if she were waiting for him to add something more. When he didn't, she sighed. "You're sure that's all there is?"

He frowned. "What else would there be?"

She bit her lip again. "I wasn't sure if perhaps you were having second thoughts about getting married. If, maybe…" She faltered then lifted her chin as if she were determined to go on. "If you didn't want me anymore."

Shock zinged through him like an electrical current. "You're joking, aren't you?"

"No, I'm not," she said, her voice husky. "You haven't touched me since the baby was born. You're always gone. What else should I think?"

"That I don't want to ravage you like some sex-starved bastard," he told her. "That I don't trust myself in the same room with you for more than five minutes."

Her eyes widened in surprise. "But you seem so detached."

"Lilli," he said, primitive need rising inside him, "I've been waiting to take you for a long time. I'm not sure how gentle I'll be."

Her gaze fixed on his, she licked her lips, sending another current of desire lashing through him. "So you really do still want me."

"Yes," he said in a voice he knew sounded rough around the edges.

Giving a sigh of relief, she moved closer to him and lifted her hand to his jaw. At her soft touch, he clenched his jaw. She rubbed her thumb over his mouth and he covered her hand with his. He slid that daring thumb of hers inside his mouth and gently bit the delicate pad.

He heard her soft intake of breath and put her hand away from him. "Don't push me."

She met his gaze for a long moment. "I go to the doctor on Friday."

"For what?"

"My follow-up visit. It's likely that I'll be released for all normal activity."

Wanting to remove any confusion on his part, he asked, "What does that include?"

"Everything," she said and lowered her voice to a whisper. "Including sex."

Max immediately felt himself grow hard with arousal. *Friday. Two days.* "I'd like you to give me a call after your visit," he told her.

"I know you told me not to push you," she said, moving closer to him again. "But can I kiss you?"

Max knew a cold shower was in his future tonight. "Come here," he said and pulled her across his lap.

She slid her fingers through his hair and gently pressed her mouth against his.

Desire raged through him. Her lips were petal soft, her body deliciously pliant. He wanted to touch her and take her every way a man could take a woman. When she dipped her tongue into his mouth, he thought he would explode.

A simple kiss, he thought, and he felt like a raving lunatic. Her breasts pressed against his chest and he wanted to tear off her dress, rip off his shirt and feel her nipples against his skin. He rubbed his hands over the side of her breasts and felt her shiver. With that small encouragement, he slid his fingers over her nipple and felt the stiff peak through her silky top.

Making a restless movement against him, she slid her tongue deeper into his mouth. His temperature rose and he began to sweat. She was so sweet, so tempting.

He knew he should stop, but he couldn't resist going a little further. He eased his hands under her top, surprised to find that she wore no bra. He wouldn't have thought he could get any hotter, especially knowing they couldn't finish tonight, but he did.

Taking control of the kiss, he slid one of his hands over her breast and swallowed her delicious gasp of arousal. "Do you want me to stop?" he asked against her mouth.

She shook her head. "It's been so—" She broke off and shuddered when he brushed her nipple with his thumb. "I never thought I could feel this way again."

"You couldn't have forgotten completely," he said in disbelief, nibbling at her bottom lip as he continued to caress her breast.

"I think I must have," she said and reached for the buttons to his shirt.

Not trusting himself any further, he covered her hand with his. "Later," he said. "Later."

Looking at her smoky eyes and lips puffy from their kisses, Max groaned. It took every ounce of fortitude not to take her mouth again.

She shook her head in disbelief. "After that last terrible time with Tony, I was sure I'd never want to be with a man again."

Max's arousal abruptly cooled. "You've mentioned this before. What was terrible about it?"

She glanced away. "I don't like to think about it. I don't like to talk about it. It's just that everything is so different with you."

"What happened with Tony?" he demanded.

She sighed. "He's your brother. There's no need to taint his memory any more than it already is."

"Lilli," he said. "I knew Tony had problems, most of which he made for himself. Heavy drinking, drugs, illegal deals. We weren't close. I'm your husband, now. You can't keep this kind of thing from me."

She twisted her fingers together. "I had already broken up with him once," she said in a low voice. "He promised things would be different, so I went out with him again. We went to a club and things were getting wild. I told him I wanted to leave. He begged me to stay for just one more dance, just one more drink. I just ordered soda."

Max got a dark feeling about what had happened with Lilli. "And?"

She bit her lip. "He put something in my drink. I woke up hours later and he had—"

Max felt a rush of nausea. He couldn't believe his own brother would do such a thing. "He took advantage of you without your consent?"

She closed her eyes and nodded. "I had told him I wasn't ready to be intimate again, that we had to take it slow. After that night, I broke things off permanently.

I realized I would never be able to trust a man who would do that to me."

Max's mouth filled with bitterness. He was so furious he wanted to break something. The strength of it caught him off guard.

Taking a mind-clearing breath, he reined in his anger and focused on Lilli. "I'm sorry he did that to you. I tried to steer Tony in the right direction, but he refused to listen." He slid his hand under her chin and guided her so she met his gaze. "I promise you I would never do something like that to you."

Her eyes were shiny with unshed tears. "You don't have to promise. I already know."

Max realized that Lilli would need to be seduced. It had been a long time for her and it would be his pleasure to remind her in every way that she was a desirable woman and that the passion between them would take her to a level she'd never experienced before. And as her husband, he would make damn sure no one ever hurt her again.

Eleven

Lilli envisioned that once she told Max the doctor had released her, the first thing Max would do was take her to bed. Instead he took her to dinner at the top of the premier Megalos-De Luca property in Vegas. With the baby in Maria's care, Lilli was free to enjoy herself.

Steeped in luxury, the resort featured an outdoor restaurant with a prized breathtaking view of the strip and beyond. "This is beautiful," she said for the umpteenth time after they enjoyed a delicious meal. "You really surprised me."

"I thought we both deserved a night out," he said, a cryptic grin crossing his face. "Think of this as the wedding dinner we skipped."

"For David," she said, laughing. Her heart skipped a beat at the sight of Max seated across the table from her. Dressed in a black suit, black shirt and tie, he looked dark and devastating. Tension and anticipation hummed between them. Every time Lilli thought about how the evening would end, her breath stopped in her throat.

She looked past the other empty tables at the night-time view of Las Vegas. "It's so sparkly," she said.

"So it is," he said and poured her another glass of Cristal.

"Why are there no other people here?"

"I ordered privacy," he said. "We can do anything we want," he added in a velvet, seductive voice.

Her heart hiccuped and she stared at the table. It was the first possibility that came to mind. "Omigoodness, you don't mean doing it here in public."

He laughed. "I said it's not public."

She sputtered. "B-but—"

Rising, he extended his hand. "Let's dance."

She distantly heard the strains of a romantic melody being piped through an outdoor sound system and immediately identified it. She stood and walked into his arms. "It's hokey, but this is one of my favorite songs."

He drew her close to him. "Old Elvis song sung by Michael Bublé. 'I can't help falling in love with you.'"

"How did you know?"

"I swiped your iPod."

"You are diabolical."

"I'll make you like it."

She had an unsettling feeling he could make her like a lot of things. She felt an achy tug in the region of her heart as she breathed in his scent and clung to his broad shoulders.

He nudged her head upward and took her mouth with his. He slid one of his hands behind her neck and she felt a sensual possessiveness in his touch. Her body immediately responded to his.

The sexy romantic song continued to play and she couldn't help feeling a little sad knowing that Max might want her, but would never really love her. The knowledge didn't keep a fire from building in her belly. The touch of his tongue and the way his body skimmed the front of hers made her blood pump with a primitive beat.

He pulled back slightly. Although his eyelids were hooded, she could still see a naked passion in them. "I've never waited this long for a woman," he said and dipped his open mouth to her neck. He drew her against him and she felt his unmistakable hardness. Sliding his hand over her bottom, he guided her against him.

"I want to taste every inch of you," he muttered against her mouth as he lifted one of his hands to her breast.

Lilli gave an involuntary shudder of anticipation.

"You like that," he said, more than asked. "I'm going to touch you all over." He slid his hand down over her hip.

The prospect took her breath away and she instinctively tried to get closer to him. She wanted to feel his skin. She wanted to slide her mouth over his chest and taste him. She wanted to see if she could make him sweat a little. Her blood pounding through her body, pooling between her thighs, she pulled his tie loose and tugged at the buttons to his shirt.

"I want to be closer, as close as I can get," she whispered breathlessly.

He swore and caught her hands against him. "This is our first time. I'll be damned if it's over in five minutes."

"You make me—" She broke off and swallowed over her dry throat. "Want."

His nostrils flared as he took several deep breaths. "Good. We'll finish this back at the house."

Burning with frustration, she allowed him to lead her from the restaurant. On the way down the elevator, she concentrated on trying to calm down. What must he think of her? That she was so easily aroused by him that she forgot about time and space?

He led her to the car and tucked her into the backseat, instructing Ricardo to take them to the house. He pressed the button for the privacy panel and turned to her. "Why so quiet?"

"I'm a little embarrassed," she quietly admitted, looking out the window.

"Why?"

She shrugged, not wanting to meet his gaze.

He slid his hand under her chin and made her look at him. "Why?"

"Because I would have had sex with you on one of the tables, and you were just—" She broke off and tried to look away, but he wouldn't allow it.

"Just what?"

"Just kidding or teasing," she said.

His dark eyes widened in disbelief. "You think I didn't want you back there?"

She bit her lip.

He swore. "Lilli, I've wanted you since the first time I saw you. I've been to hell and back a dozen times trying to keep my hands off you. You haven't had sex since you got pregnant. I don't want to rush things. I don't want to hurt you."

"Oh," she said, surprised he was so concerned about her discomfort. She'd known he had been determined to wait until the doctor released her, but this went further and oddly turned her on even more.

She impulsively slid her hands behind his neck and kissed him. She rubbed her breasts against his chest, straining to get as close as possible.

Max immediately slid his arms around her and kissed her back just as eagerly. The kiss seemed to go on and on and Lilli felt her temperature climb along with Max's.

He pulled his mouth just a breath away from hers. "I'm not complaining, but what was that for?"

"It was so sweet of you to be worried about hurting me," she whispered.

"That's your way of rewarding me for being sweet?" Max said. "Hell, no one has ever called me sweet before. Maybe I should be sweeter more often if this is how you react."

He took her mouth again and teased both of them into a frenzy by the time the chauffeur pulled into the driveway. Ricardo opened the door for them and Max helped her out of the car. After they climbed the steps to the porch and he opened the front door, he swung her into his arms and carried her inside.

"Wow," Lilli said, shocked again.

"For luck," he said. "I'm not usually superstitious, but I want to hedge my bets this time." Then he carried her upstairs to his master suite. When he set her down on the floor, he allowed her body to slide intimately down his, not hiding his arousal from her.

Lilli felt a quick shimmer of nerves and nearly suffocating anticipation. This was it. No turning back. "I bought a negligee, but it's in my room."

"Another time," he said and took her face in his hands and began to kiss her. His mouth was warm and sensual; the touch of his hands made her feel precious and sexy at the same time. Lilli felt the room begin to spin.

He unzipped her dress and pushed it down over her shoulders, waist and hips until it pooled at her feet. She pushed his jacket from his shoulders and fumbled with the buttons on his shirt. This time he didn't stop her.

Unsnapping her bra, he filled his hands with her breasts. Lilli let out a breath she hadn't known she'd been holding. Skimming his hands down her rib cage and waist, he cupped her bottom and rubbed her against his hard erection.

Taking her mouth in a French kiss, he looped a thumb beneath the waistband of her tiny silk panties and pushed them down. Lilli had thought she couldn't get any hotter, but she'd been wrong.

His fingers did maddening things to her, and she felt herself grow so swollen she could barely stand it. He made her ache. He made her acutely aware of the empty, needy sensation that she knew he could fill.

Tugging his belt loose, she unfastened and unzipped his slacks. Meeting his gaze, she pushed down his slacks and underwear.

"Touch me," he said.

She did. He was huge and hard in her hands and she couldn't help wondering if perhaps his concern about her discomfort may have been valid. She stroked him and he let out a hiss of breath. He closed his eyes while she caressed him.

"Not too much of that," he muttered and pulled her against him. Pushing away the rest of their clothes, he picked her up and carried her to his big bed. He reached over to his bed table and pulled a condom from the drawer.

Lilli took a shallow breath at the sight of him. His eyes were dark with need, his body was well-muscled, his erection huge. He reminded her of a prize stallion and some secret, primitive part of her was proud that she was the one he'd chosen.

He groaned and lowered his mouth to hers. Lilli thought he would take her at that very second. He was ready. She was ready. There was nothing stopping them. Finally.

Instead, he dipped his lips to her nipples and started making her crazy all over again. He slid one of his hands between her legs. She thought about protesting or begging. She didn't know which, but then she couldn't seem to breathe let alone say anything except the whisper that squeezed past her throat. "Please."

He drew the tip of her breast deep into his mouth and she arched toward him. "Please," she whispered again.

"What do you want, baby?" he asked her.

Shameless with need, dripping with want, she closed her eyes. "You. In me."

"Open your eyes," he said in a low, rough voice.

She did as he asked and he thrust inside her with one smooth, sure stroke.

She gasped. He moaned.

"Too much?"

She waited a few heartbeats for her body to adjust to his and shook her head. "More," she said.

Swearing under his breath, he pumped into her, driving his pelvis in a rhythm she echoed. The sensation of him filling her, stretching her, making her secret, wet places contract and shudder was almost overwhelming.

The feeling intensified with every stroke and Lilli lost control, splintering, spinning into orbit. Seconds later, she felt him stiffen and thrust one last time, groaning in release.

He lifted his head and pressed his mouth to hers, his kiss both tender and seductive. "Now, you're mine," he said.

Max kept her in bed for the next eight hours with very little sleep. At that point, he took a shower and returned some business calls. Lilli grabbed a quick shower, then took David from Maria, fed him, held him and bathed him.

Wide-awake, her baby watched her with big eyes and moved his mouth and made little sounds as if he were trying to talk with her.

"You've been such a good boy," Lilli told him. "Sleeping through the night. Maria was so happy and I am, too." She pulled a book from the basket beside the rocking chair and began to read. "'Once upon a time…'"

She alternated between reading and looking at his sweet face. The rapt attention in his big eyes made her smile. She tickled him under his chin and he wiggled. She did it again and he lifted the corners of his lips into a smile.

Joy and surprise rushed through her. "You smiled," she said and stood, bursting to share the news. "David smiled," she called down the hallway to anyone who would listen. "His first smile. David smiled for the first time."

Max rounded the corner, his cell phone pressed to his ear. "Just a minute, Jim. Something wrong?"

"No," Lilli said, rubbing her thumb under David's chin again. "David smiled for the first time."

Max looked at her first then at David, who was not smiling now. "Are you sure?"

"Yes, I'm sure. I just distracted him because I got so excited. I probably scared him," she said.

"Maybe it was gas."

"It was not gas," she said. "He doesn't smile when he has gas. He grimaces."

Max looked at her and David skeptically. "If you say so. I should wrap up this call with Jim. If David does it again, let me know."

He didn't believe her, she realized, and it bothered her. She wanted him to be as excited about David's firsts as she was. She wanted him to love David as much as— She broke off the thought. She was expecting way too much too soon, she told herself.

After a little more time, Max would grow to love David. He wouldn't be able to resist the child. It would be no time before David would be looking at Max with hero worship in his eyes. Surely a child's adoration would be able to penetrate the steel vault protecting Max's heart. Lilli just wasn't sure she could make it into his heart and maybe it was best if she didn't try.

* * *

Later that night after she fed David once more and put him to bed, she turned on the monitor and cracked the door to the nursery as she left the room. Bone tired, all she could think about was going to sleep. Max met her in the hallway holding two glasses of wine.

"Time for the rest of the honeymoon."

Despite her weariness, her pulse quickened at the seductiveness in his eyes. "If I drink a sip of that wine, I'll fall into a coma."

"Tired?" he asked, nudging the glass into her hand and guiding her down the stairs. "Baby wear you out with all his gas?"

She shot a dark look at him. "It wasn't gas. He was smiling."

"Did he do it again?" he asked.

"No, but—"

"Like I said."

"I'm the mother. I know," she said defiantly.

He lifted his lips in a half grin. "Can't argue with that," he said and clinked his glass against hers. He dipped his mouth over hers. "A meeting of the minds. Next, a meeting of the bodies. I think you might like a soak in the Jacuzzi."

It sounded wonderful. "I need my swimsuit."

He shook his head. "No, you don't."

Her heart jumped again. "Won't one of the staff see?"

"They're paid not to see."

"But still," she began.

"If your modesty is screaming that loudly," he said. "I can turn off the lights. Come on." He tugged her out the patio door and into the cool night air.

She shivered.

"The Jacuzzi will warm you up in no time."

It was easier being naked in front of him when they were in bed, when she didn't have time to think. She took a shallow breath. "You go first."

"Okay," he said and set their wineglasses beside the tub. He shucked his clothes without an ounce of self-consciousness. His tanned skin gleamed in the moonlight. His shoulders were broad, his belly flat, his buttocks firm.

Why should he be self-conscious? He had a body that should have been chiseled in marble. His face was hard, but when he smiled, he could turn her world upside down. And his eyes did things to her heart rate, her temperature, and her whole body.

He stepped into the Jacuzzi and turned to look at her. "Your turn."

She fought a rush of self-consciousness. "Turn off the light."

After he killed the light, she pulled off her shirt and jeans, then her bra and panties. Fortifying herself with another breath, she stepped into the tub. Despite the hot temperature, she plunged her body under the bubbles.

"Better?" he asked.

"Hot," she said, although she was grateful for the semicover of water.

His laugh rumbled all the way down between her legs. "You sound like Goldilocks. Too cold. Too hot. You even have the hair," he said, touching her hair before he slid his mouth over hers. His mouth was warm, his tongue seductive.

She felt some of the tension ease out of her.

"You have a beautiful body," he said against her lips. "I love the way your breasts respond to me." He lowered his hands to her nipples and plucked at them, turning them into hard orbs of sensation.

Making a sound of approval, he pulled her onto his lap. She balanced herself with her hands on his chest. His skin felt slick and sexy beneath her touch. Her thighs were slippery against his and the steamy water mirrored the heat between them.

He dipped his forehead against hers. "This wasn't such a bad idea, was it?"

Her breasts brushed against his chest, keeping her nipples taut and sensitive. "It's nice."

"I thought you would like it." Reaching behind him, he grabbed a remote and the strains of a saxophone eased around them. "Are you hungry? I can ask the housekeeper to bring something out—"

"I would drown so she wouldn't see me."

He chuckled and slid his arms around her. "I'll help you get over your shyness."

"Maybe with you," she said, her breath hitching when he fondled her breasts again.

"I wasn't sure how I would like being married, but so far I'm liking it," he said.

"So far is all of six weeks. But that reminds me of something," she said and tried to focus on something other than his muscular chest or how his hands felt on her or how his hard thighs felt under her bottom.

"What?"

"If we're going to make this marriage thing work—"

"We are," he interjected.

She nodded. "It occurred to me that I don't know what you want from me as your wife."

His eyes glinted with an irresistible sexy humor. "You've done very well so far."

"I didn't mean *that*. I mean when we're not in bed."

"We're not in bed right now," he reminded her, shifting her legs apart and pulling her intimately against him. He slid one of his hands between her thighs and moved his hand in a sensual, searching motion.

"I mean when we're not—" She broke off when he grazed the most sensitive part of her. "You're making it hard for me to concentrate."

"That's because you're concentrating on the wrong thing," he said. "I want you to concentrate on what you're feeling right now." He sank deeper into the water and slipped his hand under her bottom, pushing her upward so that her breasts bobbed directly in front of his face.

He lowered his head and took one of her nipples into his mouth. The sight of his dark head against her pale skin sent a hot current to the most sensitive pleasure points in her body. His thumb found her again and a delicious haze fell over her.

It didn't matter that things between them felt so unsettled. It didn't matter that they were outside and if someone really wanted to watch them, they could. What mattered was that she was in his arms and the water made her feel both relaxed and eager. He was looking at her as if she was his first meal in a long time, and she knew firsthand that it hadn't been very long at all.

She slid her hand down between them and found him already hard. He gave a sensual groan and leaned backward on one of the graduated steps, looking at her through hooded eyes. "How am I supposed to go slow if you're going to touch me like that?"

"You want me to stop?"

"Oh, no," he said and pulled her over him and took her mouth in a kiss that made her feel consumed and restless. "You have no idea how sexy you look," he muttered and cupped her bottom, guiding her over him. His pelvis flexed upward and she sank down onto him. With her hair spilling forward, she kissed him. His tongue filled her mouth with the same rhythm he filled her lower body. Slow and easy, the erotic motion made her dizzy with pleasure.

He squeezed her bottom. She lifted her mouth for a breath and he drew one of her nipples deep into his mouth. "You make me so greedy," he said.

He made her desperate to please him. At the same time, though, he made sure she was pleasured. She'd thought she would be too sore, too sensitive, but the water cushioned their movements.

Steam rose around them. Tiny droplets dotted his face. His dark eyes were glazed with arousal. He continued to rub and she matched his pace, her nether regions tightening with every stroke. She felt the peak start in her breasts and shower down to where she convulsed around him, her muscles contracting around his hardness.

His eyes narrowed as he gasped in pleasure, surging into her. "Oh, Lilli."

When he said her name, an aftershock coursed through her, and she realized what she craved. She wanted this to be more than good sex for Max. She wanted it to mean something to him. *She* wanted to mean something to him. Fear prickled inside her. It wouldn't be a good idea to want these kinds of things from a man who didn't believe in romantic love. She needed to figure out how to stay safe and sane.

He took her mouth in a kiss and moved sideways in the bubbling water, still inside her, her legs laced with his muscular thighs. Sanity was the last thing she could muster.

Twelve

The following morning, Max rose early. He felt an itchy sensation in his back. He felt crowded, yet at the same time, he would have liked to stay in bed and enjoy his wife's charms. Instead, he took a shower and was putting on his tie just as Lilli awakened.

She rubbed the sleep from her eyes and glanced at the alarm clock. "It's only six o'clock. You're going into the office already?"

"There's a lot waiting for me. I'll be home late tonight."

"What's late?"

He shrugged. "Maybe nine."

She nodded slowly. "Can I get you some breakfast?"

He shook his head as he straightened his tie. "I'm going straight to the office. My assistant will bring something."

Pulling the sheets up to her shoulders, she met his gaze in the mirror. Her hair was sexily rumpled and she blinked her eyes as she obviously tried to make herself wake up. The skin around her chin was pink from the effects of his beard.

He would need to be more careful in the future, he thought as he rubbed his just-shaven jaw. Her skin was sensitive and he'd mauled her from head to toe during the last two days. The vulnerability in her eyes made him want to hold her, but something else made him want to run.

He walked toward her. "Have a good day, lovely Lilli," he said in a light voice and, not trusting himself, he dropped an even lighter kiss on her cheek.

"You, too," she said. "If David smiles, I'll try to catch it with my camera phone. I'll send you a message."

The offer made his chest feel tight. "You mean if he has gas?" he teased and opened the bedroom door to leave. But not before he felt a pillow hit him in the back of the head. He whipped around, staring at her in surprise. Her hand covered her mouth as if she'd surprised herself, too. It didn't help his concentration that she'd dropped the sheets and her breasts were bared to his sight.

Steeling himself against the distraction and the hard-on growing harder by the moment, he looked down at her and shook his head. "You had me fooled. I thought you were an angel except when I got you in bed."

She bit her lip, but couldn't seem to prevent the beginning of a saucy smile. "I'm still in bed."

"So you are," he said and wished like hell he were there with her. "See you tonight."

* * *

Maybe it shouldn't have felt abrupt for Max to leave so early, but it did. Lilli pulled the sheet over her head and told herself to go back to sleep. She tried to push aside her feelings, but she felt bothered, unsettled. Was this the future for their marriage? Strangers everywhere except when they shared a bed?

Groaning, she threw off the sheet and climbed out of bed. Sore and tired, she wished she could grab a few extra winks, but she knew her mind wasn't going to let her. Grumbling to herself, she took a shower. Her body was sensitive, and she ached in secret places. She allowed the hot water to flow over her, willing it to soothe the tenderness in her muscles. And her heart.

After she dressed, she gave Maria a well-deserved break and listened for David's cry. He'd barely let out a sound before she gathered him to her and fed him. As he devoured his bottle, she noticed tiny beads of perspiration break out on his forehead.

"You are very intense about your food, aren't you, sweetie?" she said.

Moments later, he finished and she squeezed a couple burps out of him. She looked down into his face and smiled at him. He smiled back. Delighted, Lilli drank in his joyful expression. Then she remembered she needed to take a photograph, so Max would believe her. Jumping up from the rocking chair, she ran to grab her cell phone and positioned it over David's face, ready to take a photo. David, however, was less interested in smiling and more fascinated with the object in her hand. The smile had disappeared.

"Well, darn," she muttered. She smiled again and he looked at her with solemn eyes as he blew bubbles. "That's just as cute as a smile," she said and took the photo and sent it to Max anyway.

She took David for a stroll around the block. Just as she was turning into the driveway, her cell phone rang. Her heart racing, she didn't bother to check the caller ID because she was sure it was Max. "Hi there," she said.

"Hi, Lilli," an unfamiliar voice said. "This is Devon."

Lilli stopped midstep and swallowed a sudden foolish twinge of disappointment. Devon, one of the hospice attendants to her mother, he had been with them until the very end. "Oh, Devon, I haven't heard from you in a while. How are you? How are your parents?"

"Dad's not doing so well. He's in the final stages of cancer and my mother was just admitted to the hospital. They want to put her on dialysis."

Sympathy surged through her. "I'm so sorry. Is there anything I can do?"

"I didn't want to ask, but you told me to call you if things got out of control. I'm staying with my father around the clock, so I'm not making any money."

"I understand," she said. "How much do you need?"

"It depends," Devon said, his voice choking up. "On how soon my father goes. Oh, God, I can't believe I said that."

"No, I understand. I took off a lot of time to be with my mother at the end."

"I don't want him to die, but—" He broke off again and sighed. "You would think that since I work in a hospice, I would be better prepared for this."

"It's much more personal," Lilli said. "It's your father. Listen, why don't I bring you some money to tide you over? I've forgotten your address. Give it to me again."

Devon gave her the address. "I'll probably need to call you back for directions. Would you like me to sit with your father so you can get out for a while?"

"I couldn't do that to you," he said. "I feel bad enough asking for financial help."

"You forget how great you were with my mother when she so sick. You were there for us. I'd like to be there for you."

"But that was my job."

"Well, you did an amazing job and my mother and I couldn't thank you enough. So let this be a little token. I'll come over this afternoon around three. David should be napping."

"Ah, the baby. How is he?" Devon asked.

"Perfect," she said.

He laughed. "As if he could be anything else since he came from you."

She smiled. "Please keep your cell handy, in case I get lost."

"Will do, Lilli, and thanks," Devon said.

Lilli drove her little Toyota instead of the monster SUV Max had bought for her use. She left David in Maria's caring arms. After stopping by the grocery store to pick up a few things for Devon and his family, she only got lost twice, but finally arrived at Devon's apartment complex.

Devon greeted her at the door, but his father had taken a turn for the worse, so he refused to accept Lilli's offer to sit with his father so that Devon could get out for a little while.

Lilli gave the dark gentle giant a hug and left. The visit brought back memories of her mother's time in hospice. Lilli had been forced to hide the gnawing grief she'd felt in anticipation of her mother's death. Losing her mother inch by inch had been excruciating, but she wouldn't trade a moment of the time she'd had with her.

The familiar feeling of being all alone hit her as she stopped at a traffic light. She'd never known her father. Her mother was gone. Even though she was married, she sometimes still felt alone. Her chest grew heavy, her throat tightened and her eyes began to burn. Tears streamed down her face and she tried to comfort herself.

She had David. She had her little baby. She wasn't alone. The thought soothed her and she made a turn when the light turned green. Twenty minutes later, she realized she was horribly lost.

She reluctantly called Devon, but he wasn't picking up. She thought about stopping at a convenience store, but several men sat outside on the ground drinking from bottles in brown bags.

Lilli began to fuss at herself. "Should have done MapQuest. It would have taken three minutes. Three minutes." She rounded the corner and, spotting a small grocery store, she pulled into the tiny parking lot and went inside. The owner spoke very little English, but gave her directions to the interstate.

She followed the directions, or so she thought, but just found herself deeper into another area where she'd never been. At six-thirty, she gave up the fight and called Max's driver, Ricardo. He offered to come and get her, but she refused, embarrassed by her lack of a sense of direction.

Ricardo gave her turn by turn directions. Once she arrived at the interstate, she sagged with relief. Ricardo didn't want to hang up, but Lilli insisted she would be fine. She pulled into the garage an hour later and was surprised to see Max's car.

She smiled as she bounded up the stairs from the garage. Walking through the corridor, she looked for him in the foyer. She spared a quick glance into the den and noticed the patio door was open. Still dressed in his business attire, he stood outside with a bottle of water in his hand.

Lilli rushed to the patio. "Hi. You're home early," she said, unable to disguise her delight.

He turned to look at her. "And you're home late," he said in a voice that could cut glass. His eyes were cold. "Where have you been?"

Lilli winced when she remembered the discussion she'd had with Max about visiting suspicious areas of town. "I visited a friend and got a little lost driving back."

"Ricardo told me you called him from one of the worst neighborhoods in the city," Max said.

She could feel anger emanating from him. "Like I said, I got all turned around. I should have used MapQuest."

"If this was such a good *friend*," Max said. "Why would you need directions to their house?"

Lilli refused to squirm. She'd done nothing wrong. "I haven't been there very often. But I'm back now," she said cheerfully. "I need to check on David."

"Maria has him," he said. "Who was the friend?"

Lilli bit her lip. Darn, she'd hoped to avoid a confrontation. "It was Devon. His father has taken a turn for the worse, but he's lingering and Devon's mother is in the hospital."

"You didn't give him money, did you?"

"Yes, I did," she said without batting an eye. "I took him some groceries, too. I would have sat with Devon's father so he could get some fresh air, but his father was very ill this afternoon. Devon didn't want to leave him."

"You shouldn't let this guy take advantage of you."

"He didn't," Lilli said. "I was happy to write him a check." She paused a second and pressed her lips together. "I didn't take the money out of your account. I took it out of a savings account I set up with the small amount my mother left me."

"That's not the point. The point is that this man could be taking advantage of you," Max said.

"He's not. He has a heart of gold," she said, then corrected herself. "Maybe gold isn't the best description. He has a soft, sweet heart. No hard metals included."

"Unlike your husband with the steel heart," he said.

"I didn't say that," she said. "I just don't think you comprehend that Devon is a good soul."

"Who lives in a terrible area of town."

"Not everyone can afford to live up on the hill like you."

"We discussed this. You weren't going to visit him again without telling me."

"I never really agreed," she said. "But I'm an adult. I don't think I should be hassled because I want to help someone who was so good to my mother when she was dying."

"You can't put yourself in danger like that. You have a son to think about. You have people counting on you."

People? As in plural? Her heart stammered. She studied his face and moved toward him. "What are you really upset about?"

He met her gaze for a moment that seemed to last forever then let out a long breath. "I don't want anything to happen to you."

"It didn't."

"But it could have. Next time you feel the urge to go into a questionable neighborhood, will you please at least take Ricardo with you?"

"What if he's busy?"

"Then either wait until he isn't, or call me."

The worry in his voice took some of the air out of her defiance. "Okay," she said. "But if you start fussing at me, I'll stop listening."

He nodded and they stood silently watching each other. Wary. Lilli felt as if she were being pushed and tugged at the same time, as much from herself as from Max. The sound of David's cry broke the tension.

"I'd better check on him," she said.

"Have you had dinner?"

She shook her head.

"Neither have I. We can eat out here."

"Okay. I'll be back down in a little bit," she said and went upstairs to the nursery. Lilli did the bottle, bath and bed routine for David, but the baby was still wide-awake when she put him to bed. She read him some stories and rocked him, but he still didn't fall asleep.

Giving up, she took him downstairs with her and put him in a springy infant seat in a chair beside hers. Her

stomach growled at the sight of the food in front of her.
Max set down the newspaper he'd been reading. "Is
someone not sleepy?"

"I think he wants to play soccer or basketball and
he's very frustrated that he can't yet."

Max's lips twitched.

She turned on the Jacuzzi.

Max looked at her in alarm. "You're not really going
to put him in the hot tub?"

"No, I was thinking the sound of the bubbles might
soothe him."

"Good idea," he said.

"And if that doesn't work, maybe he would like to
hear a male voice."

Max lifted his eyebrows. "Mine?"

She took a bite of her dinner. "You could read to him."

"What?" he asked, pointing at the paper beside him.
"The *Wall Street Journal?*"

"Sure. That should put him right to sleep, don't you
think?"

"If you say so," he said and began to read an article
about the economy.

David kicked and wiggled. He made a neutral sound
that Lilli suspected could turn into a fussy sound. "It
would work better if you hold him."

Max looked at her. Her hair was fairy flyaway as
usual and she had a crumb on the corner of her mouth.
She gave him a huge, encouraging smile and damn if
he didn't feel tempted to do anything for her. Including
holding a potentially fussy baby.

"Okay, I'm game. Any tips?"

She set her fork down and jumped up from her chair.

"He likes to be held close," she said, picking David up from the infant seat and placing him in Max's arms. "He feels more secure when his arms and legs aren't flopping all over the place."

It presented a new challenge to hold the newspaper at the same time as he held David, but he was up for it. He'd conducted billion-dollar deals, and he'd been player of the year for his college soccer team. He had the right stuff for this. Max continued to read, but David still squirmed.

"Sometimes it helps if you jiggle him," Lilli said and took another bite from her plate, seemingly content to watch him struggle.

Max jiggled the baby and struggled to read the article from the newspaper that also jiggled from his movements. He made up a few of the words that got blurry. Actually, he began to make up entire sentences. "And then the economy got kicked on its ass due to the price of oil."

"I do not believe that statement was in the *Wall Street Journal,*" Lilli said.

Max glanced down at David, whose eyes were closed. The baby slept peacefully in his arms. He felt as if he'd just made a goal in soccer or landed a huge deal. "It doesn't matter," he said in a low voice, "because I have successfully put our son to sleep."

He glanced up and looked at Lilli. She stared at him, her eyes shiny. "Yes, you did," she whispered. "But can you put him into his crib without waking him up?"

Another challenge. His competitive spirit piqued, he ditched the paper and carefully rose to his feet. "And what do I get if I succeed?"

"A pat on the back?" she said, covering her mouth as she muffled a chuckle.

"Lower," he said. "And not on the back."

Her blue eyes lit and smoldered. "Okay. If you can lay him down in the crib and he stays asleep, you can have whatever you want. I'll warn you, though, that he usually wakes up and needs to be rocked or walked a little longer."

"We'll see," he said, more motivated than ever.

Lilli stood. "And you need to put him to sleep on his back or on his side placed against the crib rail."

"Okay," he said.

"And make sure the blanket doesn't cover his face."

"Got it."

"And kiss him good-night."

"Kiss him?"

She nodded. "It's a requirement for a good night of sleep."

"I'll remember that," he said.

He could see her cheeks bloom with color even in the moonlight. "I'll be back in a few minutes."

"If you have to pick him up again, then it doesn't count."

"For what?" he asked. "You won't go to bed with me?"

She bit her lip. "I didn't say that."

"Give me a couple minutes. I'm an amateur at this, remember?"

Her gaze softened. "Yeah, I'll be waiting upstairs."

"Don't you want to finish your dinner?"

"That won't take two minutes," she said.

He smiled and she immediately smiled in response. Then he turned and took the baby up to the nursery, coaching himself and David. "You want to stay asleep," he said to David. "You're tired. You're ready to sleep until morning. You're worn-out. You've got a full belly and you're ready for your nice bed. You'll dream of warm bottles and walks in the stroller and being held in Lilli's arms. Can't argue with that last one, big guy."

He carefully walked toward the crib and continued to hold David, studying the baby's face. The baby looked as if he were totally out. Leaning over, millimeter by millimeter, he extended his arms and David stirred. Max immediately stopped, suspended over the crib.

David quieted and pursed his lips. Max counted to twenty then moved a few more inches. David wiggled slightly and Max stopped again. Patience was clearly the name of this game. He counted to twenty and moved several more inches. This time, David didn't stir. He extended the last few inches and carefully laid him sideways on the crib, leaving the blanket wrapped around him.

David wiggled and wiggled, but Max kept his hand on the baby and surprise, surprise, his son settled down.

Then he remembered the kiss. Max swallowed an oath. Surely it couldn't be that important. The baby was asleep. That was what was important, right?

Bowing to a combination of his Type A personality and his conscience, because he knew Lilli would ask about the kiss, he carefully lowered the side of the bed. He bent over and pressed a silent kiss on David's head then rose and slowly, slowly lifted the side of the crib. It made a loud clicking noise when it locked into place, making Max grimace.

He closed his eyes, waiting for David to make a

sound. A moment passed and all was still quiet. Max opened one eye, looked down at his son and was thrilled to see that the baby was asleep.

He took a deep breath and sighed. Now to collect his reward. He left the nursery and left a sliver of a crack between the door and the jamb. Walking into his bedroom, he stepped inside and found Lilli sitting in the middle of his bed wearing a white lace teddy that managed to look both innocent and naughty. Her rosy nipples showed through the transparent lace, as did the shadow between her thighs. His fingers itched to pull the skimpy garment from her, to bare her body to his gaze. He curled his hands into a fist then forced himself to release them.

"Very nice," he said. "How did you know I would succeed in getting David to stay asleep?"

"Aside from the fact that you're an overachiever?" she asked.

He couldn't keep his lips from twitching. "Yes."

"I wanted to thank you for the effort."

He tugged his shirt over his head then shucked his jeans and underwear so he stood before her completely naked. He saw her gaze gravitate to his erection and felt himself grow even harder. "How do you want to thank me?" he asked.

"Come here," she said and opened her arms. The gesture was so artless and open that it took his breath. He slid over the bed, pulling her against him, enjoying every millimeter of her silky skin against his.

"You feel so good," she whispered.

"I was going to say the same about you," he said, and dipped his head to kiss his way down her throat. When he reached her collarbone, he gently nibbled. Her sigh made him feel as if he were ready to burst.

"You're going to make this hard for me, aren't you?" he muttered, lowering his mouth to her breast, pushing the delicate fabric aside. He slipped his hand between her thighs and found her already wet and swollen. She squirmed beneath him and he felt his heart hammer against his rib cage.

She slid one of her hands between them and captured his bare erection in her hand. "I think you already started out—" She paused and shoved him onto his back. "Hard," she said and flowed down his body like silk.

The sensation of her open mouth on his chest, followed by his belly, took his breath. She waited three breaths and the anticipation nearly made him insane. Then she moved lower and took him into her mouth. The sight of her with her fairy angel hair, good girl/bad girl teddy, and her lips wrapped around him was one of his sexiest fantasies come true.

He watched her until he couldn't stand it any longer, then rolled her over, unsnapped her teddy and plunged inside her. He couldn't get enough of her—her passion, her sweetness. It was crazy, but being with her made him believe in possibilities he hadn't considered before.

After Max took her over the top twice and finally gave in to his own release, he held her against him for several moments. Neither of them said a word, but the power and pleasure of their lovemaking vibrated between them. He gently turned her over and pulled her back against him, stroking her hair.

His touch mesmerized her and she relaxed to the point that she almost fell asleep. She felt safer and more cherished than she'd felt in her entire life.

"I missed you today," he whispered into her ear.

Her heart stopped. His admission was the closest he'd come to professing any emotion. In her heart, she hoped it was just a step away from *I love you*. It took everything inside her not to make her own confession because she knew it would only burden him. He wasn't ready to hear that sometime along the way, she'd fallen in love with him.

Max woke to the sensation of Lilli's hands on his face. "Hey, Mr. Sunshine, the alarm is on your side of the bed."

Max blinked, opening his eyes to the sight of Lilli, with sleepy eyes, sexy puffy lips and the sound of one of Beethoven's symphonies from his alarm clock. He shook his head to clear it. He must have slept so soundly that he didn't hear his alarm when it first went off. He reached over and turned it off.

He never hit the snooze button and he always got out of bed within ten seconds. Glancing over at Lilli, he paused a good sixty.

"If you're going to stare at me, you can at least make yourself useful and hug me, too."

He chuckled and rolled back toward her, pulling her against him. She snuggled her breasts to his chest and pressed a kiss to his neck. Her body felt like silk.

Growing hard, he groaned. "The problem with holding you when you're naked is that I want to do a lot more than hold you."

"What's stopping you?" she asked in a sexy sleep-husky voice.

She might as well have lit a match next to a gas pump. He took her with a thoroughness that left both of them gasping for air.

Reluctantly, he dragged himself from bed. He looked back at her, nude, with a dazed, just-taken expression on her flushed face. He couldn't resist going back for one more kiss from her petal-soft lips, then forced himself to pull away.

Just as he reached the door to the bathroom, he heard her voice. "You can call me during the day if you want. It's not required," she quickly added. "But you can if you want."

She heard him last night after all, he realized. His heart gave a strange stutter. He couldn't tell if it was pleasure or pain. He'd gone skydiving a few times, and this sensation reminded him of free-falling out of an airplane. Was this what it felt like to fall for a woman? He swore under his breath. He didn't have the time to think about it right now.

"Thanks for the invitation," he said and headed for the shower.

Over the next few days after Lilli moved into Max's bedroom, Lilli felt almost like a newlywed. Max arrived home early. They shared dinner and took care of David then retired to Max's bed for nights of amazing lovemaking. She began to hope that he would eventually love her.

Saturday night after they'd visited a park and enjoyed a gourmet picnic prepared by Max's chef, they returned home. David had been fussy most of the afternoon. She fed him part of an extra bottle, hoping he would settle down, but he continued to fuss. She noticed he felt warm to the touch and took his temperature. It was elevated, but not overly so. Still, every time she tried to put him in his crib, his little body stiffened and he cried until he shook.

Max stepped inside. "Does he need another dose of the *Wall Street Journal?*"

She shook her head. "I don't think he's feeling well."

His demeanor immediately changed. "Does he have a temperature?"

"Not much of one," she said, showing him the thermometer. "All the baby books say to keep calm. But I think I may need to take him to the doctor tomorrow."

Max nodded in agreement.

"It may be a long night," she told him. "He's only calm when I hold him."

"I can understand that," he said, meeting her gaze, making her stomach jump at his double meaning. "I'll take a turn holding him if you can't get him settled."

"Thanks," she said and sighed when he gave her and David a hug. His arms felt so solid, so strong.

"Wake me to take a turn," he told her again.

"Maybe later," she said, but she didn't ask him. She finally succeeded in getting David settled and crawled into bed. She kept the nursery monitor directly beside her and heard him when he awakened in the middle of the night with a heart-tugging wail.

Max stirred beside her. "What is—"

"No, I'll take care of it," she said, quickly climbing out of bed and heading for the nursery. She almost collided with Maria, who'd already picked David up.

"Oh, the little sweetheart, he's burning up with fever," Maria said. She made a tsking sound. "He got sick in his bed."

"Oh, no. Let me hold him," Lilli said, taking him into her arms and biting her lip at the heat emanating from his tiny body. She pressed the thermometer against his ear, aghast at how quickly it had risen.

Fear clutched at her. David began to cry. "I wish I knew what was wrong with you, sweetie. I wish you could tell me where you hurt." David gave a high-pitched scream and Lilli fought a rising tide of panic.

Max stepped inside the room. "What's wrong?"

"His fever has gone up and he got sick in his bed," Lilli said, holding him close to her as she stroked his forehead.

As David let out another scream, Max nodded his head decisively. "Okay, that's it. We're taking him to the emergency room."

Thirteen

There was no wait at the emergency room for David Maximillian De Luca. It seemed everyone knew that Max had made generous donations to the Children's Hospital. The admissions tech quickly took down the insurance information and escorted Max, Lilli and David behind a curtain.

Max looked at David, who was clearly in pain, and felt his gut wrench. His son. It was his responsibility to alleviate his pain.

A very young woman in a white coat stepped inside the curtained cubicle. She picked up the chart and glanced at it. "Are you the parents?" she asked.

"Yes, we are."

"I'm Dr. Jarrett." She extended her hand and shook his. "Let's see what's wrong with your son."

Lilli continued to hold David close, cradling his head as he let out cries and sobs. As Dr. Jarrett looked inside David's right ear, the baby howled and the doctor winced. "I think I've found the problem. An ear infection. A nasty one at that." She rubbed the baby's head. "We can take care of that, sweetheart.

"We'll start him on antibiotics right away, and I have some other recommendations for pain. The good news is that these little guys tend to respond to antibiotics within twenty-four hours or less."

"Thank goodness," Lilli said. "He's been miserable."

"And he made sure you knew it, too, didn't he?" the doctor said with a smile.

"Yes, I guess he did." Lilli met Max's gaze. "I'm glad we came."

"Me, too," he said and asked the doctor a few more questions. Dr. Jarrett left David's file open on the tray while she left the area for a moment. Max glanced at the file, seeing David's birth information, his height, weight and blood type. He digested the information without focusing on it. The doctor returned, apologizing for the interruption.

After picking up the medication from the hospital pharmacy, Max helped Lilli administer it to David. He ushered both of them to his car, and David fell asleep on the way home.

Max pulled into the driveway and Lilli put her hand on his elbow. "I'm afraid to take him out of the infant seat," she confessed.

Max chuckled. "We can't leave him in the car the rest of the night."

"It's almost morning," she said and reached closer

to touch his jaw. "You are so amazing. And I am so lucky."

His heart swelled in his chest. "Why do you say that?"

"Because I was ready to panic over what to do about David, and you knew what to do immediately."

"You would have figured it out."

"Thank you," she whispered and kissed him. "I know you don't believe in love, but you're making me fall in love with you."

He didn't say anything, but she made him feel ten feet tall. She made him feel as if he could conquer anything and he wanted to do it for her and David.

He took a breath to clear his head. "We need to put him to bed," he said.

"Yeah," she said reluctantly.

"We can do it," he encouraged her. "We can do it together."

She nodded as if she found strength in his words. "Sure we can. Okay, let's go."

Surprisingly enough, David only gave a few peeps between the car seat and the crib. He made just enough sound to reassure Max and Lilli that he was uncomfortable, but okay. Lilli placed him in the crib and appeared to hold her breath.

David continued sleeping and Lilli let out a sigh.

"Time for Mama to get some sleep," Max said, taking her hand and leading her to bed.

She insisted on brushing her teeth then fell asleep as soon as her head hit the pillow. Max wasn't so lucky. Something nagged at him. He couldn't quite put his finger on it, but something he'd seen or observed at the hospital still bothered him.

Propping his hand behind his head on his pillow, he mentally backtracked his way through the evening.

Finally he remembered viewing David's file, his birth record, his weight. His blood type. His brother's blood type didn't match David's. Lilli's blood type had been listed above David's. David's didn't match hers, either.

He shook his head in disbelief. There had to be something wrong, a mix-up. But insidious doubts poked at him. If not Tony, then who was David's biological father?

The next question hit him so hard his chest squeezed tight with the pain. If not Tony, then who had been Lilli's lover?

Max felt nausea back up into his throat. Realization coursed through him like a slow-moving poison. Sitting up, he felt himself break into a sweat. Had she deceived him? Had sweet, angelic Lilli who'd baked cupcakes for his birthday pulled off the ultimate charade?

She'd made him believe she was going to give birth to his brother's son. With her wide blue eyes and fairy hair, she'd looked so innocent, so pure. And she'd played him to the hilt when she hadn't accepted his repeated offers for money.

He looked over at her sleeping in his bed as his wife and nearly drowned in disgust for himself. Shaking his head, he rose from the bed and thought of the way his father had acted like a fool over a woman. Max had made a vow to himself never to lose his head over a woman. But he'd gone and done just that.

Caught in semisleep, Lilli struggled to open her eyes. They felt as if someone had placed sandbags on top of them. She forced them to open. It took several minutes for her to become conscious.

Her first thought was of David. Her second was of Max. She looked beside her on the bed to find her husband gone. Type-A overachiever, she thought then glanced at the clock—8:00 a.m. She immediately pushed aside the covers and headed for the nursery. No one had called her, she reminded herself, as she stepped inside to find David being fed by Maria.

The nanny smiled. "He's much better this morning. Just a little cranky. A few more doses of his medication and he will be good as new."

David was focused on his bottle, clearly intent on getting every last drop. Lilli gave a sigh of relief. "Thank you for getting up with him."

"My pleasure," Maria said. "Mister De Luca is downstairs. He asked for you to go see him after you wake up."

"He's not at work?" Lilli asked, surprised.

Maria shook her head. "No. He's downstairs."

"Thank you again," Lilli said and returned to the bedroom to throw on some clothes, wash her face and put on some concealer. She didn't want to make a practice of looking like a hag first thing in the morning.

She went downstairs and spotted him on the patio. He sat on one of the plush chairs, staring at the fountain next to the Jacuzzi. Admiring his strong profile, she felt a rush of love. She gave herself a mental pinch. *This was her husband.*

She walked toward him and smiled. "Good morning, Mr. Amazing." She shook her head. "I don't see how you can go to sleep after I do, and still get up earlier than I do."

He met her gaze, but his eyes were cold. "I have things on my mind." He set his coffee cup on the patio table. "I saw David's medical file at the hospital last night."

"Is he okay? Is there something wrong that they didn't tell us?"

He lifted his hand. "No, no. Not that. What I noticed was David's blood type. It didn't match yours."

Max watched her carefully.

"Then it must match Tony's," she said, as if she were certain.

Feeling his gut begin to twist and turn, he shook his head. "No, it doesn't."

Lilli frowned. "It has to. There must be some mistake."

Max sat silently for a long moment. Awed by her ability to lie without so much as a twitch, he continued to study her. "There's no mistake, Lilli. David's blood type doesn't match Tony's. Tony cannot be David's biological father."

She stared at him for a long moment. "He is," she said her voice rising. "There's no other possibility. There's no—"

"Are you sure?" Max asked. "Who else did you have sex with while you were seeing my brother?"

Her mouth dropped wide in horror. "No one, I mean—" She broke off. "I wouldn't—"

She was still sticking to her story, but he was beginning to see some cracks in her composure. "Funny, that's what I thought, too."

"No, really," she said, knitting her fingers together. "I didn't have sex with anyone else. Tony has to be David's biological father. There's no other possibility," she said. "There was no one else. How could it be anyone else?"

Max stared at her in silence. Disappointment stabbed at him. Some part of him had held out hope that she would be honest with him. That she would give him that much.

Panic shot across her face and she ran to him. "You must believe me. You must. That blood test is wrong. It has to be. It has to—"

He stepped aside before she could touch him. He didn't want her to touch him. He didn't want his body to betray him. There was only one explanation for her hysteria. She had indeed lied to him and she was terrified of losing her meal ticket.

"I need to leave," he said and headed for the door.

"Max," she called after him, her voice full of tears and desperation.

But Max kept on walking.

Watching him leave, Lilli felt her throat and chest close so tight she could hardly breathe. He didn't believe her. He thought she had deceived him. Her heart died a little with each step he took away from her.

She sank into her chair, feeling as if she were going to splinter into a million pieces. How had this happened? *What* had happened? *Who* had done this to her?

Her mind reeled and she tried in vain to remember more details of that last fateful night with Tony. It had been hard enough for her to deal with the idea of Tony taking advantage of her, but knowing some anonymous faceless monster had done this to her made her feel more victimized than ever.

How could Max believe her when she couldn't believe it herself? And now he hated her. She'd read it on his face as clear as the writing on their prenup, on their marriage certificate and on the adoption papers.

She closed her eyes and felt her stomach and chest twist so hard she feared she would get sick. She broke into a cold sweat. Her mind raced. If he hated her, then how much more would he hate David?

Her first instinct was to leave. To get as far away from Max and this house as she could.

But why? She had done nothing to be ashamed of. She was the victim.

But she wouldn't be the victim any longer.

All day at work, Max tried to wrap his mind around the idea that Lilli had deliberately deceived him. But as his anger had cooled, he had trouble believing it. If she was acting, she could win an Academy Award.

She'd been stunned when he'd confronted her, certain there'd been a mistake. Her face had been full of confusion, horror and disbelief. Everything he'd been feeling.

If she'd truly been after his money, wouldn't she have insisted on more in the prenup agreement? He sat in his office, gazing blindly at the mountains in the distance. None of this added up. She had looked at him in complete disbelief when he told her Tony couldn't be David's father.

Pinching the bridge of his nose, he knew what the only explanation could be. Tony had not taken advantage of Lilli that night she'd been drugged. Some other man—some perverted stranger—had violated her. The only consolation he could find was that at least Lilli had no memory of the event.

He thought of little David and felt a surge of protectiveness. The baby *was* his. In every way that mattered. That child had burrowed into Max's heart so deeply he'd never be able to extricate him. Nor would he ever want to.

And Lilli. Max took a deep breath.

They'd made irrevocable vows to one another. He'd sworn to care for David as if he were his own. Now that the harsh emotions of the moment had passed, he knew he needed to go to her again. This time, he *would* listen.

After Lilli brought David back from his stroll, she rocked him for a long time. His soft warm body and sweetness were the only thing that reminded her she was alive. Setting him into his crib, she bent over to kiss his forehead and stared at him for a long while.

Softly closing the door to the nursery, she walked downstairs. Halfway down the steps, she heard a sound and saw Max standing just inside the front door. Her breath just stopped. She stared at him for a full moment, wondering if he was real.

"We need to talk," he said.

Her heart squeezing tight with dread, she followed him out onto the patio. The sunny afternoon provided a stark contrast to the desperation she felt inside her. She swallowed over a lump in her throat. "I understand if you want David and me to leave. I don't expect your support, especially now."

He held up his hand. "Lilli, I'm sorry I jumped to so many conclusions. I can guess what happened."

She closed her eyes. She couldn't look at him as she

recalled that terrible night she'd tried to forget. "Like I told you before, I told Tony I wanted to leave that night. He begged me to stay for just one more song, one more drink. I ordered a soda. I remember feeling dizzy, then nothing…until I woke up hours later in the back room of the club. I could tell something had happened," she said in a halting voice. "Tony was passed out next to the door. I couldn't get out of there fast enough. I got home and sat under the shower until the water turned cold." Opening her eyes, she shook her head, her tight throat reducing her voice to a whisper. "I'm so sorry, Max, but I swear I didn't know. I don't remember anything. And now there's this image of a faceless monster—"

"That's enough." He moved toward her and wrapped his arms around her. "No more," he said. "You've been through enough."

Lilli was afraid to believe her ears. Yet his strength surrounded her. His warmth, the scent she knew and loved. Could it be real?

Swiping at her tears, she cautiously searched his face. What she saw there almost made her knees buckle in relief. He believed her. She could see it clear as the sunlight. "You believe me, don't you?"

He nodded. "Yes, I do. I should have given you a chance to explain, but—"

She sniffed. "You thought you were looking after your brother's child and—" She lifted her shoulders. "And you're not." She took a deep breath and tried to steady herself. "If you want David and me to leave, we will."

"No," he said, the word as hard as steel. "I want you and David to stay. You two belong to me."

Lilli felt a surge of relief, but had to make sure. "But

won't you resent us? Won't you feel as if we're a burden that's been pushed on you?"

He shook his head. "I chose to marry you. I chose to adopt David. None of that has changed." He paused, slicing his hand through his hair. "The only thing that has changed is that now I know how vital you are to me, to my life. I never thought this would happen to me, but I love you. I don't want to live without you. Either of you."

Lilli felt as if the room turned upside down and this time her knees did buckle. Max caught her against him, sank into a chair and pulled her onto his lap. She lifted her trembling hands to his hard, but precious face. "I thought I was going to be all alone in my feelings. Loving you, but never having your love."

"But you married me anyway."

"How could I not? If there was a chance that I could make your life happier by being in it, then I wanted to be there for you. I love you so much."

He closed his eyes and shook his head as if he was overcome with emotion. "I kept saying I didn't understand how Tony could have been so damn lucky to find you. But I'm the lucky one. I get to keep you. Forever," he said, sealing the words with a kiss.

"Forever," she echoed, "But I'm the lucky one. I got the man of steel who has a heart of gold."

* * * * *

BILLIONAIRE'S
MARRIAGE BARGAIN

BY
LEANNE BANKS

This book is dedicated to Tami. Thank you.

One

"She needs a husband."

Alex Megalos looked at the man who had made the statement, sixty-year-old Edwin James, owner of the extremely successful James Investments and Wealth, Inc. Alex wondered if Edwin was hinting that Alex should take on the job.

Alex had successfully avoided commitment his entire thirty years, although things with his most recent girlfriend had gotten a bit dicey and that relationship was headed for the end. The fact that it didn't bother him made him feel a little heartless, but he knew it was best to end a relationship that was doomed. Plus he'd known enough women to realize that they all wanted something. As far as he was concerned, love was fiction in its purest form.

He swallowed a sip of Scotch and glanced across the ballroom at the woman under discussion. A sweet brunette with ample curves, Mallory James was no man-eater like most of the women Alex dated. She wore a modest deep-blue cocktail dress that cradled her breasts, and featured a hem that swung freely at the tops of her knees. Nice legs, but what appealed most about her was her smile and laughter. So genuine.

"Mallory should have no trouble finding a husband. She's a lovely girl with a lot of charm."

Edwin set his empty squat glass on the bar and frowned. "On the outside. On the inside she's a pistol. Plus, she's picky."

Alex did a double take. "Mallory?" he said in disbelief.

"Her mother and I have tried to match her up with a half-dozen men and she passed on all of them. I had some hope for that Timothy fellow she's with tonight, but it doesn't look good. She says he's a great *friend*."

Alex nodded. "Friend. The kiss of death. Just curious. Why do you want her to get married?"

"She's out of college and she wants to work in my company."

"Is that bad?"

Edwin glanced from side to side and lowered his voice. "I hate to admit it, but I can't handle it. She could be a perfect employee but I can't handle the possibility of having to correct her, or worse yet, fire her. The truth is when it comes to my daughter, I'm a marshmallow. You can't be soft if you want to achieve what I have."

"No, you can't. You think marriage will solve things."

"I want her safe, taken care of. She works with a bunch of charity foundations, but she says she wants more. If she's not kept occupied, I'm terrified she'll end up like some of her peers. In jail, knocked up, on a nude sex tape."

Surprised, Alex looked at Mallory again, a wicked visual of her dressed in skimpy lingerie coming out of nowhere. "You really think she's that kind of girl?"

"No. Of course not. But everyone can have a weak moment," he said. "Everyone. She needs a man who can keep her occupied. She needs a challenge."

Alex was at a rare loss as to how to respond. He had approached Edwin to casually set up a meeting to discuss finding an investor for his pet resort project. "I'd like to help, but—"

"I understand," Edwin quickly said. "I know you're not the right man for Mallory. You're still sampling all the different flowers out there, if you know what I mean," he said, giving Alex a nudge and wink. "Nothing wrong with that. Nothing at all. But," he said, lifting his finger, "you may know someone who would be right for my Mallory. If you know some men with the right combination of drive and character, send them my way and I would be indebted to you."

Alex processed Edwin's request. Having Edwin in his debt would put Alex in a better position of strength in gaining the funding he wanted. One of the first rules of wealth was to use other people's money to achieve your goals.

Alex glanced at Mallory. It wouldn't hurt anyone to help Edwin in this situation. In fact, all parties stood to gain.

He caught Mallory's eye and shot her a smile. She gave a slight smile then her gaze slid away and she waved to her father. "I haven't had a chance to talk with Mallory in a while. I'll go over and get reacquainted. I'll see what I can come up with for you, Edwin."

Over six feet of pure masculine power, with dark brown hair and luminescent green eyes that easily stole a woman's breath, Alex Megalos turned women into soft putty begging for the touch of his hands. His sculpted face and well-toned body could have been cut from marble for display in a museum. He was intelligent, successful and could charm any woman he wanted out of her clothes. His charm belied a sharp and tough businessman. As a hotshot VP for Megalos De Luca Resorts, International he was prized for his dynamic innovative energy and making things happen.

So why was he looking at her? In the past, Mallory had always felt he'd looked through her instead of at her. When she'd first met Alex, she'd turned into a stuttering, clumsy loon every time he'd come close. He was so magnetic she'd instantly developed a horrible crush and flirted with him.

And that awful night when she'd actually tried to seduce him… Mallory cringed. Even though Alex had been chivalrous by catching her so she didn't get a concussion from falling on the floor when she'd blacked out, it had been one of the most mortifying moments of her life. Although Alex had thought her fainting spell had been due to her drinking her cocktails too quickly, the incident had been a wake-up call.

Good sense had finally prevailed. She was over the crush now. She knew good and well he was out of her league. Plus she wasn't sure Alex Megalos had the ability to stay focused on one woman for more than a month. Talk about an invitation to heartbreak.

Mallory exhaled and turned toward some guests of the charity event she'd planned. "Thank you so much for coming, Mr. and Mrs. Trussel."

"You've done a marvelous job," Mrs. Trussel, a popular Las Vegas socialite raved. "The turnout is so much better this year than last year. I'm chairing the heart association's event. I would love to get together with you to hear some of your ideas."

"Give the poor girl a break," Mr. Trussel, a balding attorney said. "She hasn't even finished this project."

"I feel like I need to call dibs." Mrs. Trussel

paused and studied Mallory for a long moment. "You aren't married, are you?"

Mallory shook her head. "No. Too busy lately."

"I have a nephew I would like you to meet. He's earned his law degree and been working for the firm for the last year. He'd be quite a catch. May I give him your number?"

Mallory opened her mouth, trying to form a polite *no*. If she had one more setup, she was going to scream. "I—"

"Mallory, it's been too long," a masculine voice interrupted.

Her heart gave a little jump. She knew that voice. Taking a quick, little breath, determined not to embarrass herself, she turned slowly. "Alex, it has been a while, hasn't it? Have you met Mr. and Mrs. Trussel?"

"As a matter of fact, I have. It's good to see you both. Mrs. Trussel, you look enchanting as ever," he said.

Mrs. Trussel blushed. "Please call me Diane," she said. "We were just saying what a wonderful job Mallory has done with the event tonight."

"I have to agree," Alex said. "Would you mind if I steal her away for a moment?"

"Not at all," Mr. Trussel said, ushering his wife away.

"I'll be in touch," the woman called over her shoulder.

As soon as they left, Mallory turned toward Alex. "If you're being nice to me because my father asked you to, it's not necessary."

Alex narrowed his eyes a millimeter. "Why would you say that?"

Mallory moved a few steps away to keep check on the crowd milling through the giant ballroom. She noticed Alex stayed by her side. "Because you were talking with him just a few minutes ago and I know he's trying to make sure I get more friends so I don't move back to California."

"California?" Alex said. "He didn't mention that. Besides, why wouldn't I want to come say hello to you on my own? We've met before."

"Just a couple of times," she said.

"I can even tell you that the first time we met you spilled wine on me." He lifted his lips in a sexy smile designed to take the sting out of his words.

He would remember that. Mallory tried very hard not to blush. She looked away from the man. He was just too damned devastating. "I didn't spill wine. The server did. Even Lilli De Luca said the server was moving too fast."

"That's right. You're good friends with Lilli. Have you seen her and Max's baby?"

"All the time. Even though she has a mother's helper, she lets me take care of David sometimes. Such a sweetheart. He's sitting up on his own now."

Fearing she wouldn't be able to sustain her airy, you-don't-impress-me act much longer, she took a step away from Alex. "Great seeing you," she said. "Thank you for coming to the event tonight. Your donation and presence will mean a lot to inner-city children and their parents." She lifted her hand in a gesture of goodbye. "Take care."

Alex wrapped his hand around hers. "Not so fast. Aren't you going to thank me for rescuing you?"

Her heart tripping over itself at his touch, she looked at him in confusion. He wasn't talking about the time she'd blacked out, was he? "Rescuing me? How?"

"I've met the Trussels' nephew. Nice guy, but boring as the day is long."

Mallory bit the inside of her lip. "That could just be your opinion. Not everyone has to be Mr. Excitement. Not everyone drives race cars in their spare time. Not everyone keeps three women on the string at one time while looking for number four."

Alex's narrowed his eyes again. "I believe I've just been insulted."

Mallory shook her head, wishing she'd been just a teensy more discreet, but Alex seemed to bring out lots of unedited thoughts and feelings. "I was just stating facts."

"You should get your facts straight. Yes, I've had a few girlfriends, but I generally stick to one at a time unless I make it clear that I'm a free agent and the women should be, too."

A few girlfriends. Mallory resisted the urge to snort. "It's really none of my business. Again, I do appreciate your presence and—"

"You keep trying to dismiss me. Why? Do you dislike me?" he asked, his green gaze delving into hers.

Mallory felt her cheeks heat. "I—I need to watch over the event. The headline entertainer will be appearing in just a few minutes."

"Okay, then let's get together another time."

She stared at him for a full five seconds, almost falling into the depths of his charisma then shook her head. Those were the words she'd dreamed of hearing from him eight months ago. Not now. "I'll check my—"

"Hey, Mallory. You're looking hot tonight," a man said in a loud voice.

Mallory glanced at the man with the bleached-blond shock of hair covering one of his eyes as he sauntered toward her. She braced herself. "Oh, no."

"Who is he?" Alex asked.

"Brady Robbins. He's the son of one of the resort owners. He wants to be a rock star and was hoping my father would underwrite his dream. Bad setup," she whispered. "Very bad setup."

"Hey, babe," Brady said, putting his arm around Mallory and pulling her against him. "We had a great time taking that midnight swim in the pool that night. You were so hot. I couldn't get enough of you. Tell me you've missed me?"

Mallory felt her cheeks heat. She'd worn a swimsuit and nothing hot had happened. She tried to push away from him. "I've been so busy," she said, disconcerted by Brady's ability to hold her captive despite his tipsy state.

"The lady's not interested. Go sober up," Alex said, freeing Mallory in one sure, swift movement.

Brady glanced up at Alex and frowned. "Who are you? Mallory and I have a history," he said and tried to reach for Mallory again. Alex stepped between them.

"She doesn't want to share a future with you," Alex said.

"She didn't say that to me," Brady said in a loud voice. "You don't know it, but she has a thing for me. She likes musicians."

Mallory cringed at the people starting to stare in her direction. She didn't want this kind of situation taking the focus off the purpose of the event. She cleared her throat. "Brady, I don't think we're right for each other," she began.

"Don't say that, baby," he said, lunging for her.

Alex caught him again. "Come on, Brady. It's time for you to leave," he said and escorted the wannabe rock star from the room. Mallory said a silent prayer that she wouldn't have to face either man again.

A week later, Mallory's Realtor friend, Donna Heyer, took her to view a condominium at one of the most exclusive addresses in Vegas. The facility boasted top-notch security, luscious grounds with pools, hot tubs, tennis courts and golf courses.

"I love it. Let me see what I need to do to make it happen," Mallory said after they left the spacious condo available for lease. The truth was she would love a closet at this point, as long as she wasn't under the same roof as her loving, but smothering father.

"Just remember," Mallory said as they walked toward the bank of elevators. "This is top secret. I don't want anyone to know, because if my father figures out that I'm determined to move out, he'll have a cow and find a way to sabotage me."

"No one will hear it from me," said Donna, a discreet forty-something woman whom Mallory had met through charity work. "I'm surprised he doesn't understand that you need your independence."

Mallory sighed. "He's afraid I'll turn all wild and crazy."

Donna gasped. "But you would never—"

"I agree I would never, but within the last year, he has developed high blood pressure and an ulcer. When I told him I wanted to move back to California, he had an episode that sent him to the hospital, so I hate—" The elevator doors whooshed open and Mallory looked straight into the green gaze of Alex Megalos. Her stomach dipped. *No, not now.*

"Mallory," he said.

"Alex," both she and Donna chimed at the same time. So Donna knew Alex, too. That shouldn't surprise her. Didn't everyone in Vegas know who Alex was? He was constantly featured in both the business and social pages. Glancing at Donna as she entered the elevator, she bit her lip.

"Good to see you, Donna," Alex said then turned to Mallory. "If you're considering buying here, it's a great property."

"Just looking," Mallory said.

Donna shot Mallory a weak smile that was more of a wince. "I sold the penthouse to Alex."

"Oh," Mallory said, unable to keep the disappointment from her voice. If Alex mentioned it to her father... The elevator dinged its arrival to the street floor and the doors opened. "Donna, could you give me just a second to talk to Alex?"

"No problem," Donna said. "I'll wander around the lobby."

Dressed in a perfectly cut black suit with a crisp white shirt and designer tie, Alex looked down at her expectantly. "You wanted to apologize for not getting back to me?" he said, more than asked.

"Sorry. I've been busy and I knew you would be, too," she said, catching a whiff of his cologne.

"Shopping for a new condo," he said.

"About that," she said, lifting her index finger. "I would really appreciate it if you could keep that on the down low for me. Please," she added.

"You don't want your father to find out," he said.

"At this rate, I'll be lucky to get out of the house by age thirty."

His lips twitched. "You could always get married."

She rolled her eyes. "Ugh. You sound like him. Besides, think about it, what would you have done if your father insisted you get married at age twenty-five in order to move out of the house?"

"Point taken, but you're female. My father would have done the same if he'd had daughters."

"But you can't really agree with the philosophy?" she asked, unable to believe he would share such a point of view. "You're more modern and liberated than that, aren't you?"

"In business, I am. I have to be. But my father is Greek. I was raised to protect women."

She gave him a double take. "Protecting them? Is that what you call what you do?"

He threw back his head and laughed. "Let's discuss this in the car. I can drop you off at home then go to my dull meeting where I have to deliver a speech."

"If you're the speaker, I'm sure it won't be dull. You don't need to take me home. Donna will drop me off at the mall where I parked my car."

He lifted his eyebrows. "This sounds like a covert OP. I can drop you off at the mall. Before you say no, remember you owe me."

"I don't owe you," she said, scowling.

"I helped you ditch your wannabe rock star ex-boyfriend."

"He was never my boyfriend," she told him. "Just a bad setup."

"Yet you took a midnight swim with him and he describes the evening as very hot."

"Probably because he doesn't remember it. If you must know, he had too much to drink and I had to get home on my own."

"I'm beginning to understand why your father wants to keep you locked up."

Alex helped Mallory into his Tesla Roadster, noticing the diamond anklet dangling from her ankle. She wore sandals with heels and her toenails were painted a wicked frosty red. She had nice ankles and calves. Her hips were lush, her breasts even more lush. Her body was more womanly than that of any woman he'd dated, but there was something about her spirit, the sparkle in her personality that got his attention. Despite the fact that women often described him as charming, he'd been feeling old and cynical lately.

"You must exercise," he said as he slid into the leather driver's seat and nudged the car into gear.

"Yes. Why?"

"You have great legs," he said, accelerating out of the condominium complex.

"Thank you," she said and he heard a twinge of self-consciousness in her voice. "I walk and I've started doing Zumba and Pilates. Now back to the discussion about my father, I really would like your promise that you won't discuss my visit to this complex with him."

"I don't see why he needs to know. You haven't taken any action yet, have you?"

"No, but I hope to." She skimmed her fingertip over the fine leather seat. "I wanted this car. It's sporty and green. Once my father read that it goes from zero to one hundred in four seconds, he freaked out. I should have started out telling him I planned to get a motorcycle. Maybe then he would have agreed."

Alex laughed. "You really are trying to drive him crazy, aren't you?"

"Not at all. I just want to live my life." She looked up at the roof. "Can we lower the top?" She glanced at him. "Or are you afraid of messing up your hair?"

He felt a jerk in his gut at the sexy challenge in her words. "I can handle it if you can," he said and pressed the button to push back the roof.

Mallory lifted her head to the sun and tossed back her hair. The sun glinted on her creamy skin and his gaze slid lower to the hint of cleavage he saw in her V-neck blouse. Alex was beginning to get a peek at the wild streak her father had mentioned. He wondered how deep that streak went.

"What do you do with your time?" he asked.

"Plan charity events, volunteer at the hospital and the women's shelter, visit friends, steal away to the beach when I can." She hesitated. "I'll tell you more if you promise not to tell my father."

"You have my word as a gentleman."

"I don't often hear you described as a gentleman," she said.

He threw her a sideways glance. "What do you hear?"

"Lady killer," she said. "Player."

"And what do you say?"

"I don't know you well enough," she said. "I just know I'm not in your league."

He shot her another quick glance. "Why not?"

"I'm not a model or a player. I'm just—" She shrugged. "Me. Average."

"You're far from average."

"Yeah, yeah," she said, waving aside his compliment.

Her dismissal irritated him. "I gave you my word. Now tell me your secret."

"I'm working on my master's degree online."

"What's so bad about that?"

"My father wants me to get married." She lifted her hand. "Take this exit for the mall, please. Oh, and my other secret is that I'm learning to play golf. Now that's funny."

"I'd like to see it."

She shook her head. "No, no. You probably have a handicap of something outrageously good, like ten."

"Nine, but who's counting," he said.

She laughed and shook her head again. "I'm sure you are." She glanced outside the window. "I'm parked near Saks. The white BMW."

He pulled beside the brand-new model luxury car. "That's not a shabby ride," he said.

Opening the door, Mallory turned to stroke the leather seat. "But it's not a Tesla," she cooed.

Amused by her enthusiasm for his car, he couldn't help wondering about her enthusiasm in bed with the right man who could inspire her.

She leaned toward him. "Now, remember you promised you wouldn't discuss any of this with my father."

"I won't say anything."

Her lips lifted in a broad smile so genuine that it distracted him. "Thanks," she said. "I'll see you around." She got out of the car.

"Wait," he called after her.

Turning back, she leaned into the car. "What?"

"Meet me for lunch," he said.

She met his gaze for several seconds of silence then wrinkled her brow in confusion. "Why?"

Alex's usually glib tongue failed him for a half-beat. "Because I'd like to see you again."

"Aren't you involved with someone?"

"No. I broke up with her."

Mallory's eyes softened. "Poor girl."

"Poor girl? What about me?"

She waved her hand. "You're the heartless player."

"Even players need friends," he said, trying to remember the last time he'd had to work this hard to persuade a woman to join him for lunch, for Pete's sake.

She looked at him thoughtfully. "So you'd like me to be your friend." She sighed. "I'll think about it."

Damn it. Negotiations were over. Time for hardball. "Lunch, Wednesday, one o'clock at the Village Restaurant," he said in a voice that brooked no argument.

Her eyes widened in surprise. Her mouth formed a soft O. "Okay," she said. "See you there."

He watched her whirl around, her hips moving in a mesmerizing rhythm as she sashayed to her white BMW. He hadn't realized that Mallory James could be such a firecracker.

If he was going to help poor Edwin find Mallory a husband, he needed to get some more questions answered. Mentally going through his list of acquaintances, he dismissed the first few men as contenders. Whoever he recommended for Mallory would need to be able to stay one step ahead of her. Otherwise, she would leave him eating her dust.

Two

Alex adjusted his tie as he returned to his office after a series of meetings that had begun at seven this morning. His conscientious assistant, Emma Weatherfield, greeted him with messages. "Three calls from Miss Renfro," she said in a low voice.

He nodded because he'd expected as much after he'd broken off with Chloe last week. "I'll take care of it."

Emma nodded, keeping her expression neutral. That was one of the many qualities he liked about his young assistant. She was a master of discretion.

"Ralph Murphy called. I asked him the purpose for his call and he wanted to know if Megalos-De Luca was still acquiring any additional luxury properties."

Alex's interest inched upward. If Ralph, a minor competitor, was calling him, then maybe he wanted to sell. Alex smelled a bargain. "I'll call him before I take lunch. Anything else?"

Emma flipped through the message slips. "Rita Kendall wants you to attend a benefit with her, and Tabitha Bennet wants to meet you for drinks on Thursday. Chad in marketing wants five minutes with you to get an opinion on a new idea." She paused. "Oh, and Mallory James called because she can't make lunch today. She sends her apologies."

Alex stared at Emma in disbelief. "Mallory ditched our lunch date?" He had women practically crawling over broken glass to be with him and Mallory had blown him off. His temper prickled. "Did she leave an alternate day? Did she offer an excuse?"

Emma gave him a blank look and glanced at the message again, shaking her head. "I'm sorry, sir. She was only on the line for a moment and was very polite, but—"

He waved his hand. "Never mind." He took the messages and turned toward his office then stopped abruptly. "On second thought, get Mallory's cell number and find out what her schedule is for the next few days, day and night."

Mallory had been certain Alex Megalos would forget about her after she canceled their lunch meeting. After all there was always a line of ready and willing females begging for his attention. Mallory knew better than to spend any more time with him. He was too seductive and she was too susceptible. He might as well have been the most decadent chocolate she'd never tasted. Truth told, he was the perfect man for an exciting fling, but he'd said he wanted to be friends. It wouldn't take much time with him for her to turn into a pining sap again.

Stunned when he called and left a message on her cell, she procrastinated in responding, not sure what to say. Between her undercover classwork for her online master's degree, her charity obligations and quest to move out of the house, she was too busy for Alex, anyway. He was the kind of man who would take up a lot of space in a woman's life.

She'd agreed to fill in as head greeter for a charity event organized by one of her friends on Saturday night. As guests entered the ballroom event with music flowing from a popular jazz band, Mallory checked off reservations and directed staff to guide the guests to assigned tables.

As the last of the guests arrived, she tidied up the greeter table and tossed out the trash, still undecided whether she would remain much longer. She was tired and she needed to begin work on a research paper.

Glancing at the crowd of people and the beautiful display of flowers, she wavered in indecision.

"Room for one more?" a smooth male voice asked from behind her.

Fighting the havoc that his all too familiar voice wreaked on her nervous system, she whirled around. "Alex," she said in surprise.

Dressed in a dark suit that turned his eyes a shade of emerald, he pointed to the sheaf of paper on the table. "Isn't my name on the list?"

"Well, yes, but—" She'd noticed his name, but she'd assumed he wouldn't attend. Alex's name was always on the guest lists for these events. He was a high-profile businessman and bachelor. Every hostess wanted him at her party. She swallowed over a nervous lump in her throat and glanced at the seating chart. "There are two reserved seats on a front table just left of center. Will that work?" She waved toward the staff escort.

"As long as you join me," he said.

Surprised, she glanced behind him, searching for a woman. "You don't have a date?"

"I was hoping you would take pity on me," he said, but he reminded her of a sly wolf ready to raid the henhouse.

She gave an involuntary shiver of response. "I hadn't decided if I was going to stay for the entire event."

"Then I'll decide for you," he said and took her hand in his.

Mallory stuttered in response but was so caught off guard she couldn't produce an audible refusal. As Alex led her to the front table, she felt hundreds of eyes trained on her and Alex. Alex may have been accustomed to this kind of attention, but she was not. She quickly took the seat he pulled out for her.

The combination of the rhythm and blues band playing sexy songs of want and longing, the warm flickering candlelight and the close proximity of Alex's chair to hers created a sensual atmosphere. Two glasses of wine appeared for them in no time.

He lifted his glass and tilted it toward her. "To time together," he said. "Finally."

He stretched out his long legs and she felt the brush of his leg against hers underneath the table. He glanced at her again with those lady-killer green eyes of his and her chest tightened. She instinctively rubbed her throat and saw his glance fell to her neck and then to her breasts before he met her gaze again.

"You like this band?" he asked.

Forcing her gaze from his, she looked up at the stage and nodded. "The music is moody and the lyrics are—" She searched for the right description.

"Sexy."

The way he muttered the single word made her whip her head around to look at him. He was staring at her, studying her, considering her. She felt a rush of heat and took a quick sip of wine. "Yes," she said. "Do you like them?"

"Yes. Looks like the dancing has started. Let's go," he said and stood.

She blinked at him and remained seated. "Um."

He bent down and whispered in her ear. "Come on, we can talk better on the dance floor."

Confused, she followed him and slid into his arms. Why did they need to talk? she wondered. For that matter, why did they need to be together at all?

"How is your online class going?"

"Good, so far," she said, catching a whiff of his yummy cologne. "But I need to begin a research paper. That's why I was considering leaving early tonight."

"I'm glad I caught you," he said with a hint of predatory gleam in his eyes. "You're a difficult woman to catch. Do you treat all men like me? Blow off lunch dates, don't return calls…"

Embarrassed and then contrite that she'd been rude, she shook her head. "I'm sorry. I didn't mean to be inconsiderate. I just didn't take your invitation seri—" She broke off as his eyes narrowed and she realized her apology wasn't helping.

"You didn't take me seriously?" he echoed, incredulous. "Don't turn all polite on me now."

She sighed. "Well, you're such a flirt. I just didn't believe you."

"No wonder no man can get close to you. Is that one of your requirements? That whoever you date can't flirt? Sounds boring as hell to me."

"I didn't say that. It's that you flirt with every woman. I wouldn't want someone so important to me flirting with every other woman on the planet."

"Does that mean you want someone with very little sexual drive or appeal?"

"I didn't say that, either. Of course, I want a man with a strong sex drive. I just prefer that his drive be focused on me," she managed to say, but felt her face flaming. "But that's not all. He also needs to be intelligent and liberated enough to encourage me to do what I want to do."

He nodded. "You say you want someone you can walk over, but the truth is you want a challenge. I bet if a man played golf with you and took it easy on you that you'd be furious."

Surprised he'd nailed her personality so easily, she felt another twist of confusion. "This discussion is insane. I'm not looking for a long-term relationship right now, anyway. Just like you aren't," she added for good measure.

"That's where you're wrong. When the right woman comes along, I'll seal the deal immediately in every physical, legal and emotional way imaginable."

A shiver passed through her at his possessive tone and she couldn't help wondering what it would be like to be *the right woman* for Alex. Underneath all his charm, could he ever be truly devoted to one woman?

Mallory caught herself. She was insane to even be thinking about his right woman. Heaven knew, it wasn't *her*. Her thought patterns just proved she needed to create some distance between her and Alex.

She glanced at her watch. "I should help the hostess with the extra collections. You don't mind, do you?"

"If I did?" he said.

"Then because this is for charity, you would be a gracious gentleman and allow me to help the hostess," she said firmly.

"Damn, you're good," he said, admiration and something dangerous flickering in his gaze. Mallory supposed she was imagining both.

She smiled. "Excuse me. Good night."

He caught her before she left. "See me before you leave."

His intensity put her off balance. "I'll try," she conceded because she suspected he wouldn't let her leave until she promised that much. She walked out of his arms in the direction of sanity. She'd manufactured an excuse to get away from him. The hostess probably didn't need help, but Mallory sure did.

Mallory did end up helping the hostess with an assortment of last minute minicrises. Just as she was walking down one of the long halls toward the ballroom from one of her errands, she saw Alex approaching her.

"I had to track you down again," he said. "Why are you so determined to avoid me?"

She swallowed over a nervous lump in her throat. "I'm not—avoid—" She stopped when he lifted an eyebrow in disbelief.

"Oh, Mallory," a woman from the lobby called. "Is that you Mallory? My nephew…"

"Oh, no, it's Mrs. Trussel about her nephew. She's been calling me every other day."

"Come with me," he said, taking her hand and urging her down the hallway.

"Oh, Mallory." The voice grew fainter.

"I should at least respond," Mallory said as Alex tugged her around a corner.

"Did you avoid her, too?" he asked, opening a door and pulling her inside a linen closet.

"No. I called and made my excuses. Besides, you're partly to blame."

"Me? How?"

She pointed her finger at his hard chest. "You're the one who told me he was a total bore."

"I should have let you waste your time with him instead?"

"Well, no, but..." She bit her lip and looked around the small, nearly dark room. "Why are we in this closet?"

"Because this appears to be the only way I can get your undivided attention," he said. "You didn't answer my question. Why are you avoiding me?"

She sighed. "I told you. You're a huge flirt."

"Try again," he said.

She closed her eyes even though it was so dark it wasn't necessary. "Because you have this effect on women. You make women make fools of themselves. I don't want to make a fool of myself again," she whispered.

A heartbeat of silence followed. "Again? When did you make a fool of yourself?"

She bit her lip. "I know you remember that night I fainted," she said. "In the bar."

"You'd just drank your cocktails too quickly. It can happen to anyone," he said.

She took a deep breath. May as well get it all over with, she thought. "When I first met you, I was like everyone else. I thought you were gorgeous, irresistible, breathtaking. I—" She gulped. "I had a crush on you. That evening I was trying to—" She lowered her voice to a whisper. "Seduce you."

Silence followed. "Damn. I wish I'd known that. I would have handled the situation much differently."

"As if it would have mattered," she said. "Stop teasing. You know I'm not your type."

Suddenly she felt his hand on her waist. "I'm getting tired of your assumptions."

Mallory felt as if the room turned sideways.

"I can't tell if you're underestimating me or yourself. Damn, if you haven't made me curious," he said and lowered his mouth to hers.

If the room had been turning sideways before, for Mallory, it was now spinning. His hard chest felt delicious against her breasts, his hands masterful at her waist while his lips plundered hers.

Her heartbeat racing, she couldn't find it in herself to resist this one taste, this one time, this one kiss. With an abandonment she hadn't known she possessed, she stretched on tiptoe and slid her fingers through his wavy hair and kissed him back.

She wanted to take in every sensation, his scent, the surprised sound of his breath, the way his hands dipped lower at the back of her waist and urged her closer, his tongue seducing hers.

His kiss was everything and more she'd ever dreamed all those months ago. Hotter, more seductive, more everything... She drew his tongue into her mouth, sucking it the same way...

He abruptly pulled his head back and swore, inhaling heavy breaths. After a second, he swore again. "Where did that come from? I didn't know you—"

Thankful for the darkness in the closet, she bit her still-buzzing lips. "You didn't know what?" she whispered.

"I didn't know you would kiss like that. Hot enough to singe a man, but keep him coming back for more."

Mallory couldn't help but feel a twinge of gratification. After all, Alex was the master seducer.

He lowered his mouth and rubbed it over hers, making her shiver with want. "You could make a man do some crazy things. Who would have known little Mallory—" He broke off and took her mouth in another mind-blowing openmouth kiss. One of his hands slid upward just beneath her breast.

He nibbled and ate at her lips. "Can't help wondering what else is cooking underneath that sweet-girl surface."

A dozen wicked thoughts raced through Mallory's mind. Wouldn't she like to show him what was underneath? Wouldn't she like to feel his bare skin against hers? Wouldn't she like to get as close as she possibly could to him right now?

In a linen closet, some distant corner of her mind reminded her.

And afterward she would have to face the people outside.

She reluctantly pulled back. "I don't think that finding out what's underneath my sweet-girl surface is in the immediate future."

A moment of silence followed. "Why is that?"

"Because I would never want to have a public affair with you."

"This closet is hidden," he said, so seductively he tempted her to leave her objections behind.

"There will be people outside with questions and speculations. I should leave and then you can follow later."

"Later," he echoed.

"It was your idea to pull me in here."

"You would have rather faced Mrs. Trussel?"

She shifted from one foot to the other. "It doesn't matter. I just know I would never want to get involved with you, especially publicly."

"Why the hell not?" he demanded, his voice and body emanating his raw power.

She fortified her defenses. "Because after it's over,

I don't want anyone saying, 'Poor Mallory. Alex took advantage of her.'"

He gave a chuckle that raced through her blood like fire. "What about the poor guy who gets scorched by your kiss?"

She couldn't help feeling flattered, but she pushed it aside. "I should leave."

"I'll be right behind you," he said.

"I don't want to have to answer questions," she said.

"Then grab a towel and say you're cleaning up a mess."

"And you?"

"I'm making plans for the next time you and I get together."

"I don't think that's a good idea."

"I'll change your mind," he promised, and she shivered because she knew if anyone had the ability to change a woman's mind, even her mind, it was Alex.

The following day, Alex's mind kept turning to thoughts of Mallory. She piqued his interest more than any other woman had in ages. Women had come easily to him. The trademark Megalos features had served as both a blessing and a curse for Alex.

With his older brothers committed to medicine for their careers like their father, Alex had always been viewed as the lightweight because he was determined to pursue gaining back influence in the family-named business.

What his father and brothers didn't grasp was that when the tide was rolling against a man, he had to use everything to fight it off—intelligence, charm and power. Alex had used everything he had to rebuild the influence of the family name in Megalos-De Luca Enterprises. He'd butted heads more than once with Max De Luca, but lately the two had become more of a team and less adversarial.

Max had even expressed dismay over the board's decision not to support Alex's plan for a resort in West Virginia near Washington, D.C. Since Alex had secured legal permission to develop the resort on his own, he was determined to make it a success. He would show the board he knew what he was doing, and in the future they wouldn't fight him.

As an investor, Mallory's father could be important to Alex's strategy. Mallory could be the key to unlocking the door to her father.

Funny thing, though, the woman made him damned curious. He pushed the button for his assistant. "Emma, please come into my office."

"Of course, sir."

Seconds later, she appeared, notebook in hand. "Yes, sir."

"I want you to send flowers to Mallory James for me."

Her eyes widened. "Oh. She's lovely," Emma said. "So polite on the phone."

"Not my usual type," he said.

She paused a half-beat. "Much better."

His lips twitched in amusement. Emma was extremely discreet and rarely expressed her opinion unless he asked for it. "How well do you know her?"

"Not well at all. But she's very personable and gracious. You'd never know that her father could pay off the national debt."

"Send her a dozen red roses," he said.

Emma nodded slowly and made a note.

"What's wrong with a dozen red roses?" he asked, reading her expression.

"It's terribly clichéd," she said. "You're dealing with a different quality of woman with Mallory. Something personal might make more of an impression," she said, then rushed to add, "not that you need to impress her."

Alex thought for a moment as several ideas came to mind. "Okay send her a dozen roses in different colors with a Nike SasQuatch driver and a box of Titleist Pro V1 gold balls."

Emma blinked at him.

"She's learning to play golf," he said. "In the note, tell her I'll pick her up for a round of golf on Tuesday at 7:00 a.m."

Three

Tuesday morning at seven-thirty, Mallory was awakened by a knock on her bedroom door. Groggy, she lifted her head and groaned. She'd been up until 4:00 a.m. finishing a paper for her class.

"Miss James," the housekeeper said in a low voice through the door.

Mallory reluctantly rose from bed and opened her door. "Hilda?" she said to the housekeeper.

"There's a man downstairs and he insists on seeing you. Mr. Megalos."

Mallory groaned again. "Oh, no. Not him. I called his assistant to cancel."

"He's determined to talk to you. Shall I tell him you'll be down shortly?" Hilda asked.

"Okay, okay," Mallory said and closed the door. Thank goodness her mother and father were out of town for a business meeting in Salt Lake City, one of the few times her mother left the house. Otherwise, she would be grilled like her favorite fish.

She padded across the soft carpet to her bathroom. Her hair in a ponytail, she washed her face and brushed her teeth. She thought about applying makeup, fixing her hair and dressing up, then nixed the idea. If Alex saw her au naturel, that should really kill his curiosity.

Pulling on a bra and T-shirt and stepping into a pair of shorts, she descended the stairs where he was waiting at the bottom, looking wide-awake and gorgeous.

"Good morning, sleepyhead. Did you forget our date?"

"I called your assistant and gave her my regrets. I had a late night last night."

"Partying?"

"Ha. Finishing my paper until 4:00 a.m.," she corrected and yawned. "I'm sorry if you didn't get my message, but as you can see I'm not ready for a round of golf."

"We may as well squeeze in nine holes," he said. "You won't be able to go back to sleep, anyway."

Frowning at his perceptiveness, she covered another yawn. "How do you know that?"

"I'm just betting you're like me. Once I'm awake, I can't go back to sleep."

She studied him for a long moment. "You have me at a disadvantage. You've obviously had a full night of sleep."

"So I'll give you a few pointers," he said.

A lesson, she thought, her interest piqued. Although she was already taking lessons, it might be interesting to get another approach.

"Nine holes," she said.

"Until you can do the full eighteen," he said, clearly goading her.

She shouldn't give in to his challenge. Although she was tempted, she absolutely shouldn't. "Give me five minutes."

"A woman getting ready in five minutes?" he said. "That would really impress me."

She smiled as she thought about what her finished appearance would look like. No makeup, ponytail, shorts, shirt, socks and golf shoes. "We'll see," she said and headed back upstairs, feeling his gaze on her.

After Mallory took a rinse and spin shower, slapped on sunscreen and got dressed, she joined Alex as he drove to the golf course. She told herself not to focus on her attraction to him. Even though the sight of his tanned, muscular legs revealed by his shorts was incredibly distracting, she tried not to think about how sexy and masculine he was. She tried not to think about how it would feel to be held in his arms, in his bed, taken by him. She tried not to think about how exciting it would be to be the woman who drove him half as crazy as he drove her. Used to drive her, she firmly told herself.

Mallory knew Alex wasn't a forever kind of man, but she'd always thought he would be a great temporary man, amusing, passionate, sexy. If a woman decided to have an affair with him, she would need at all times to remember not to count on him for a long-term relationship. That would be a fatal, heartbreaking mistake.

Not that she was going to have an affair with him, anyway, Mallory told herself as she teed off. She watched her ball fly a respectable distance toward the hole and sighed in relief.

"Not bad," he said. "Just remember to lead with your hips both ways," he said and he swung his club and hit the ball.

His ball soared beyond hers. "What do you mean both ways?" she asked. "How?"

"First get balanced," he said. "Then lead with your hips in the backswing and the downswing. Get behind me and put your hands on my hips," he instructed.

"What?"

"Don't worry. I'm not going to seduce you on the golf course. Unless you want me to," he said and laughed in a voice that made her feel incredibly tempted.

Gingerly placing her hands on his hips, she felt the coil of power as he swiveled his hips and swung the club.

He turned around to face her and glanced down her body. "It's what women have always known. The power comes from the hips."

She felt a heat that threatened to turn her into a puddle of want, but stiffened her defenses and walked toward her next shot. "Thank you for the reminder."

Alex wondered if Mallory was making all those moves deliberately to distract him. After he'd mentioned the tip about hips, she swung her backside before each shot. When she wiggled her shoulders to stay loose, he couldn't help but notice the sway of her breasts.

"Visualize where you want the ball to go," she whispered to herself, and without fail she would bite her lush lower lip, reminding him of how her lips had felt when he'd kissed her.

By the time they reached the ninth hole, he had undressed her a dozen times. He knew she would be in his bed soon, but since she was Edwin's daughter, he figured he may have to play this one a little more carefully.

After she made her last putt, she turned to him with a smile on her face that made the sunny Nevada day seem even brighter. "Thank you for twisting my arm. This was more fun than I'd imagined."

"If you don't enjoy it, then why did you decide to learn to play?"

"The challenge," she said as they walked toward the clubhouse. "I like to learn new things." She laughed to herself. "And my father thought it was a good way to attract a husband."

"But that's not part of your diabolical plan," he said.

"No. But the golf course *is* where a lot of business is conducted," she said.

"Ah. I'm impressed," he said and he was. "The problem with you trying to do business on the golf course is that men will be distracted by your body."

She shot him a sideways glance. "You're not trying to flatter me again, are you?"

He moved in front of her and stopped. "Whatever is between us is more than flattery. I made that clear the other night in the closet. I can make it clear again."

Her eyes widened and she bit her lip. He lifted his finger to her mouth. "Don't do that to your pretty lips," he said. "Let me take you to dinner."

He watched a wave of indecision cross her face. She hesitated an extra beat before she shook her head. "No. I told you I'm not getting involved in a public situation with you where people could misconstrue that we're involved."

He lifted his hand to push back a strand of her hair that had come loose from her ponytail. "We already are involved."

Her eyes widened again. "No, we're not."

"You're not attracted to me," he said.

She opened her mouth then shut it and sighed. "I didn't say that. But I already told you that I don't want to be known as one of your flavors of the month. Wherever you go, you draw attention, so there's no way we could have dinner without people talking about it or it ending up in the paper."

"You really don't want to be seen with me," he mused and shook his head. This was a first. Usually women wanted to parade him in public at every opportunity. Alex switched strategy with ease. "No problem. We'll have dinner at my condo tonight."

Mallory felt a shiver of forbidden anticipation as she stepped inside the elevator that would take her to Alex's penthouse condominium. She shouldn't have agreed, but the more time she spent with him, the more she wanted to know about him.

And who knew? Perhaps Alex could be a resource for helping her get started professionally. As much as she loved her parents, she craved her independence. She needed to succeed on her own.

The elevator dinged her arrival at the penthouse and she took the few steps to Alex's front door. Before she pushed the buzzer, the door opened and Alex appeared, dressed in slacks and a white openneck shirt. He extended his hand. "Welcome," he said and led her inside the lushly appointed condo.

"This is nice," she said, looking around. Although

Mallory was accustomed to the trappings of wealth, even she was impressed with the architectural design and masculine contemporary furnishings.

"I own a home farther out of town, but this is more convenient during the week," he said as they walked toward a balcony with a stunning view.

"It's gorgeous," she said and closed her eyes for a second. "And quiet."

"I chose it for that reason. After a busy day, I can sit here and let my mind run. It's often my most productive time of the day. I come up with some of my best ideas up here or at my cabin in Tahoe." He waved his hand toward a table set with covered silver platters, fine china and crystal. "I sent my staff away just for you. That means we're on our own except for my full-time housekeeper Jean. She'll take care of cleanup."

Mallory sat down at the patio table and wondered how many other women had sat in this very chair. More beautiful, more sophisticated women determined to capture Alex's heart, perhaps even to marry him.

Her stomach twisted at the thought, so she deliberately pushed it aside. This could very well be the only evening she spent with Alex. She may as well enjoy it.

Alex poured a glass of wine and she studied his hands. His fingers were long, and like everything about him, strong and masculine-looking. She wondered how they would feel on her body. She would bet Alex knew exactly how to touch a woman. A twist of awareness tightened inside her, surprising her with its intensity.

Shaking her head at the direction of her thoughts, she took a sip of wine and latched on to the first subject that came to mind. "You mentioned that your father is Greek," she said. "Your family is obviously part owner of Megalos-De Luca. Do you have other relatives working for the company?"

He shook his head and lifted the silver cover from his plate and motioned for her to do the same. "My grandfather only had one son, my father, who chose to go into medicine. His decision infuriated my grandfather so much that he refused to speak to my father."

"Oh, no. That's terrible," she said. "What does your father think of your career choice?"

He took a bite of the lobster dish the chef had prepared. "He hasn't spoken to me since I dropped out of premed, majored in business and got involved in the family business again. My two older brothers went into medicine and the same was expected of me. Business isn't noble enough. It just pays the bills."

"You and your father don't speak?" she asked in disbelief. "What about your mother?"

"My mother sneaks a call to me every now and then, but she feels her job is to support my father."

"My mother takes a back seat approach to marriage, too. She goes along with my father's whims. I don't think I could do it. I don't want to do it," she said more firmly.

"Maybe if you met the right man…"

Mallory swallowed a bite of dinner and shook her

head vehemently. "The right man will encourage me to follow my own goals and ambitions. Isn't it ironic that your father decided to buck his father's trend? Yet when you did the same thing, he reacted the same way as his father."

"The same thing has crossed my mind more than once," he said in a bitter voice.

Mallory felt a surge of sympathy for him. She never would have dreamed Alex's family had totally cut him off. "That's got to be difficult. What do you do for holidays?"

"Ignore them," he said, his gaze suddenly cool. "What about you? You're an only child, aren't you?"

She nodded, wondering if his estrangement with his family truly bothered him so little. "I begged for a sibling until my eighteenth birthday."

He chuckled. "You finally realized it wasn't going to happen."

She nodded, thinking back to that time in her life when everything had changed. "Everything was different after the accident. My mother changed. My father changed some, too."

Alex met her gaze. "What accident?"

"I was seven at the time. My mother was taking my brother and me with her for a quick trip to a nail salon."

"I didn't know you had a brother," he said.

Her stomach suddenly tightening, she pushed her food around her plate. "Not many people do. It's too painful for either of my parents to talk about. He was two years older than me. His name was Wynn and he was a pistol," she said, smiling in memory. "He was the adventurous one. My father was so proud of him."

"Was," Alex prompted.

"My mother ran a stop sign and we were hit by a pickup truck. All three of us had to be taken to the hospital. My brother took the brunt of the collision. He died in the emergency room. They told me I almost died. They had to remove my spleen and I broke a few bones. I stayed in the hospital for a couple of weeks, ate gelatin and ice cream and got out and wanted everything to go back to normal. But it couldn't. I remember how quiet the house was without Wynn around."

"What happened to your mother?"

"She had a few cuts and bruises. They released her after one night, but she has never been the same. She never drove again and I had to push when it came time for me to get my license. The accident frightened both my parents, and she blamed herself for my injuries. Both of them were, are, terrified of something happening to me."

A thoughtful expression settled on his face. "Now it all makes sense."

"What does?"

"Why your father is so protective," he said. "They almost lost you. They don't want that to happen again."

"But you can't wrap yourself in cotton and climb

into a box because you're afraid something bad will happen," she said.

"*You* can't," he said, his lips twitching in humor.

"I love my mother, but I don't want to live my life that way. I sometimes feel as if every time she looks at me, she remembers losing Wynn."

"That's tough," he said.

She nodded. "It has been. She won't really let me get close to her."

"Maybe she's afraid of losing again," he mused.

"Maybe, but I don't want to make all my decisions based on what could go wrong."

"Caught between being the dutiful, devoted daughter and wild woman hiding underneath it all," he said.

"Parental guilt is a terrible thing," she said with a sigh, taking another sip of wine.

"I don't have that problem," he said.

"What about brotherly guilt?" she asked.

"My brothers followed my father's lead. One of them is a researcher," he said and gave a sly smile. "I donate to his foundation anonymously."

She smiled, feeling as if she'd just been given a rare treat. "You just told me a secret, didn't you?"

"Yes, I did. Don't spread it around," he said, shooting her a warning glance that managed to be sexy, too.

So Alex cared more about his family than he pretended, she realized. He was more complicated than the player she'd thought he was. Mallory wondered what other secrets lay beneath his gorgeous surface.

"I won't tell your secret as long as you don't tell my father about my plan to move out and get a job."

"What will you do if he cuts you off financially?"

She shrugged. "I'm Edwin James's daughter. He's taught me how to invest. I have a cushion. Speaking of employment, do you think Megalos-De Luca could use me on staff?"

He paused for a few seconds, a flicker of surprise darting through his green gaze. He quickly masked it. "I hadn't thought about that. Let me get back to you on it."

"Oooh," she said, shaking her head. "Complete evasion. And I had such hopes."

"You didn't really think I invited you here to interview you for a job, did you?" he asked in a low, velvet voice.

She felt a rush of heat and glanced away.

"Are you blushing?" he asked.

She shook her head. "Of course not," she lied. "Dinner was delicious. Let me take my plate to the—"

"No. My housekeeper will take care of it. You're my guest." He stood and extended his hand. "Let's go up to the second level." He led her up a set of stairs to another terrace. This one featured an outdoor pool, hot tub, bar and chaise lounges.

Sensual music so clear the band could have been

right there on the deck flowed around them. A slight breeze sent warm air whispering over her skin. Looking out into the horizon, she felt as if she could see forever. She drew in a deep breath and felt her burdens and dissatisfaction slip away for just a moment. For just a moment, she felt free.

The moment stretched to two, and because Alex was a man, he didn't feel the need to fill the silence with useless conversation. He hadn't made a sound, but she was aware of him. She knew he stood closer, yet not quite touching her, because his warmth radiated at her back.

"If you sold tickets for this, I would buy a hundred," she said.

"For what? The view?" he asked, sliding his hand down her arm.

"Yes, and the temperature, and the breeze, and the feeling of freedom. Do you feel this way every night?"

"No," he said and closed his other hand over her other shoulder. "But you're not here every night."

"Flattery again," she said, unable to keep from smiling. Even though she knew he was just flirting, she couldn't help but be charmed by him. It had been that way since the first time she'd met him.

"Not flattery," he said. "You need a review." He turned her around and lowered his mouth to hers, taking her lips in a kiss that made her feel as if she were a sumptuous feast.

Sliding his fingers through her hair, he tilted her

head for better access and immediately took advantage. He kissed her like he wanted her, like he had to have her. The possibility threw her into a tailspin.

Her heartbeat racing, she felt a shocking surge of arousal that nearly buckled her knees. She kissed him back and his low groan vibrated throughout her body to all her secret places.

"Say what you want, Mallory, but you make me feel free and hungry at the same time. How do I make you feel?" he asked, dipping his head to press his mouth against her throat.

Another rush of arousal raced through her. She couldn't lie. "The same way," she said, her voice sounding husky to her ears.

"What are you going to do about it?" he asked, but it was more of a dare.

A visual of what she wanted to do scorched her brain. "I don't know," she said. "I thought I had you figured out, but there's more to you than I thought there was."

"It's the same for me," he said, sliding his hand upward to just below her breast.

Mallory sucked in a quick breath. "How am I different?"

"I thought you were a sweet girl, quiet and shy."

"And?"

"And you're sweet, but you're not quiet or shy. You've got a wild streak a mile wide and I want to be there when it comes out."

His fingers grazed the bottom of her breast, making her want him even more. It was a feeling she knew that would roar out of control if she let it. She just wasn't sure she was ready for it.

"So what does Mallory want to do tonight?" he asked.

Her limbs melting like wax, she struggled with her arousal. She wanted to let go, but she didn't want to lose herself to Alex. That would be too dangerous.

She grasped through her brain for something else, something that would give her more time. "Your car," she finally managed to say. "I want to drive your car."

Four

Sweet little Mallory had a lead foot.

She rounded corners and made hairpin turns at breakneck speed. Alex began to understand Edwin's anxiety. If it had been his choice, he would put the woman in a nice, big Buick. Or a Hummer.

"This is wonderful," she said, the wind whipping through her hair. "I love that it only has two gears. I can keep it in second gear all the time. I know there were only seven hundred and fifty models of this car made for this year. Who did you have to bribe to get it?"

"No one. I just had my assistant make a few calls and the deal was done."

"Maybe I could order one and hide it," she mused.

Alex laughed. "Do you really think you could hide a purchase like that from your father? You know he has people watching you 24/7."

She shot him a sideways glance. "He's not supposed to hover," she said. "The agreement is if I keep a low profile on the party scene, then the bodyguards must remain invisible to me."

"He'll have my hide when he finds out I let you drive my car like a bat out of hell," he said, but wasn't concerned.

"Bat out of—" She broke off. "And I thought I was taking it easy."

He noticed her skirt flipping around her thighs in the wind and slid his hand over her knee.

She swerved and popped forward. "Oops, sorry," she said, pushing her hair behind her ear. "We should go back."

He slid his hand away, pleased that his touch had flustered her. "I know a place that has a great view not far from here."

"Which way?" she asked. "I have a weakness for a great view."

So did he, Alex thought, looking at her skirt still dancing over her thighs. He gave her the directions and minutes later, she pulled into a clearing on top of a hill that overlooked the Las Vegas strip.

"This is beautiful," she said as she killed the engine and leaned her head back. She inhaled deeply. "I'm surprised you let me drive your car."

"I am, too," he said, reaching for her hand.

She turned her head to look at him. "Why?"

"I haven't let anyone drive that vehicle except me. Sure a Ferrari is more expensive, but I had to wait for that electric roadster for over a year. If you wrecked it—"

"You'd just get another one," she finished for him.

He met her gaze. "True." He sat up in his seat and leaned over her. "So you've driven my Tesla. What do you want to do next?" He dipped his mouth to her luscious, pale neck.

She sighed and he slid his hand over her knee.

"The way you act, I almost think you really want me," she said, turning her lips toward his as he skimmed his mouth across her jaw.

"Almost," he echoed, his voice sounding like a growl to his own ears.

"Like I said, I'm not your usual type," she said, shifting toward him.

"Maybe that's a good thing," he said and rubbed his mouth over her sexy, soft lips. He loved the texture and taste of her. He slid his tongue over her bottom lip.

"But you've dated models, actresses," she protested, at the same time opening her lips to give him better access.

"None of them had a mouth like yours," he said and couldn't put off taking her mouth in a kiss. He slid his tongue inside, tasting her, relishing the silken sensation of her lips and tongue.

She gave a soft sigh and lifted her hands to his head, sliding her fingers through his hair. She massaged his head and welcomed him into her depths. With each stroke of her tongue, he felt himself grow more aroused.

He slipped one of his hands beneath her blouse and pushed upward toward her ample breasts. He touched the side of one of her breasts, stroked underneath. He wanted to touch her all over. He wanted to taste her all over.

He felt her heat and arousal begin to rise. She arched toward him and he knew she wanted more. Giving the lady what she wanted and what he wanted, too, he unfastened her bra and touched her naked breast.

She quivered beneath his touch. Her nipple already stiff, she wiggled against him. Her artless response made him feel as if he would explode.

He continued to kiss her, playing with her nipple and slipping his hand beneath her skirt, closer to her core. Reaching the apex of her thighs, he stroked the damp silk that kept her femininity from him.

"You feel so good," he muttered. "So good." He dipped his fingers beneath the edge of her panties and found the heart of her, swollen and waiting for him.

It was all he could do not to rip off both their clothes and drive into her hot, wet, sweetness. She would feel like a silk glove closing around him.

Groaning, he rubbed her sweet spot until she

bloomed like an exotic flower. She began to pant and it became his mission to take her to the top.

"You're so sexy," he said. "I can't get enough of you." Still rubbing over her swollen pearl, he thrust his finger inside her.

She gasped and he felt her internal shudder of release, her delicious shudder of pleasure. "Oh—Al—" She broke off breathlessly as if she couldn't form another syllable.

She clung to him, dropping her head to his shoulder. Seconds passed where her breath wisped over his throat. Finally she let out a long sigh.

"I don't know whether to be embarrassed or—"

"Not embarrassed," he said, still hard as a steel rod. He closed his arms around her.

"Amazed," she said. "We're not even in bed," she said, awe in her voice.

"We will be," he said. "It's inevitable. I have business at one of our island resorts next weekend. I'm taking you with me."

"Next weekend?" she said, pulling her head from his shoulder to gape at him. "But I have papers and I promised to help at a charitable auction."

"Get your paper done before the weekend and find a substitute, Mallory. I won't take no for an answer."

She opened her mouth to protest then closed it. "It's crazy," she whispered.

"Just the way you like it," he said.

"What if I don't—" She broke off. "What if you

don't—" She frowned. "What if we change our minds and decide we don't want to take this further?"

"We can just treat this like it's an extended date."

"No expectations?" she asked.

"If that's what you want," he said, but he knew what would happen.

Relief crossed her features. "Okay."

He brushed another kiss over her irresistible mouth. "I'll send one of my drivers to pick you up and take you to the airport. My assistant will call with all the details."

She looked at him as if her head was spinning. "That, uh, that might not be a good idea. My father—"

"Don't worry. I'll talk to him," he said.

She blinked. "Talk to him? What will you say?"

"I'll tell him the truth—that we're seeing each other," he said.

"I'm not sure that's a good idea," she said. "He may try to push you to—" She broke off and cleared her throat. "He really wants me to get married and he may try to push you to make a—" She cleared her throat and looked away. "Commitment."

"Mallory," he said, sliding his index finger under her chin. "Do you really think anyone could succeed in pushing me to make a commitment I don't want to make?"

She met his gaze for a long moment. "No. I guess not."

"I can take care of me and anyone else who is important to me. I'll talk to him." The poor woman looked dazed. He took pity on her. "Would you like me to drive back to the condo?"

Relief washed over her face. "Yes. Thank you."

Alex cleared his schedule to meet with Edwin James the following evening. The wily Californian poured Alex and himself a glass of whiskey and stepped away from his desk to a sitting area furnished with burgundy leather chairs and mahogany tables. Edwin's office oozed old wealth, but Alex knew the old man had started with nearly nothing. He'd started his own business, expanded, turned it into a franchise operation and began investing, first for himself then others who paid him handsomely.

Alex knew that he and Edwin had a lot in common. He allowed the older man to start the discussion.

"You told me you wanted to build a resort in West Virginia and you'd like me to find you some backers. Why West Virginia?"

So began the interview. Alex answered all of Edwin's questions with a minimum of spin and an abundance of facts and figures.

"Why did Megalos-De Luca turn this down?" Edwin asked.

"Other than the fact that they're blind as bats, and you can quote both me and Max De Luca on that, they're focusing on expanding in current proven markets."

Edwin nodded. "I would think they wouldn't let you do this on your own. Don't you have some kind of noncompete agreement?"

"I do," Alex said. "But I told them I would walk if they didn't make an exception."

Edwin lifted his bushy gray eyebrows. "So you can play hardball when you want. I like that."

"You're not surprised."

"No," Edwin said. "You don't get as far as I've gotten without being able to read people." He paused for a moment. "I've got three or four investors who would be right for this. I'll get back to you by the end of this week." He rose from his chair and extended his hand. "I look forward to doing business with you."

Alex nodded as he shook Edwin's hand. "Thank you. Same here," he said. "On another subject, you asked me to recommend some men who might interest your daughter."

Edwin's eyes lit up. "You have someone in mind?"

"Yes. Me," Alex said. "Mallory and I are seeing each other."

Edwin stared at him for a long moment. "I already knew that," he said. "I have a couple guys who watch over her. They told me about her driving your car. She lost them on one of the turns." He shook his head. "You're a brave man. Just so you know, I would want to show my gratitude in a substantial way to the man who can get my daughter happily down the aisle."

"That would be down the line," Alex said. "We're

still just getting to know each other. In fact, I have to go to one of our island resorts this weekend and I'm taking her with me."

Edwin nodded slowly. "She loves the beach. Just don't let anything happen to her. She's my little girl."

"She always will be even though she's turned into a smart, adventurous and very capable woman," Alex said. "I wonder where she got that adventurous streak."

Edwin cackled and shook his finger at Alex. "You're a smart one, yourself. Maybe she's finally met her match."

Mallory decided not to join Alex for the long weekend. Staring at her unpacked suitcase, she felt like a wuss. A smart wuss, though, she told herself. Even though Alex was unbelievably hot, had allowed her to drive his car and invited her to go on a weekend adventure with him, she knew he was trouble. She knew she would have a hard time hanging on to her sanity.

Rising from her bed, she paced a path from one end of her room to the other and back again. Biting her lip, she glanced at the small stacks of clothes on the bench next to the suitcase. She'd gathered the items necessary for a trip to an island.

Although deep down, she'd ultimately known that she had no business even thinking about going to a fast food joint with Alex, let alone an island resort, she'd been tempted. How could she not be? She loved the beach.

The fact that she would have Alex's attention away from the glare of Las Vegas shouldn't make her shiver with anticipation. The prospect of walking along a beach with Alex, her hand laced with his, the ocean breeze rippling against their skin. A taunting visual filled her mind of sharing a kiss with Alex under the moonlight with the waves lapping at her toes.

Mallory sighed, looking at the stacks of clothes again. It would take so little. Just a few swift motions to lift and lower them into the designer suitcase. She would be insane to do it. Completely and totally insane.

A knock sounded at her bedroom door, startling her. Her heart jumped into her throat. "Hilda?" she said, knowing it was the housekeeper announcing the arrival of Alex's driver. She went to her door, trying to drum up some mental fortitude. She wouldn't make Hilda do the dirty work. Mallory would calmly tell Alex that she had changed her mind.

Taking a deep breath, she opened the door.

To Alex.

"Ready to go?" he asked.

His eyes met hers and his magnetism hit her like a tidal wave. Her throat closed up and she tried to squeak out the word *no.*

He glanced around the room and his gaze landed on the stacks of clothes and the open suitcase. "Sweetheart, you're running behind," he said, lifting the stacks of clothes in his hands and setting them in the suitcase.

Swallowing over the lump in her throat, she found some semblance of her voice. "I was thinking it would be best if I didn't go."

He searched her face. "You were going to chicken out."

"I was not going to chicken out," she said, automatically lifting her chin. "I was just going to make a wise decision."

He walked toward her and her stomach danced with butterflies of expectation.

"This is your chance to let down your hair. Even your dad has given his okay."

She still considered that miraculous. "Yes, but my mother has freaked out. She said she's too upset to get out of bed."

"It's not as if I'm taking you to some war-torn country."

"Alex," she chided him, but couldn't put a lot of oomph into the emotion because she secretly agreed with him.

"You want me to talk to her?" he offered.

Mallory shook her head vehemently. "No, no, no. You don't have a calming effect on women."

He rested his hands on his hips. "I'm not going to try to push you to do something you don't want to do," he said. "I'll walk down to my car and give you five minutes to join me. But don't blame this one on your parents. Make your own decision," he said and left the room.

Mallory stared after him, her heart hammering against her rib cage. She'd spent most of her life forced to be sensible and ultracareful out of consideration for the most important people in her life.

Alex was right. This was her opportunity to taste a little of the freedom she'd been craving, so why was she stalling? Was it because she was afraid of what he brought out in her? Was it because she was afraid of breaking her hard and fast rule to not fall for him?

Taking a deep breath and telling herself to stop overthinking, she put another stack of clothes in her suitcase. She went to the bathroom and grabbed her travel bag of toiletry items and tossed them into the suitcase. She opened the lowest drawer in her dresser and paused, her hand hovering over the bits of silk and lace that she had *never found the nerve to wear in front of another human being.*

Her door burst open again, startling her. Alex and a big beefy man wearing a chauffeur's uniform stepped inside. "I decided you might need some help," he said and glanced down at her suitcase. "Is it ready?"

"Yes, but—"

"Okay, Todd, you mind closing it up and carrying it downstairs?"

"No, sir," the man said and followed Alex's orders.

Alex met her gaze. "And now for you," he said, moving toward her.

Mallory felt her stomach dance with nerves.

"Where's your passport?" he asked.

"The top left-hand drawer in my bureau, but I can get it," she said.

He opened the drawer, pulled out her passport and flipped through the empty pages. Mallory felt a twist of embarrassment at the lack of places she'd been.

"I don't see a lot of stamps," he said.

"No."

"You don't like to travel?" he asked, turning back toward her.

"I love to travel. I just haven't—" She broke off and squealed as he hauled her over his shoulder and walked out of her bedroom. "What are you doing?"

"Carrying you to my car."

Embarrassed, but oddly thrilled, Mallory bounced against his shoulder as he carried her down the staircase. Hilda stood by the front door wearing an expression of shock and confusion.

"Miss James?" she said, clearly unsure what she should do.

"I'm okay," she said to Hilda. "Just don't tell Mom about this. Alex, I thought you said you weren't going to push me."

"Mallory," he said in a sexy, chiding voice. "This isn't pushing. It's carrying."

When he stopped outside a Bentley and allowed her to slide down the front of him, so that she was acutely aware of his hard, muscular body, Mallory looked into his green gaze and relearned what she'd already known. Alex was trouble.

Five

Mallory flipped through a magazine during the flight to Cabo San Lucas on Alex's private jet. She stole a glance at Alex and tried to push aside her edginess. Alex appeared to be working on a redesign of an existing resort, complete with construction plans and artist's renderings.

"Looks nice," she said.

He glanced up and nodded. "These are for a redevelopment for a resort off the coast of South Carolina. I just bought out a competitor last week. It was a steal.

"And you already have plans?" she asked, surprised because she'd heard so many stories about the drag time associated with construction.

He smiled and at that moment, he reminded her of a shark. "The people I work with know not to drag their feet. Otherwise, they won't be working for me."

She nodded. "I wish I'd brought my laptop. That way I could have done some classwork."

He shook his head and leaned back in his seat. "I want this to be a weekend of total relaxation and ir-responsibility for you."

She couldn't swallow her humor. "That's not exactly equitable. You're working now and you'll be working at the resort."

"Briefly at the resort," he corrected her. "I'm de-livering a keynote because Max De Luca didn't want to go without his lovely wife, Lilli. She wouldn't go because the baby got a cold earlier this week."

Mallory frowned. "I hadn't heard. Poor thing. I know Lilli refuses to leave David when he's sick. She's very protective."

"As is Max," Alex added and glanced down at the drawings again.

"I like that about him," she said thoughtfully.

"What?" he asked.

"I like that Max is protective of David even though David isn't his biological son."

Alex nodded. "Max is tough. Lilli's made him human."

"You like her?" Mallory asked, feeling a twinge of envy.

"She's a lovely woman on the outside and the

inside. She brought cupcakes to the office for Alex's birthday. I thought he was going to fall over, but he loved it. And the cupcakes were damn good. I tried to talk her into making some for my birthday, but Alex told me to call a bakery. SOB."

Mallory laughed. "Are cupcakes your favorite?"

"Anything baked homemade is my favorite," he said. "I like cookies, cupcakes. My favorite is apple pie with ice cream."

She laughed again. "You just don't seem like the all-American apple pie kind of guy."

"Why not?"

"You're too—" She broke off, feeling heat rush to her cheeks.

"Blushing again?"

"I don't blush," she said.

"No?" he said, leaning toward her and lifting his fingers to her cheeks. "Then what is this pretty pink color I see—"

"A gentleman wouldn't make a big deal out of it," she said.

"You've said I'm not a gentleman. And you like that about me," he said, rubbing his index finger over her lips, sliding it inside against her teeth.

Mallory instinctively opened her mouth and he slid his finger onto her tongue. It was an incredibly erotic moment that came out of nowhere. Her gaze held by his, she curled her tongue around his finger and gently suckled.

Alex's eyes blazed with desire and he pushed aside his papers and pulled her onto his lap. "You like to tempt me, don't you?" he asked her. "I think you want to see how far you can push me."

"You started it," she said, her hands resting on his strong chest and loving the sensation of his muscles. He slid his fingers beneath the bottom edge of her blouse and stroked her bare skin.

"Does that mean you want me to stop?" he asked.

Her heart hammering in her chest, she slipped her hands up to his shoulders. "I didn't say that."

"I can't help wondering what you're like when you really cut loose," he said, lowering his mouth to her jaw and kissing.

Craving more, she lifted her head to give him access to her throat. He immediately read her invitation and responded. She sighed at the delicious sensation of his mouth on her bare skin.

"You will be in my bed," he told her. "It's inevitable."

She felt herself sinking under his spell. She wanted him, but she would be a fool to give him her heart.

Five hours later, Alex had delivered one speech and he would give another one during dinner. After that he could attend to his female guest who had followed his advice to make use of all the resort facilities.

As he changed his shirt and tie for dinner, he returned a call to Todd, his chauffeur/bodyguard.

"What's up?" Alex asked, glancing out the window to the wide beach and blue ocean.

"So far, she went snorkeling, spent a little time in a kayak, drove a Jet Ski. Now she wants to go Para-Sailing."

"What the—" Alex stared out the window this time, looking for Mallory and Todd. "You told her she couldn't do it, right?"

"I did. She wasn't very happy about it. Said you and I were as bad as her father," he said.

"Where the hell are you?"

"At the Rigger Resort," Todd said. "It's about four hotels west of the Megalos complex. I bought her a drink in the Tiki bar to distract her, but I don't think it's going to work."

"Okay, I'll be there in a few minutes," Alex said.

"But I'm your driver," he said.

"I'll be there in five," Alex insisted as he left the suite.

Alex easily commandeered a hotel shuttle and walked into the Tiki bar. He spotted Mallory immediately. Dressed in a scant black bikini that emphasized her curves she wore a joyous smile on her face and her long, dark hair was slick against her back. She was riveting. Blinking, he noticed other men were equally riveted. The land sharks were moving in while Todd tried to push them back.

Alex parted the crowd and stood in front of Mallory. As soon as she recognized him, she jumped from her stool and stopped just sort of throwing her arms around him. "Oops. I don't want to get you wet."

"Hey, baby, you can get me wet anytime," a male voice called from a few feet away.

Alex shot the man a quelling glance that sent a hush over the crowd. Then he turned back to Mallory. "You've been busy."

Her eyes sparkled. "I've had so much fun. Loved the Jet Ski. I definitely want to do that again. And snorkel. And snuba. You said you would take me to snuba. I'm almost ready for deep-sea diving." Her brow furrowed and she leaned closer to him. "The only thing is that Todd here is being a spoilsport. I was all set to Para-Sail, but he nixed it. Now it's too late."

He pulled her to the side. "You don't need to do everything in one day," he pointed out. "We can snuba and Para-Sail tomorrow, together."

She searched his face. "I didn't know if you would be busy tomorrow, too."

He shook his head. "Not a chance. And I want to make sure we get the best Para-Sail group. I won't have you risking your gorgeous body with some fly-by-night company."

Her lips curved in a slow smile. "So *you* were the one who nixed the Para-Sail excursion."

"Damn right," he said offering no excuses. "You can wait one more day and do it tandem with me. That way, you'll always associate the experience with me."

"That sounds a little possessive," she said.

"Does that upset you?" he asked.

A moment of silence passed between them where he felt a fist of longing build in his gut, surprising him with its force. He saw the same dark longing reflected in her eyes.

"No," she finally said.

"Good," he said. "Now put on a T-shirt or a robe or something. You're sending the poor locals into a frenzy."

She laughed with delight. "Omigoodness, if I believed half of what you say, then I would be convinced I'm the most desirable woman in the world."

"By the end of this trip, you will be," he told her and slid his arm around her for the benefit of everyone who was watching. He wanted them to know she was with him. "Any chance you could do something boring like shopping or getting one of those spa treatments women like so much."

Biting her lip, she looked into his eyes and he felt an unexpected jolt. "Am I making you nervous? Am I making the man who drives race cars for fun nervous?" she asked in disbelief.

"I wouldn't use the word nervous," he said.

"Then what word would you use?"

"Let's just say you're keeping me on my toes," he said and gave in to the urge to brush his lips over hers. "I'll see you after the dinner meeting and my speech.

Order anything you want from room service then put on a beautiful dress and get ready for a walk on the beach."

"What if I didn't bring a beautiful dress with me?"

"Then go shopping," he said. "I need to leave. Todd will take you anywhere you want to go within reason," he added when he remembered the Para-Sailing.

Within minutes, Mallory finished her fruity beverage and went back to the hotel. She'd packed some cute dresses, but nothing she would consider beautiful, so the pressure was on to find something. She showered and left the resort, and Todd took her to several recommended shops. Nothing grabbed her, so she returned to the resort and looked through the shops there.

Surprisingly enough, she found a hot-pink silk halter-neck dress with sparkles at the bodice and a few scattered throughout. The shopping goddess was on her side. The shop had the dress in her size.

She took it upstairs and immediately changed into it. She curled her hair and added a touch of exotic eye makeup and lip gloss. Hungry, but too excited to eat, she turned on the television and sat on the bed.

Thirty minutes turned into an hour. An hour turned into two. Restless and wondering what had held up Alex, she turned off the television and walked onto the balcony. She closed her eyes as the sea breeze brushed over her. The sound of the surf soothed her.

If her mind weren't whirling a mile a minute, the sound would lull her to sleep.

She couldn't help wondering what she was doing here in Alex's suite. Yes, the suite featured five bedrooms, four bathrooms, full kitchen, formal dining room and a large living area that offered every convenience imaginable, but she was starting to think she'd lost her mind by joining him.

Inhaling a deep breath in search of calm, she caught a hint of his cologne. She opened her eyes and found him standing in front of her.

"You looked so beautiful," he said, lifting his hand to touch a strand of her hair. "So peaceful."

"The sound of the ocean helps," she said, looking at him, noticing that his tie was askew and his shirt pulled loose. "Everything okay?"

"It could be better. I finished my speech and was leaving the ballroom when my ex came out of nowhere."

Mallory stared at him in shock. "Your ex?" she echoed. "Which ex?"

He shot her a dark look. "Chloe Renfro."

"Oh," Mallory said, recalling a willowy blonde. She felt a stab of jealousy, but refused to give in to it. "How did that happen? Does she live here? Have a place here?"

"No to both. She must have found out about my appearance from someone." He pulled his tie the rest of the way loose. "I knew she was going to have a difficult time with the breakup, but I never predicted this."

"You can't totally blame her for having a hard time getting over you. I mean, if a woman grew accustomed to receiving your undivided attention, it could be pretty difficult when your attention goes elsewhere."

"I never gave her my undivided attention," Alex said. "I made it perfectly clear from the beginning that there would be no strings for either of us. Our relationship was not headed for anything permanent."

Ouch. "I wonder how she knew to find you here." An uneasy thought occurred to her. "Unless you brought her here another time." The image tainted the trip for her so swiftly that she tried to push it aside. "But that's none of my business."

He put his hand on her arm. "Mallory, I haven't brought any other woman here but you."

She exhaled, feeling a trickle of relief. "What did you do about her?"

"I arranged for her to get on a flight back to the States," he said with a grim expression on his face.

It dawned on Mallory that this was the flip side of the positive attention and adoration Alex received. "Do you have to deal with this kind of thing often?"

He shook his head. "Despite your impression, I've grown very selective with my dating partners. Just because I'm photographed with a woman doesn't mean I'm intimate with her." He shook his head and shrugged off his jacket. "Enough. I won't allow this to spoil the rest of our evening."

She watched him pull off his socks and step into a pair of canvas shoes. He extended his hand to her. "Ready for that walk on the beach?"

She smiled slowly and accepted his hand. "Sure, let's go."

They took the elevator down to the lobby. At the luxe lounge, Alex bought her a fruity drink and a beer for himself and excused himself from employees who approached him.

Feeling their curious gazes, Mallory was relieved when they stepped outside. "So much better," she said when her feet encountered cool sand.

Alex kicked off his shoes and left them at the foot of the steps leading to the resort. "Beautiful woman, beautiful night. What could be better? Come here," he said and pulled her into his arms. He pressed his mouth against her and tasted her with his lips and tongue, making her feel delicious.

"Mmm," he said in approval. "More."

Her heart tripped over itself. She pulled back and laughed breathlessly. "After our walk."

"I'm surprised you have the energy after all you did today," he muttered as they walked toward the shore.

"I had some downtime while I waited for you."

"Second thoughts about coming," he said.

"How did you know?"

"I could tell," he said.

Surprised, she frowned at him. "How is it that you read me so easily?"

He shrugged. "It's mostly because I want to," he said. "I watch your face and body for signs. I do the same kind of thing when I'm negotiating. You're just a lot more fun to watch," he said, sliding his hand to the top of her opposite hip.

Mallory couldn't deny how wonderful she felt at this moment. With the ocean beside her, the sand at her feet and Alex's arms around her, she couldn't imagine anywhere she would rather be.

"I had a wonderful time today. Thank you for bringing me," she said, looking up at him.

"You were supposed to say you missed me desperately," he said in a mocking tone.

"Just as you missed me," she said innocently.

"Trust me, you had more fun than I did." He shook his head. "Poor Todd couldn't keep the men away from you. It's a wonder I didn't have to fight off a few of them to get to you."

She laughed. "Would you have really done that?"

"You like that idea, do you?" he asked, squeezing her against him.

Heaven help her, she did, at least in theory. How crazy was it that she was preaching liberation on one hand yet loving it when Alex went primitive on her? She couldn't admit it aloud, though. She heard the strains of beach music coming from a resort up ahead. The romantic sound tugged at her.

Alex came to a stop and swung her against him. "Dance?"

Her heart skipped and stuttered. "Yes," she said and began to follow his lead. "You're a good dancer," she said. "When did you learn?"

"When I was young. It was a requirement in my family. My mother was determined that her sons would be civilized and have good manners. I hated every minute of it until I started noticing the opposite sex. Then I figured out that dancing is a damn good way to get close to a woman you want to get to know better. But there's an even better way," he said, sliding his hand down to the back of her waist and drawing her intimately against him.

He felt so good, so strong, and Mallory was so tired of resisting him. She'd always told herself he was the perfect man for a fling. He brought out a wildness in her and made her feel as if it were okay.

She felt something inside her rip so strongly she could almost hear it. Restraint, resistance, she was impatient with living under her code of caution.

"If you and I get closer," she began, her heart beating like a drum in her chest.

"We will," he said, dipping his mouth over hers and away, revving up her temptation.

"I want to keep it confidential," she said. "Secret."

He paused a half-beat. "You want me to be your secret lover?"

"I don't want my parents hurt by any sort of publicity," she said. "And that's the last sensible thing I want to say."

"Are you ready to go wild?" he asked and lifted the inside of her wrist to his mouth. "You taste so good. I can't wait to taste every inch of you."

"Then don't," she whispered. "Don't wait."

Six

But he did wait, and the waiting just made the tension inside her stronger. Mallory had expected Alex to whisk her back to the hotel and immediately devour her. Instead he continued to dance with her on the beach, taking her mouth in long, drugging kisses that made her knees turn to liquid.

The darkness surrounded them like a cocoon of privacy. No one else was anywhere within sight. She wasn't aware of anyone else. She was solely focused on Alex.

He slid one of his hands all the way up her side to the outer edge of her breast and caressed her from the outside of her dress. She felt her nipple harden from the indirect touch. She craved feeling his skin on hers.

An edginess built inside her. "Shouldn't we go back to the suite?" she asked, biting her lip against a moan as he slid one of his fingers just inside her dress to her bare breast.

"We will," he said. "Trust me. I want to take my time with you. Once we get back to the room and I take off your clothes, it will be hard for me to slow down.

"Your skin feels so soft, so edible," he murmured, dipping his mouth to her throat again.

Her pulse spiked.

"I love the way your body responds to me," he whispered. "When I touch you, you take a little breath and hold it. Is that because you want more? Or less?"

She bit her lip at the sharp wanting he caused inside her. "More," she whispered and boldly pulled at the buttons at the top of his shirt. She splayed one of her hands across his smoothly muscled chest. "I want to feel you, too."

He sucked in a sharp breath as if she'd surprised him. Tipping her head backward, he slipped one of his hands through her hair and took her mouth again. This time his kiss was more aggressive, more purposeful. He slid his thigh between hers, and Mallory's breath just stopped.

Feeling his arousal pressed against her, she reacted purely on instinct, undulating against him.

Alex swore under his breath. "Time to go. But if

this were a private beach," he said, and a shocking visual raced through her mind of Alex, naked and taking her right there. The power of it shook her.

She stumbled as he led her toward the resort. He caught her against him. "Okay?"

Mallory had never been this aroused in her life. Never wanted so much to take and be taken by a man. "Yes. No." She swallowed over the emotion building in her throat, a combination of apprehension and anticipation. "I—just—really—want you."

He met her gaze and she saw the same hunger mirrored in his eyes that she felt in every pore of her body. He took her mouth in a quick, but thorough kiss. "You're going to get me," he promised in a gritty, sexy voice and urged her toward the resort.

As soon as they stepped inside, he took a right down a different hallway. "Let's take the back elevators. I'm not in the mood for small talk with one of my employees."

As if even the elevator knew not to impede Alex, it immediately appeared and Alex pulled her inside. As soon as the doors closed, he took her mouth again, urgency emanating from him.

Dizzy from his touch and the heat he generated inside her, Mallory clung to him as the elevator door swept open. A man stepped inside, giving her a second and third look before he got off the elevator three floors later.

Self-consciousness trickled through her and she closed her eyes.

"Did you know him?" he asked.

She shook her head and met his gaze. "Does it show on my face? How I feel?" she asked. "That I'm so turned on I can't—"

He covered her lips with his finger. "You're not alone," he told her, and the elevator finally arrived at their floor.

Alex led her to the suite and before he'd closed the door, he was pulling her into his arms. "There's something about you," he said in a rough voice. "It must be in your skin, in your voice, deeper. I just know I have to have you. All of you."

Tugging her farther into the suite, he pulled her down on the sofa with him and took her mouth in a consuming kiss that made every cell inside her buzz with need and pleasure.

Skimming one of his hands up her side, he found the side zipper of her dress and pulled it down. With his other hand, he untied the knot of silk at the back of her neck. He pulled the soft, sensual material down, baring her breasts.

She felt a whisper of coolness from the sudden exposure, but the heat of his gaze warmed her. He lifted his hands to her breasts, taunting her already sensitized nipples and she looked away, swallowing a moan.

"Oh, no," he said, putting his hand under her chin

and drawing her gaze back to his. "No hiding," he said. "No holding back. I want to see every look, feel every response, hear every sound you make."

Shoving aside her doubts and insecurities, she reached for his shirt and unfastened the rest of the buttons. "Fair is fair," she said, her heart racing like the wind. Urged on by his gaze and her need to be close to him, she pushed his shirt down and pressed her swollen breasts against his chest.

Her moan mingled with his. She felt the muscles of his biceps tense beneath her hand. He swore and took her mouth in a searing kiss.

In the middle of that endless kiss, he pushed her dress aside and slid his hand between her thighs. With unerring instinct, he found her most sensitive, most secret place.

His groan vibrated throughout her. "You're so hot, so wet," he said, his low voice full of approval and need. "I want you everywhere at once," he said and pushed her against an oversize pillow. He skimmed his mouth down her throat to her chest and then he slid his tongue over one of her nipples. A second later, he drew the aching tip into his mouth and she felt a corresponding twist of sensation low in her belly.

As he stroked her between her thighs at the same time he consumed her breasts, Mallory felt her head began to spin. Tension, need and a wanting so vast it shook her to the core. She felt herself climbing to a precipice. He'd taken her there before in the car. But this time, she didn't want to go without him.

"Alex," she managed to say, pulling herself upward. "I want—" She broke off and swallowed. "I need you to—" Meeting his gaze, she lowered her hands to his slacks and tugged his belt loose. "Inside me," she said in a voice that sounded husky to her own ears.

His eyes nearly black with arousal, he stood, stripping off his slacks and underwear. Transfixed by the sight of him, she stared at his muscular body from his strong, wide shoulders over his well-built chest, flat abdomen and his large masculinity jutting from his pelvis.

His size made her wonder if she was ready for him.

Still watching her, he pulled a packet from his pocket and put on the protection. Then he slowly covered her body with his. She felt his erection between her thighs and everything except being with him fled her mind.

He rubbed against her intimately and she arched to take him inside. Sliding his hand between their bodies, he played with her again. Each stroke made her more desperate for him. "Please," she whispered, but she didn't want to beg.

"Hold on," he told her and pushed her thighs apart and thrust inside her.

His invasion stole her breath. "Alex," she breathed and they began to move in an age-old rhythm of possession and surrender. She could feel how much he wanted her, how much he craved her. It was as if he wanted to capture her spirit and soul to light the darkness in his, and Mallory knew nothing would ever be the same for her again.

The next morning, Alex awakened early as he always did. Propping his head on his elbow, he looked down at Mallory, stretched out on her side with the sheet wrapped around her waist. Her brown hair fell in shiny, sensual waves over the top her chest and shoulders. The sight of her voluptuous bare breasts taunted him. During their multiple rounds of lovemaking last night, he'd noticed how her nipples hardened just by him looking at them. Everything about Mallory's body responded to him.

Her responsiveness seemed to go deeper than her skin, although he sensed she wanted to hold some part of herself back. The more Alex was around Mallory, the more he wanted all of her.

He liked the way she pushed back at him. She didn't need his money, and wasn't at all interested in the notoriety her relationship with him could bring her. Her desire to keep their affair secret amused him at the same time that it pinched his pride. If he decided he wanted more from her, though, he would change her mind. Some might consider him arrogant, but for Alex it was just the truth. It was very rare that he didn't get what he wanted. He wanted Mallory and he intended to enjoy every minute of their secret lover weekend. He would make sure she enjoyed every minute, too, but he would give her a little break, noting the violet shadows under her curly eyelashes. He knew he'd worn her out last night.

Sliding out of bed, he went into the den and called room service for breakfast. The newspaper would be delivered in mere minutes, so he grabbed a quick shower and pulled on a pair of shorts. As expected, breakfast, along with three newspapers, arrived shortly. He directed the staff to set the breakfast on the large wraparound balcony.

If Mallory didn't awaken soon, then he would read the papers and reorder for her when she rose. He'd barely finished his first article from the *Wall Street Journal* when she appeared, wrapped in a fluffy robe with sexy, sleepy eyes, as she peeked from the bedroom sliding doors.

"Good morning," he said. "You're just in time for breakfast."

"There's some for me?" she asked, moving toward the table. "The smell of something heavenly woke me up."

"Coffee?"

"Bacon," she corrected, sitting down in the chair opposite him. "The most useless food on the planet."

"But too good to resist," he said, lifting a slice and offering it to her.

She took it and devoured it, closing her eyes as she

ate it as if it were a sensual experience. He wondered how a woman could make eating bacon so arousing, but damn if she didn't.

"I'm starving. I didn't eat dinner last night—"

He frowned. "Why not? I told you to order anything you wanted from room service."

She met his gaze. "I was a little nervous," she confessed.

Something inside him tugged and twisted at her admission. "The prospect of Para-Sailing didn't bother you, but I did?"

"Oh, being with you is much more—" She broke off. "Much more everything than Para-Sailing. They told me Para-Sailing is over in five minutes."

"I hope I lasted longer than that."

She giggled, covering her eyes. "Oh, wow."

Her response was addictive. He tugged her hand and pulled. "Come here. Have some breakfast."

She sat on his lap with no protest. Surveying the plates he'd ordered, she made a little moan of approval. "I want a bite or two of everything," she said and took a bite of the omelet. "Delicious. Have you ever noticed how everything tastes like gourmet food when you're starving?"

He nodded. "Even a stale sandwich from the deli because you don't have time to get anything else."

"Exactly. But since you're a big whoopty-doo VP, I would think your employees would always make sure you get perfectly fresh food."

"Contrary to rumor, I don't force my employees to work the same hours I do. I sometimes work late nights and have been known to grab a package of crackers from the vending machine."

She made a tsking sound of false sympathy. "Poor big whoopty-doo VP."

"You're heartless."

"That's me, heartless Mallory." She smiled then glanced at the food again. "Oh, don't tell me that's a chocolate croissant."

"It is," he said, enjoying every minute of having this woman on his lap.

She sighed. "I may have to eat more than two bites of that."

He snatched the croissant from the plate. "You may have to kiss me to get it."

She met his gaze with soft, but searching eyes. "I would have thought you'd gotten so many kisses last night that you wouldn't want anymore."

"In that case, you would have been very wrong," he said and took her mouth with his.

Mallory was in beach and man heaven. She'd known Alex's attention could be intoxicating, but she'd really had no idea how intoxicating. Doing snuba, a combination of snorkeling and scuba diving, with Alex, Mallory felt as if she were discovering a whole new wonderland. The vibrant colors of the reefs and fishes were spectacular and joining hands with Alex while twenty-five feet underwater upped the thrill exponentially.

As promised, they Para-Sailed tandem. Surprisingly when they hovered above an inlet, it felt more peaceful than frightening. Alex took her mouth in a kiss that sent her heart soaring into the stratosphere. Every once in a while, she wondered how she could possibly return to her claustrophobic existence after experiencing so much freedom.

After their busy morning and early afternoon, they enjoyed a gourmet picnic lunch on a private beach. Mallory guzzled an ice-cold bottle of water.

"You're turning pink," Alex said, pressing his finger against her arm. "Get under the umbrella. Do you need more sunscreen?"

She moved to the double chaise lounge underneath the umbrella. "I've applied it a gajillion times today."

He joined her on the lounge, his skin gleaming bronze from their time in the sun. "Not exaggerating, are you?"

"No," she said, admiring and resenting his tanned skin at the same time. "It isn't fair that you don't burn."

"My ancestry. I guess it's one thing I can thank my father for," he said with a dry laugh and pulled out a bottle of sunscreen. He poured some cream into his palm then rubbed it onto her shoulders.

"Do you miss him?" she asked after a long moment.

"Who?"

"Your father. I can't imagine not being able to talk to my father whenever I want." The idea actually hurt her heart.

"I've gotten used to it," he said with a shrug, rubbing the sunscreen onto her belly.

"I think that's a lie," she said.

He met her gaze and lifted a brow. "And who made you the expert on me?"

Her heart twisted like a vise and it hit her that she wished she could be an expert on Alex. She wished she could know him in every possible way. "Am I right?" she asked.

He laced his fingers through hers. "You keep surprising me," he said. "One minute you're wild, the next you're deep and thoughtful."

"You didn't answer my question," she said, willing him to meet her gaze. A long silence followed, and she resisted the urge to fill it.

"I miss what could have been. Sometimes the death of dream is worse than a real death." He met her gaze and the naked emotion in his green eyes took her breath and stole a piece of her heart. "Satisfied?"

She wondered if she would ever be satisfied. If she could ever know enough of him and not want more. She rose and pressed her lips to his. It seemed the right thing to do.

When she pulled back, he trailed his finger between her breasts. "You know this is a private beach. There's no one else but you and me here." He slid his finger around the edges of the cups of her bathing suit. "You could take this off…."

Her pulse raced at the invitation in his voice. It was more an invite than a dare. "I've never gone topless on a beach before."

"Have you wanted to?" he asked.

"Not before," she said, but she liked the idea of taunting and tempting him. With his experience, he always seemed to have the upper hand.

"And now?" he asked, sliding his finger beneath the edge of the top of her bathing suit, just a fingertip away from her nipple. She felt her nipple grow hard and fought against the urge to arch against him.

"I could get burned even worse since that skin has never seen the sun," she said, her voice husky to her own ears.

"I would be happy to put sunscreen on you," he said. "Every inch."

Mallory closed her eyes, wondering if she wanted to be this wild, wondering if she could. Still keeping her eyes closed, she lifted her hand and untied the strings at the back of her neck. She pushed the cups down and reached behind to unfasten the other strings at her back, then pulled the top of her bathing suit from her body.

She finally opened her eyes.

Alex gazed at her possessively, his nostrils flaring slightly in sudden arousal. She was surprised, but gratified by the speed of his response.

He met her gaze. "You have no idea how you affect me."

An illicit thrill raced through her. "Maybe you should show me."

He slid his hands over her breasts. "My pleasure," he said.

He taunted her with his hands, then replaced his hands with his mouth. He nibbled at the hard, sensitive tips of her breasts, making her want more and more. He took her mouth in a French kiss and rolled on top of her, pushing her thighs apart.

In the afternoon sun, shielded only by the umbrella, he took her with a glorious, consuming intensity. She reveled in the sound of the waves as he thrust inside her. The scents of salt, sand, coconut oil and musk filled her head. She wanted him to take her. She wanted him to fill her completely and in his taking, she wanted him to feel completely full. It was the most carnal yet spiritual experience in her life, and she wondered how she would possibly survive being separated from him.

The next day, they had to return to Las Vegas. Both she and Alex were quiet. He studied designs and reports. Mallory looked through the same magazine for the fifth time, not seeing a single image, not reading a single word. The weekend had been the most glorious of her life, but she was searching for a way to pull herself together. She'd been stretched sexually and emotionally. How was she supposed to go back to her parents' home and be the Mallory she'd been before? How could she?

Thirty minutes before they were scheduled to land, she sensed Alex looking at her. "I want you to move in with me," he said.

Her heart leaped in her chest. She couldn't. Not for her peace of mind, not for her parents' peace of mind. "I can't do that. Right now," she added.

"Why not?" he asked.

"My parents are old-fashioned. They would be horrified and hurt. Besides, you and I need to be sensible. I told you before I didn't want a public affair." She shook her head. "I need to get my own place. If you still want to see me—" She broke off, floundering.

"Want," Alex echoed, taking her hand in his. "You've given new meaning to the word. You can't believe social conventions are bigger than what is going on between you and me."

Her heart twisted and she met his gaze. "This isn't about conventions. I've got to recover from being with you. I don't want to be one of those women who can't get over you. I'm starting to feel more and more sympathy for them," she said.

"This is different," he said, swearing. "It's wrong for you to not be with me."

Every cell in her urged her to say *yes*. Her connection with Alex had been so powerful it had seemed almost otherworldly. Her brain stepped in like a sharp elbow-jab. Alex was a player. This could be over in a second and she would be picking up the pieces of her heart. By herself. "It's too fast," she said, meeting his green gaze, rocked by the emotion she saw there. "I need more time."

Seven

"You're glowing," Lilli De Luca said, two days later, as she joined Mallory for lunch at an outdoor café shielded by umbrellas. "If it's a new spa treatment, please tell me what it is. My sweet little David is wearing me out with his teething."

Mallory smiled, thinking of Alex. "I took a trip to the beach over the weekend. Maybe you should try to do the same soon."

The waiter refilled their glasses of mint iced tea. Mallory remembered how good the iced bottle of water had felt on her throat the afternoon she and Alex had spent on the beach.

Lilli made a face. "Max and I were supposed to

go to the beach this past weekend, but David got sick and I just couldn't leave him."

"I know," Mallory said then tried to take back the words. "I mean, I heard something about David being sick."

Lilli lifted her eyebrows in surprise. "Really? From who?"

Mallory shifted in her wrought-iron chair. "Um, I think Alex Megalos may have mentioned it."

Lilli's eyes widened farther. "Alex? When did you see him?"

"Oh, he's everywhere," Mallory said, waving her hand. "You know, Mr. Social, in the spotlight."

"Hmm," Lilli said, studying Mallory. "I remember how you used to have a crush on him."

"Most single women do," Mallory said, her stomach tightening. "Probably some married women, too. He's charming, good-looking and sexy," she tried to say in a matter-of-fact voice.

Lilli took a bite of her sandwich and swallowed it. "Is there something you're not telling me that you want to tell me?"

Mallory's throat tightened. "I'm not sure. Off the record, just how much of a hound dog would you say Alex Megalos is?"

Lilli furrowed her eyebrows. "Aside from my husband, he is one of the most charming men I've ever met. He actually hit on me when I was pregnant. Very flattering."

"But you were gorgeous when you were pregnant," Mallory said, pushing aside a stupid twinge of jealousy. "And gorgeous when not pregnant, too."

Lilli smiled. "You're such a good friend." She paused. "Here's the thing. Alex is a paradox. He's a terrible flirt. But do you know what he gave David as a gift? A year of tuition at any college and a Tonka truck he can ride. And get this, Alex made me swear that I would support David if he decided to be a sous-chef instead of a tycoon for Megalos-De Luca. How can you not love him for that?"

Mallory thought of Alex's unrelationship with his own father and tears filled her eyes. "How can you?" she echoed.

Lilli studied Mallory for a long moment. "You're still not telling me something."

Mallory blinked her eyes against the tears. "I've kinda gotten involved with Alex," she confided.

Lilli's eyes widened. "How involved?"

Mallory bit her lip. "Pretty involved. Too involved. I'm scared."

"If he hurts you, I'll kill him. I'll make Max kill him, too."

Mallory shook her head. "No murder needed. He asked me to move in with him."

Lilli stared at her, speechless. It took her a full moment to find her voice. "Move in? As in his house?"

"Or condo," Mallory said. "I told him no. My parents would freak. I don't want to make Dad's blood pressure spike through the roof. And my mother is finally coming out of her bedroom since I spent the weekend with Alex. At the beach."

Lilli shook her head. "One surprise after the other. I always thought there was more to Alex than met the eye. He's so good-looking and charming you're tempted not to look any further."

"And once you do, you're hooked," Mallory said.

"Oh," Lilli said and gave a sympathetic smile. "I don't know what to say."

"Just say you'll be my friend whatever happens," Mallory said, unable to avoid an impending sense of doom about her relationship with Alex. She couldn't imagine being able to hold his attention for long.

Lilli covered Mallory's hand. "Always," she said. "I'm always your friend, just as you've been mine since the first time we met. Just remember, both Max and I will kill Alex if he hurts you."

Twenty-four hours later, Alex called her. "You and I need to meet. There's been a development. Come to my office immediately."

Entrenched in research for her term paper, Mallory frowned into her cell phone. "Development?" she echoed. "That's a little vague. I'm in the middle of this paper. Can't you give me more information?"

"Mallory," he said and she could hear the stretched

patience in his voice. "I won't discuss this on the phone. I'll send my driver to—"

She sighed. "No, no. I can drive myself. Give me an hour."

"Thirty minutes," he countered and hung up.

Mallory stared at her cell phone and felt a frisson of fear. Alex had never sounded like this before. There was an eerie calm to his voice. A chill passed over her and she took a deep breath. Saving her file, she shut down her computer, changed her clothes, applied lipstick and mascara and headed for Megalos-De Luca Enterprises.

A valet attendant greeted her and took her car. Mallory walked inside the skyscraper, and security took her name and immediately allowed her to pass. Alex had clearly prepared everyone for her arrival.

With each passing second, she felt her tension increase. What could possibly be so important that he couldn't discuss it with her on the phone? As she took the elevator to the top floor, she tried to conjure the worst scenario. Her heart sank. If he wanted to banish her from his life, this was an odd way to do it.

The steel elevator doors opened and she stepped outside. She spoke with a receptionist who pointed her toward a corner office. She approached a woman outside the corner office. "I'm looking for Alex Megalos's office."

The young woman nodded. "And you are?"

"Oh, I'm sorry. I should have introduced myself. Mallory James."

The woman smiled. "Miss James. It's nice to meet you. I'm Alex's assistant, Emma. Please go on in. He's waiting for you."

"Thank you," Mallory said and took a deep breath as she opened the door to Alex's office.

Alex looked up, then immediately stood. "Come in. Please close the door behind you."

Mallory did as he asked. "I can't tell if I feel like I've got an appointment with the CIA or the principal from my elementary school."

He didn't smile at her remark. That made her more nervous. "Have a seat," he said.

She gingerly sat in the chair across from his desk. "I'm already nervous and you're not making it better."

"Unfortunately it's going to get worse before it gets better," he said.

Her heart sank further. "I can't stand it, Alex. Just tell me."

"You remember that day we spent on the beach on the island," he said.

She nodded. "We ate and talked and…"

"Made love," he said for her.

She nodded again. "Yes."

"We were supposed to be alone. It was supposed to be private."

She frowned in confusion. "There was no one around."

His eyes turned to chips of green ice. "No one we could see. Someone using a long-range lens took photos."

Shock coursed through. She lifted her hand to her mouth. "Oh, my God. You can't mean…"

"The photographs are grainy, but they've shown up on the Internet."

Alarm turned her blood to ice. "The Internet?" she echoed, trying to comprehend what he was saying. "Our pictures are on the Internet. *We* are on the Internet?"

His face grim, he nodded. "Yes. We're putting together a number of action plans to counter the negative impact of—"

"*We?*" she said weakly. "Who is *we?* How many people know about this?"

"So far, just the company's top PR official, your father and me," Alex said. "I'll handle this," he said. "I'll protect you."

"How can you?" she asked, numb and humiliated at the same time. "And my father." She shook her head.

"I will," he promised and his phone buzzed.

He picked up the receiver. "Yes, Emma." His face turned more grim. "Let him in."

Seconds later, Edwin James, Mallory's father, walked through Alex's door with murder in his eyes. "You've destroyed my daughter's reputation," he said to Alex. "What kind of man are you to take advantage of a young lady like Mallory?"

"Daddy," Mallory exclaimed.

"I'm going to take care of this," Alex said in that eerily calm tone.

"There's only one way you can do that," her father said.

"I know."

"The two of you have to get married."

Mallory gasped. "That's ridiculous."

Alex met her gaze. "No. It's not."

She shook her head, feeling as if the whole situation had turned completely surreal. "This is the twenty-first century. It's true my reputation may suffer a little," she said.

"A little," her father said.

Mallory's stomach dipped. "This will just be the scandal of the moment. It will pass. There's no reason to make a permanent decision because of it."

"You want people thinking you're some kind of—" Her father broke off as if he couldn't say the words. "Loose woman. You want people thinking you're a—" He shook his head again as if he couldn't stand the very notion of it. "I won't have it. You were a sweet and innocent woman until you hooked up with Megalos here. He's ruined you."

"He hasn't ruined me," she protested.

"There's only one solution to this problem," her father interjected. "You and Megalos need to get married and soon. Now don't argue, Mallory," he said, shaking his finger at her. "Even Alex agrees with me. I just hope I can keep this from your mother. The disappointment would devastate her."

Guilt sliced through Mallory. In this, her father was right. Her mother was fragile. Although Mallory chafed against the constraints her parents had placed on her, she loved them both deeply and hated that she was causing them pain. She bit her lip. "This is such a huge move to make just for the sake of covering a scandal. Neither Alex nor I were anywhere near ready to make that kind of commitment."

Alex moved from behind his desk, his green gaze wrapping around hers and holding tight. "I can't agree with you. You know I'd already told you I wanted you to move in with me."

Her father swore under his breath.

Mallory's stomach knotted. "Did you have to say that in front of him?" she whispered even though she knew her father could hear her.

"This discussion is a waste of time," her father said, pounding his fist on the desk. "The solution is obvious to everyone." He pursed his lips at Mallory. "It should be obvious to you."

Confused and overwhelmed, she looked at her father. "Daddy, could I please have a moment alone with Alex?"

He clenched his jaw. "Seems to me you've had a few too many moments alone with him."

"Daddy," she said in a chastising voice.

"Please, Mr. James," Alex said, surprising Mallory with his support.

"Okay," her father said. "I'll be outside."

"You don't need to go all the way downstairs," Mallory said.

"I need a cigar," he said.

"You're not supposed to be smoking," she called after him as he stormed out of Alex's office. Her heart swirling with a dozen different emotions, she turned to Alex. "This is crazy."

"Lots of things that happen in this world are crazy. Who would have thought the photographers would have followed us onto that beach?"

"They couldn't have been interested in *me*."

He raised his eyebrows. "Wealthy heiress takes off her shirt for tycoon."

She cringed. "Was that the headline?"

"No, but it could have been." He shook his head. "What I'm saying is these are the cards we've been dealt. We need to do the best we can with this hand." His gaze darkened and he laced his fingers through hers. "In my mind, it could be a winning hand."

Her heart stuttered and she swallowed over a lump in her throat. "How can you feel that way? My father is practically forcing you to marry me."

"No, he's not. I told you before that I'm not a man to be forced into anything by anyone. Especially marriage." He lifted one of his hands to her jaw. "We have something between us. Yeah, the sexual chemistry is outrageous. But there's something else. I like how I feel when I'm with you. I like who I am when I'm with you."

"You're serious," she said, searching his gaze. "But don't you feel trapped? That's what I couldn't bear. The idea of trapping you."

"Before you walked in that door today, I knew we needed to get married."

"But it's so archaic," she said, fear and hope warring inside her.

"It's not archaic," he said. "It's right. Tell me that deep down there isn't something inside you that feels good about this idea. You feel good about being with me all the time, about having me as your husband. Down the line, having babies together," he said, putting his hand on her belly.

Mallory's breath froze somewhere between her lungs and her throat. "I always thought you were trying to avoid marriage. Why would you be willing to make a commitment now?"

"I told you. Because it's the right thing to do. You know it, too."

Mallory closed her eyes. Her head was spinning. Alex wasn't professing undying love. In fact, he hadn't mentioned love at all. She felt a twist of longing inside her. This wasn't what she'd pictured for her marriage.

She forced her eyes open. "What if this is a disaster?"

He gave a rough chuckle and pulled her into his arms. "Mallory, in our own way, you and I are over-achievers. There's no way this will be a disaster."

She buried her head in his shoulder. "I just wish things could be different."

"They will be," he said. "After we're married."

Just like that, the decision was made and wedding plans were put into motion. Exhibiting more enthusiasm than she had in years, her mother plunged into making the arrangements. Her father insisted the wedding take place in ten days.

Alex presented her with a ring that felt strange on her finger. Mallory enlisted Lilli's assistance to help her find a dress.

Standing in front of a three-way mirror after she'd tried on six dresses, Mallory shook her head. "I look like I'm wearing meringue. None of these seem right," she said.

Lilli chuckled, adjusting the gown slightly. "Are you sure it's the dresses?" she asked gently. "Or is it the man?"

"I can't think about that," Mallory said, returning to the dressing room. She hadn't told Lilli about the scandalous photographs of her and Alex. It was too humiliating. "Just trust me, when I tell you that Alex and I have our reasons for getting married."

"But so quickly," Lilli said, following her. "Why can't you take your time?"

"There's a good reason," she said, pushing the gown down and stepping out of it.

Lilli shook it out and returned the garment to the hanger. Then she turned to Mallory. "Are you pregnant?" she asked in a quiet voice.

"No," Mallory instantly replied. "Pregnancy would be easier than—" She broke off and shook her head.

Lilli gave her a blank stare. "I'm dying of curiosity, but if you don't want to tell me, I won't force it."

Mallory sighed and closed her eyes. "It's just so embarrassing. When Alex and I took our trip together, we visited a private beach and…" She opened her eyes and waved her hand.

Lilli's eyes widened. "Oh." She paused. "But I still don't see why you would need to rush into marriage."

"Because someone took pictures of us," Mallory whispered, misery and shame rushing through her again.

"Oh, no," Lilli said, putting her arm around Mallory's shoulder in sympathy.

"They've shown up on the Internet on an obscure site, but it's just a matter of time before someone figures out who the couple in the photos are. My father wants Alex and I married before the story really comes out so it will seem like old news."

Lilli nodded. "And what do you want?"

Mallory shook her head. "I don't know. Alex and

I had begun to connect in a way I'd never thought possible, and I mean more than sexually. But we weren't ready for this."

"He'd asked you to move in with him," Lilli pointed out.

"Yes, but—" Mallory broke off, feeling a sharp twist in her stomach. "He hasn't said he loves me," she admitted.

"Have you told him that you love him?" Lilli asked.

"No," Mallory said and fiddled with the elaborate skirt of the slip. "It seemed too soon."

"I can tell you from personal experience that just because a couple doesn't say I love you before the wedding doesn't mean they will never say it," she said with a soft smile. "It also doesn't mean their marriage can't become a dream come true."

Mallory looked into Lilli's clear blue eyes and found a drop of hope that soothed some of her doubts. "How can we make this work?"

Lilli smiled again. "Just take it one step at a time."

A knock sounded on the dressing room door. "Hello, ladies," the bridal consultant said. "I have some more dresses for you to try."

Mallory met Lilli's gaze and gave a wry smile. "Step one, find a dress I can live with."

Eight

"This was supposed to be simple and small," Mallory said to her father, gaping at the number of people packed into the chapel as she peeked from a tiny window. "How many people are in there?"

Her father patted her hand. "I don't know. Your mother said the guest list kept growing. I haven't seen her this excited about anything in a long, long time," he said.

Mallory met his gaze. "Since Wynn died," she said, feeling a tug of sadness.

Her father nodded. "I know it's been difficult for you to become our only child. We probably didn't handle everything the way we should. And your mother's depression—" He broke off as if he were overcome with emotion.

Mallory was caught off guard by the display. "You two have been wonderful parents."

Her father smiled. "You're so sweet. You sure as hell didn't get that from me." He inhaled deeply. "I just want you to know that I've always been proud of you, and you are a beautiful bride. Megalos is a lucky man."

Her heart twisted with emotions she hadn't expected to feel. She'd been in such a rush to prepare herself for today that she hadn't had much time to think about her parents' feelings. Her eyes swelled with tears. "I love you, Daddy. I hope you'll always be proud of me."

"Always," he said and kissed her cheek. He pulled back and stood taller. "It's time."

She nodded, her stomach fluttering like a hummingbird's wings. Her father gave a soft tap on the door and it immediately opened. At the sight of everyone in that chapel turning to look at her, then standing, her throat tightened with anxiety. She bit the inside of her lip to keep it from quivering.

Then she looked ahead and saw Alex. Gorgeous Alex with so many more layers than she'd dreamed. Wearing a classic black tux, he stood with his feet slightly apart, his hands folded in front of him. With his gaze fixed on hers, she felt as if she was the only other person in the room.

His lips lifted just a bit, giving a hint of his pleasure at seeing her as she walked down the aisle. She smiled and gave her mother a tiny wave just before she arrived at the front of the chapel. Her mother smiled broadly in response.

She finished the last few steps and looked at Alex as he joined her and her father in front of the chaplain. Her heart turned over like a whirling tumbleweed.

"Dearly beloved," she heard the minister say, but her awareness of Alex squeezed everything else from her mind. She was only aware of him, his height, his strength, his incredible magnetism. Was she really going to be his wife?

"Her mother and I," her father said in reply to something the chaplain had asked. Mallory blinked as her father kissed her cheek and joined her hand with Alex's.

His hand felt strong wrapped around hers. Today, more than ever, she needed that strength. She wondered if he suffered from doubts. Surely he did. This had been as much a surprise to him as it had been to her.

Seconds passed and Alex turned her toward him. She stared into his handsome face and wanted to know his heart. She wanted to be in his heart.

His eyes burned into hers. In his green gaze, she saw encouragement, support, strength and…possibilities. Oh, how she wanted those possibilities to come true for both of them.

"Do you, Alex, take Mallory to be your wife? To have and to hold…"

"I do," Alex said, and she felt the click of a lock. She knew he was tying himself to her and her to him. Heaven help them both.

The reception was held in an exquisite private ballroom with marble floors, gold mirrors and crystal chandeliers. Her parents had spared no expense. The menu was sumptuous and the room dripped with white roses on every available surface from the tables to the piano.

She thanked another couple for coming and felt her cheeks ache from smiling. All the tension of the previous ten days was catching up to her and more than anything, she craved a quiet corner. But there was still the first dance and the cake to cut.

Alex dipped his mouth to her ear. "How are you doing?"

She smiled at his timing. It was as if he'd known her energy was starting to flag. "How much longer do we have to stay?" she whispered.

He chuckled. "As far as I'm concerned, we can leave now."

Severely tempted, she shook her head. "We need to do some of the traditional things for the sake of—" She shrugged. "Of whoever cares. We should dance."

"That I don't mind," he said and led her to the dance floor. He spoke with the band for a second and then took her in his arms. The strains of the song that had been playing on the beach began. An old song that had been remade again and again, the tune and words made her smile.

"Up On The Roof," she said, her heart twisting at the romantic selection. "Nice choice."

"I thought so since we'll be spending a lot of evenings on the roof of my penthouse." He spun her around and she laughed. "That's the first real smile I've seen on your face today."

She nodded and closed her eyes so she could seal this moment in her mind. Opening her eyes, she met his gaze, full of hope and wishes. She wondered if he could see them written on her face. She wondered if he felt the same way.

The first dance of their married life together and Mallory whirled from Alex's arms to her father's to partner after partner. The wedding planner finally rescued her, pulling her aside for the cake-cutting.

"It's that time," the woman said in a cheerful voice. "Now if we could just find your groom."

Mallory looked around the room, unable to find Alex. "I don't see—" She double tracked over a corner where a tall blond woman and Alex appeared to be engaged in an intense conversation. The woman lifted her hand to his cheek and Mallory felt as she'd been stabbed. She looked away. "I'm sure he'll be here soon. I would love a sip of water, please," she said.

"Let me get that for you," the woman said. "Can't have our bride getting parched."

Mallory bit her lip, wondering who the woman was. She looked familiar, but she couldn't quite place her. A guest approached her and she plastered on a smile.

Minutes later, the wedding planner returned with Alex, who wore an inscrutable expression. She felt him studying her face, but couldn't bear to look him in the eye.

"I think we need to call it a night," Alex said to the wedding planner. "Mallory is tired."

The wedding planner pressed the bottle of water into her hand. "Just a little longer, I promise. Cut the cake and ten minutes of pleasantries, then out the door."

"Five minutes," Alex said in a firm voice. "My wife is tired."

The wedding planner raised her eyebrows in surprise, but nodded. "This way, then."

Alex led Mallory to the table and she still couldn't look at him. "What's wrong?" he asked in a low voice.

"I could ask you the same," she said and accepted the knife. Alex placed his hand over hers and they cut the first piece. Cameras flashed.

Alex lifted a bite to her lips and Mallory wondered if she would be able to swallow even that small bite. She took it into her mouth and forced it down her dry throat then offered his bite to him.

He surprised her, capturing her hand and kissing

it after he swallowed his bite. The wedding guests roared in approval.

Mallory was filled with confusion. A champagne glass was placed in her hand and she looped her hand through Alex's. Forced to look at him, she saw the possessiveness in his gaze and felt her stomach drop to her knees. What had she let herself in for?

Alex took her glass and his, placed them on the table then pulled her into his arms. She stiffened.

"It's almost over," he promised and covered her mouth with his, surprising her again with his passion. When he pulled away, she was trembling.

Alex lifted his hand to the applauding crowd. "Thank you for coming. Please enjoy the rest of the party. Good night," he said and guests tossed rose petals as he led her out of the room.

Alex had arranged for them to stay in the resort's penthouse suite for the night. He guided her to the private elevator. As soon as the doors whooshed closed, he turned to her. "What's wrong?"

She leaned her head back against the cool steel wall and closed her eyes. She didn't know whether to cry or scream.

"Mallory, why are you upset?"

She sucked in an indignant breath and met his gaze. "Why in the world would I be upset when you are in the corner with a beautiful blond woman at our wedding reception?"

Realization crossed his face and he sighed,

rubbing his hand over his face. "You weren't supposed to see that."

She blinked. "That makes everything better." The elevator doors opened and she stalked toward the doors decorated in ivy and roses.

"Dammit, wait a minute," he said, catching her arm. "I meant I didn't want you upset. That was Chloe. She crashed the reception. I was trying to avoid a big scene by having security remove her from the room."

Mallory met his gaze. "Really?"

He nodded. "Really."

She took an extra breath. "Do you always have this kind of problem when you break up with a woman?"

"Never like this. I'm starting to see the reason for restraining orders," he said, his gaze troubled.

"Should we do something about this? About her?" Mallory asked.

Alex looked at her for a long moment and lifted his hand to her cheek. "You just gave me an amazing gift."

"What?" she asked, confused.

"You said *we*. Should *we* do something? Even though you're miffed," he said, rubbing his finger over her mouth as if it were a lush flower.

Mallory felt some of the fight drain out of her. "Just imagine if the tables were turned," she said. "If you'd seen me in the corner with another man at our wedding reception."

"That's easy," Alex said. "I would have made a scene and given him a bloody nose. You handled it with much more class." He glanced at the door. "Why are we standing outside?"

With no warning, he picked her up and carried her to the door, pushed it open and brought her inside where the room was lit with oodles of candles and dozens of white roses. "What are you—"

"The threshold tradition," he said. "It's supposed to bring good luck. Everyone can use good luck."

He looked down at her and took her mouth with his in a searing, possessive kiss that left her breathless. "What was that for?"

"Because I've been wanting to kiss you all night," he said, sinking onto a white leather sofa and holding her on his lap.

"You've already kissed me several times today."

"Not like I wanted," he said. "Not enough." He rubbed his lip over hers from side to side in delicious, sensual movements. "You feel so good," he said, sliding his tongue over her bottom lip. "Taste so good."

"It's the cake," she said. "I taste like wedding cake."

He gave a dirty chuckle. "Trust me. It's not the cake," he said and took her mouth in another kiss. After a moment, he pulled back and tugged off her shoes. "Bet you're ready to get rid of these."

She nodded and it began to sink in that she had gotten married. She was now his wife. The notion made her chest tighten with a strange mixture of emotion.

"And your dress," he said with a devil's look in his eyes. "Bet you're ready to get rid of that, too."

She couldn't keep a smile of amusement from her face. "Good luck. This dress has fifty buttons."

He shot her a look of disbelief then glanced at her book. "What idiot thought of that?"

"A very famous designer."

"Who is clearly a man-hater," he said and lifted his hand to the buttons. "Good thing I've got staying power."

She lifted her hand to his shoulder and met his gaze. "Do you?" she asked. "Do you really have staying power?"

He paused, clearly hearing her serious tone. "Yes, I do."

Mallory bit her lip, but felt a resolve strengthen inside her. "I don't want to be married to you if you're going to have other women."

His face turned dead serious. "There will be no other women for me, no other men for you," he said in a low, rough voice.

His latter comment caught her off guard. She would never consider being with another man. Now that she'd been with him, now that she'd been his wife, how could she think of anyone but Alex?

"Do you understand?" he asked, lacing his long fingers with hers.

She nodded. "Of course."

"I take my wedding vows seriously, Mallory. I'm committed to you," he said.

She nodded, but her mind was still full of questions. The biggest was would he ever love her?

"I'm your husband," he said, his hands moving over her buttons, releasing them with a speed that surprised her. "Soon enough, there won't be an inch of you that doesn't know that you are my wife."

They spent the night making love until Mallory was too exhausted to continue. She fell asleep in Alex's strong arms and awakened to his kisses. He made love to her again and they shared a delicious meal before it was time to leave.

Alex's job made it impossible to leave his work for a honeymoon. He swept her off her feet and carried her inside his condo. "Welcome home, Mrs. Megalos," he said and allowed her to slide down his body until her feet touched the floor. "The movers will bring anything you want from your parents' place. Just give instructions to the housekeeper and she'll handle everything. I want you to feel comfortable here, so feel free to convert one of the other bedrooms into an office if you like. I'll leave a charge card for you in the morning. Something's up with the board of directors, so I'll need to go in early."

Her heart twisted at the notion of him leaving, which was silly. Having his undivided attention for the last twenty-four hours had knocked her equilibrium completely off-kilter.

He studied her face as if he could read her mind. "You'll be okay, won't you?"

"Of course," she said, refusing to give into her weakness for him. Alex would need a strong woman for his wife, so she needed to buck up and pull herself together. "I have plenty to do to get settled here and make-up work for my class. We can have dinner tomorrow night on the upper terrace."

"Sounds good," he said. "But it may need to be late. I only got half the story from Max at the reception, but it's sounding like we may be in for a major reorganization. I'll send in the housekeeper to unpack for you while I check my messages and give you a chance to relax."

Two hours later she sat propped up in bed, staring at her laptop screen. Feeling a shadow cross over her, she glanced up to see her husband leaning over her wearing a towel looped around his waist and, she suspected nothing else.

His green eyes full of seduction, he shot a quick glance at the laptop. "Anything you need to save?" he asked.

She nodded tearing her gaze from the sight of his amazing body. She wondered if the time would ever come when he didn't take her breath away. She marked the Web site for future research, saved her notes and turned off her laptop.

He immediately took the laptop from her and set it on the dresser. Dropping his towel seconds before he turned off the bedside lamp, he climbed into bed, covering her body with his.

Mallory shivered in anticipation.

"You're not cold, are you?" he asked, sliding his warm hands under her pajama tank top.

"No."

"Good, because you're wearing entirely too many clothes," he said and pulled her top over her head. His hard chest rubbed deliciously against hers, causing a riot in all her most sensitive places. He took her mouth in a hot kiss and pushed her shorts and panties down her legs.

He immediately found her sweet spot with his talented fingers. After a few strokes, he had her panting. "Open up, sweetheart," he told her and as she slid her thighs apart, he thrust inside her, claiming her again, all the way to her core.

Alex left before she woke the next morning. Their days fell into a pattern where Alex left early, arrived home late, worked a couple hours after dinner, made love to Mallory and fell asleep.

An uneasiness inside her began to grow. Was this going to be their future? A distracted dinner followed by late-night sex? It almost seemed as if they talked less now than they had before they'd married.

She wanted to get through to Alex. She wanted him to see her. She wanted him to, heaven help her, love her. Mallory racked her brain for ways to get to him. She tried to meet him for lunch during the day. She invited him to play golf. He was always apologetic, but always too busy.

One evening when Alex was working late again and Mallory was trying her best not to sulk, the condo phone rang and when she answered it, she knew she'd found a way to get Alex's attention.

"Thursday night's not good for me," Alex said absently to Mallory as he made a mental note to himself about the resort in West Virginia. "I'm working late."

"Not on Thursday night. Change your plans," she said in an airy, but confident voice as she sipped her wine during their late dinner.

Surprised that she would disagree with him, he shook his head. "I can't change them. I have a late meeting with marketing then I have a conference call with three contractors in West Virginia."

"Reschedule," she said, surprising him again with her insistence.

"Sweetheart, you don't understand—"

"No," she corrected. "You don't understand. I need you to be available on Thursday night. I need you to go somewhere with me."

"Mallory, be reasonable."

"I am. Do you know how many evenings you've spent with me since we got married?"

"I told you this month was going to be tough. I have an unusually heavy workload partly due to the construction project in West Virginia. Maybe we could schedule something for Sunday night."

She shook her head stubbornly. "No. It has to be Thursday."

"Tell me what it is," he said.

She took a deep breath. "A surprise."

She was such a tenderhearted woman, he thought. Lord he was lucky he hadn't married one of those sharp, brittle women he'd dated during the last several years. "That's sweet," he said. "But I really can't cancel—"

"You have to," she said. "Or I—I'll have to do something desperate."

Alex blinked at her. "What the hell—"

She rose from the table, her meal nearly untouched. "I mean it. I've made plans. I need your presence on Thursday night, and as your wife, I shouldn't have to—" Her voice broke and she bit her lip. "Beg."

Swearing under his breath, Alex stood and reached for her. "You're feeling neglected. Dammit. I can't change my schedule."

She pulled back and lifted her hands. "Don't try to charm me. Don't use seduction. Do you realize I've seen you for an average of sixty waking minutes each day since we got married? I'm just asking for one night," she said, her voice breaking again. Clearly appalled at herself, she spun around and ran from the dining room to the terrace, whisking the door closed behind her.

Alex swore under his breath and rubbed a hand

over his face. The downside of marrying a woman with heart was dealing with her sensitivities. Alex's primary focus was his career. His role at Megalos-De Luca Enterprises was his destiny. Everything else came second. Relationships, his needs, his desires. Everything. Now that he was forging ahead on his individual resort project, more was demanded from him than ever.

As his wife, she would need to grow accustomed to his schedule. His first mistress was his work. This once, however, he would bend, but he would make it clear that in the future, she should never make plans that required his presence without consulting him first.

Thursday night arrived and Alex's chauffeur drove Alex and Mallory to the address she'd given him. Mallory was scared spitless. Her palms were clammy, her heart raced. Her only saving grace was that Alex was distracted by a call he'd received on his cell phone. For once, she was thankful for the interruption.

The more she thought about it, the more she feared this may not have been such a good idea after all. Alex might not appreciate his new wife interfering. By the end of the evening, he could very well be furious with her.

Her stomach twisted into another knot and she tried to rein in her fear. Her instincts had screamed that this was the right thing for her to do. She prayed she was right.

Todd pulled in front of the entrance to the lecture hall and he opened the door for Alex and Mallory to exit the Bentley. Alex wrapped up his call and curiously glanced at the building. "Thanks, Todd," Alex said then turned to Mallory as he escorted her inside. "Are you going to tell me what this is all about now?"

"No," she said, forcing a smile to her face as they approached an auditorium. "You'll know soon enough."

Alex gave a long-suffering sigh. "Do we have assigned seats?"

"Yes," she said, her stomach twisting and turning. "Near the front."

They took their seats and Mallory held her breath.

"You're really not going to tell me," Alex murmured in her ear.

"I'm really not," she said and prayed this would all turn out right.

Finally the lights dimmed and a gray-haired man mounted the platform. "Ladies and gentleman, as director of bio-genetic studies for the University of Nevada, it is my honor and pleasure to introduce this evening's speaker, Dr. Gustavas Megalos…"

Mallory slid a sideways glance at Alex as his brother's name was announced. His eyes rounded in surprise and his gaze was fixed on the podium as a man with dark hair and glasses climbed the platform.

"Gus," he whispered, leaning toward her. "How the hell did you know he was coming to town?"

"He called and said he wanted to see you," she said, trying unsuccessfully to read her husband.

"You couldn't just tell me," he said.

"I didn't know how you would respond. It was too important to risk you saying no."

His jaw tightened. "That's why you said you would do something desperate."

She swallowed over the knot in her throat. "Yes. Are you angry?"

"I'm surprised," he said and focused on his brother.

Mallory suffered in limbo as Alex's brother discussed the importance of genetic studies and the advancements that had been made. She stole glances at Alex throughout the lecture, trying to read him, but his expression was inscrutable.

She hoped she'd made the right decision. That time Alex had opened up to her, she'd glimpsed a longing for his family. She prayed this would be a turning point, and that Alex could reconnect with his family.

Alex's brother finished his speech and the crowd applauded. Alex turned to Mallory. "You want to tell me the rest of the plan now?"

"There's a bar next door. You and your brother can go there and have a beer together," she said, feeling a spark of hope.

"What about you?" Alex asked.

"I'll go home."

Alex shook his head. "I want my brother to meet my wife," he said, standing and extending his hand to her.

Her heart dipped at his words and the emotions she read in his eyes. Maybe, she felt herself begin to hope more and more, maybe Alex could grow to love her after all.

Nine

One week later, Mallory and Alex attended a charity gala held at the Grand Trillion Resort and Casino. After Alex's successful visit with his brother, Mallory's confidence had begun to climb. Although Alex still worked late, he'd begun to call her during the day, and if she wasn't mistaken, she was seeing a new light in his eyes when he looked at her. As for her own feelings, she felt as if she was glowing from the inside out. Her heart was traveling in uncharted waters with him. She'd never felt so strongly about a man, but now she had reason to hope their marriage would work.

Unable to keep a smile from her face, she glanced

around the room and saw her father wave. She and Alex visited him at the bar.

Mallory kissed her father on the cheek. "Hi, Daddy. How's business? Ready to hire me?"

Her father choked on his whiskey, pounding his chest. He scowled at her. "You shouldn't frighten an old man like that when he's got half a glass of whiskey in his throat."

"I'm not that scary," she said.

"No, but you don't need a job," he told her giving her a quick squeeze. "You have a husband to take care of you now."

Getting married hadn't changed Mallory's desire to prove herself professionally, but she could see that it would be futile to argue with her father. "Where's Mom?" she asked, looking around the beautiful room.

"She's over there talking to one of our neighbors. I have to tell you, Mallory. Your wedding did wonders for her. She's getting out more, taking some kind of exercise class. Plating or something."

"Pilates," Mallory said, trading a smile of amusement with Alex.

"She's trying to get me to go with her," he said, clearly appalled.

"You should try it," she said. "It would be good for you."

He shook his head. "I'll stick to golf. Go give her a kiss. She'll be glad to see you."

Spotting her mother in a cluster of women, Mallory walked toward her. Her mother glanced up and smiled, breaking slightly away from the other women. "Hi, sweetheart. I told your father I was looking forward to seeing you tonight."

"Thanks." Mallory kissed her mother on her cheek. "It's good to see you, too. You look wonderful."

"You look wonderful, too," her mother said. "Something about seeing you get married made an impact on me. Life does go on, doesn't it?" she asked, with a hint of her former fragility in her eyes.

Mallory knew what her mother was saying. She still suffered over Wynn, but after all this time, it seemed she finally saw the need to start living again. "Yes, it does. I know I've told you this before, but thank you for all the work you did for my wedding."

Her mother smiled. "That was my pleasure. You're my only daughter, so that was my only chance. I'm doing pretty well. I've even started exercising."

"That's what Daddy told me. That's great," Mallory said.

"Now if I can just talk him into quitting cigars and Scotch," her mother said.

"Then you'll be performing a miracle," Mallory said.

Her mother laughed. Although it was an odd rusty, unfamiliar sound, Mallory felt a rush of tenderness.

"You may be right," her mother said. "I should let you get back to your handsome, new husband."

Mallory looked over her shoulder at Alex and felt her heart skip over itself. Longing, deep and powerful, twisted through her. As every day passed, she found herself wanting his love more and more. "I'm sure I'll see you again later," she said and kissed her mother once more.

She walked toward her father and Alex. With their backs facing her, she decided to surprise them. As she crept closer, she heard her father talking.

"I told you I would reward the man who could get my daughter happily down the aisle. It may have taken some extra pushing, but you succeeded. Her mother and I are very pleased. Mallory just doesn't understand that she needs a protective influence in her life. You provide that for her."

Mallory frowned at her father's words. *Reward? Happily down the aisle? A protective influence?* Had her father actually offered Alex a reward to marry her? Her stomach twisted with nausea. She stared at the two men in disbelief. It couldn't be true, she thought. It couldn't be.

"She's more adventurous than I originally thought," Alex said. "When you first talked about matchmaking, I thought she would need a much milder, more conservative man than me. After spending some time with her, I wasn't sure any of my friends could keep her busy enough to stay out of trouble."

Mallory gasped, unable to keep the shocked sound

from escaping her throat. Alex must have heard her because he immediately turned around. His gaze met hers and she instantly knew she'd caught him at his game. The terrible secret was out. He'd never really wanted her as his wife. He'd obviously just wanted something from her father, although she couldn't imagine what Alex could need because her so-called husband was plenty wealthy.

"Mallory, don't misunderstand," Alex began.

"I don't think I do," she said, torn between humiliation and devastating pain. She felt like such a fool, and she'd hoped he would eventually love her. He had no intention of loving her. She was just a game piece he'd used to win something obviously more important to him.

He moved toward her and she shook her head, backing away.

"You didn't want to marry me because of any feelings for me," she said, her throat nearly closing shut from the pain.

"Baby, don't overreact," her father said.

She shot him a quelling glance. "And you made it all happen. I was so stupid," she said, hating that her voice broke. "So stupid. I actually thought you wanted me," she said to Alex. A horrible pressure at the back of her eyelids formed, making her feel as if she would burst into tears any second. She refused to give into it.

"I feel like such an idiot. And here I was trying my

best to be a good wife when it was all a sham." Her voice broke again. "I want a divorce," she said and fled the room.

The hurt Alex saw in Mallory's eyes stabbed him like a dagger. He turned to Edwin James. "Are you okay, sir?" he asked.

Edwin's face was pale. "I could be better, but I'll be okay. I'm not as sure about my daughter," he said then grimly met Alex's gaze. "I'm not so sure about you."

"If you're okay, then I need to go talk to my wife," Alex told him.

Edwin lifted his eyebrows. "By all means, do."

Alex immediately clicked into crisis mode and left the ballroom. He ruthlessly pushed back his emotions, putting a plan together and executing it at the same time. Dammit, he wished Mallory hadn't heard that conversation. Lengthening his stride, he headed for the front door, suspecting she would try to get the car or grab a cab. He took the stairs instead of the elevator and rounded two corners before he arrived at the resort entrance. Mallory was stepping into a cab.

He quickly jogged toward the cab and grabbed the door as she began to close it.

Mallory stared up at him. "What are you doing? Go away. Leave me alone. I don't want anything to do with you." She let out a squeak when he wouldn't let her close the door. *"What are you doing!"* she shrieked.

"I'm getting in this cab with *my wife*," he said and slid into the back seat, pushing her over and pulling the door closed behind him.

Mallory immediately darted for the other side of the cab and reached for the door handle. Alex reached across her to hold down the lock. "Drive," he said to the cabdriver.

"Where?" the driver asked with a wary expression on his face.

"Let me go!" Mallory yelled.

"Around," Alex said, absorbing the ineffective blows from Mallory's pelting hands.

The driver glanced at him doubtfully from the rearview mirror. "I'm not sure I should—"

"I'm her husband," Alex said, lifting his head when Mallory aimed her hand at his face. "Please note. She's hitting me, not the other way around."

The cabdriver nodded. "Oh, okay," he said and moved the car forward.

"Damn you," Mallory said. "I have nothing to say to you. The only reason you married me was to get something from my father. I have nothing but disgust for you."

"I didn't marry you just because of your father," he said, determined to remain calm.

"But that was part of the reason."

He shook his head. "As you know, there were several factors. The photos from the beach pushed things along," he said.

"If there even were photos from the beach. I never saw them," she retorted.

"I can show you if you'd like to see them. I was trying to protect you from embarrassment," he said.

"Protection," she echoed vehemently. "Who are you protecting? Yourself or me?"

Alex gritted his teeth. "As I said, I can show you—"

"But the photos weren't really the big deal, were they? The dealmaker for our marriage was my father," she told him, her eyes full of hostility.

"You're upset. You're not thinking clearly," he told her. "There's no way I would have married you if there wasn't something between us, something strong," he said.

"But not love," she said bluntly. "And don't tell me I'm not thinking clearly. This is the first clear thought I've had since I met you. So tell me, did it all work out well for you? Was the deal you made with my father really worth being tied to me? After all, you could have easily been through a dozen women since you met me."

He took her wrist in his hand. "Our marriage wasn't about your father. Have you forgotten that I asked you to move in with me when we were in the islands?"

"You'd already negotiated some kind of deal with my father," she said and looked away, shaking her hand. "I should have known. It was just so easy and you were so attentive. It couldn't have been real."

"It was real," he told her. "Everything you and I did was real. It was between you and me."

"You never took a second look at me until you made your deal with my father," she said, her gaze damning him with the disillusionment he saw there.

"The truth is your father told me you needed a husband and he flat out told me he knew I wasn't the right man for you," he told her.

Her eyes widened in surprise. "What?"

"He asked me if I knew anyone who would be a good match for you. In the beginning, when I first tried to get you to meet with me, it was so I could find out your likes and dislikes and introduce you to some men who might work for you."

Her jaw dropped. "You've got to be kidding."

He shook his head. "Trouble was the more I got to know you, the more men I eliminated from the list. I decided I was the right one for you."

She stared at him for a long moment as if she were trying to digest his explanation. She shook her head. "That's ridiculous. I don't believe it."

"Fine. Ask your father," he said.

"As if he would tell the truth," she said. "He would agree with anything you say."

"*Your father* would agree to *anything?*" he said more than asked.

She met his gaze for a long moment then looked away. "This is still ridiculous. And I'm still getting a divorce. I won't stay in this sham of a marriage."

Despite the fact that Alex was known as a master persuader, a master negotiator, he was rock-solid on some issues. Marriage was one of them. "There will be no divorce," he said quietly.

She looked at him as if he were crazy. "Excuse me? You can't force me to stay with you. It's perfectly reasonable that I wouldn't want to stay in a marriage based on lies."

He gave a harsh laugh. "Every couple who gets married is lying to each other. The woman lies about liking sports. The man lies about liking her family. Marriage is often based on a pack of lies. The deception may be made with good intentions, but it's still deception."

She shook her head, looking at him as if she didn't know him at all. "You're so full of cynicism. No wonder you don't believe in love." She glanced away. "How stupid of me to hope that you and I—" She broke off and stared out the window. "I still want a divorce."

"I've already said that's not an option. A Megalos never divorces," he said.

"Interesting time for you to pull out the family card given the fact that you don't even speak to your family anymore," she said.

He withstood the low blow. "That wasn't like you, Mallory."

He watched her take a deep breath. "Perhaps not," she said. "This situation isn't bringing out the best in me. *You* aren't bringing out the best in me. The wisest thing to do is for us to quietly divorce and get on with our lives. It would take very little time to—"

"I told you we're not getting a divorce. I'll fight you every inch of the way."

"Why?" she demanded, turning around, full of fire and fury. "I could name a dozen reasons why we shouldn't stay together."

"We've made a commitment," he said. "We've taken vows. Those are the reasons we'll stay together."

"But those vows have nothing to do with love, past, present or future. You don't even really believe in love. Why be miserable?"

"Misery isn't necessary. Just because you're facing reality instead of relying on romantic wishful thinking doesn't mean we can't be happy. We can work it out and reach a deal to make a happy life for ourselves," he said.

She made a face. "You make it sound like a business negotiation."

"Ask you father. Ask your friend. Ask anyone who's been married. Marriage is one negotiation after another."

"And the reason you married me is because you thought you could win them all because I was so easy," she said, full of resentment. "I need to be away from you. I need some space." She turned to the cabdriver. "Drop me off at the Bellagio, please."

"No. Take us here instead," he said and gave the

address for his house on the outskirts of town. He wanted privacy.

"I'm not staying with you," Mallory said. "I can't. And you can't make me. I can't bear to be with you one more night."

The change from her adoring, loving attitude cut him to the quick, but he didn't give into it. "There are plenty of bedrooms in my home. Choose one. We can discuss this in the morning."

As soon as Alex opened the door to his home, Mallory flew past him hardly noticing the beautiful decor. She was so upset she barely took in the sight of lush, intricately designed carpets, antique wooden furniture and the sparkle of crystal and mirrors.

"Would you like something to drink?" he asked from behind her.

She quivered at the intimate sound of his voice and despised herself for her reaction to him. She refused to look at him. "While I'm tempted to ask for the biggest bottle of wine you have, I'll just take water," she said. "Can you please point me in the direction of your kitchen?"

"It's down the hall to the left, but all the bedrooms have small refrigerators and bottled water," he said.

She nodded. "Thank you. Now, if you could point me in the direction of the master bedroom?"

His eyebrows lifted in surprise. "Upstairs, far left."

She nodded. "I'll be sleeping at the other end of the house. Good night," she said and felt his gaze taking in her every step. Taking a sharp right at the top of the stairs, she walked all the way to the end and opened the door to a guest room decorated in shades of restful green.

She might have appreciated it more if she weren't so upset. After some searching, she found the mini-fridge discreetly hidden in a cabinet. She pulled out a bottle of water and took several swallows as she paced the carpet.

Mallory rubbed her forehead. How had she gotten herself into this situation? Her father had deceived her. Alex had deceived her. A bitter taste filled her mouth. Perhaps she had even deceived herself.

Sure, in the beginning, she had kept her guard up around Alex. She'd continually reminded herself that he was a player and she would never hold his interest. The more time she'd spent with him, though, the more she'd wanted to believe he was sincere. *What a fool.*

A knock sounded on the door. Alex, she thought and scowled. "Go away."

A brief silence followed. "Mr. Megalos asked me to bring you some things for your stay," said a timid female voice.

Cringing at her rudeness, Mallory rushed to the door. "I'll just leave them—"

Mallory opened the door to a woman dressed in a black uniform with a hesitant expression on her face. The woman held a large basket that contained toiletries and a robe.

"I'm so sorry. I thought you were—" Mallory broke off. "Someone else. Thank you. This is lovely."

"You're very welcome," the woman said, smiling cautiously. "I'm Gloria, and may I congratulate you on your recent marriage to Mr. Megalos."

Please don't, Mallory wanted to say, but swallowed the urge. "Thank you."

"May I get anything else for you?" Gloria asked. "A snack?"

Mallory's stomach was still upset. She didn't know when she would want to eat again. "No, thank you. This will be fine. Thank you again, and good night," she said and closed the door. Waiting a few seconds for Gloria to walk away, Mallory locked the door. She didn't want a surprise intruder, particularly one that stood six feet tall and was entirely too handsome and charming.

She couldn't believe the two most important men in her life could have done such a thing to her. Did her father truly believe she was incapable of making good decisions for herself?

Her stomach twisted into another knot.

She felt so betrayed. She would do anything to escape to somewhere far, far away from both Alex and her father. Europe, she fantasized, or Australia.

Not likely. Mallory frowned. Both Alex and her father would have their goons watching her every move.

Sinking onto the bed, she crossed her arms over her chest. Everything inside her ached. It was a wrenching sensation as if she were being ripped apart. Even though she and Alex had only been married for a month, she'd become his wife in her mind, and heaven help her in her heart and soul.

And it had all been a trick.

Remnants of the first overwhelming rush of anger still lingered, but other unwanted emotions trickled through her fury. Bone-deep sadness and gaping loss the size of a black hole sucked her downward.

Her chest and throat tightened like a vise closing around her. She felt so lost. A sob escaped her throat, then another. She'd been determined not to cry in front of Alex, but it was as if a dam broke and unleashed her tears.

Stripping off her clothes, she crawled into bed and cried herself to sleep.

A sliver of dawn crept through the window the next morning, waking Mallory. She lay in bed in a semisleep state, wondering if Alex was already up and drinking his coffee. He rose earlier than anyone she knew, even her father.

Her eyes still closed, she sniffed the air for the

scent of coffee, but the only thing she smelled was the unfamiliar scent of lavender. She frowned to herself.

Any minute he would walk back in the room and look at her. She would pretend to be asleep for a maximum of thirty excruciating seconds, then she would open her eyes and smile, and he would lean over her and kiss her good-morning….

Mallory sighed, waiting for the sound of his footsteps. She heard nothing and forced her eyes open even though they felt weighted down with concrete blocks.

Everything that had happened last night hit her at once. Emotions jabbed at her ruthlessly. Humiliation. Loss. Anger.

She pulled the sheet over her head to hide. Oh, heaven help her, what was she going to do now?

She'd seen the expression on his face. He wouldn't let her go. Alex possessed the personality of a conqueror, and he knew far more about winning than she did. Any chance of her resistance was doomed.

She burrowed deeper under the covers. All she wanted to do was hide. How long, some rational part of her mind asked. How many years would she hide?

The same way her mother had.

Mallory immediately tossed back the sheet and sat up in one swift motion. "Damn it," she said. "Damn him."

Alex may have destroyed one of the deepest wishes in her heart, but she had other goals, other dreams. Mallory refused to stop living.

Ten

"I want a job," Mallory said, her hands folded in her lap, her gaze steadfast. Her glorious wavy hair was pulled back into a ponytail at her nape and she emanated as much warmth as an icicle.

Alex could hardly believe the change from his sweet, adoring and passionate bride to the cool, remote woman sitting on the chair opposite him.

"A job," he echoed, rolling the word around his mouth as he stood.

"That's right. If you insist on us remaining together, then the least you owe me is the opportunity to pursue some of my dreams." She paused a half-beat and her eyes flickered with deep sadness.

"Since some of my dreams will never come true, helping me get a job is the least you can do."

Alex stuffed his hands into his pockets in frustration. "Why do you want to work? You can lead a life of leisure. Or at the least, you can set your own schedule. That's the dream of most American women *and* men."

"This isn't a new goal for me. I mentioned it to you some time ago. If you're deadset against it, you better tell me now. This is a deal breaker," she said in a crisp voice.

Alex was stunned at her inflexibility. He didn't want his wife working. He didn't want his wife to feel it was necessary to work. "You're making this difficult."

"In the grand scheme of things, I'm not asking for all that much."

Resting his hands on his hips, he looked down at her, wondering where the sweet woman who'd been his wife had gone. "I can provide for you. You don't need to work."

"Yes, I do. I *need* to feel as if I'm accomplishing something. I don't want to feel like I'm under someone's thumb." She took a quick breath.

"A job," he said again. Alex hadn't spent much time thinking about his future wife, but he'd always expected his wife to retire from her job once they married. After all, he could provide everything a woman could wish for.

He looked into Mallory's eyes and saw the combination of hurt and determination. The hurt made him feel restless. Resting his hands on his hips, he considered options.

"I'll have to think about it. It's not as if any job would do since you're my wife," he said.

"I'll give you two weeks," she said, coolly meeting his gaze.

He lifted an eyebrow. "Or what?" he asked, surprised again that she would have the nerve to give him a deadline. Daddy's little girl was pushing back.

"Or I walk," she said, rising from her seat. "You may not agree to a divorce, but I don't have to agree to live with you, either."

Even though Alex knew he would eventually win any arguments she presented about living apart, he couldn't help feeling a shocking illicit thrill at the challenge in her eyes, her voice, her body. She oozed a dare to him.

"Fine," he said. "I'll find a position for you. You'll be reviewed by someone other than me. If you don't cut it, then it's back to charity work and being my wife."

She glowered at him. "I can cut anything you throw at me. And as far as being your wife, this has become a business arrangement. It was from the beginning. I just didn't know it. If we're going to have a loveless marriage, it's going to be a sexless marriage."

Alex blinked. She couldn't be serious, not with the chemistry they shared. He laughed. "Good joke."

"I am not joking," she said, looking so furious he

wondered if steam would come pouring out of her ears any minute. "Why should I continue to humiliate myself—"

"I didn't know you found sex with me humiliating," he cut in. "I could have sworn those were sounds of pleasure you were making."

She inhaled sharply. "This marriage is a sham. Everything between us is a sham."

"That's not true and you know it. You're exaggerating because you're still upset," he said and shook his head when she opened her mouth. "This argument is unnecessary. You can stay in another bedroom if that's what you want, but it won't last. Now, is that all?"

She silently met his gaze for a long moment, her hands knotted in fury, her cheeks pink from barely restrained temper. She looked like she wanted to slap him. "Yes," she hissed.

"Then I need to get to work. You can either ride with me or I'll send a driver for you."

"I'm not riding with you," she said. "In fact, I think I'll stay here for the next two weeks."

Alex shook his head. "No. I said you may choose another bedroom, not another house. Besides, we have appearances scheduled for this weekend."

"You can't really expect me to appear with you in public and act as if everything between us is all lovey-dovey."

"I can and I do," he said. "I'll leave you with

something to think about. We didn't profess our love to each other before we were married, and you had no aversion to sharing my bed then. I'll see you tonight at dinner." He leaned toward her to kiss her goodbye, but she turned her head.

Even though Alex had won the argument, the victory was hollow. He hadn't realized how much the affection in Mallory's gaze had felt like a ray of sunshine.

Malloy rode to the condo in a sedan driven by Todd. Scowling at the sunny day, she pumped her foot as she crossed one leg over the other. What she wouldn't give to wring Alex's neck and wipe that insufferable confidence off his face.

She'd never felt more trapped in her life. She felt as if the very life was being choked out of her. How could he possibly expect her to pretend their marriage wasn't just a big show? How could she possibly act as if she adored him when she was already fantasizing about fixing a dinner that would cause him a week's worth of indigestion?

After a while, she would wear him down. He would tire of having a wife in name only. He may not love her, but he wanted her to warm his bed. She scowled again at the thought. She'd been so easy, so eager to please. Now Alex would see a different side of her. A side that would make him give her the freedom she deserved.

Mallory allowed herself to stew over the situation

until she arrived at the condo. Then she chose her new bedroom, the one farthest away from Alex's. No need to tempt him. She wouldn't need to worry about being tempted by him. Now that she knew the truth about him, she couldn't possibly feel even a spark of lust, let alone love. She moved all her clothes and belongings to the room and studied how she could make her new bedroom a place of comfort and solace.

She decided to go shopping for candles, pillows and anything else that caught her attention. At the mall, the local animal league was holding a fund and adoption drive. Mallory stroked the soft fur of the dogs and cats. She'd always wanted a pet, but her mother had been allergic.

But she no longer lived in the same house as her mother. An idea occurred to her as she petted a kitten. If she was looking for comfort, a pet would be perfect. She wondered how Alex would feel about having a pet. It would be inconsiderate to get one without asking his opinion.

On the other hand, it had been incredibly inconsiderate for him to marry her for business reasons, too. Mallory smiled to herself as she looked at the animals. Alex would probably hate having a pet. All the more reason for her to get one, although Mallory would never adopt an animal out of spite. Adopting a pet would be one little dream of hers that she could still make come true. If she and Alex remained married, there would be no children. The realization saddened her. She would need to give her affection to some other living being.

Mallory spent the rest of the afternoon shopping for her new bedroom and the two cats she adopted from the animal shelter. New collars, cat food, an electronic litter box, cat carriers.

As she pulled up to the entrance of the condo, the valet opened the door for her and glanced in her back seat. "Would you like some help taking your bags upstairs?"

"Yes, please. That would be wonderful," Mallory said, grabbing the two cat carriers while her new furry friends made plaintive cries. "I don't think they like the carriers, but I don't trust them loose yet."

The nice valet helped her carry everything up to the penthouse.

As she opened the door, she caught the scent of dinner cooking. Surprised because she hadn't requested anything, she wondered if Alex had called from work with instructions. The prospect of seeing him again almost destroyed her good mood, but when she looked at her new kitties again, she had to smile.

Jean, the housekeeper, walked into the foyer and blinked at the sight of the cat carriers. "Cats?" she said in disbelief.

"Yes, aren't they darling?" Mallory asked. "I'll put them in my room for now, but later—"

"Your room," Jean echoed, grabbing several bags

the valet had deposited at the front door and trying to keep up with Mallory.

"Yes," Mallory said, walking through the den and down the long hallway to the end. "I guess Alex didn't have a chance to tell you, but this will be my room. I may redecorate, but I'll figure that out later." She bent down to let out the long-haired black cat with glowing green eyes. "His name is Gorgeous," she said as she stroked his silky, soft fur.

The other cat mewed in envy and Mallory laughed. "I know. It's your turn, Indie," she said, releasing the short-haired calico and rubbing her under her chin. "Aren't they sweet?"

The housekeeper shot a wary eye at Gorgeous, who'd sprang onto an upholstered chair. She cleared her throat. "Mrs. Megalos, I'm not sure Mr. Megalos is a cat lover."

"That's okay. I'll take care of them," Mallory said.

Jean cleared her throat again then nodded. "Mr. Megalos asked me to tell you as soon as you arrived that the two of you are having dinner on the upper terrace. He asked the chef to prepare your favorite dish."

I'm sure he did, Mallory thought as she narrowed her eyes. If Alex thought Crab Imperial on the terrace was going to be enough to win her back to his bed, then he was sadly mistaken. "Thanks. How soon will it be ready?" Mallory asked.

"He requested that you join him as soon as you arrive," Jean said.

Mallory nodded. "Please tell him I'll be upstairs as soon as I set up the litter box and wash up."

"You want me to mention the litter box?" Jean asked in a strained voice, clearly reluctant to be the bearer of that news.

"Good thinking," Mallory said. "Ask him to come in here so I can surprise him."

The housekeeper looked at her as if she'd lost her mind, but nodded. "As you wish."

As Indie circled around her, Mallory pulled out the litter box and poured the litter into it.

"What the hell—"

Mallory glanced up to find Alex staring at Indie. He met her gaze and even though the real reason she'd gotten the cats was for her own edification, she got a tiny thrill at the look of shock on his face. "A cat?"

"Two," she said with a smile that was completely sincere. She pointed at Gorgeous sitting in the chair. "The volunteers at the animal rescue league told me cats are happier in pairs. I was going to get kittens, but I decided on adults because not as many people want them. Meet Gorgeous and Indie," she said and picked up the calico. "I love cats. Don't you?"

He opened his mouth then rubbed his hand over it. "Tell me again why you got two," he said.

"So they won't be lonely while I'm at work," she said.

Alex clenched his jaw and gave a short nod.

"Dinner's ready. I asked the chef to prepare your favorite."

"Yes, thank you. Jean told me. I'll wash up and join you," she said, feeling the strain between them pull like an overstretched rubber band. She hated the sensation.

Leaving her new furry friends in her new room, she freshened up and climbed the stairs to the upper level of the terrace. A light breeze softened the blazing heat. Alex stood, looking over the balcony, his mind seemingly a million miles away. The wind ruffled his wavy hair and his white shirt. He appeared so isolated. She wondered if he would ever admit to feeling lonely. She wondered if he would ever admit to needing someone. Needing her?

Slamming the door on such useless thoughts, she lifted her chin. She could and would get through this. "The Crab Imperial smells delicious," she said, taking a seat at the table.

Alex glanced up and walked to the table. It struck her that he moved with the grace of a primitive, wild animal. A tiger, she decided. He moved his chair next to hers and sat down, his leg immediately brushing hers.

Mallory's heart skipped and she moved her leg away from his. She wished she wasn't so aware of him. She shouldn't be, she thought, taking a sip of white wine. Not after what he'd done.

"You've been busy today," he said, picking up his fork and taking a bite.

"I had a lot to do," she said and took a bite of the Crab Imperial. It tasted like sawdust.

"You didn't need to move into another room so quickly," he said. "You could have slept on your decision."

"No, I couldn't," she said, suspecting that if she'd slept on her decision she would have never moved out. She would have simply remained under Alex's spell forever, feeling and acting like a weak fool.

She took another bite and it tasted the same, sawdust. Blast it. "What did you find out about jobs for me today?"

He took a long sip of wine and speared a piece of crab with his fork. "Technically nothing."

Mallory's blood pressure immediately rose. "I really meant it when I said I wanted a job. I can interview for one on my own."

"That won't be necessary. I've decided you'll work for me," he said.

She blinked. "How?"

"I've been working double time because of the resort I'm developing in West Virginia. Your father has supplied the investors."

"In trade for you being my husband," she said, a bitter taste filling her mouth.

"He would have done it, anyway. It's a good investment."

"Why was it necessary? You have enough money on your own," she blurted out.

"One of the rules of wealth management is that you use other people's money to accomplish your goals. You don't risk your own."

She was surprised at his acumen, but shouldn't have been. "Where do I fit in with this?"

"I want you to interface with my contacts in West Virginia. There will be very limited travel," he said. "I don't want my wife spending most of her time away from me. I'm balancing several demands at Megalos-De Luca Enterprises and the personal resort start-up, so I won't be able to get your job in place for another week or so."

"As long as it's within two weeks," she said, feeling as if she had to hold the line. Alex had made her forget everything but him. She couldn't let that happen again.

"I'll make it worth the wait," he said in such a sexy way that it sent a shiver down her all the way to her toes.

Upset by her reaction to him, Mallory rushed down a couple of bites of the dish and gulped some wine. "That was delicious. I'm full. If you don't mind excusing me—"

"Already?" he said with a raised eyebrow that could have made her back down in other circumstances. But not now.

"The cats," she said. "I need to get them acclimated to their new home."

He gave a slow nod that made her feel as if she

may have won round one, but the game was far from over. "We have a cocktail party with the other VPs, CEO and board members of Megalos-De Luca Enterprises the day after tomorrow."

She blinked in surprise. "That's not much notice."

"No, it isn't," he said. "The board is introducing a reengineering specialist."

"You don't sound happy," she said.

"I'm not. Neither is Max De Luca."

She shivered at the cold expression on his face. "I can't imagine anyone in their right mind who would want to go up against the two of you."

He lifted his mouth in a smile that bared his teeth like a wolf. "I always thought you were a clever woman."

She stood. "Just not clever enough to see through the ruse you and my father cooked up."

Alex shot from his chair and snagged her wrist. "There was always something between us, Mallory. You can't deny that."

She knew she'd always had feelings for him. That was all. She shook her head. "I have no idea what your true feelings, if any, are for me."

"I can show you," he offered and lowered his head.

She turned her head away and his mouth seared her cheek. Her heart was hammering a mile a minute. "I want more than a man who's interested in me for the money my father can find for him. I want more than sex."

Eleven

The tension at the Megalos-De Luca cocktail party was so thick it reminded Mallory of trying to breathe in a dust storm. The room vibrated with such suspicion she couldn't wait to leave.

Spotting Lilli De Luca, she felt a smidgeon of relief and waved. Lilli smiled in return and moved toward Mallory. "Hi," she said, giving Mallory a quick hug. "This is horrible, isn't it?" she said in a low voice.

Mallory gave a short laugh, nodding in agreement. "I couldn't agree more. It feels like we're waiting for the gallows."

Lilli's pretty features wrinkled in concern. "I know. Max has been very upset about this. He won't talk about it, but he's not sleeping well at all. What about Alex?"

Mallory felt a twist of self-consciousness. She didn't know how Alex was sleeping because she wasn't sharing his bed. "He's bothered, too."

Lilli nodded. "The two of them are talking more and more. It's interesting how something like this can turn two men who were competitors into more of a team. You find out a lot about a man by how he acts when the pressure's on."

The discussion made Mallory even more uncomfortable. She would examine why later. "How's David?"

Lilli lit up. She lifted her hand and showed a miniscule of space between her thumb and forefinger. "He's this close to crawling. Max is egging him on even though I keep telling Max we'll both be doing a lot more chasing once David is mobile."

Mallory felt a stab of loss as she thought about the babies she wouldn't have with Alex.

"I'm sure you're still enjoying your honeymoon period," Lilli said with a knowing smile. "What's new at the Megalos house?"

"Cats," Mallory said. "I adopted two cats."

Lilli gaped. "Oh, my gosh. How did Alex react to that?"

"Surprisingly well," Mallory said and shook her head. "And they seem to love him. They wind around his ankles every night when he comes home." She still couldn't believe it, but she supposed she shouldn't have been surprised. Alex could turn every woman to putty. She just hadn't known his powers extended to felines.

Lilli glanced at the other side of the room. "It looks like there's going to be an announcement. We should join our husbands."

Mallory walked to Alex's side. He held a glass of Scotch in his hand and appeared attentive, but relaxed. She knew better, though. He hadn't touched his drink and every once in a while his jaw clenched.

She shouldn't care, and she told herself it was just human nature not to want to see another human being suffer, but Mallory knew that the first wave of her white-hot anger and indignation against Alex had finally cooled. "Are you okay?" she asked in a low voice.

He met her gaze and she saw a flash of turbulence before he covered it. "Yes. You're drinking water. Did you want something else?"

She shook her head, thinking she would just like to leave the oppressive atmosphere. "Who is he?" she asked, nodding toward the man getting ready to speak.

"James Oldham, one of the board of directors," he said.

"He has shifty eyes," she whispered.

Alex chuckled. "You continue to delight me."

His statement was so natural it caught her off guard. Mallory often dismissed Alex's compliments because she assumed a hidden agenda. This time there was none and she couldn't suppress a burst of pleasure.

"Ladies and gentlemen, thank you for joining us on such short notice," James Oldham said. "As you know, Megalos-De Luca Enterprises has long provided travelers all over the world with the ultimate resort luxury experience. We continue to do that. We also continue to refine the bottom line so that we keep our stockholders happy. To best facilitate that continued refinement, we are bringing in the best of the best in reengineering consulting firms to help us improve our financial edge in this complicated world market. Please welcome Damien Medici," he said and the door to the room opened, revealing a tall, dark man with black hair, olive skin and dark, watchful eyes. His lips lifted in the barest of smiles. He turned his head and she glimpsed a jagged scar along his jaw.

Mallory watched Alex give a nod and a soundless clap of his hands while the rest of the room applauded. Max leaned toward Alex and said something. Mallory felt the tension in the room grow exponentially and took a sip of her water.

"No relation to Santa Claus, is he?" she said to Alex.

His lips twisted in humor and he slid his hand behind her back. "Not exactly. He goes by a couple nicknames. The Terminator. Switch for switchblade. Here he comes," he said.

Mallory turned to find Damien Medici studying

the four of them intently, with particular interest in Alex and Max. He extended his hand. "The two namesakes of the company. I've heard much about you. Max, Alex," he said, shaking each of their hands. "We have more in common than you probably think. I look forward to working with you."

Damien turned to Lilli. "Mrs. De Luca?" he enquired and smiled. "Max did well." He then turned to Mallory and extended his hand. "As did Alex, Mrs. Megalos."

Mallory reluctantly accepted his hand. "Mr. Medici," she said.

"I'll be meeting with each of you individually soon," Damien said to Max and Alex.

"Welcome to Megalos-De Luca Enterprises," Alex said in his regular charming voice, but Mallory didn't miss the emphasis on the company name. Alex and Max would protect the company. Damien might not know it, but he would be facing the fight of his life if he wrangled with the two of them.

Damien nodded and walked away. Alex and Max exchanged a look then Alex glanced down, pulling his BlackBerry from his pocket. He frowned. "We should go," he said to Mallory and escorted her from the gathering.

Alex was completely silent during the drive to the condo. That should have been fine, but Mallory couldn't stop herself from being concerned. She knew he was bothered about Damien Medici, but she wondered if there was something else bringing that dark look to his face. Could it be something about the development in West Virginia?

He absently wished her good-night, and Mallory went to bed, but didn't sleep well. Rising early despite her lack of sleep, she showered and got dressed. Entering the kitchen, she was surprised to see Alex seated at the table talking on the phone.

As soon as he caught sight of her, he cut off the conversation. "Please have a seat," he said, standing and pulling out a chair for her.

Mallory felt a ripple of uneasiness. Although she glimpsed slight shadows beneath his eyes, Alex seemed almost too controlled, too calm. She took the seat he offered. "Okay."

He took a deep breath. "I'll give you the divorce you want."

Shock hit her like a cannonball. Surely she hadn't heard him correctly. "Excuse me?"

"I said I'll give you a divorce," he said in that too calm voice.

Shock hit her again, followed by confusion. "I don't understand."

He shoved his hands into his pockets, one sign that he wasn't as calm as he seemed. "I don't expect you to understand. That's why I'm giving you the divorce. Chloe," he began.

"Your ex-girlfriend?" Mallory could hardly forget the woman since the willowy blonde had shown up during her trip to the islands and the wedding reception.

"We were briefly involved, which was a terrible mistake on my part," he said in a cold, crisp voice. "I can't allow you to suffer as a result of my mistake."

Mallory shook her head, still confused. "I don't understand. Would you please sit down? This is a strange enough conversation without my having to crane to look up at you."

Alex reluctantly sat. "Chloe is threatening to go to the press with a story that she's pregnant with my child. She's claiming she got pregnant while you and I were seeing each other."

Mallory's heart stopped. "Oh, my God," she whispered. "She's pregnant with your child?"

He shook his head. "No, she isn't."

"How can you be sure?"

"I always wore protection and we were only together twice," he said.

"But condoms don't provide perfect protection," Mallory said more to herself than to Alex, her mind spinning with the news. She felt a deep twist of resentment and jealousy at the thought of Chloe bearing Alex's child.

"The woman is a pathological liar," Alex said. "I wouldn't be surprised if she's not pregnant at all."

Mallory stared at him. "Really?"

"Really," he said and finally swore. "She showed up uninvited at our wedding reception, for God's sake."

"Were you still seeing her when you and I—"

"Absolutely not," he said and took her hand in his. "I swear it. I broke up with her before you and I got involved. Once there was you, there was no one else."

Mallory felt a shiver run down her body at the naked honesty in Alex's eyes. Her emotions running all over the place, she looked at him helplessly. "If she's lying, then why do you want to divorce me?"

"I can't put you through this kind of scandal. I refuse to do it. You don't deserve it. The only way I can protect you is to divorce you." He drew in a slow breath. "I'll take care of it quickly and quietly. I have to leave town on business for the next few days. While I'm gone you can choose where you'd like to move. I think it's best that you leave Vegas, at least for a while, so you won't have to answer questions." He paused. "I'm sorry. Divorcing you is that last thing I want to do, but it's the only choice. Chloe is promising a long, drawn-out fight, and I know you would never escape the whispers. Chloe was my mistake, not yours. You deserve the fresh start that I can't give you."

Fifteen minutes later, she watched him walk out of the condo. Mallory felt as if she'd been sucked into a killer tornado and spit out in pieces. She wandered the condo, shell-shocked.

She should be happy, shouldn't she? This was what she'd wanted, no, demanded of Alex. Now she could be free to pursue her own life, her own dreams. Freedom was what she'd been craving for years.

Why did she feel like crying? Why did she feel as if someone important to her had died? Biting her lip, Mallory walked to her new bedroom and felt tears stinging her eyes. She blinked furiously to make them stop, but they streamed down her face.

Sinking onto the bed, she tried to come to terms with what Alex had told her and his solution. Her cats hopped onto the bed and rubbed against her. She grabbed Gorgeous and held him against her. He mewed in sympathy.

She glanced at the books for her online class sitting on her dresser. She'd had a hard time concentrating lately. How much harder would it be now?

She tried to formulate a plan. While she packed her belongings, she would figure out where to go. California, she thought, and immediately rejected the idea. Somewhere different. Somewhere that no one knew her. The East Coast. Florida. A remote, sunny island. A downpour of images of the time she and Alex had shared in Cabo stormed through her. The memories were so sweet she ached from them.

She pulled a suitcase from the closet and began to fill it with clothes. Heaven help her, she was confused. She'd spent most of her life doing what everyone else had told her to do. During the last month, she'd been tricked into marrying the man of her dreams. Now she was getting a divorce. She hadn't wanted to get married. She didn't want a divorce.

The thought took her by surprise. She opened

another drawer and dumped the clothes into the suitcase then stopped. A question echoed in her mind, throughout her body. What did she *really* want?

Four days later, Alex returned from his business trip. Riding the elevator to the penthouse, he dreaded walking into his home. He'd been tempted to stay at the resort downtown. Even though Mallory had been furious with him during the last week they'd been together, he'd still looked forward to her presence.

He despised the fact that his life had become tabloid fodder. He despised the fact that he'd been forced to cut Mallory out of his life for her protection. He felt gutted, empty. He'd always been so sure a woman couldn't get to his soul. Until Mallory.

He'd even started liking her cats.

The elevator stopped at the top floor and the doors opened. Swearing under his breath, he braced himself for utter quiet. He opened the door to the condo and gritted his teeth. He had never known he could be this miserable.

Closing the door behind him, he dropped his suitcase in the foyer and walked into the den. The calico sprinted out to greet him with the black male at her heels. He stared at the cats in confusion.

"What the—"

The cats wove around his ankles, mewing. Untangling himself, Alex raced to Mallory's room. Empty except for the furniture that had been there before she moved. His heart fell to his stomach.

Why the hell were the cats here? Had she left them with him for some sick reason? He backtracked to the kitchen, searching for Jean, but there was no sign of the housekeeper. He noticed, however, that the sliding door to the deck was slightly ajar. He stood very still. Was that music playing?

Confusion and anticipation coursed through him. He stepped outside and heard the music coming from the upper deck. He couldn't imagine why she would still be here. He'd made it perfectly clear to Mallory that he would give her a divorce. He hadn't softened the scandal he was facing.

Climbing the stairs to the upper terrace, he didn't know what to expect. It certainly wasn't finding Mallory reclined on a chaise lounge wearing a silky gown.

She glanced up to meet his gaze and smiled. A knot of longing formed in his throat. He wondered if he was dreaming.

"Welcome home," she said and sat up in the chair. "I poured a glass of Scotch for you. It's on the bar if you want it."

He did. Lifting the small glass from the bar, he took a long sip, feeling the burn all the way down. He met her gaze again. "I thought you would be gone."

"I almost was," she said, rising to her feet. "I packed up everything. But the whole time I couldn't stop asking myself what I really wanted." She moved toward him.

His heart pounded hard and deep. "And what was your answer?"

"I want to be the woman of your dreams," she said. "I want to be the woman you choose above all the other women. I want to be the woman you love even though you never thought you would fall in love."

He narrowed his eyes, steeling himself against the temptation to take her in his arms. "Love won't fix the mess with Chloe."

Her eyes flashed with sadness then she lifted her chin in determination. "Do you love me?"

Stunned by her boldness, he stared at her for a full moment before responding. "It doesn't matter. I won't put you through this scandal."

She pressed her lips together. "Afraid I can't take it, right?"

"I didn't say that," he said.

"You may as well. Are you going to underestimate me like everyone else has?"

Surprised again, Alex felt as if she were taking him on a ride with hairpin turns and gut-wrenching drops. "I don't underestimate you. I know you're an amazing woman. Adventurous, kind, sexy."

She made a moue of her lips. "Sounds like you might like me a little bit."

"A little bit," he echoed and swore. He took

another swallow of his drink. He didn't know how it had happened, but he was tied up in knots over her.

"I wouldn't have thought you were the quitting kind," she said. "Not if it was something you really wanted."

"I'm not," he said.

"Then you must not want me very much," she said.

His breath left his body. "Dammit," he said reaching for her. "I want you too much. I can't stand to see you hurt by all this. I finally find a woman who makes me feel like a human being, who makes me feel alive inside and I have to give her up. Dammit, it's killing me, Mallory. Don't make it any harder."

Mallory blinked, dropping her jaw and working it for a few seconds. She shook her head. "I'm going to make it very hard. I love you and I'm tired of being told what I should want and what I should do. You and I got married and I can stomp my foot and scream and rail at you because of the deal you made with my father, but the truth is I wouldn't have married you if I didn't want to." She took a deep breath. "And I don't think anyone, including my father, could have forced you to marry me. So, Mr. Megalos, consider yourself stuck with me."

Alex stared at her in amazement, not quite able to believe her. "Are you sure? This is going to get messy."

"Life is messy," she said. "I want to spend mine with you."

In that moment she made all Alex's dreams come

true at once. He pulled her against him. "I love you more than I can tell you. You really are the woman of my dreams."

He took her mouth in a soul-searing kiss that went on and on. He felt dampness against his cheeks and realized she was crying. Pulling back, he searched her face. "Mallory?"

"I was so afraid," she said. "So afraid that maybe I was wrong, that maybe you didn't love me."

"Oh, sweetheart," he said, pulling her against him. "I guess I'll just have to spend the rest of my life telling you and showing you how very much I love you."

She took a trembling breath. "Starting now?"

He swung her into his arms and headed down the steps. "Starting now."

Epilogue

Six weeks later...

Poring over lists, charts and plans for Alex's resort in West Virginia, Mallory sneaked a peek through the glass oven door and felt a twinge of relief. Good, she hadn't burned anything this time. Cooking wasn't her forte, and even though it wasn't technically necessary for her to cook, she wanted to be able to fix something special for Alex. He'd been working so hard, engaged in a constant corporate battle with Damien Medici. The master of reorganization had been a major pain in the rear and she just wished he would go far, far away. The planet Jupiter sounded like a good place for him.

With both her kitties snoozing at her feet, she glanced back at her work. She took her job for Alex very seriously. In fact, Alex joked that she took it too seriously sometimes when she was glued to her cell phone getting answers to questions and smoothing out rough spots. She could tell, however, that he was proud of her. It was amazing how much their relationship had changed once they'd admitted their love to each other. The difference was night and day.

Hearing the front door open, she watched the cats race out of the room. Seconds later they began to mew in welcome.

"Good afternoon, you spoiled, beautiful felines," Alex said in an affectionate voice at odds with his words. "What have you been up to today? Shredding curtains, ripping upholstery? Mallory?" he called.

Her heart still hiccupped at the sound of his voice. "In the kitchen," she said, rising from the table and peeking into the oven again. So far, so good.

Alex strode into the room and pulled her into his arms. If she didn't know better, she would say he was even more gorgeous than the first day she'd seen him. "How was your day?" he asked. "Tell me you're finished with your work," he said before she could answer, and lowered his mouth to hers.

Mallory bubbled with laughter, then sank into his kiss and his embrace. He kissed her as if she were the only woman on earth, and she was starting to believe that maybe she was for him.

She pulled back and took a couple of quick breaths. "I had one more thing I wanted to do before—"

"No," he said, shaking his head. "You're done. I have plans for you."

She wondered what was behind the mysterious glint in his green eyes. "Really?"

"I do, and there'll be no stalling, no excuses due to homework or anything else," he said firmly and paused a half-beat. "What is that amazing smell?"

Mallory smiled. "Apple pie. I made it myself. And we have ice cream."

His gaze softened. "You didn't have to do that. You could ask the cook—"

"I know. I wanted to." She glanced over his shoulder. "Time to take it out," she said, and pulled the pie from the oven and set it on a hot pad. "You've been working so hard lately in so many ways," she said, her mind drifting to the problems with Chloe. "I thought you deserved a little treat."

He came up behind her and put his arms around her waist. "We may have to take the pie with us. I've arranged for a celebration."

She turned in his arms and searched his face. "Why? Did Damien move to the other side of the world?"

Alex's face hardened. "No, but he's taking some time away from Megalos-De Luca to handle a crisis somewhere else." He gave a deep sigh. "My good news is that Chloe submitted to a pregnancy test and she's not pregnant."

Relief washed over Mallory. She knew how much Alex had suffered over this. "She can't threaten to sue you anymore."

"Exactly. So I've decided to celebrate by getting your passport stamped."

Mallory dropped her mouth in amazement. "How? When?"

"Tonight," he said. "We'll take my personal jet. We can sleep or do other things on the way," he said in a suggestive voice. "We'll take the pie with us, too."

Mallory's mind flew in a half-dozen different directions. "But I really do have a paper due and I've got to stay on top of those people in West Virginia or they won't get things done the way they should—"

Alex placed his index finger over her mouth. "This is part one of our honeymoon. We're gong to Paris."

"Paris," she echoed. "I've never been."

His lips curved in sexy *gotcha* smile. "I know. I see it as my personal duty to fill up all the pages in your passport the same way I fill up…"

Her face flaming at his intimate suggestion, she covered his mouth with her hand.

He kissed her fingers. "Not blushing, are you?" he teased.

"Stop it. You're making it hard for me to think straight."

He lowered his mouth to a breath away from hers. "One of my other jobs," he said.

She groaned. "Part one. Why did you say this is part one of our honeymoon?"

"Because numbers are infinite," he said, his face turning solemn. "They go on forever. The same way our love will."

"Pinch me," she said. "I can't believe I'm this lucky. Pinch me."

Alex shook his head. "Wait until I get you on the plane. I'll do a lot more pleasurable things than pinch you."

Mallory sighed as he kissed her. She knew he would deliver on his promise. Loving Alex and being loved by him would be the greatest adventure of her life.

* * * * *

BILLIONAIRE
EXTRAORDINAIRE

BY
LEANNE BANKS

This book is dedicated to all those who have helped me
along the way, with special love to my mother,
Betty Minyard. I am so blessed that you are
my mother and my friend...

One

All she had to do was fake it.

All she had to do was act as if her insides matched the calm, competent, loyal, efficient and discreet surface she worked hard to maintain. Emma Weatherfield had been faking it since she was six years old. This should be no different.

At 6:45 a.m., the door to the corner office suite at Megalos-De Luca Enterprises opened and in walked a tall man with black hair and black eyes that seemed to sear her with appraisal.

Emma's stomach clenched. She hadn't expected him until later. She felt goose bumps rise to the surface of the skin on her arms as she stood to greet the man. She'd been told he looked like a handsome version of Satan and she couldn't disagree. She didn't see a millimeter of pity or softness in his hard face or hard body. The scar on his cheek only punctuated his ruthless reputation.

Her pulse raced, but she ignored her reaction. "Mr. Medici," she said.

"Emma Weatherfield," he said and extended his hand to hers.

She hesitated a beat before taking it. After all, he was here to take the company that had provided the only stability she'd experienced in her life and rip it to shreds. Despite protests from Megalos-De Luca's top management, the current chairman of the board, James Oldham, had insisted on hiring an outside firm to conduct a reorganization. Damien Medici had made his fortune eliminating jobs.

She had a job to do, she reminded herself, and slid her hand inside his warm, strong palm. He squeezed her hand with just the right pressure and held her gaze as she noticed the texture of his skin. The calluses on his palm surprised her. He was president of his own company; there was no need for him to perform any sort of manual labor.

She would learn the answer to that question. She would learn the answers to all her questions and those of her previous bosses. It was her job to learn everything she could about Damien Medici and report back to the people of Megalos-De Luca, to whom she owed her new life.

"Call me Damien when it's just the two of us. Mr.

Medici can be reserved for other times. I was told you were efficient, but I didn't expect you to arrive at the office so early on a Monday," he said with a hint of admiration.

"Habit," she said, removing her hand from his. "Since this was a new position, I wanted to be prepared."

"And are you?" he asked, glancing around the office suite.

No, she thought, and wished she weren't so viscerally aware of his power. "I'll let you be the judge of that."

He nodded and pushed open the door to the corner executive office that gave a sweeping view of the craggy, snowcapped mountains outside of Las Vegas. "Come in," he said. "I understand you've been with the company for six years."

"Yes, I have," Emma said. She followed him inside the large inner office, watching as he wandered around the room, checking out the equipment and the desk and giving a cursory glance to the view.

"According to your résumé, you climbed the ranks quickly, working for Alex Megalos for the last two years. MD," he said, shortening the company name by using the initials of the founders, "has been good to you. They've paid your tuition and given you flexible hours to complete your degree."

"All true," she said.

"I'm sure you're grateful," he continued, unbuttoning his jacket. "Perhaps so grateful that you don't want to see MD make any significant changes."

"I want MD to thrive. The current economy is difficult. I want only the best for MD's future," Emma said, giving her planned response. She sounded stilted to her own ears.

He studied her. She felt a shiver race through her, but refused to let it show.

"Even if it's necessary for MD to cut jobs?" he asked. "Even if I need to turn the regular way of business on its ear?"

"You're legendary in your field. I'm certain you will be looking out for the company's best interests. After all, that's what you're paid to do as an unbiased, professional contractor."

He paused a moment and a ghost of a smile crossed his face again. "Good," he said, as if he knew she was giving a performance. "In that case, I'd like to start with financial reports from all the company divisions."

She blinked. "I thought you might want to meet with some of the vice presidents first."

He shook his head and pulled a laptop computer from his bag, ignoring the first-class computer on his desk. "The VPs will try to clutter my analysis with emotion. I'll take the reports."

"Yes, sir. If you prefer a different desktop…" she began.

"I always use my own computer. I prefer the ease of taking it with me."

"We have memory sticks available for that if—"

He shook his head. "No problem. Give it to someone else and it will be one less expense for your company."

She nodded slowly. True, but it also meant she would have difficulty gaining access to his electronic files when the time came. She'd known this assignment was going to be difficult, but she hadn't realized just how difficult.

"Yes, sir," she said again, determined to learn something about him. "How do you take your coffee?"

"I prefer to have a coffeepot in my office. I pour my own."

Now that surprised her. He must have read her reaction on her face.

He gave a short laugh. "I'm not like your previous bosses. I wasn't raised in a home filled with servants. I can take care of myself."

She nodded, wondering if she'd heard just a drop of resentment in his voice about the affluent upbringing of Max De Luca and Alex Megalos. "Is there anything else I can get for you?"

He shook his head. "Thank you. Just the reports."

Poring over the initial reports, crunching numbers, Damien felt the quiet vibration of his Black-Berry and debated picking up. A call would break his focus and he despised that. Glancing at the caller ID, he recognized his brother Rafe's number and answered.

"What's up, Rafe?" he asked, stretching as he

glanced outside the window and saw the sun begin to set.

"I'm chilling on a yacht in Key West. When are you going to pry yourself away from your job and come down and let me beat you at pool?"

Damien rose from his desk. "You're as much a workaholic with your yacht business as I am in my field."

"You must be afraid I'm gonna beat you bad," Rafe said.

Damien chuckled. He and Rafe had traded wins and losses playing pool since the two had reconnected as adults. "I won last time."

"Rematch," Rafe said crisply.

"Not anytime soon. My current contract will demand all my attention. James Oldham, Megalos-De Luca's new chairman of the board, has contacted me to reorganize Megalos-De Luca Enterprises."

Silence followed. "You always said you would find a way to pay back the De Lucas for what they did to our grandfather. I wondered how you'd pull that off."

"Funny how hard you have to work for some things, while others practically fall into your hands," Damien said. He'd dreamed of this day, this opportunity to bring down the De Luca name. The impact of the De Lucas' destruction of the Medici heritage had repercussions in future generations. Damien had always felt it was his job to make the De Luca family feel the same pain.

"Have you started yet?"

"Today," Damien said, feeling a surge of adrenaline at the realization. "I've been given an office at the Megalos-De Luca headquarters for my convenience."

Rafe laughed. "Talk about letting the fox in the henhouse."

"You could say that. I've also been supplied with a pretty little assistant," Damien said. "She's as loyal as the day is long."

"You have plans to change that," Rafe ventured.

"I'll do whatever is necessary," Damien said, intrigued by the thought of finding out what was underneath Miss Weatherfield's proper exterior. With forget-me-not-blue eyes, silky brown hair and a body he suspected held dangerous curves, she made him wonder what she was like in bed. Finding out could be a secondary bonus.

"Be careful," Rafe said.

Damien frowned at the odd remark. "Of what?"

"You've made your reputation and fortune by your ability to make unemotional decisions. You've got a lifetime of revenge riding on this contract. That's a helluva lot of emotion."

Damien considered his brother's advice, then firmed his resolve. "No need to worry about me, little brother. I've always led with my mind. This time will be no different."

"Okay. I've got your back if you need me," Rafe said. "Except when we're shooting pool."

Damien cracked a slight grin. "Thanks. Maybe I'll

take you up on your offer after I'm done here. We'll have something to toast. Take care," he said, and turned off his phone.

By the following afternoon, Damien had slashed seventy-five positions on the organizational chart. He planned to pull two of his best employees off their current assignments so they could perform individual analyses on each work group. The board had offered to give him MD employees to do the reviews, but Damien knew objectivity was key.

At four o'clock, a knock on his door interrupted his evaluation. "Yes," he said.

Emma peeked through the door and shook a paper bag. "I'm sorry to bother you, but I noticed you hadn't eaten, so…"

Her thoughtful gesture took him by surprise. He'd been clear that he would take care of himself. He waved his hand. "Come on in. What do you have?"

"I didn't know what you liked," she said, walking through the door.

He noticed she wore a conservatively cut black jacket and skirt that hinted at curves underneath. No sign of cleavage, and the skirt hit just below her knee, exposing shapely calves. He couldn't help wondering how she would look in something more revealing. "Then how did you choose?"

She opened her pink mouth and stared at him for a beat as if he'd caught her off guard. "I guessed. Roast beef on rye with brown mustard, lettuce and tomato."

His lips twitched. "Red meat," he said. "You didn't think I was a vegetarian."

She bit her lip and smiled tentatively. "Wild guess. I passed up the quiche, too."

He chuckled, reaching for the bag. "Thank you. You did a good job. Plain chips," he noted.

"I played it safe," she said in a neutral tone.

"So you did. If you've always been so adept at reading your employers' appetites, I can see why you were promoted."

Her eyes widened. "It was just food. It isn't that difficult. Alex liked anything with olives. Max skipped pasta and carbs at lunch because he always wanted to be sharp for the afternoon."

"And what about you?"

"Whatever I pack," she said. "May I get anything else for you?"

"Whatever you pack," he repeated, ignoring her question. "There's a company cafeteria."

"Habit," she said with a shrug that drew his gaze to her slim shoulders. "I've been packing my lunch since elementary school."

"Same here," he said. "When there was food available."

She gave him a silent, questioning glance.

"Foster homes," he said.

"Oh," she said, a combination of sympathy and confusion flitting through her eyes. "My father died when I was young, so it was just my mother and me."

He met her gaze and felt a lightning-fast connection that took him by surprise. He saw the same surprise cross her face as she blinked and looked away.

"I hope you like the—"

"Emma," a male voice called from the outer office. "Emma, are you there?"

Damien watched her cringe. "Just a second," she whispered and walked to the doorway. "Brad, I'm assisting Mr. Medici—"

"You can go ahead and—" Damien broke off, surprised when she desperately waved her hand behind her back for him to stop speaking.

Surprise lashed through him at her silent order. Or, was it a plea?

"No, tonight's not good. I need to work on a paper for one of my classes. Please excuse me," she said and turned back to Damien, closing the door behind her.

She met his gaze for a moment, then bit her lip. "Sorry about that. I'll just—"

Curious despite himself, Damien lifted his hand. "Who's Brad?"

She gave a heavy sigh. "He's a very nice man in accounting. Very kind. I can't think of a bad thing to say about him."

He nodded silently. "Except he doesn't take a hint well."

She closed her eyes and nodded. "He's very nice—"

"You've said that twice," he said.

"I don't like hurting people's feelings," she admitted. "Especially nice people."

"He's not all that nice if he's ignoring your rejections," he said. "I've learned that most nice people prefer honesty even when it hurts."

"I haven't been dishonest," she said.

"I'm sure you haven't."

Silence hung between them as she gnawed her lip. "He's asked me out at least a dozen times."

"And you've said no each time?" Damien said, incredulous. "The guy's head must be made of concrete."

She winced. "I might have visited his mother in the hospital once."

A soft heart beneath that crisp suit, he decided, and found the quality appealing. He shrugged. "You want me to see if he's on my list for terminations?"

Emma gasped. "Oh my goodness, no. I couldn't live with myself if I ever—" She shook her head. "No. He's an excellent employee. Honestly."

He regarded her silently for another long moment. She blinked and cleared her throat as if she were gathering her composure. "Well, I, uh, should let you eat your sandwich. If you need anything…"

"You'll know," he said.

Emma closed the door to Damien's office behind her and wanted to melt into the hardwood floor. Mortified, she covered her face with her hands. What was wrong with her? She prided herself on her ability to present a calm demeanor in every situation. Yet she'd been *babbling* to Damien Medici.

She'd worked for Max De Luca, who'd been called

the man of steel. She may have felt intimidated at times, but she'd managed to hold her own. For Alex Megalos, she'd maintained the highest level of discretion. Given his playboy reputation before he married Mallory James, she'd encountered more than a few phone calls from overzealous wannabe girlfriends.

Yet here, she'd glimpsed slices of humanity, even humor, when she'd expected Damien to be a block of ice. She found his strength and complexity compelling, almost seductive.

Appalled at the notion, she castigated herself. "Ridiculous," she muttered. Damien Medici was going to slice MD to shreds. He was the enemy.

TWO

The next morning, Emma walked into Max De Luca's office suite to give him an update on Damien Medici. She felt a combination of nerves and disappointment as she faced Max, a tough VP whose heart had softened because of his wife Lilli and his son David.

"The only thing I know is that he has already begun to put together a termination list and that he asked for information from these departments." She handed her former boss a typed report.

Max glanced over the report. "What about the computer?"

"He's using his own laptop and told me to give the desktop to someone else who needs it. He uses his cell phone for all his calls, except for people inside the company. I included those calls on the report."

"I see," he said, thoughtfully reviewing the information. "Based on this, I think he'll start cuts in middle management."

Emma bit her lip.

Max shrugged. "I agree that MD needs to streamline. I just want to make sure we don't cut anything vital to our future. Middle management isn't a bad place to start, as long as he doesn't want to cut too deeply," Max conceded. "Both Alex and I agree that Medici isn't the right man for this job, but James Oldham is determined to stay on the side of the stockholders. He has won the position of chairman of the board, and he clearly intends to keep it. He is the most dictatorial chairman I've ever encountered at MD. Keep me posted. Let's meet next Tuesday at the same time."

"I'm sorry I don't have more information," she said.

Max gave a cynical smile. "Medici's no fool. He clearly trusts no one. If you learn anything new, use your cell to call my cell or Alex's."

"Of course," she said and left his office. She took the elevator down two floors to Damien's office suite.

As she entered the office, she was surprised to see a light shining from beneath the door to the inner office. The door was slightly ajar and she could hear Damien's voice. Stepping closer, she listened.

"Mr. Oldham, if you truly want Megalos-De Luca to be at the top of its game, you'll have to give me free rein on the cuts. I accepted this contract with you based on your promise to let me do what I do best. If you're finding our agreement difficult, I can leave today."

Emma dropped her jaw in shock. James Oldham was chairman of the board. *No one* dared speak to him in such a way.

"I've been through this many times, Mr. Oldham. I understand you're concerned about bad PR. A well-publicized termination package and a reemployment assistance program will go a long way to softening the blow." Damien paused for a second. "What's your answer? Will you give me the latitude you promised or not?"

Several seconds passed and Emma held her breath. If only James Oldham would just say *no,* then no one at the company would need to deal with him, including her.

"I thought you would see it my way," Damien said in a triumphant tone.

Emma's heart sank.

"I'll be in contact soon," Damien said, his voice louder as he moved closer to the door.

Emma fought a sliver of panic. He could *not* find her eavesdropping. She quickly moved to her desk and began to hum an off-key version of a song by Fergie as she turned on her desktop and set down her lunch and purse.

"Emma," Damien said from behind her.

Despite the fact that she knew he was there, she jumped. "Oh, hello. You're here very early."

"As are you," he said, studying her.

She prayed he couldn't read her mind. "I have this new boss who is even more of an early bird than I am. It's a real challenge to out-early him."

His lips twitched. "I don't expect you to work the kind of hours I do. I've been described as a workaholic by more than one person."

"And are you?" she asked, thankful for the diversion.

"I've never been afraid of hard work. That attitude has served me well. My work is my passion. My mistress."

"But don't you want human companion—" She quickly realized she'd stepped outside the line of professionalism and broke off. "I apologize. That's none of my business."

"You're correct. It's not, but I could ask you the same question."

Emma thought of her mother and all the money and effort it had required to get her out of trouble. Time and time again. "I have family."

"So do I. Brothers," he said. "We made contact again after we became adults."

The way he looked at her made her feel as if he could see inside her. There was a terrifying sexiness to his power. She suspected that he was the kind of man who could make a woman do anything he wanted and make her like it, too.

She wanted to withdraw from his appeal. She wanted not to feel the pull toward him, the forbidden attraction. She wanted to be able to be perfectly professional, perfectly removed. And she would.

"So you do," she said. "Forgive me. I've gotten off track. What can I get for you?"

For just three seconds, his gaze flicked over her with a heat that burned through her gray Ann Taylor suit, white blouse and maybe even through her department store bra and panties to the soft flesh beneath.

Emma held her breath.

"I'm still making evaluations based on the reports I've received. I'll be asking for information from other departments later today."

Emma's breath came out in a whoosh which she attempted to hide. She clasped her hands together. "Okay. Just let me know," she said and watched Damien return to his office and close the door.

"Get yourself together," she told herself. The only difference between Damien and her previous bosses was that Damien was worse, far worse. And far more forbidden.

The following day at lunch, Lilli De Luca burst through the door to Damien's outer office suite with her baby David in her arms. "Hi, Emma! We've missed you."

David, with his curly hair and bright blue eyes, beamed. "Mmm," he said as he looked at Emma.

Emma couldn't help smiling back at him. "What a sweetheart. Omigoodness, look at how he's grown," she said, extending her arms.

David went to her willingly. Emma dipped slightly under his weight and glanced at Lilli. "He's gained."

Lilli smiled and groaned at the same time. "Tell me something I don't know."

"He's so friendly, though. I thought he would be clingy," Emma said, bouncing as the baby stuffed his fist into his mouth. "Teething?"

Lilli nodded. "I'm told he's in that in-between stage. A few more months and he'll get clingy."

"He's gorgeous," Emma said. "And such a sweetie."

Lilli smiled with pride. "I couldn't agree more. Max is busy on a conference call. He told me a visit from David and me would cheer you up. How's it going?"

"It's going," Emma said because nothing else really seemed appropriate.

Damien's door swung open and he glanced at the three of them. He lifted his eyebrow in inquiry at Emma. "Mrs. De Luca," he said.

"And David," Emma added.

"Call me Lilli," Max's blond wife said. "How are you?"

"Fine, thank you. And you?"

Lilli smiled, glancing at David. "Busy. I see you won the lottery and got Emma assigned as your assistant."

He gave a slight nod. "Yes."

"Alex and Max have been locked in warfare over who gets Emma as their assistant. Consider yourself very lucky," she said.

"I do," he said, glancing at Emma and then at the baby. "This is Max's son?"

Lilli nodded. "The joy of our lives."

David looked at Damien curiously and Damien

extended his hand toward the baby. David grabbed the man's thumb and tugged.

Damien smiled. "Strong grip," he said. "He will have a strong will."

"Not too strong, I hope," Lilli murmured. "Would you like to hold him?"

Damien hesitated. Something inside Emma forced her to move before he could respond. She pushed the baby against his chest and he instinctively cradled David in his arms.

"Hello, there," he said.

David stared at him, transfixed, then blew a bubble.

Damien's lips curved slightly. "David is a good name for you. I can see you throwing a rock and felling Goliath."

"A modern-day Goliath," Lilli said. "Who would that be today?"

Damien met her gaze. "Interesting line of thought," he said and passed the baby to his mother. He nodded. "It's a pleasure to see you again."

"And you," Lilli said. "You have a difficult job. I don't envy you."

"I lead with my mind, not my emotions," Damien said. "I perform best that way." He glanced at Emma. "I need reports from some additional departments."

More terminations, she thought, but schooled her expression. "Let me get my notepad."

"I should go," Lilli said. "It's good seeing you again, Emma. Call me sometime. We could meet for lunch."

"Thanks," Emma said, feeling a tightness in her

stomach. "That sounds great. Thank you for stopping by." She picked up a pad and headed for Damien's office.

Moments later, after he'd listed the departments, she nodded and rose from the chair in front of the desk.

"You look pale," he said. "You hate what I'm doing."

"You see revenue," she said. "I see people's lives and families."

"Ultimately," he said, "revenue affects people's lives and families."

"I suppose," she said, feeling tired.

"Take the rest of the day off," he said.

She snapped her head up. "I couldn't."

"Yes, you could and you will. I take care of my own. I've been a manager long enough to know when one of my employees needs a break. And you need one now." He waved his hand. "Go shopping, take a nap, sit by the pool. Do whatever women do to relax."

She smiled. "I don't shop to relax. I'm not a big napper. And in case you didn't notice, I'm not chasing a tan."

"I noticed," he said, his eyes slightly hooded. "Find a way to take a break. You need it." He glanced down at his laptop screen as if he were dismissing her.

She rose slowly, unable to look away from him. He was right, but sometimes she didn't know *how* to relax. "What about you?" she couldn't help asking, even though she should. "How do you relax?"

He lifted his head, meeting her gaze. Had she really dared to ask him that?

"I don't," he said. "It's not necessary for me."

She tried to bite her tongue, but her reply escaped despite her better judgment. "Pot. Kettle."

His eyes narrowed. "Go home."

"I will," she said. "But pot. Kettle. G'night."

Emma arrived home and checked her voice mail, bracing herself as she heard her mother's voice. She sounded fine, but Emma could never be quite sure. She dialed her mother in Missouri. "Hi, Mom. How are you?"

"Good," her mother said. "I worked at the drugstore today. There was a big sale on ibuprofen, so everyone was stocking up. It kept me busy. You'll be happy to know I didn't do any gambling."

"I am," Emma said.

"But it sure is boring as hell," her mother retorted when Emma failed to rise to the bait.

Emma's stomach twisted. "Boring as hell" was a red flag. It was one of the first signs that her mother was falling off the gambling wagon.

"Would you like me to come see you?" Emma asked. "I could probably come this weekend."

Emma's mother laughed. "No. I'm not in any trouble. You can stay where you are."

"Are you sure?" Emma asked. "Because I can—"

"No, no. You don't need to interrupt your schedule for me. We'll see each other in June. That will be just fine for me. Have you been out with any new men lately?"

"Work has been busy for me, too," Emma hedged. "I need to get used to my new boss." Emma wasn't sure that would be possible with Damien.

"Is he young and handsome? Maybe you could go out with him. I never understood why you didn't date your other bosses. They were young, handsome and rich."

Her mother just didn't understand. "Mom, part of the reason I've succeeded is because I keep my professional life separate from my personal life."

"What personal life?" her mother countered. "All you do is work or take classes. When are you going to do something fun?"

Emma bit her tongue. She hadn't had time for a lot of fun with her mother's gambling addiction. "When things settle down a little bit," she said and switched the subject. "Is everything okay with your apartment? You mentioned a problem with your garbage disposal."

Ten minutes later, she hung up and released a heavy sigh, but she couldn't escape her uneasiness. Emma's mother had left Las Vegas three years ago after Emma had bailed her out of another bad debt. The goal had been to remove her mom from temptation. So far, it had worked, but Emma never felt as if she could let down her guard.

With her salary, Emma could be living in a luxurious condominium if she chose. Instead she always felt as if she needed to save it all away just in case her mother faltered again.

At times her worry had consumed her—she'd only found relief in work or the classes she took. Lately, however, she'd found herself craving something more. Not gambling, thank goodness, but perhaps friendship or companionship. She'd shied away from close relationships partly because of her shame over her mother's problems, but it had been three years since her mother's last gambling incident. Maybe she should try going out. Emma pictured herself hitting the club scene and cringed. Doing laundry or charity work would be easier and more productive.

Despite the fact that she was aware of every move Damien made during the next week, Emma kept her professional facade firmly in place. Inside, she was insatiably curious. His scar fascinated her. She wondered how he'd gotten it. She wondered where he got those calluses on his hands and how they would feel touching her.

There was a ruthless, dangerous streak about him that intrigued her. He was clearly a predatory male—there must be a woman or *women* in his life. His sexuality was too strong for him to be a monk.

Exhausted by the time she arrived home at the end of the week, she went to bed early only to dream of him. In a steamy vision, he held her with his dark gaze, then took her into his arms. Her heart hammered against her chest and she knew she should pull back, but she couldn't find the energy or the will.

Suddenly his muscled chest was bare against hers,

his tanned skin gleaming in the moonlight. Her breasts grew heavy with arousal. Restlessness hummed in her blood. She arched against him, wanting more, wanting that firm mouth of his on hers. Standing on tiptoe, she opened her mouth as he dipped closer to her. Closer, closer… Anticipation vibrated through her. Almost…

The image turned black.

He disappeared.

Like magic, one second he was there, the next gone. Frustration coursed through her. Where had he gone? Why—

She made a muffled sound of dissatisfaction and was suddenly aware of her rapid breaths and the sheet twisted at her waist. Her eyelids fluttered and she opened her eyes to the semidarkness of her room and the whir of the ceiling fan overhead. Her body was hot, aroused, ready.

Emma covered her head with her hand and groaned. "Oh, no." It was bad enough that she couldn't stop being aware of Damien every second she was in the office. Now he was invading her dreams. She was going to have to do something drastic. She was going to have to take Mallory Megalos up on her offer to set Emma up on a blind date. Emma needed a distraction. A male one.

Three

A rare rainstorm hit the Las Vegas area as Damien left the MD parking lot in his Ferrari. The car was one of his indulgences and the only times he didn't drive it were during a hailstorm or in snow. About a mile from the office, he braked at a stoplight and caught sight of a stranded motorist on the side of the road.

Taking a second look, he realized the person wearing the bright yellow rain slicker looking beneath the hood of the subcompact was his assistant, Emma. Checking his rearview mirrors, he motioned for the driver in the next lane to let him pass. Moments later, he pulled into the parking lot and lowered his window.

"Need some help?" he asked.

Emma whipped her head around to gape at him. "Damien?"

"Yes. Do you need some help?" he repeated.

Her eyes wide with surprise, she shook her head. "No, I can handle it. I was just seeing if it was something obvious like a loose battery cable or something."

"And?" he prompted.

"And it looks like I'm going to have to call the car service. They guarantee to arrive in an hour, so I'll just wait in the car. Thanks, though."

"How were you planning to get home?" he asked.

She paused, then smiled. "Didn't think of that."

"I'll call my service and you can ride with me. Slide in," he said, unlocking the passenger door and pushing it open.

Emma hesitated, looking at the door with what appeared to be trepidation in her eyes. He wondered what could be going through her brain.

"Come on," he said. "You're just getting wetter."

"Okay," she said and he called his car service as she slammed her hood shut. He hung up just as she scooted into the leather seat. "Yikes, now I'm getting your seat wet."

"It'll dry," he said with a shrug and noticed her gaze lingering on his shoulders. She quickly glanced away, but he couldn't prevent a quick surge of pleasure at her admiration, although he suspected it was reluctant. She'd seemed remote to the point of skittishness this week. He'd thought it was due to her antipathy at his role in cutting jobs at MD. Now he wasn't so sure.

Her cell phone rang, interrupting the silence. She grabbed it from her bag and winced. "Oh, no." She pressed the call button. "I'm so sorry," she said. "I got stranded with car problems. May I reschedule?" She paused. "As late as possible," she said. "Next Wednesday at six-thirty, thank you so much."

"You sure I can't get you there tonight?" he asked.

She shook her head. "No. It's a gift certificate for a birthday present I never used. Hair, makeup, a makeover kind of thing. I decided I should finally take the plunge."

"Why? You look beautiful," he said.

Her cheeks flared with color. "Thank you. I just thought it was time for a change. You and I talked about how we don't have much of a social life, so I decided maybe I should try to get one. A social life," she clarified. "But don't worry. I won't let it interfere with my job."

"I'm sure it won't," he said. "Is Brad finally going to get a break?"

Emma shook her head. "No, but Mallory Megalos has been trying to set me up for ages. I may regret it. We'll see," she muttered and looked out the window. "Oh, look. The car service is already here."

"Do you have a garage you regularly use?" he asked, pushing open the driver's-side door.

"You don't have to go out there. You'll just get wet," she protested.

"I've been in worse situations. Give me your keys

and stay where you are. I'll handle this. What is the name of your garage?"

She oozed reluctance, but he felt a spurt of victory when he saw her cave. "Ray's Auto Service."

Emma sat in the car, stewing over her predicament. If her goal was to stay as far away from Damien as possible and to squelch her hyperawareness of him, she'd just lost what little progress she'd made over the last week.

Everything about him felt sexy and forbidden to her, and sitting so close to him in the car just made it worse.

He ducked inside the car and slid his fingers through his damp, dark hair. Droplets of water clung to his high cheekbones. She knitted her fingers together to keep from reaching to wipe the water from his tanned cheeks. Mere inches from him, she couldn't help staring at the sensual shape of his mouth.

She took a deep breath to clear her head and instead inhaled the combination of leather, rain and just a hint of his cologne.

He turned to meet her gaze. "It's all taken care of. You should get a call from the garage tomorrow morning."

"Thank you," she said, taking another deep breath in an effort to curb her frustration.

"Have you had dinner?" he asked.

"No, but—"

"I haven't either. Would you like to grab a bite?"

She bit her lip. "That's not necessary. You've already done enough."

"We may as well eat," he said. "Unless you had other plans."

"No," she said reluctantly.

"Okay. Do you like seafood?"

"Love it," she confessed.

His mouth turned upward into a sexy smile that made her stomach dip. "Good. I do, too."

He drove to one of the most exclusive restaurants in Vegas and pulled his car to the valet at the entrance. Three young men stepped toward the car, appearing to salivate at the chance to drive the vehicle. One opened the door for her. "Welcome, miss," he said.

Rising from the car, Damien nodded toward the young man who had greeted Emma. "You," he said and tucked a large bill in the man's hand along with his key. "The name is Medici. Treat her nicely," he said.

The young man smiled and handed Damien a valet parking ticket. "Like a baby."

Damien stepped beside Emma and escorted her through the door. "How did you decide which one should take your car?"

"Easy," he said. "The one with the best manners. He helped you out of the car."

The maître d' took her coat and handed it off to an assistant hostess.

"Hmm," she said, impressed. "I feel a little under-dressed," she said. "When you said a bite to eat, I didn't expect this."

"You don't like it?" he asked.

"I didn't say that," she said, glancing around at the chic, sophisticated décor and the chic, sophisticated clientele. "I've never been here."

"And you live in Vegas?" he said in surprise. "Even I knew about this place and I'm new to town."

She shook her head, but couldn't help smiling. "You forget. I pack my lunch."

"Ah, well, not tonight," he said. Seconds later, they were guided to a table for two next to a window with a view of a fountain.

"This is lovely," she said. "I feel guilty."

"Don't. It will be nice for me to look at something besides reports while I eat dinner at my desk."

"I don't think you would have a difficult time finding someone to fill this chair," she said.

"But they wouldn't fill it like you do," he said, then glanced at the wine list. "White or red?"

"Either," she said, still hanging on his comment about how she filled the chair. What did he mean by that? "Whatever you prefer."

"What do *you* prefer?" he asked, meeting her gaze across the candlelit table.

"White," she said.

"Good," he said, and the candlelight glinted off his scar. Although she didn't want to stare, the jagged line captured her attention and curiosity. She caught his quick glance and tried to look away.

The waiter arrived and she forced herself to look at the menu. After they placed their orders and the waiter returned with their wine, Damien lifted his glass to her. "To a rare rainstorm, car trouble and a mutual appreciation for seafood."

She smiled and nodded, lifting her glass to clink against his. "Here, here," she said softly and swallowed a sip of the fragrant Pinot Grigio. "Very good."

"Yes," he said as she took another sip. "I noticed you staring at my scar."

The wine caught in her throat and she coughed. She cleared her throat several times, wishing he hadn't seen her looking at him so intently. "I'm sorry," she finally managed. "That was rude."

"No, it wasn't," he said. "Natural curiosity."

She couldn't think of a good response, so she said nothing and didn't attempt to push any more wine through her tight throat.

"You wonder how it happened, don't you?"

She sucked in a quick breath. "It's none of my business."

One side of his mouth lifted in a cryptic smile. "But you still want to know. How do you think I got the scar?"

She blinked at his question. How in the world should she know? But she had imagined. She'd visualized several scenarios. Dare she share them?

"Your mind is turning a mile a minute," he said, far too accurately. "Go ahead, tell me how you thought I got the scar."

Emma closed her eyes for a second, then for some wild, unreasonable reason, she decided to play along.

"You were in a bar fight and a drunk went after you with a broken bottle."

He cocked his head to one side and lifted his wine-glass for a sip. "Who won the fight?"

"You, of course," she said. "Or, you were a pirate on a ship and someone cut you with a sword."

He chuckled. "I like that one. How did I get off the ship?"

She shrugged. "You swung on some ropes and swam ashore. I loved Johnny Depp in his pirate movies."

He nodded. "Any other scenarios?"

"You faced a shady guy in an alley outside a night-club. He went after you with a switchblade because you'd stolen his girlfriend."

"Interesting," he said. "How come I wasn't the shady guy?"

"Well, in a way you were because you stole his girlfriend," she said.

He lifted a dark eyebrow. "You think I'm shady?"

She winced, realizing she'd gone too far. "This was all supposition. Crazy scenarios."

He nodded and took another sip. "Your first scenario was closest. I got into a fight with one of my foster fathers. He was beating my foster mother. I was thirteen. I had my fists. He had a beer bottle. My foster mother stayed. I was reassigned."

"Oh," she said, feeling the weight of that moment on her chest. "That's horrible."

He shrugged. "I survived my childhood. Not everyone does."

Emma couldn't help wondering what other scars he carried as a result of his upbringing. His effort to protect his foster mother had been heroic, but it hadn't been rewarded.

"Now I've frightened you," he said.

"No," she said quickly, shaking her head. "The thought of you going through that as a young man," she said, taking a quick breath. "It hurts."

"You have a tender heart. Your mother must have loved you well."

"She did the best she could," Emma said.

He wrinkled his brow slightly as he studied her and she felt compelled to explain. "You know how some people have a drinking problem?" she asked and he nodded. "She had…has a gambling problem."

He gave a slow nod. "That must have been tough."

"It was. Sometimes, it still is. But she doesn't live in Vegas anymore, so that's a good start." Emma felt uncomfortable beneath his scrutiny. "Enough of that. Where did you live before you came here? How are you dealing with our lack of humidity?"

"I had a long-term assignment in Minnesota, so I find this a nice change. I build houses for charity," he said.

"Really?" she said. "I'd wondered where you got those calluses on your hands."

"You noticed," he said, his dark eyes glinting with sensuality again.

Her breath stopped somewhere in her chest. "Yes, I guess I did," she reluctantly admitted.

"With my job, I strip away the excess. To balance that, I help build up. The combination keeps me balanced."

She was caught off guard that he would feel the need to build anything. Ruthlessness seemed to come so easily to him.

"Your face is so easy to read. You look surprised."

Irritated that he seemed to have the ability to read her thoughts, she frowned, blurting out her thoughts. "Yes, I'm surprised. I thought you were a descendant of one of those pirates we were discussing a moment ago. I wouldn't have thought someone who cuts the livelihood of dozens of people without batting an eye would be interested in any kind of charity." She was horrified that he provoked her so easily. "I can't believe I just said that to my boss."

Damien gave a low chuckle. "I was told you're discreet and respectful. Is this how you talked with your previous bosses?"

"No," she said, shaking her head. "I'm extremely discreet. Ask Alex Megalos or Max De Luca. And I've always been respectful. It's you," she said. "You bring it out in me. This is crazy. I shouldn't be here. Perhaps I shouldn't be your assistant." She rose to her feet because she couldn't stand embarrassing herself further.

"Sit down," he said. "Our dinner is on the way.

There's no need to waste a good meal just because you think I'm the kind of man to eat small children for breakfast."

When she didn't immediately comply, he lifted an eyebrow.

Sighing, she sank into her chair. "I wouldn't have said small children."

"Okay," he said. "Pretty assistants who tell the truth."

He'd just called her pretty. She felt a rush of pleasure. Heaven help her, this was crazy. She felt like a double agent. She'd prejudged Damien and he was scrambling her preconceptions of him. He was scrambling her hormones, too. She couldn't help wondering what it would be like to kiss him, and more.

The waiter served plates with presentations of gourmet fish and vegetables.

"Tell me more about you," he said. "You've made me curious."

She felt a clench and swallowed. "No need to be curious. I'm boring. Really boring."

"Favorite music," he countered.

She shrugged. "Maroon 5. Fergie. Michael Bublé. Van Morrison. Delbert McClinton."

"Van Morrison and Delbert McClinton," he echoed. "They don't fit."

"They're wonderful. They don't need to fit," she said, unable to squelch a smile.

He slowly lifted his lips in a return smile. "I like that."

He said it as if he found her interesting, perhaps

even alluring. The notion was as heady as three glasses of champagne, but Emma was determined not to sink further under his spell. Focus on the meal, she told herself. Not the man.

Two hours later, with the rainstorm at an end, Damien drove her home to her safe, modest apartment complex on the outskirts of town.

"Maintenance should repair that light," Damien said as he pulled to a stop just outside her apartment.

"I'll remind them tomorrow. Thank you for everything," she said. "Rescuing me in the rain, dinner. Thank you."

He cut the engine. "No problem. I'll walk you to your door."

Surprised, she shook her head. "Oh, that's not necessary. My door is in sight."

"I wouldn't be a gentleman if I didn't walk you to your door," he said.

"I thought we had established that you are a pirate, not a gentleman," she whispered.

He chuckled. "I'll walk you to your door," he said and got out of the car.

Emma sighed, wishing he weren't so attractive, wishing she weren't fascinated by him. He opened her passenger door and helped her out. His hand was strong, his body emanated a heat that tempted her to lean into him. She resisted the urge.

Feeling the light touch of his hand against the small of her back, she walked toward her door.

Rattled by his effect on her, she rummaged inside her purse for her key, finally locating it. She jammed it into the lock and turned. It took a few tries, but the lock finally released and her breath did the same.

She opened the door and turned to him. He was far too close. "Thank you again," she murmured, hyperaware of his tall, muscular form. "For everything."

"My pleasure," he said.

Eager to escape his effect on her, she scrambled forward, falling. She was certain she would land flat on her face, but Damien caught her. His strong arms wrapped around her, drawing her back against his muscular body. Her breath stopped in her chest.

Whoa, girl. Get yourself under control. She put her hand on one of his forearms to remove it, but was immediately distracted by the way his muscles rippled beneath her touch.

"Are you okay?" he asked, his mouth inches from her ear. The sound was low and intimate, filling her with instant heat.

Emma swallowed over her dry throat and nodded. "Yes, I'm fine. I just lost my balance." She deliberately stepped away from him and turned around. "Thanks," she said. "Again. I'll see you tomorrow."

"Not unless you have another ride," he corrected. "I can pick you up. Is seven-thirty okay?"

Emma blinked, remembering that her car was in the shop. "Oh, that's not necessary. I can—"

"Do you have another ride?" he cut in.

"Not at the moment, but—"

"Then there's no reason for you to reject my offer, is there?"

His gaze could melt steel, she thought, and heaven knew she wasn't steel. "I guess not. I'll see you in the morning. Good night," she said, closing the door and leaning against it, praying for sanity.

Four

The next morning, Damien barely pulled into the parking lot just outside Emma's apartment before she opened her door and strode toward him. As usual, she wore a suit, this time dark slacks and a jacket with a white blouse underneath. Her silky light brown hair was tugged away from her face in a ponytail, emphasizing her delicate features and the contrast of her rosy lips with her pale skin.

Although he suspected her pantsuit was designed to disguise her long legs and feminine curves, he could see the promise of her feminine form beneath the business attire…creamy pale shoulders and breasts with rosy tips just a shade darker than her lips, a slender waist, round inviting hips and long, lithe legs that would wrap around a man's waist while he…

Putting his car in park, he got out and opened the car door just as she reached the car. "Good morning."

"Good morning," she said, her gaze skimming over him in appreciation before she glanced away and slid into the car. "Thank you."

Returning to the driver's seat, he felt her assess him again before she turned her head. It was as if she had a hard time resisting the urge to look at him. The knowledge shot through him with a secret pleasure.

Emma Weatherfield intrigued him more with each passing day. He'd already intended to get information from her regarding Max De Luca and Alex Megalos. Now that he knew she was attracted to him, he'd decided to satisfy his curiosity and hers in bed. MD had no rules against fraternization among employees, so there was no reason the two of them couldn't indulge.

"Did you sleep well?" he asked, putting the car into gear and driving out of the parking lot.

She slid a quick sideways glance at him, but kept her head facing forward. "Well enough. I don't require a lot of sleep."

"Neither do I. That helps when you're a workaholic."

Her lips turned upward slightly. "I guess it would. Did you work more last night?"

"For a while," he said. "Several things need to be in place when a company is making employee cuts, such as employment counseling, instructions for how to apply for unemployment, recommended programs for additional training and relocation information. Despite your belief that I'm a ruthless pirate with no consideration for human beings, I know there's a right way and a wrong way to make cuts. The people giving the notices will also need to be properly trained."

She gave a slow, reluctant nod. "If the cuts are absolutely necessary, then the employees need as many resources at their disposal as possible." She grimaced. "I wouldn't want to be the one delivering the news."

"With your soft heart, it would be difficult. But there are ways that make it easier for the person being released."

"I can't imagine what," she said.

"A matter-of-fact approach that offers the laid-off employee a measure of dignity is vital. There are even days of the week to try to avoid."

"Terminations on Friday?" she asked. "To give people a chance to recover from the blow."

"No, Friday is the worst day. The terminated employee is left to stew all weekend without an opportunity to receive support."

"You almost make it sound humane," she said, meeting his gaze with her blue eyes.

"I'm not out to destroy everyone's lives," he said, and thought of Max De Luca. He was just determined to settle a score with the family who had destroyed his.

Thirty minutes later, after he and Emma had

arrived at the office, Damien was clarifying some figures with one of his assistants who worked from home when he heard a loud voice in the outer office.

"He's a hatchet man. He's going to destroy our lives. All I want is one minute with him," a man said.

Damien immediately rose from his desk and rushed to open the door. Emma stood with her back to him.

"Mr. Harding, Mr. Medici is busy right now. He cannot take visitors without an appoint—"

"Let me at him," the heavyset man said, his face gleaming with perspiration.

"I'm Mr. Medici," Damien said, stepping in front of Emma, motioning her aside.

The man immediately turned his attention to Damien. "You," he said, pointing his finger at Damien. "You're going to ruin us."

"I have no intention of ruining you. Excuse me, we haven't met. My name is Damien Medici. And you are?"

The man blinked as if he were surprised at Damien's politeness. "I'm, uh—I'm Fred Harding and I heard my name is on your termination list. How am I supposed to feed my family if you fire me?" he demanded, rubbing his damp brow with his hand.

"The termination list hasn't been finalized. However, if your employment is terminated, then you will be given at least two weeks pay with employment and training counseling, plus you'll receive assistance on how to apply for unemployment benefits provided by the government."

Fred Harding met Damien's gaze, then glanced away and took a deep breath. "It's still tough."

Damien nodded. "It is, but I have to tell you that plenty of people turn this situation into a good change. I don't know if your position is on the line, but you can be one of those people who make this kind of change a positive one for yourself."

"We'll see," Fred said, wearing a look of resignation.

"Good luck," Damien said, extending his hand.

Fred accepted the handshake. "Thanks. I'll take it."

After the man walked out of the office, Emma audibly exhaled. Damien glanced at her.

"I thought I was going to have to call security," she said.

"So did I," Damien said. "This is crazy. I'm speaking to a board member today. The VPs have wanted to keep the reorganization quiet, but the uncertainty is just making everyone nervous. Productivity will go into the toilet. This kind of thing can't be kept secret. An assistant, cafeteria worker or janitor could find out and start spreading false rumours."

"What are you saying?"

"I'm saying I want an announcement to go out to all MD employees that a reorganization is taking place and what the minimum severance package will be. The first cuts should be taken no less than three weeks after that."

Emma's eyes widened. "Isn't that fast?"

"According to Fred, apparently not fast enough," Damien said. "I'm also going to get security on this floor. I'm not going to have you providing guard duty. If you get even a hint of a threatening attitude in a call or e-mail, then I want you to let me know immediately. In the meantime, the open door policy is over. From now on, lock the door and you and I both will use a key. Do you understand?"

Emma bit her lip. "Yes."

Damien returned to his office and Emma sank into her chair. She hated to admit it, but she had begun to feel a bit frightened by Fred Harding's desperation before Damien had intervened. From her experience with her mother and her mother's lenders, she'd learned that desperate people used desperate measures to protect themselves. Or irrational ones.

She was amazed at how quickly Damien had diffused the man's blustering, threatening demeanor. He'd stepped right in front of her. What if Fred had been carrying a weapon? The possibility made her break into a cold sweat.

His protectiveness did something to her, sent her into a whirl of confusion. She tried to remember when a man had been so blatantly protective of her, but she couldn't. Sure, Alex and Max had gone to bat for her professionally, but she couldn't recall when a man had come to her defense so readily.

Determined to collect herself, she poured a cup of coffee and booted up her computer, her mind speeding a mile a minute. The image of his strong back and the low but authoritative voice he used with Harding was stamped on her brain.

Damien was the kind of man who made other men back down simply by virtue of being. He oozed confidence and clarity.

She took a sip of her coffee as he returned to the outer office. "Have you locked the door?"

She shook her head. "No, I—" She didn't want to show how much the incident had affected her. "I'll do it right away."

She rose and he snagged her wrist. "Are you okay?"

"It just took me off guard," she said. "It's not something that happens every day." She forced a little laugh. "Well, there was that one woman who stalked Alex for a while…" When he lifted his eyebrow, she rushed to correct herself. "Just kidding."

He looked into her eyes with deadly intent on his face. "I won't let anyone hurt you," he said.

A tremor shook her all the way to her toes. She knew with certainty that he could and would protect her. It tripped off wishes she'd kept locked away for years—the fantasy that a man would stick with her through the rough times.

He was talking about work, she reminded herself. It wasn't personal, but his hand wrapped around her wrist certainly felt that way. Maybe she secretly wanted it to be personal.

Appalled at the direction of her thoughts, she pulled her hand from his. "Hopefully, it won't be an issue."

He nodded. "It won't be," he said in a crisp voice. "If you're recovered—"

"I am," she quickly said, stiffening her spine against his effect on her.

"Then I'd like you to draft a letter for all of the employees informing them of the reorganization plans. After it's finalized, I'll discuss it with a board member and we should send it out no later than tomorrow."

Taken off guard yet again, she forced a nod. "Okay. I'll just need the details."

"I've already e-mailed them to you," he said. He walked to the outer office suite door and turned the lock.

The room immediately seemed to shrink, and as he walked closer to her, the oxygen seemed to disappear. Was she trapped in here with the devil or the man in her fantasies?

"I'll be on the phone for the next hour, but if you run into any problems, don't hesitate to interrupt."

Fighting the sense that she was aiding and abetting a slasher, Emma constructed the letter and revised it twice after suggestions from Damien. Her stomach remained in a knot the entire morning. She knew she had to inform Max or Alex about this latest development, but the earliest she could manage it would be during her lunch hour.

Scooting out of her office a few minutes early, she left a note for Damien and rushed to Max's office, but he wasn't there. She tried Alex, but he was also out of the office.

Fretting, she went outside for a walk and called Max's personal cell phone number as he'd asked. When the call went immediately to voice mail, her frustration spiked. Her lunch hour nearly over, she visited Max's office once more, only to find him still gone. She swung by Alex's with matching luck and, despairing, headed for the elevator.

The doors opened and Alex appeared, smiling when he saw her. "Emma, what a nice surprise to see you. Mallory's been after me to make sure you're attending that charity gala she's planning in a few weeks. She's determined to hook you up even though I told her that you're the most content single woman I know."

"Mallory's a sweetheart. I've got the charity gala on my calendar." Emma glanced at her watch. Her time was running out. "Do you have a minute?"

"Sure. What do you need?"

"In your office?"

Alex must have picked up on her nervousness because his expression sobered. "Of course," he said and led the way to his office. "Marlena, hold my calls for the next few minutes," he said to his assistant. As soon as Emma stepped inside his private office, he closed the door. "News?"

She nodded, feeling a knot form in her throat. Her sense of loyalty was torn. On the one hand, she owed Alex and Max her college education and her future. On the other hand, Damien was her boss and he believed he was doing the best thing for MD.

"He's going to the board. He's determined to send a letter to all employees informing them of the impending layoffs and the minimum compensation they can expect. I think he wants to make the first cuts within a few weeks."

Alex stared at her in shock. "I didn't think he would move this quickly."

"I've never seen anyone so focused. He has very specific ideas about how the layoffs should be announced and conducted, down to the day of the week."

"Which day?" he asked.

"Not Friday," she said. "He seems to prefer Tuesday or Wednesday to give people a chance to access support services."

"Unless we find a way to stop him, he's going to change the entire culture of the company," Alex said grimly. "How can MD continue to progress with all these cuts? Granted the stock dividends are down, but whose aren't? A panic cut is going to bite into our chances for future profits."

Emma couldn't disagree. "Unless you can find a way to get someone on the board to agree with you…" She felt duplicitous even saying such a thing. "I'm sorry I don't have better news."

"No," Alex said. "You did what you were supposed to do. Keep us posted."

Nodding, she left his office. She'd thought she could do this job without it bothering her, but now she felt ripped in half, dirty almost. Distracted as she walked down the hallway, she pushed the button for the elevator. Seconds later, the doors opened and she found herself face-to-face with Damien.

Damien felt the slightest twist in his gut at the expression on Emma's face. Guilt, he saw it in her clouded blue eyes, her eyebrows knitted with worry. Poor thing, she made a terrible double agent.

"Miss Weatherfield," he said, because he always addressed staff formally when in public. "What a surprise to meet you here on the executive floor."

"I—uh, I ran into Mr. Megalos and he wanted to discuss the invitation his wife had extended to me for a charity gala in a few weeks," she said.

He nodded. The truth was she'd run upstairs to tell Alex what Damien was planning to do. As if Alex or Max could change it. Damien knew they couldn't. "What charity gala is this?"

"Uh, I believe it's for cancer research. It's on a Saturday, the week after next."

"I've intended to participate in a charity drive since I've been in Vegas, but I've been busy. Perhaps you would allow me to escort you," he said.

Her jaw dropped and she moved her mouth, but no sound came out. She cleared her throat. "I—uh—"

"Unless you already have an escort," he said.

"No, but—"

"But?" he echoed.

"I may be helping Mallory, so I wouldn't be able to give you the attention you deserve," she said.

"I'm not high-maintenance," he said with a

slight smile. "I can look after myself once we arrive. Date?"

She bit her lip and looked at him with a frightened expression. "I guess so. I'll uh, head back to the office, Da—" She broke off. "Mr. Medici."

He gave a short nod and watched her step quickly into the elevator. The doors closed and he stood there for a moment. He wasn't surprised that Emma was reporting to her previous managers. Heaven knew, this had happened to him many times before.

Her guilt was actually a promising sign. It meant he had begun to chip away at her loyalty. It meant she felt conflicted, which meant she didn't see him as a total sonovabitch out to destroy MD.

It meant he could possibly win her over to his side. She had the information he needed to take down Max De Luca. Emma was highly intelligent and had a knack for reading people. Her calm attitude encouraged disclosure, and Damien was certain she knew secrets about both her bosses. Secrets he intended to learn. He would use any method to gain her assistance, including seduction. In fact, seducing Emma could very well be the best side benefit of taking this assignment.

Five

Emma spent the entire weekend cleaning and re-cleaning her apartment, but she still felt scummy. She suspected this was some sort of Lady Macbeth-esque response to her subterfuge at work. She had a hard time looking herself in the eye in the mirror, let alone meeting Damien's gaze on Monday morning.

With the doors locked, she was even more aware of him than usual. Was she imagining it or was his body brushing hers more often? Did he notice how his hand covered hers on the doorknob?

She found herself desperate to turn down her internal heat and maintain a business attitude toward him. Why did her mind persist in imagining him shirtless with his chest pressed against hers, his strong arms wrapped around her? Why did she find herself forcing her gaze from staring at his mouth, wondering how his lips would feel on hers?

None of this made sense. She'd been assistant to two very attractive and powerful men before. Why did Damien affect her this way? She felt as if she had suddenly gone man-crazy, except her lunacy was very specific.

Thank goodness, a distraction appeared. She grasped at it. The salon offering her a full makeover called to schedule an appointment since they'd had a cancellation for Monday. During her pedicure, Mallory called and set Emma up with a date on Tuesday night.

Emma didn't care if the guy was an axe murderer. She just needed someone to get her mind off her boss. Staring into the mirror at the end of her make-over, she was stunned at the transformation. With a few sunny streaks and her hair styled in a sexy shoulder-length cut, smoky eyes and plump lips, she actually looked hot. Gulp. Although she wasn't sure she could duplicate the job the experts had done on her, she would give it her best try since she was meeting her blind date for cocktails and dinner.

The following day, she walked into the office with an extra little bag that contained her cosmetics and change of clothes for her date. She heard Damien on the phone, but he finished before she had a chance to discern anything about his conversation.

He entered the outer office and nodded at her. "Good morning," he said as he reached to lock the door.

"Good—" She noticed the white bandage around his left hand. "Oh, no, what happened?"

He shrugged. "A minor accident last night. It was teen night for Rebuilding Vegas. The idea was to teach practical construction skills to local kids."

Emma grimaced. "Sounds like it was dangerous."

"Someone dropped a saw from the second floor. I tried to catch it so no one would get hurt."

"But you got hurt."

"A few stitches. I'll live."

"Bet they offered pain medication, and you wouldn't take it," she ventured.

His lips twitched. "It wasn't necessary."

"Of course it wasn't," she said. "You probably need to chew glass in order to be happy."

He gave a low chuckle. "You're in a snappy mood today. Any reason why?"

"Not really," she said, thankful that she had a date tonight. A date that would hopefully take her mind off Damien. Heaven help her, the man was burning up her dreams and fantasies. She could only hope that whoever she met tonight would be able to distract her.

He narrowed his eyes. "Your hair looks different," he said.

"Very observant," she said. "I got it cut last night."

"That's not all. There's something else."

"The hairstylist added a few highlights," she said, uncomfortable under his intent gaze.

"Nice," he said. "But it looked good before. Ah, this was your makeover. I thought you weren't going until Wednesday."

He'd remembered, she thought, and her discomfort grew. "They had an opening."

"They changed your hair. What else?"

She cleared her throat. "Just chose a couple new outfits for me to wear and some different makeup. The makeup is more appropriate for after work. I have some for to—" She broke off, not wanting to reveal any more. "I'm sure there are more important topics for us to discuss. Did you want me to gather any reports for you today?"

Feeling him watch her in silence, she fought the urge to fidget.

"Yes. As a matter of fact, I do. I want to do a closer study on the San Diego resorts."

"I'll get them for you," she said. "You had mentioned you hadn't wanted to talk to any of the VPs involved with the departments you're studying. Should I assume you prefer to take the same approach with this one?"

He shook his head. "No. As a matter of fact, I want to talk with Alex or Max, but I'll arrange that myself."

Frustration rippled through her. "As you wish. Is there anything else?"

"Not right now," he said.

Without realizing it, she released that sigh she'd been holding as she turned away.

"You're displeased," he said.

"I'm sorry. I didn't mean to come across that way," she said, sliding into her seat, damning herself for giving away her emotions. She really was supposed to be much better at conveying calm. She always had been before Damien had arrived.

"Any chance you can give me an honest answer to an honest question?" he asked, his bandaged hand resting on his lean hip.

"Of course I can," she said.

"Why did you sigh just a moment ago when I told you I have nothing else for you to do right now?"

Darn it. She should have held her breath. She reluctantly met his gaze. "If I'd known you were going to give me so little work to do, then I would have taken an extra online course this semester. You don't want me to make your coffee. You don't want me to set up appointments. I feel guilty spending so much time twiddling my thumbs."

His lips twitched. "A first," he said. "You're upset because I'm not giving you more work to do."

"Well, would you be happy?" she asked, her courage stemming from frustration.

He paused, looking at her in silence. "You have a good point. Okay, fine. I want you to take a look at the performance, expenses, employees—everything in connection with the San Diego resorts. And I want you to make a recommendation for job cuts."

She dropped her jaw. "Excuse me?"

"Yes. I'd like your recommendations within two days."

"Two days?"

"Do you have a problem with that? You've been trained to read a profit and loss statement. Despite the fact that you're an executive assistant, you've earned a degree in business. I think this assignment will help you gain some perspective."

She worked her mouth, then closed it and cleared her throat. "No. No problem. Thank you very much." She watched him walk into his office, the V-shape of his body distracting her. Until he closed his door.

Emma shook her head. *Crap.* This was what happened when she let down her guard. Damien now expected her to give him suggestions on his hatchet job. How was she supposed to do that?

Hours later, after skipping her lunch break, Emma felt as if her eyeballs were spinning. She had begun her assessment of the San Diego properties and tentatively put an X beside a few positions only to mark out her original X.

Just as she made the decision to cut a position, she began to think about the person in that position and how they would feel about having their job cut, what kind of family they supported. Several scenarios for each person came to mind, all of them making her feel like the Grinch.

Absently glancing at the clock, she was shocked by the late hour. She was supposed to meet Mallory's setup guy in thirty minutes. She had to stop working. Even though she'd essentially made zero progress, she had to stop. Hopefully a good night of sleep would provide her with a clear mind tomorrow so she could properly perform this assignment. In the meantime, she needed to remember how to make her eyes smoky, she thought as she grabbed her cosmetic bag and headed for the restroom.

Twenty minutes of swearing and perspiration later, she'd changed into her makeover outfit of a little black dress that showed a bit of cleavage and clung to her curves and returned to her desk to turn off her computer.

Hearing a sound in the outer office, Damien glanced away from his laptop, noting the tightness in his shoulders and neck. The sensations weren't unusual. He'd been known to go for hours completely focused on his task. He'd learned, however, that even he should take short breaks. He opened his door and glanced into the outer office, stopping short.

The sight of a woman wearing high heels and a body-skimming black dress that hugged her curves—in particular the backside currently facing him—took him off guard.

"Emma?"

She whirled around, her eyes wide and her plump lips parted in surprise. "Oops. I didn't hear you."

He stared at her face, taking in her sexy blue eyes and luscious mouth, pink and tempting. "Special occasion?"

She shrugged her shoulders, drawing his attention to her generous, creamy breasts. "One of Mallory's setups," she said with a lopsided smile. "We'll see."

"One," he echoed. "There's more than one?"

"That's up to me," she with a slight grimace as she grabbed her purse and a plastic bag. "She's very determined. She says crazy things like I'm an undiscovered treasure. Nice of her," she said, clearly embarrassed. "I should go. I'll see you in the morning."

He nodded. "Yeah. Have a good time."

"Hope so," she said with a smile and walked out of the office, her hips drawing his attention. He thought about putting his hands on her hips, taking her breasts into his hands and mouth, sliding between her thighs and feeling her femininity close around him like the most intimate, wet embrace.

Feeling himself grow hard, he was surprised at the force of his reaction to her. Plus, for some reason, he felt damn annoyed that she was seeing another man tonight. He was usually as detached about his sex life as he was about his professional life. He chose his partners for their ability to please him, and he'd never had a problem providing a woman with complete sexual satisfaction.

The truth was, however, that he tended to choose a more sophisticated woman than Emma, a woman who would respond to his needs and the passion of the moment and be satisfied with a brief affair, with perhaps an expensive trinket as a souvenir.

Despite her professional demeanor, he could

feel her curiosity about him growing stronger every day. She was drawn to him, he could see it in her eyes and hear it in her breath when he stepped close to her. He couldn't help wondering how hot he could make Emma, how she would feel in his arms, in his bed.

Damien gave a mental check of his calendar and a plan quickly formed in his mind. A surge of anticipation and satisfaction slid through him. Emma Weatherfield would be in his bed by the end of next week.

After a date where she could not stop comparing her setup guy to Damien, Emma felt like banging her head against the wall. Any wall, but especially her office wall because the next morning she found to her great disappointment that the setup date had provided her with zero distraction. A baby-faced blond sales rep for a paper company, Doug Caldwell had been full of smiles and eager to please. He reminded Emma of a puppy where Damien reminded her of a mysterious predator.

In addition, today she faced the ugly task of recommending which employees should be let go from their positions. By Thursday afternoon, she felt as if she may as well be playing Pin the Tail on the Donkey with the organizational chart. She hoped against hope that Damien was too busy and would forget to ask for her recommendations.

As if on cue, he opened the door to his office and shot her a look of inquiry. "Ready to give me your list?"

Dragging herself into his office with her final draft, she instinctively held the paper behind her back. "I feel I should warn you that I don't have your experience, so my recommendations may not be as helpful as you or I would like them to be."

He waved his hand. "Let me see them."

She reluctantly surrendered the paper to him and clenched her teeth as she waited for his response. He glanced at the paper, then at her. "Where are the rest of the recommended cuts?"

"Those are all," she said and cleared her throat.

"Two?" he said in astonishment. "You recommended two cuts?"

"Yes. Two," she said.

He rubbed his hand over his face and chuckled. "You do know that if you were ever promoted into management you would need to be able to fire an employee."

Her stomach knotted. "Yes."

"What was your major?"

"Business administration," she said.

He shook his head.

"But I think my natural skills are better in the areas of organizing and reducing expenditures through practical economic measures."

"Turn out the lights when you leave the room," he said.

"Yes. No new hires before you begin downsizing. No pay raises for executives. With the actual properties, initiating new incentive programs and perks for repeat customers. Since most of our properties are top-of-the-line luxury resorts, finding a way to lure new guests during the off-season would give new customers a taste of what it's like to stay at an MD resort. Once they've experienced it, they will want to repeat it."

He gave a slow nod. "Have you talked about these ideas with your former bosses?"

She shook her head. "I thought it would have been considered presumptuous."

"Do you want to advance at MD?"

"Of course I do," she said, unable to keep a trace of indignation from her voice.

"You underestimate yourself. I suggest you put together a report with your suggestions." He shrugged and sat down. "That's all."

She stared at him with an open mouth for several seconds before he raised his eyebrows at her. "Did you have a question?"

Blinking, she pulled herself together and backed away. "No." Returning to her desk, she fought a wave of confusion. Had Damien Medici just offered career guidance? Had he paid her a compliment? She felt a rush of pleasure. He certainly hadn't gushed, but he hadn't criticized her ideas, either.

Sinking into her seat, she was puzzled. If he thought she underestimated herself, why didn't he allow her to do more for him?

At the end of the day on Friday, Damien called her

into his office again. "What time should I pick you up tomorrow night?"

"Tomorrow night?" she echoed, confused.

"For the charity gala," he said.

She'd hoped he'd forgotten. "Oh, that. I'm going to volunteer, so I actually need to be there early. I can just meet—"

He shook his head. "No. It won't be a problem. I can pick you up early. What time works best for you?"

Emma barely resisted the urge to squirm. Showing up with Damien would be like linking herself with the enemy. She narrowed her eyes, wondering if he were doing this precisely to make her squirm. But what choice did she have? "Five-thirty should be fine," she said, preparing herself for disapproving expressions from the De Luca and Megalos couples. "I promised Mallory I would assist with any last-minute problems. I understand if you want to bow out since my attention will be divided."

"I wouldn't think of it," he said, his dark eyes glinting with determination.

She swallowed a sigh. "I'll see you then," she said, and turned.

"One other thing," he said, and she turned back around.

"Yes?"

"I've been asked to review a property in South Beach that MD wants to purchase."

She nodded. "Yes?"

"You and I are going there next week to review the

property in person," he said, as if he was informing her that she would be joining him at a business luncheon in a diner.

She stared at him in disbelief.

"You need to call my private jet. We'll leave on Wednesday and return on Sunday. I'll make the hotel reservations under a different name so they won't know they're being observed."

She nodded, stunned by the news, but determined to keep her composure. "Okay. You'll give me the number," she said. "For your private jet?"

He scribbled it on a piece of paper and handed it to her. "There it is. Pack like a tourist. Swimsuits, dresses. No business attire required." He handed her a credit card. "Buy everything you need and put it on my card."

"Oh, that's not necessary. I have dresses. I have a swimsuit," she said, remembering she'd bought one at a discount store three years ago…or was it four?

"We're going in disguise," he said. "I'll book adjoining suites, but we'll be a couple. Use my card. I want you to dress the part. Dress like my woman would."

Six

Although she'd bought it on sale, Emma spent more than she would have preferred on a black full-length gown with a discreet halter top that plunged in the back. Stepping into kitten-heel sandals, she grabbed the small beaded clutch she'd bought at her favorite thrift store and checked the mirror once more. With smoky eyes, shiny lip gloss and her hair swinging free to her shoulders, she almost didn't recognize herself. She looked almost glamorous.

She hoped she didn't look as if she were trying too hard. For the fifth time, she thought about ditching the dress, scrubbing off her makeup and calling in sick. Calling in sick, however, was something she'd never done in her life, and she refused to start now.

The doorbell rang, and she nearly jumped out of her skin. Taking a deep breath to calm herself, she walked to the door and opened it. She looked at Damien, dark and dangerous in a black tux. The breath she'd just taken stuck in her throat.

He seemed taller, she thought, and the way he looked at her made her stomach dip and sway.

"You look beautiful," he said, extending his hand.

"Thank you," she said, reluctant to take his hand, fearing she might get burned just by the sensation of his skin on hers. Crazy, she thought, and took his hand. "You look very nice, too," she said in a brisk tone that sounded at odds with her compliment, even to herself.

She was thankful the sun was still shining to help her ward off any forbidden fantasies her mind might conjure. She blinked at the sight of a driver holding the door to a limo. "I didn't expect—"

"I couldn't have you crawling out of a Ferrari when you're dressed for a ball."

He helped her into the limo and followed her inside.

"Thank you," she murmured, feeling like Cinderella. She'd ridden in a limo before, but she'd been taking notes from Alex Megalos during the drive.

"Something to drink?" he asked, waving his hand toward the bar.

"Oh, no, thank you," she said and took another deep breath, inhaling a hint of his cologne. The silence inside the limo was deafening. She supposed she should try to make small talk, but she was too aware of the fact that his thigh was mere inches from hers.

"Have you had a chance to go shopping for our trip?" he asked, adjusting one of the cuffs of his shirt.

Distracted by the contrast of his white shirt against his tanned skin, she again noticed the bandage around his hand. "How is your hand?"

"I don't pay much attention to it. The stitches will be out next week."

"Good," she said.

"You didn't answer my question," he said with a hint of amusement in his deep voice.

She met his gaze. "Shopping," she echoed and shook her head. "No. I haven't had a chance. Maybe tomorrow."

"You don't sound very enthusiastic," he said.

"I'm not comfortable using company money for my wardrobe, especially when I know job cuts are on the way."

"It's not Megalos-De Luca money. It's my company's money, and trust me, we're not hurting." He shook his head. "I'm surprised. Most women would jump at the chance."

Most women weren't her. "With my background, being thrifty was necessary for my survival. You should understand that from your own experiences."

"True," he said. "But I can loosen the purse strings when necessary."

"I'm definitely not at your level and I always feel as if I need to be prepared—" She broke off, not wanting to reveal the rest.

"Prepared for what?" he asked.

"The worst," she said.

He nodded. "Something we have in common. Who knows," he said, his gaze falling over her with sensual curiosity. "There may be more."

As Emma and Damien entered the grand ballroom at the casino, Emma caught the expression of shock and confusion on Mallory's face.

"Emma," Alex Megalos's wife said, clearly searching for words.

"Hi, Mallory. Have you met Damien? He's working for Megalos-De Luca. Apparently he hasn't had a chance to get out much since he's been in Vegas, so he asked if he could come with me and drop a bundle at the gala tonight."

Mallory blinked, still confused, but game. "How generous of you, Mr. Medici. You may not remember me. I'm—"

"How could I forget you," Damien said, taking her hand and lifting it to his lips. "You are the enchanting wife of Alex Megalos."

Mallory smiled, but she didn't appear to buy his charm. "Thank you. And thank you for contributing to the success of our charity gala tonight. Your donation will mean a lot to us. I hope you don't mind if I borrow Emma for a bit. We have some last-minute tasks," she said and grabbed Emma's hand.

"Just make sure you return her to me," he said, looking at Emma.

"Oh, count on it," Mallory said and pulled Emma away.

Mallory dragged Emma across the ballroom and into a back room. She pushed Emma against the wall, her eyes wide with consternation. "What the—"

"He insisted on joining me. I'd just been in Alex's office telling him—" She shrugged "—giving a report and Mr. Medici showed up at the elevator just as I was leaving. I tried to discourage him, but no luck."

Mallory shook her head. "Wow. Do you think he's interested in you?"

"Oh, no," Emma said, feeling herself grow warm. "I'm sure he's got another agenda. He's that kind of man," she said, giving voice to what was always in the back of her mind.

Mallory's eyebrows shot upward. "Sounds like you're getting to know him pretty well."

Emma winced. "Not really. Not as much as I'm supposed—" She broke off again, because she didn't know how much Alex had told his sweet bride. "So," she said as brightly as she could. "Tell me how I can help."

Mallory frowned. "Are you okay?"

"Uh-huh," Emma said, quickly composing herself. She wondered why it was so easy with Mallory and so difficult with Damien. "Are you?"

Mallory gave a start. "Well, yes. So how was your date last week?"

"He was very nice."

Mallory's face fell. "Okay, I get your message.

We'll move along to bachelor number two. Is next Tuesday good?"

"Let's try the week after. Next week is busy for me," she said, her heart skipping a beat when she thought about the trip to Miami. Should she tell Max or Alex? Why did she feel so conflicted? Emma shook off her craziness. "I'm waiting. How can I help?"

Mallory paused for a moment, then nodded. "We got some last-minute big rollers and they've totally messed up my seating arrangements. Help."

Emma smiled. Now she was on familiar ground. "Give me the list."

Damien took a seat at the bar and ordered a scotch. Struck by the sumptuous luxury of the ballroom, he couldn't help remembering that lean time when he'd been declared an independent child and lived hand to mouth. Even before his father had died, his family had never been wealthy. They'd never owned their own home.

He caught sight of an advertisement on the wall for Megalos-De Luca proudly announcing their charitable contributions and felt bitterness roil through him like acid. The irony of the De Luca family being the least bit connected to anything charitable was a joke.

When Damien thought about how the De Lucas had cheated his grandfather out of the Medicis' beloved estate, the fire roared inside him again. The once solid family had scattered, and were still scattered. One of his uncles had committed suicide, an aunt betrothed to a prince had been dumped. Children had been orphaned. Someone had to make this right. That someone was him.

Emma caught his eye as she passed him by. She glided with confidence through the ballroom and smiled at the waitstaff in a much friendlier, more open way than she did him. That fact stuck in his craw. He wondered what it would be like if she were that open with him. He felt an odd growl in his gut and watched her through narrowed eyes. Why should it bother him?

He would have her. In every way a man could have a woman, he was determined to have her, and he would. He took another swallow of whiskey and felt the burn all the way down. Not only would she give him herself, she would give him all the information he wanted to make Max De Luca pay.

"What do you want to drink?" Damien asked her as he played blackjack at the charity high-roller table.

Emma noticed he was winning against the house. No surprise there. "I don't drink very often. I'm always the DD."

"No need tonight," he said. "A limo will safely transport you home."

She met his gaze and felt the frisson of something between them. How could that be? He was the devil. The obscenely wealthy devil and she, well, she was just Emma. "Something with peach schnapps," she admitted in a low voice, leaning toward him. "A lady's drink."

"Got it," he said and turned to the waitress in the ultra-short black dress. "Sex on the Beach," he said. "Water for me."

Emma frowned at him and he lifted his hands. "Hey, I'm gambling," he said. "I have to keep my head."

"Does winning matter that much?" she asked as the dealer shuffled the deck for another game. "Since the money goes to charity anyway."

He gave a low, dirty chuckle and shook his head. "Winning always matters," he said.

Sipping her fruity drink, Emma watched him rack up the chips until it appeared he'd accumulated a mountain of them. "I'll cash them in now," he finally said to the dealer and rose from the table.

"That's a lot of money," she said after he cashed in his chips and collected a receipt for charity.

"It's deductible." He shot her a sideways glance. "Plus I had to deliver on your promise to Mallory that I was going to drop a bundle."

Emma fought a twist of discomfort. It had been presumptuous of her to promise Damien's money. On the other hand, it had been presumptuous of Damien to insist on attending the event with her.

"Don't worry. I know you were protecting me," he said.

"Protecting you," she echoed in disbelief. "Why would I do that? Why would you of all people need protection?"

"Because Mallory Megalos wanted to scratch off my face."

"I can't believe you would be concerned by Mallory."

"I'm not. I learned long ago not to rely on anyone's opinion but my own, but it's good to know you were looking out for my best interests."

His comment was so far from the truth it was all she could do not to correct him. She remembered, however, that it was part of her goal to get him to trust her so that she could get information for Alex and Max.

Managing a tight smile, she glanced at the buffet and moved toward it. "After all that gaming, I bet you're hungry. See anything you like?"

"Yes, I do," he said in a low, intimate voice that snagged her attention. She looked at him and his gaze was focused totally on her. She felt a rush of heat. "The food does look delicious," she said, attempting to distract him.

His gaze didn't budge. "Delicious," he said, but he clearly wasn't referring to the food.

Emma felt as if she needed a fan.

A hand brushed her back and she turned to find Doug Caldwell, her blind date from the previous night. "It's good to see you. Mallory didn't tell me you were coming tonight."

"Probably because I was going to be helping her. Damien Medici, this is Doug Caldwell."

"Good to meet you," Doug said. "You don't mind if I borrow Emma for a dance, do you?"

Wearing an inscrutable expression, Damien remained silent for a long, uncomfortable moment.

Doug gave an uneasy laugh. "Just one," he promised. "Unless you're engaged."

"Of course not," Emma replied. "Excuse me and enjoy the buffet."

Inwardly fuming, she allowed Doug to guide her onto the dance floor.

"Who is that guy, anyway?" Doug asked.

"My boss," she said and watched him lift his eyebrows. "Well, not exactly my boss. I've been assigned to work with him while he performs a service for the company."

"He seemed territorial about you. Maybe he's interested in more than business."

"Oh, no. He's just one of those men who come across as intimidating the first time you meet him." And the second time, and the third....

"If that's the case and you're up for it, I'd like to take you to dinner next weekend."

She wasn't, but she also didn't want Doug to think anything romantic was happening between her and Damien. "I wish I could, but I'm going to be out of town next weekend."

"Then how about the weekend after that?"

"My schedule is tight right now, but maybe we could meet for cocktails again."

"I was hoping for something more," he said.

"I'm sorry. I'm taking some classes, so I'm very busy."

He gave a put-upon sigh. "Okay, I'll take what I

can get. Cocktails on Saturday night in two weeks. Don't forget."

She nodded and the music stopped, saving her from further discussion. Just a few feet after parting with Doug, she felt a warm, strong hand close over hers and looked up to find Damien.

"Hello," she said, taken off guard, distracted by the sensation of his closeness.

"My turn," he said and as another song began, he pulled her into his arms.

She quickly glanced over her shoulder, wondering who was watching. "Are you sure this is a good idea? I wouldn't want to start rumors."

"I've never been bothered by rumors. Are you worried that all the MD people are going to think you're making nice to the hatchet man?"

She gasped at his bluntness. "I've always made it a practice to keep my professional relationships completely professional."

"You're telling me you weren't attracted to your previous bosses," he said.

Feeling his crisp tuxedo jacket beneath her hand, she couldn't help wondering how his naked shoulder would feel. How would his skin feel? She tried to squelch her curiosity. "Well, I didn't mean to say they're not attractive men. They are and they're very good men, but my relationships with my bosses have always been work-focused."

"But they didn't affect you like I do."

Her breath stopped in her throat. She swallowed hard.

"You're not denying it," he said.

Emma grasped for her usual rational, cautious mind. "Just because there's some sort of odd, fleeting, marginal chemistry doesn't mean anyone should act on it."

He lifted a dark eyebrow. "Marginal, fleeting," he echoed.

"Exactly," she said, wishing her heart wasn't racing so fast. "Chemistry is just chemistry."

"One of the things I noticed about MD is that they don't have a policy against employees fraternizing with each other."

"Yes, but fraternization just muddies the water." And the mind, she thought, determined to keep her own mind clear as the sound of a saxophone oozed through the room.

"You don't need to be afraid," he said.

"What do you mean?"

"I would never force you. I've never had to force a woman." He leaned closer, brushing his mouth just an inch from her ear. "You would come to me."

Fighting his knee-weakening effect on her, she pulled back. "I'm not that easily seduced," she whispered.

"I never said you were easy," he told her. "I just said there was something between us. Not the usual attraction. At some point, we're going to need to explore it to get past it. We may as well enjoy it."

Part of her may have felt he was right, but she refused to give into it. She stepped backward. "We won't have an affair. I won't come to you. Count on it," she said and turned away. Florida was going to be oh-so-great, she thought as she stalked toward the bar to get a bottle of water. She might as well be walking through hell.

Later that evening, Mallory Megalos announced the winners of the raffle items. One person won a vacation to Greece, another to Italy, another to France. Someone else won a sports car. Emma wasn't paying attention to the names of the winners because she hadn't entered any of the drawings. With her mother's problems, she never gambled.

"The winner of the Tesla Roadster, with taxes absorbed by an anonymous donor, is Emma Weatherfield," Mallory announced.

"Emma!" a coworker exclaimed.

She snapped her head around to meet the manager's excited gaze. "Excuse me?"

"You just won a car."

Emma frowned. "That's not possible. I didn't enter. I didn't buy any raffle tickets…"

"Emma, you won a Tesla Roadster," Mallory announced from the platform. "Come and get the keys."

Confused, she shot a quick glance around her and walked toward the platform. "I'm sorry," she whispered to Mallory. "There must be some mistake. I didn't buy any tickets."

"Well, someone must have entered your name,"

Mallory said, lifting the ticket with her name scrawled on it. "This is the coolest car in the world. I would be jealous if Alex didn't let me drive his."

"How—"

"Congratulations, Emma Weatherfield!" Mallory said.

Still disbelieving, she reluctantly accepted the keys. "Thank you. Thank you so much." Glancing into the crowd, she caught sight of Damien. He wore a mysterious yet knowing expression on his face, and she immediately suspected he was behind her win. She also knew she couldn't accept the car.

Seven

Emma pressed the keys into Damien's hand as he assisted her into the waiting limo.

Following her inside the car, he looked down at the keys. "What's this?"

"Those are the keys to the car that you won from the raffle tonight," she said.

"Couldn't be mine. I didn't enter the raffle." He extended his arm to drop them into her lap. "I'm not big on counting on luck."

"I didn't enter the raffle, either. The tickets were too expensive. Twenty-five dollars each," she said, her frustration rising. "It had to be you."

"Why?" he asked. "Don't you have other friends and

admirers? Couldn't someone else have just decided to buy several tickets and put names of friends on them?"

Emma studied his face, her gaze sliding to the scar. The mark of imperfection was incredibly sexy to her and the fact that she knew he'd gotten that scar protecting someone got to her every time she looked at his face. She tried to read his expression, but it was inscrutable.

Narrowing her eyes, she shook her head. "Something about this is fishy. I almost feel as if I should give the car back."

He lifted his eyebrows. "I wasn't aware that your current mode of transportation was in such great condition that you could throw away a brand-new car."

"Well, a roadster isn't very practical," she countered.

"True. It's only a two-seater. You don't have children, do you?"

"You know I don't," she said. "But there's also not a lot of space for packing things in the trunk."

He nodded. "You take a lot of driving trips?"

"Not really," she admitted. "But I do visit my mother in Missouri sometimes."

"I hear it will go two hundred and twenty miles on one charge," he said casually.

"I know all about the specs. I was in charge of making sure Alex Megalos got his the first possible second."

"Nice company car," Damien said in a tone brimming with disapproval.

"The company didn't pay for the car," she quickly

told him. "He paid for it out of his own money. Which leads me back to my original point. I didn't buy a raffle ticket, so how could I have won it?"

"Apparently someone entered for you," he said. "Someone wanted you to have the car."

She frowned, crossing her arms over her chest. "I'm not comfortable with this at all."

"Many people aren't comfortable with change," he said.

She glanced at him again, wondering if he was talking about the changes that would be taking place within MD. Or other possible personal changes. Her gaze dipped involuntarily to his mouth and she felt an unbidden rush of warmth. She forced her gaze away, but was still aware of him, the scent of his cologne, the closeness of his body. His hip was mere inches from hers. She glimpsed his long legs in her peripheral vision. His hand rested on the leather seat just above her shoulder.

He confused her. If he was trying to buy her loyalty or something else, wouldn't he have taken credit for entering her in the lottery and held it over her head?

She turned toward him, looking up into his face. "If some mystery person had bought a lottery ticket on your behalf and you'd won, what would you do?"

"I don't have personal experience. No one has ever bought a lottery ticket on my behalf," he said in a dry tone. "I've had offers for free headstone markers—"

"You haven't received death threats?" she asked, feeling a chill.

"Too many to count, but that wasn't your original question. If I won a car and liked it, I would keep it. If I'd won this car and didn't want it, I would sell it because the demand for the car is so high."

"Sell it," she echoed. "That sounds almost mercenary considering I got it because of a charity drive."

"If you sell it, you could buy yourself a new car and put the rest of the cash in the bank."

The idea tempted her. "If I bought a good used car…"

"I didn't suggest you go that far," he said. "If you insist on selling it, the least you can do is get yourself new, reliable transportation."

She threw him a sideways glance. "Considering you didn't enter the lottery for me, you seem to have a strong opinion."

"You asked my opinion."

True, she thought.

"Do you like the car?"

"I haven't even driven it yet. I was told it could be delivered as soon as Monday. I don't even know how to drive the thing."

"I'm sure the person who delivers it will be glad to show you." He paused a moment. "You could wait to make your decision after you've taken the car for a ride. It's often wise not to judge before you've had a chance to evaluate the car for yourself."

His gaze held hers and she couldn't help comparing him to a fast, dangerous sports car. *What kind of ride would he give?* Emma should have been horrified by the direction of her thoughts, but when he lowered his fingers to brush back a strand of her hair, all she could do was stare.

He lowered his head and she held her breath. *Was he going to kiss her?* She should turn away, push him away, but she couldn't move.

"It's your call, Emma. No one is going to force you. You can give the keys back before, or you can take a ride and decide for yourself."

His voice was low and intimate, the same way he would talk to a lover. She felt an ache start in her breasts and slide lower into her nether regions. She couldn't remember feeling this aroused by a man, and he'd barely touched her. What if he'd kissed her? Would she be able to resist him? Would she want to?

The limo pulled to a stop, distracting her. Glancing out the window, she saw that they had arrived at her apartment's parking lot. She cleared her throat and decided to say goodbye here before he made her have another sensual meltdown. "Well, thank you for your generous contribution to charity this evening."

"I'll walk you inside," he said and gave the chauffeur a quick nod. The chauffeur opened the door. Damien got out and extended his hand to help her.

"It's really not necessary," she said.

"I insist," he said, and she knew it was useless to argue.

She released his hand as quickly as possible, but the sidewalk was too small. With each step, her bare shoulder brushed against his arm. Determined to escape him as soon as possible, she pushed her key into the door lock and turned it, glancing over her shoulder. "Again, thank you for—"

The door whisked open, taking her off guard. Her mother stepped into view. "Surprise! I found a deal on a flight and took an extra day off. I've been missing my baby girl."

"Mother," she said, surprised, noting that her mother had changed her hair color again. Violet-red this time. "How did you—"

"I have to go back on the red-eye on Monday night, but it was worth it. It's been too long," her mother said, then glanced past Emma to Damien. Her blue eyes rounded. "Oh, my, I've interrupted a date. You actually went on a date." She craned her neck to get a better look. "Is that a limo? Why didn't you tell me?"

Emma felt a rush of embarrassment. "This wasn't a date. It was a charity gala. This is my boss, Damien Medici."

Her mother's eyebrows sprang upward and she pursed her lips into an O.

Damien extended his hand. "It's a pleasure to meet you, Ms.?"

Her mother glanced at Emma. "What nice manners. My name is Kay Nelson. And it's my pleasure to meet you. I don't usually get to meet Emma's coworkers, so this is a treat."

"He's not a coworker," Emma quickly said. "He's my boss."

"Oh," Kay said. "Well, would you like to come

inside? I brought Emma a bottle of wine and baked her favorite cookies as part of her surprise."

Emma stared at her mother in dismay. "Oh, no, I'm sure Mr. Medici is too—"

"I'd love to," he said, and Emma swallowed an oath.

Damien wouldn't dare give up this golden opportunity to get a different view of Emma outside work. Her mother was a charming, but fidgety, little magpie. She seemed unable to sit for more than a few minutes before jumping up for one reason or another. "Would you like more wine, Damien?" she asked.

He held up his hand at her offer of the pink beverage. He'd managed to swallow a few sips for the sake of being sociable, but he preferred dry red wine to white and never, ever pink.

"I'm sure you can imagine how proud I am of Emma. She's always been a good girl. Much more conservative than I am, and look at her now. Working at Megalos-De Luca. Do you know she has worked for two vice presidents?"

"Yes, Mother, he knows," Emma said.

"Well you can't blame me for bragging about you. That gown is just beautiful. You've done something different with your hair, too, haven't you?"

"Mother," Emma said. "I think Mr. Medici needs to leave."

"There's no need to rush," her mother protested. "Do you need to leave, Damien? If you're worried about running up the bill with the limo sitting out there, I'm sure Emma would be happy to drive you home."

Emma's mouth dropped open in protest.

"I'm in no rush," Damien said, leaning back in his chair, ignoring Emma's hostile glare. "Tell me more about Emma as a child."

"She was so thrifty. I swear that girl could make a penny squeal." Kay sighed. "But you know we didn't always have it easy, so that was a good thing. I nick-named her Goddess Hestia. Can you guess why?"

"That's the goddess of hearth and home, right?"

"Yes," Kay said. "We moved a lot and Emma was quick to make anywhere we lived into a home. What a life. Remember the pony I got for you that Christmas?"

Emma nodded with a soft smile. "Peanut."

"She loved that pony. Unfortunately we ran into a little difficulty and could only keep him for a year."

Emma's smile turned strained. "That was one of the good years," she said.

"She always loved animals. What was the name of the last dog we had?"

"Sheba, a golden retriever. We had to give her away because we moved to a place that didn't allow pets."

"I'm surprised you don't have a pet now that you're on your own," Damien said.

"I'm gone too much. It wouldn't be fair."

"Always practical," Kay said, lifting her hands. "Too busy to date in high school. Too busy to do much dating at all. I'm happy you went out tonight."

"It wasn't a date, Mom," Emma said, standing as if she couldn't bear the conversation one minute longer. "Thank you again, Damien."

He rose to his feet. "My pleasure," he said. "Perhaps your mother can help you shop for your upcoming trip."

"Trip," Kay said, immediately perking up. "What trip?"

"I'm going on a business trip to South Beach to evaluate one of the resorts down there. I'll be buying a few new things because I'll be posing as a resort guest."

"I've told her to put it on my account," Damien said.

"Oh, my, how generous. South Beach is so romantic. I went there once with my third husband." She frowned. "Or was it my fourth?"

"Your third," Emma said in a low voice and moved swiftly to the front door. "Oh, my goodness, look at the time. We didn't mean to keep you so long, Damien."

"Oh," Kay said, jumping from her perch on the sofa. "I should leave so the two of you can say good-night privately."

Emma's eyes rounded in horror. "No." She barely got out the word before her mother disappeared into a back room. "I apologize for my mother. She means well."

"I found her charming," he said. "And I wouldn't want to disappoint her by not saying good-night to you privately," he added, stepping so close to her it was all he could do not to take her into his arms, all he could do not to take her mouth and slide his tongue over hers so she wouldn't be able to deny the heat between them any longer.

Damien knew, however, that Emma would have to come to him. It would take every ounce of his self-control, but it was necessary. He lowered his head, closer and closer. Her eyes fluttered and he heard the soft intake of her breath. He moved his mouth so close he could feel her breath. Her body hummed with expectation. Her eyes fluttered again.

It would be all too easy to pull her against his chest, to kiss her every objection away. He wanted to strip her of her reserve and poise until she was begging for him. To fill his hands with her breasts and explore all her secrets. He would tease her until she called out his name again and again. Then he would thrust inside her and give them both the satisfaction they craved.

Hard with desire, he fought against temptation.

"Good night, Goddess Hestia," he said. Then he walked away.

It took a full moment of the cool night air drifting over her skin where Damien had been radiating heat just seconds earlier before she realized he'd left. And he hadn't kissed her. Her body screamed in protest. Her nipples were taut buds straining against her dress and she was wet with wanting.

Chagrined by her response, she forced herself into her apartment with one last glance at the taillights of the limo as it left her parking lot. She felt like an idiot. She'd practically melted into the doorjamb.

She should be relieved that he hadn't kissed her. It would have been completely unprofessional. Instead, she was peeved. How could he get so close to her, nearly rubbing his body against hers, close enough to give her the kind of kiss that sent rockets around the world, and not touch her?

A strangled groan escaped from her throat just as her mother entered the room. "Oh, sweetheart, I'm so sorry. Did you have a romantic evening planned with Damien? I hope I didn't interrupt."

Emma couldn't quite swallow another groan. *"He's my boss, Mother. Nothing more."*

Her mother shook her head. "He is gorgeous and he clearly thinks a lot of you. There's no reason you shouldn't enjoy yourself with him. Trust me, you don't meet men like him every day."

"I'm aware of that, but—"

"I mean I can see why you might find his facial scar frightening. It does look a little savage and—"

"He was defending his foster mother when he got that scar."

Her mother lifted her eyebrows. "Oh. It sounds like the two of you have gotten to know each other quite well considering he's *just your boss.*"

Emma sighed. "Can we please talk about something else? Like when did you decide to visit me?"

"I know I'm imposing, but I've missed you."

"You're not imposing," Emma said, putting her

arms around her mother and giving her a hug. "You know I'm always happy to see you. But I do like a little notice so I can meet you at the airport."

"To make sure I don't stop at the slot machines," her mother said. "Don't worry. I resisted temptation."

"I'm proud of you."

"Thank you, baby. I wish I could be closer to you. Missouri is so slow compared to Vegas."

"Peaceful," Emma corrected. "Remember, when you first moved there, you said it was peaceful. How's Aunt Julia?"

"She's doing fine. She loves her grandbabies. I would love to have some of my own," her mother hinted.

"Not for a long time," Emma muttered. "I'm really tired. I'll fix you banana pancakes in the morning. Would you like that?"

"You're so good to me," her mother said. "You've been making banana pancakes for me since that Mother's Day when you were eleven years old."

"Eight," Emma said, smiling at the memory. "But who's counting?"

"After breakfast, we can go shopping," her mother said. "I can't wait. Sweetie, this time you don't even need to look for sales since it's not your money."

The next morning, after Emma made banana pancakes with real maple syrup for her mother, the two of them went shopping.

"We can go to the Versace store," her mother said.

"Hmm," Emma said.

"Louis Vuitton," her mother continued, rapturous. "Roberto Cavalli."

Or not, she thought as she pulled into an outlet mall.

"Darling," her mother said. "Why are we going to an outlet mall when you could shop at any designer store in Vegas?"

"Because I'm not using Damien Medici's money," Emma said, delighted to find a parking space close to an entrance.

"But he offered. I'll bet he even insisted. Why do you deprive yourself this way?" her mother asked.

Emma didn't want to remind her mother of all the times they'd overspent only to have to return the luxury items they'd purchased. She didn't want to tell her mother that she still lived in fear that her mother would gamble again, fall into debt, leaving Emma to cover the losses.

"This is like a hunting expedition," she told her mother. "You and I are looking for several prize animals." Emma watched her mother, seeing something click in her gaze.

"You like the challenge of bagging the big one on your own terms. I'm in," her mother said, and got outside the car, her tennis-shoe-clad feet ready to pound hard, unforgiving floors for the prizes that awaited them.

Eight

Thank goodness Damien was out of the office during most of Monday and Tuesday. He sent a town car to collect her on Wednesday morning. The driver opened the car door for her to slide onto a luxurious leather seat while he loaded her luggage into the trunk.

Emma's heart pounded, but she told herself to be calm. Damien had proven that he wouldn't force himself on her. If he could control himself, then she should be able to control herself.

She hoped she had the right clothes. Her mother had insisted on several purchases that Emma wouldn't normally have chosen. Emma had agreed to them only because her mother had visited South Beach and she hadn't.

Currently dressed in designer jeans, a silk tank top and crocheted sweater to keep her warm during the flight, she bit her lip, trying not to feel insecure. She pumped her foot, idly noticing her wedge-heel sandals and pearl and sterling silver anklet. She hoped she looked touristy enough.

Damien was probably accustomed to being surrounded by women who dropped thousands of dollars on revealing clothes without batting an eye. Emma couldn't imagine ever being that kind of woman. Instead of going to the main terminal, the driver took an alternate route. She glanced at her watch, worried that he may put her behind schedule.

"Excuse me," she said. "Don't we need to go to the main terminal?"

The driver shook his head. "No, Ma'am. Different terminal. You're flying on a private jet."

"Oh," she said, leaning back in her seat. Soon enough, he pulled in front of another terminal and unloaded her luggage. Her walk through security was effortless and quick. Afterward, she followed an attendant to a corporate jet and boarded.

"We'll be leaving very soon," the attendant told her. "What can I get you to drink? Juice, water?"

"Water would be fine," she said, glancing past the woman and spotting Damien. She felt a kick in her stomach.

He glanced up from his paperwork and shoved it aside. He stood. "Prompt as ever," he said with a slight smile.

She walked toward him, feeling an odd sense of relief at his presence. "I forgot we weren't going to the main terminal."

"I fly commercially sometimes, but more for trips to Europe, Asia or Australia. This is one of my indulgences," he confessed. "I like traveling on my own timetable. I can get more work done in a more comfortable environment." He smiled in a conspiratorial way. "See. I don't have to chew glass to be happy."

She couldn't swallow a laugh.

"There you go," he said. "You're not a nervous flyer."

She shook her head. "Not unless there's a lot of turbulence."

"I'll tell the pilot to avoid it," he said.

"Is that like fries?" she asked. "I'd like a burger with fries. I'd like a smooth flight with no turbulence."

He chuckled. "I never thought of it that way, but yes, maybe. Have a seat. Are you hungry? Thirsty?"

"The attendant already asked me what I wanted to drink," she said, sitting down. At that moment, the perky attendant brought out chilled bottled water for both Emma and Damien, and juice for Damien.

"Would you like breakfast?" he asked her.

"I grabbed a bagel before I left home."

He nodded. "I'll take my regular," he said and sat down.

Curious, she leaned toward him as she sat across from him. "What's your regular?"

"Breakfast is two scrambled eggs, bacon, whole wheat toast, grape jam and breakfast potatoes."

"Lunch?"

"If I take it, club on whole wheat, salt and vinegar chips, dill spear."

"Dinner?"

"Filet mignon, rare, baked potato, broccoli, Caesar salad. Scotch."

"You reward yourself if you have to travel at night," she said.

"Damn right."

"I've learned more about your diet in the last two minutes than I have the entire time I've worked for you," she said.

"Some people say that flying eliminates boundaries that concrete emphasizes."

"In what way?"

"You're secluded above the atmosphere with one other person. No distractions unless you invent them. No interruptions. Just time with little space separating you from that one other person," he said.

The expression in his gaze sent a montage of hot visuals through her mind. This was way too early in the morning and during the trip for her to be thinking about Damien…that way. Taking a quick breath, she deliberately tried to break the hum between them that seemed to grow louder with each passing second.

"Except when you're stuck in the center seat with a child on either side of you," she said.

He chuckled. "That's when noise-canceling earphones are required."

"That won't stop bathroom trips and spills," Emma said.

"You say that as if you have experience," he said.

"I do. I've had to take a few last-minute flights that were packed."

"None of that today," he said.

Emma relaxed slightly into her leather seat. "So true."

The attendant peeked into the lush passenger area. "The pilot says we're ready for takeoff. Please fasten your seat belts."

A few hours later, the jet landed in Miami and a limo pulled alongside the plane. Although Emma had made the travel arrangements herself, she couldn't help but appreciate the efficiency. Within forty-five minutes, they'd checked into the resort they were to evaluate, and she was wandering around her private suite located next door to Damien's. The lavish suite featured a sitting area with a wall of windows that opened onto a balcony that overlooked the resort's three pools, Jacuzzis and the turquoise ocean. She took a deep breath of the ocean air and enjoyed the breeze as it played over her skin. Hard to believe this was *work*.

"What do you think so far?" a voice said from the balcony beside her.

She glanced over to find Damien looking at her.

He'd already changed out of his business clothes and wore a tight black T-shirt that emphasized his broad shoulders and well-developed chest and biceps. She couldn't seem to stop her gaze from following down the rest of his body to lean hips encased in swim trunks. Her mouth went dry and she licked her lips. What had he asked her?

"Pardon me?" she said in a voice that sounded strained to her own ears.

"What do you think of the place so far?"

"It's beautiful. Check-in was smooth and the bellman was friendly. So far, my suite appears immaculate."

"Same here," he said. "It's almost as if they knew we were coming."

Emma felt a twist in her stomach. It was likely the staff had indeed known because she'd told Max about Damien's plans.

"We're just getting started. I haven't had time to review my checklist, but I will—"

"Later," he said. "We're burning daylight. Put on your swimsuit and meet me downstairs."

"Uh—" She started to protest because she had actually planned to conduct a thorough inventory of the suite, but he was the boss. "Okay. Give me just a few minutes," she said and walked inside the suite.

Even though Damien had been a perfect gentleman, she couldn't escape the barely hidden predatory watchfulness in his gaze. Try as she might, she couldn't ignore the simmering attraction between them.

Unpacking her swimsuit, Emma told herself she would just have to push her curiosity about Damien aside. Holding up the black string bikini her mother told her she must buy in order to fit in with the other tourists, Emma had second, third and fourth thoughts. Grabbing her sunscreen, oversize sunglasses, baseball cap and checklist, she told herself this was just business.

Damien lounged by the pool, responding to messages on his BlackBerry as he waited for Emma. He was counting on making this trip a turning point. By creating some distance between her and corporate headquarters, he planned to increase her sense of loyalty to him—mentally, physically and sexually.

Glancing upward, he spotted a pale woman wearing a baseball cap, huge sunglasses and a mesh cover-up that didn't conceal a tiny black bikini or the voluptuous body beneath it. Spotting her silky brown hair swinging over her shoulders, he realized it was Emma. Since she always hid herself beneath tailored suits, he'd only been able to imagine her naked.

Swearing under his breath, he took in every delicious inch of her. Her baby-pale skin would fry in this sun, he thought, immediately deciding to get an umbrella to shield her. Her full breasts bounced with each step. Her hips swayed invitingly.

Then she stopped suddenly as if she were looking

for him. He caught her nervousness as she licked her lips then bit her upper one. He withheld a groan while he mentally stripped her of those tiny pieces of fabric.

Damien stood and moved toward her. She immediately caught sight of him. "Hi," she said breathlessly. "It took me a little extra time because I had to put on sunscreen."

Damn shame, he thought. He would have loved to apply it himself. "No problem. I thought we'd go out to the beach since we don't have much time left today. We can check the pools and hot tubs later."

"Sure," she said and followed him to the towel hut. Holding the wooden door from the pool area for her, he took a lingering glance at her backside as she stepped in front of him.

Uh-huh. He had plans for her. They walked onto the beach and one of the beach staff approached them. "May I help you?"

"We'd like a cabana with two lounge chairs," Damien said.

"Right away, sir," the beach staff said and led them to a cabana, brushed sand off chairs and situated them underneath.

"Thank you," Emma said.

Damien nodded and tipped the man.

"Excellent service," she said, sitting down on the chair.

"Yes. Like I said, it's almost like they know they're being evaluated. But that couldn't be possible, could it?" he asked, studying her face.

She looked away. "Maybe they're always conscientious."

"Maybe," he agreed, but he already knew that Emma had informed Max about the trip. Ultimately, it wouldn't be his loss. It would be MD's loss because they wouldn't get an unbiased view of the resort. "Of course, here comes the cocktail waiter. What would you like?" he asked Emma.

"Something from the bar?" the waiter asked.

"I don't need anything. I brought water," she said, pulling a bottle from her bag and taking a sip.

"You must order something," he said. "How can you comment if you don't try everything?"

"You order for me, then."

"Beer for me and Sex on the Beach for the lady," he said and met her gaze dead-on.

Emma made a little choking sound. Damien took the opportunity to rub her back and gently squeeze one of her shoulders. "Okay?"

"Fine. Just fine," she said in a husky voice, leaning back in her chair. She covered her face with the cap from her head.

The waiter quickly filled the order and Damien drank half his beer while he urged Emma to polish off her mixed drink. He pulled off his T-shirt and baseball cap. "Would you like to go in the ocean?"

She sat up, but paused. "It's been a long time since I've been in the ocean."

"How long?"

"I live in Vegas, remember, so ten or more years."

He grabbed her hand. "Then we need to fix that right now," he said and led her toward the water.

"There's no rush," she said with a slight protest in her voice. "I don't have to do everything the first day."

"This isn't everything. This is just a little dip."

"Yes, but I think I might prefer the pool."

"It's been so long. How would you know?" he asked, tugging her into the surf.

"Whew! It's cool, isn't it?"

He smiled, finding her shyness appealing. "Are you afraid of the water?"

"Oh, no," she protested, but continued to grasp his hand like a vise.

"No problem. We can take it as slow as you want," he said, coming to a stop. He felt her gaze on him for a long moment, but couldn't read her expression because of her sunglasses.

"I can go a little further," she said in a low voice that had Damien visualizing her naked and beneath him again.

Oh, heaven help me, I'm standing next to Damien and he's half-naked. How in the world did he maintain that body? She shuddered at what he might think of her body. No one would call her reed-thin. A man like Damien must be accustomed to dating women with model-perfect figures.

Emma tried to push those thoughts from her head. It didn't matter if Damien thought she wasn't thin enough. In fact, it was all the better. With the cool water fluttering over her ankles, she stepped deeper into the ocean. The water splashed against her calves.

"Okay?" he asked, and she abruptly noticed that she was clasping his hand with a death grip.

"Oh," she said and tried to loosen her grip, but a wave took her by surprise. She gave a little jump.

He gave a low chuckle.

"Don't laugh at me," she scolded him and bit her lip as she forced herself to move forward. Another wave broke, licking at her thighs. She clasped his hand. "Are there jellyfish?"

"Probably not in May," he said.

"Probably," she echoed.

"I'll pick you up and carry you back if you see one," he offered.

Emma didn't know which prospect was worse— a jellyfish or being in Damien's arms. "Thanks," she muttered and inched forward. "Why do the waves seem to be getting bigger so quickly?"

"High tide," he said. "Do you want to go back?"

"Not yet," she said, refusing to give in to her fear. The last time she'd visited the ocean there'd been a strong undercurrent and she'd inhaled saltwater while she tried to determine which way was up. It wasn't a pleasant memory and she wanted to replace it with a better one. She walked further and the bottom seemed to fall out. Slipping into water up to her chin, she automatically clutched at Damien, wrapping her arms and legs around him. "What—" she gasped "—happened?"

"You're okay," he said, closing his strong arms around her. "We were on a sandbar and the bottom suddenly dipped. I've got you."

Surprisingly, the water was calmer. "Where did the waves go?" she asked.

"We're past them now," he said. "This is where it gets nice and calm. Do you like it?"

Taking in all the lovely sensations, she felt buoyant, yet protected. Her body had grown accustomed to the cooler temperature and she felt warm and safe against Damien's strong chest. Her legs dangled in the water while he made sure their heads stayed above the ocean.

She took a deep breath and something inside her eased. His skin was smooth beneath her fingers wrapped around the back of his neck. His chest glistened from the reflection of the sun.

"We should probably go back towards shore," she said, deferring to her logical, rational side.

"Yeah," he agreed. "Is that what you want?"

He felt deliciously strong and the sensation of the water washing over them was sensual in a way she'd never experienced. "Not really," she said, meeting his dark gaze. "It's nice."

"Yes, it is," he said, sliding his hands over her back. "Were you scared?"

"Nervous. It's been awhile and the last time I took a good dunking." She glanced out at the blue water, the sun making it sparkle like diamonds. "It's so beautiful."

"Have you ever been on a yacht?"

She shook her head. "No. Why?"

"My brother lives down here. He owns a yacht business."

She smiled. "Rough life."

He laughed. "That's what I say. Would you like to go for a ride?"

Intimately aware of the fact that he stood between her thighs, her breasts just below his chin, she already felt as if she were on a ride, a very dangerous one. "It's not part of our evaluation of the resort, is it?" she asked, but the idea of spending some time out on the water nearly made her drool.

"No, but we don't have to spend every minute evaluating the actual resort…"

"I'd love to," she said impulsively and hoped she wouldn't regret it later.

Nine

After a delicious dinner in the hotel's gourmet restaurant, Damien took Emma for a stroll down Lincoln Road to enjoy the night air and the outdoor mall. Emma had been a charming dinner companion, tasting and rating every dish. When she'd closed her eyes and licked her lips after sampling the chocolate cake, it had been all he could do not to carry her up to his room. "I've called my brother and he's taking us out on one of his yachts tomorrow. But you can go shopping the day after tomorrow while I'm catching up on some of my work. Use my card."

"Oh, I keep forgetting about your card," she said and abruptly stopped, her brown knee-length skirt swishing around her curvy legs. Her silk top emphasized her delicate shoulders and draped over her breasts. Damien was enjoying Emma's South Beach dress far more than her conservative office attire. She pulled out his credit card and held it toward him. "I don't need this anymore. Actually, I never did. I was able to find a few things on sale, so…"

"You didn't use my card?" he asked in disbelief.

She gave an uncomfortable shrug. "No. It just didn't seem—" She seemed to read his expression of disapproval. "I found bargains, so it wasn't necessary."

"I told you to use my card," he said, torn between dismay and anger. He'd never had a problem getting a woman to use his credit card for shopping before. "I knew you would need different clothing for this trip and it was appropriate for me to provide for that."

"I'll wear it again," she said.

"When?" he asked.

"Maybe on a date," she said, lifting her shoulders and smiling. "Mallory's determined to match me up with her friends."

Her reply irritated him. "So you'll wear that black bikini on a blind date?"

Her mouth opened and she paused before she closed it and bit her lip. "Well, maybe not, but I needed a new swimsuit anyway. Why is this such a problem? I was trying not to take inappropriate advantage."

Yet, she wouldn't bat an eye before betraying him to her former bosses. "It's insulting."

Her eyes widened. "I certainly didn't mean it that way." Her brow furrowed. "How could it be insulting?"

"I offered to provide clothing for a mandatory business trip and you rejected it."

"I apologize. I didn't look at it that way." She took a quick breath. "This trip has been wonderful so far. I just appreciate being able to be in this amazing place with—" She broke off suddenly as if she didn't want to finish the sentence. She didn't want to be happy being with *him*.

Another step closer, he realized with a sliver of satisfaction. He was making progress. Soon enough she would give him everything he wanted—her passion, and the information he needed to get De Luca. "Keep the card," he said. "Maybe you'll find something when you get a chance to go shopping. A souvenir."

After their walk, they returned to the hotel's night-club, which featured subdued lighting, white sheetlike drapes that extended from the high ceilings to the floor, couches and free-flowing martinis. A band played Cuban music, luring listeners onto the dance floor.

"I know Vegas has some hot nightspots, but like most natives I don't get out to them," Emma said as she sipped her martini. She glanced around. "There's something sybaritic about this place. How is your mojito?"

"A little sweet. I prefer my drinks dry. How is your martini?"

"Delicious and generous," she said. "After my full day, I'm almost afraid to drink it."

"It would be a shame to waste it," he said, looking at her mouth, wanting to taste it. The restless, irritable feeling inside him grew, but he tamped it down. "We should dance," he said.

"We should?" she echoed after taking another sip from her martini.

"We have to make our charade believable," he said and extended his hand. She followed him onto the dance floor and allowed him to pull her against his body.

The music shifted to a rhythm-and-blues tune and Damien decided, for once, to enjoy the moment. For just this song, he would steep himself in the scent and sensation of her and seduce her just a little further. Damien knew that anticipation was half the game.

He dipped his lips to her shoulder and glided them over her bare skin. She gave a delicate shiver, but didn't pull away. In fact, she lifted her arms and looped them around the back of his neck. Gratifying, he thought.

He slid his hand down to the small of her back and drew her intimately against him. Her breath caught, but still she didn't move away.

Every time she submitted to his physical approach, she bumped up his arousal another notch. He was already hard and allowed her to feel it.

He wanted nothing more than to take her mouth with his, but he waited. It killed him, but he waited, instead caressing her smooth neck. She felt pliant and willing in his arms. He decided to go a little further and slid his thigh between hers.

She gave a little whisper of a groan that intensified his arousal another degree. "Do you want me to kiss you?" he whispered against her ear.

She sighed, arching against him as if she wanted to be closer.

"If you want me to kiss you, lift your mouth," he told her, his voice sounding gritty with desire to his own ears. He waited and the seconds beat inside his head like a low-pitched bell that vibrated through his body. One, two, three…

She finally lifted her head, her eyes dark with need. "Kiss me," she whispered, and he lowered his head.

Her mouth felt like silk and satin and every sexy, soft thing he'd ever tasted. He lingered on her lips, savoring the sensation of her pliant mouth beneath his. Soon enough, though, it wasn't enough and he slid his tongue between the seam of her lips to taste her.

She gave a sexy little sigh, and allowed his entrance. She tasted sweet and forbidden. Her tongue wrapped around his, drawing him deeper. She may as well have been stroking him intimately for the effect she had on him. He couldn't remember a woman making him this hot. He wanted to touch all of her at once. Sliding his hand up her rib cage, just brushing the side of her breast, he continued to take her mouth.

She rubbed against him and he wanted to pull up her skirt so he could touch her sweetness. He wanted to drop his mouth to her breasts. Despite the fact that they were dancing in a darkened corner, he restrained himself.

"I want to put my mouth all over you," he muttered

against her mouth. "I want to taste you. I want to make you so hot you can't stand it and beg me for more. I want to slide deep inside you and fill you all the way."

She pressed her open mouth against his in sexual invitation. He kissed her once more, taking her mouth in only a fraction of the way he wanted to take her body. "There are beds with curtains by the pool. I could take you there."

"Oh," she said, taking in a quick, sharp breath. She met his gaze, her eyes full of wanting. "I don't know. It's so—"

"Decadent," he said. "Primal."

"Yes." She took another breath.

"It's up to you. I won't force you. I'm going outside to one of those beds. I have protection," he assured her. "We won't go any further than you want to go."

She licked her lips and he couldn't withhold a groan.

Her eyes widened at the sound. "I can't promise—"

"No promises," he said. "Just pleasure. I'll wait there for fifteen minutes," he said and pressed his mouth against hers before he walked away.

She would join him. He was confident of it. He should be feeling more of a sense of triumph. Especially for the larger goal of getting information from her. Instead, though, what he wanted more than anything was to feel her arms and legs wrap around him while he plunged inside her with nothing between them but skin and pounding blood. Damn, if he could explain it, but he wanted her affection and devotion, too.

* * *

Emma felt as if her brain had been scrambled. During the last three minutes, all her mental electrical circuits had fried to smithereens. "Come on, rational brain. Save me," she muttered as she glanced in the direction of the deserted beds by the pool. The beds featured curtains that shielded against prying eyes.

Damien Medici had just issued the wildest invitation she'd ever received in her life. Did she have the nerve to accept it? Perspiration dotted her forehead. Did she have the good sense and fortitude to turn him down or, if necessary, just run away to her suite upstairs?

Emma took another sip of the martini, despite the fact that she knew it wouldn't help clear her mind. Every fiber of her being craved Damien. She wanted to feel his skin against hers. She wanted him to make her moan. She wanted to make him groan.

If she followed her sensible self, she would run. It was insane.

It was also a once-in-a-lifetime opportunity.

She knocked back the rest of her martini and pushed aside her professional concerns. For the next hour or two, she wouldn't think about MD. She would think about Damien and her.

Walking toward the beds by the pool, she had second and third thoughts. She kept walking, though, glancing at the loungers, roped off from the crowd inside and on the patio. A little further and she began to feel uneasy. Perhaps she should go to her room.

Perhaps this was totally insane. It *was* totally insane, but maybe he was worth the insanity.

Emma walked past one more bed and felt the chicken in her start to squawk. Stopping, she took a deep breath and tried to calm herself. She felt her nerve begin to dissolve.

Maybe…

"Emma," Damien's voice, low, but strong, reached out to her. "I'm here."

Sucking in another deep breath, she slowly turned toward him. He stood just outside one of the poolside beds, the light outlining his tall, powerful frame.

Wanting washed over her. She wanted to be with him. She wanted to touch him. Gathering her nerve, she walked toward him. "I almost left," she confessed, looking into his face, half shielded by the darkness.

"I'm glad you didn't," he said and lifted his hand to her hair.

"Come inside," he coaxed.

With only his hand on her hair, she followed him inside, distantly aware of the swish of draperies closing behind her. The music from the live band played from a speaker in the pool area, adding to the sensuality of the atmosphere.

"Put your arms around me," he told her, and she did.

"This is crazy," she said, inhaling his scent from his open shirt.

"Yeah," he said, rubbing his forehead and nose against hers as he slid one hand underneath her hair and the other around the back of her waist. "Wanna stop?"

Her heart tripped over itself. "No," she whispered.

He pressed the small of her back, guiding her pelvis against his arousal. She felt herself grow hotter with each movement. The air inside the curtained area grew more steamy with each passing breath.

His movements were carnal and suggestive. She wasn't the least bit threatened, though. She wanted more. Lifting her head, she met his gaze and he guided her against him in a rhythm as old as time.

He swore, pulling her mouth against his and squeezing her bottom. Her heart raced and she felt light-headed. She had never felt this much want, this much need.

Tugging blindly at his shirt, she fumbled with his buttons. He pushed her hand aside and loosened them himself. She spread her hands over his warm, muscled flesh. So strong, so male.

His strength was an aphrodisiac. Distantly sensing his hands on the buttons of her blouse, she felt a draft of air on her back and her chest as her blouse dipped to her chest. One, two, three more seconds and her bra seemed to dissolve.

Her breasts meshed with his chest and she couldn't withhold a moan. He thrust his tongue into her mouth while he stroked the sides of her breasts. Her nipples peaked even though he hadn't touched them. Lower, she grew wet and swollen.

"So sweet, so good," he said, sliding his mouth down her throat, down her chest to her breast.

Emma held her breath, wanting, aching for more.

He gently pushed her back on the lush lounge and followed her down, taking one of her nipples into his mouth.

She arched toward him in pleasure and need. "Oh, Damien."

"I love the sound of my name on your lips," he muttered, sliding his lips down to her abdomen, pushing away her skirt. He skimmed his hand beneath her satin panties and found her most sensitive spot with unerring ease.

Emma shuddered at his intimate touch. She felt her body tighten with each stroke of his fingers, each breath that blew over her bare belly. He dipped lower and took her with his mouth.

Pleasured in a way she'd never experienced, she felt as if he were claiming her with his hands, with his mouth. Of its own volition her body shook with the beginning waves of climax.

Pulling away just before she soared, he skimmed his mouth back up her body. Every cell inside her was begging for him to finish her, to fill her up and take her the rest of the way. Her craving for him stole her breath.

"Inside," she said, clinging to his shoulders, drowning in his black gaze full of potent arousal. "Inside."

He pushed down his slacks and pulled on protection, then pushed her thighs apart. "Hold on tight," he said in a voice rough with need. Then he thrust inside her in one mind-blowing stroke.

He filled her, stretching her so that she could

barely catch her breath. The way he took her, the way he looked at her felt somehow primitive, as if he was laying claim to her and she would never be the same. Her heart pounding with overwhelming sensations and feelings, Emma couldn't tear her eyes from his. She lifted her hand to his face, touching his scar. He closed his eyes for a heartbeat, then rubbed his mouth over her hand.

He began to pump and the pleasure inside her quickly built again. The need edging toward desperation tightened. With each thrust, he took her higher and higher.

"I want it all, Emma. Give it all to me," he muttered.

His demand, his powerful thrusts and all the feelings she was experiencing were too much. Her body clenched him and a deep spasm of pleasure shot her into a realm of ecstasy she'd never experienced. A second later, he stiffened and swore, shuddering in climax. The experience was so powerful it took her a full moment to begin to breathe again.

Feeling his heartbeat pound against hers, she opened her eyes, half wondering if the earthquake that had taken place between them had brought down their outdoor boudoir if not the entire hotel.

She met his gaze to find him looking at her with an expression of primitive possession and a twinge of surprise. "I knew there was something between us, but—"

"It surprised me, too," she said, breathless.

"I want you to join me in my suite," he said and

pulled an extra key card from the pocket of his slacks as he got dressed. He handed her the key. "I want more time with you."

Taking his cue that it was time to get dressed, she gathered her wits, pulled on her clothes and slipped his key into her small purse. She met his gaze. "Is that an order?"

"Not at all," he said, leaning toward her and rubbing his mouth against hers. He arranged her blouse and smoothed her hair. The considerate gesture took her by surprise. "An invitation. You go first. I don't want to leave you here by yourself."

Her heart squeezed at his admission. "Why not?"

"Because you're wearing the irresistible expression of a woman who's just been thoroughly—" He broke off. "Trust me. One look at you and the hounds will be at your heels. Leave first and I'll catch up with you."

Feeling off-kilter, she stepped into her sandals and took a few deep breaths. She glanced back at him.

"I'll catch up in just a minute," he said.

She peeked out of the curtain and, seeing no one, she walked outside. The tropical breeze played over her skin, soothing her as she walked on the concrete next to the pool. What had she just done? she asked herself. Although Emma's sexual history was rather sparse, she couldn't recall any experience that had exploded with such passion. Physically, it had been unbelievable, but there'd been something deeper going on between them…unless she'd imagined it. And should she dare go to his room? Was she out of her mind?

Seconds later, she felt him step to her side and slide his hand around her back. "Okay?"

"Yes," she said, but her hands were trembling.

He caught one of them and slid his strong hand over hers. "Liar."

"I'm working on it," she said defensively. "I don't have that much experience with this kind of thing."

"Sex?" he asked, as he guided her toward the elevators.

She didn't want to admit just how limited her experience was. "With my boss in a cabana. New for me."

He chuckled. "I'm glad I got you carried away."

She took in a deep breath and entered the elevator as the doors whooshed open. She closed her eyes, hating how vulnerable she felt.

"What is it?" he asked.

They were the only people in the elevator. "This is going to sound really crazy, but I don't want you to think I'm easy."

He gave a bark of laughter. "Easy? I felt like I was breaking into Fort Knox."

Her heart lifted and her lips twitched. She threw him a sideways glance. "Slight exaggeration."

He shook his head. "I would have taken you in the office, in my car, in the limo, at the charity event…"

His confession squeezed her heart. "Why me?"

"You have something," he said, his eyes darkening. "You have something I've never had before and I want it."

The elevator dinged as it reached the top floor

and he glanced at the doors as they opened. "But it's up to you. You have the key to my suite," he said and walked out of the elevator.

Emma followed him outside of the elevator and slowly walked to her room. Standing outside her door, she looked further down the hall to Damien's room. She'd thought he was heartless and cold, but he was hotter than a fire on the coldest, scariest night of her life.

She wondered what she had that Damien could possibly want so much. Her heart did a strange flip-flop. Did she have the nerve to go to his room? Did she have the nerve *not* to go to him?

Ten

Two hours later, after they'd made love again, they sat together on the balcony with a blanket wrapped around them and the stars shining down. Her body was silky and warm within his arms.

"Have you ever done this before?" Emma asked, then shook her head. "Don't answer."

The truth was Damien had never felt magic the way he did tonight. "I haven't done this before, sat on a balcony with a beautiful woman in the middle of the night."

"I wouldn't say beautiful," she said.

"I would," he said.

"That's the sex talking," she said.

But it wasn't. Damien had glimpsed Emma's

sweetness and not only was she beautiful on the outside, she was beautiful on the inside. She was so loyal. He craved receiving that loyalty for himself.

"A lot of stars up there. What kind of wishes would you make?"

"If I believed in making wishes?" she asked.

"Yeah, I know," he said. "I made too many when I was a kid."

"Blowing out candles on a birthday cake," she said.

"Shooting star," he said.

She nodded.

"What kind of wishes would you make?"

She took a deep breath and nuzzled against his chin. "I would wish that my mother would never gamble again. That she would never *want* to gamble again."

"That makes sense." He slid his hand over her silky hair. "Name something frivolous."

She gave a soft chuckle. "Oh, wow. That's tough."

"So much has been about survival."

"That's right. You know, don't you?"

He felt her looking at him. "Yeah, I do." He paused. "So tell me something frivolous."

"I'm guessing world peace isn't acceptable."

He laughed, hugging her against him. "Not frivolous."

"Okay," she said, closing her eyes. "This is hard."

"You can do it."

She sighed and smiled. "A new apartment with a Jacuzzi and a wonderful pool."

"Sounds good."

"Losing ten pounds," she added.

"Don't even think about it. You don't need to lose anything."

She looked at him in disbelief. "You could have models, women with perfect bodies."

"Yours is perfect," he said, sliding his hands over her soft skin. "Name something else."

She closed her eyes. "A vacation somewhere exotic."

"Keep going."

"A dog."

"You mentioned that before. So you need a dog nanny, too," he said.

"Oh, I think that's going a bit far. Your turn. Name some wishes."

"I don't have wishes. I set goals. I give myself targets and exceed them."

"Spoken like a true tycoon," she said. "Okay, let's go further back, back to the time when you believed that blowing out the candles on that birthday cake meant your wish would come true."

He shook his head, lifting his hand to rub his jaw. "That's so far back. I don't know if I can remember. The first few years the family was split up, I made wishes that we could get back together. Wishes that my father and brother hadn't died in that train accident. Wishes that we hadn't been too much for my mother to deal with after it happened."

"That had to have been horrible," she said.

"Yeah, kinda hard to find something frivolous when your entire world has blown apart," he said.

"But you eventually decided you wanted a Ferrari," she said, with just enough humor to lift him out of his gloom.

He chuckled. "Yeah, I did, but you can be damn sure I didn't count on getting it by blowing out candles on a birthday cake."

"No, but it proves you've had some wishes," she said.

"Okay, back in the day, I wished for a bike where the chain didn't fall off every half mile."

"Did you ever get one?"

"Hell no. By the time I could afford one, I didn't care that much. I waited a long time to buy my first car because I used public transportation. That first car was a piece of—" He broke off and laughed. "Let me put it this way. It was no dream machine. The roof liner hung down on my head, the color was silver, metal and rust, and it drank oil like an alcoholic drinks booze."

"How did you accomplish so much with no support at all?"

He shrugged. "I worked," he said. "All the time. When I wasn't working, I was in school. By the time I hit twenty-two, I had three sideline businesses— commercial coffee service, accounting for small businesses and microstorage—when I started working for a firm that helped companies streamline and downsize when necessary. I worked my way to the top of that firm and they offered me a VP position. I passed and started my own company. My three sideline ventures exploded, demand for my services shot through the roof. I still lived like a poor foster kid and invested my money. All of a sudden I had more money than I knew what to do with."

"What a story," she said. "Talk about self-made. Has it been a total blur?"

He nodded. "A lot of it. The first time I celebrated Christmas in a long time was two years ago on my brother's yacht. My brother from Atlanta came down for the day."

"How was that?" she asked.

"Pathetic," he said, shaking his head. "It might as well have been a funeral. Until we started drinking and playing pool."

She chuckled. "Sounds interesting. Who won the game?"

"I did, of course. The two of them got way too sloshed. Rafe is always trying to do a rematch. I beat him almost every time."

Emma sighed and sat silently.

"What are you thinking?"

"I'm thinking at least you made a start at getting your family back together," she said. "And at least you have each other. That's more than a lot of people have. Nobody has a perfect life."

"Except for maybe Alex Megalos and Max De Luca," he said, his resentment rising suddenly.

"Neither of them has had a perfect life. Alex's father disowned him when he joined the company. And Max's father nearly ruined the company. On top of that, Max had to deal with his half brother. He was involved in criminal activity. Max's marriage didn't start out on the best foot, either." She stopped suddenly as if she realized she'd revealed far too much. "Of course, it's all better now and Max is a wonderful father."

Damien digested the information, filing each detail away for study at a later time. Emma may have just given him the key he needed to finish Max De Luca. He felt Emma give a little shiver. "Cold? I think it's time for me to take you back inside and warm you up."

Dressed in shorts and a tank top over her bikini, Emma accepted Damien's brother's hand as she boarded the yacht. She felt Damien just behind her.

"I'm Rafe. Welcome to my humble home at sea," he said and Emma saw the resemblance between brothers. Dark hair and dark eyes. At first glance, Rafe seemed to have a lighter air about him.

"Emma Weatherfield," she said. "I'm Damien's assistant at Megalos-De Luca. Thank you for inviting us."

She turned her attention to the large gleaming boat. Thankful that her expression was hidden by her sunglasses, Emma tried not to gawk.

Damien gave a rough chuckle. "Humble home? You wouldn't know humble if it jumped up and bit you."

"Nice to see you, too," Rafe said, shaking his brother's hand.

"It's generous of you to invite us on such short notice."

"It's not as if I had a choice. My brother is a dictator at heart. But it's my pleasure. If you should decide you'd like a change in environment, I'm certain I could use a woman with your talents in my organization."

"Don't start, Rafe," Damien said in a low voice with inlaid steel.

"I'm much more fun than he is," Rafe grumbled. "Let me show you around."

Rafe instructed one of the staff to get their drinks, then led them on a tour of the yacht, the upper level, below deck which included bedrooms, a well-equipped kitchen, an elegant but comfortable living area with a large-screen TV, and last, but not least, a game room with a pool table.

"I'm always trying to get your boss to come down and take some time off, shoot some pool, but he's married to the job," Rafe said.

"He just can't stand it that I beat him last time," Damien said.

"You're afraid of a rematch," Rafe goaded him.

"You always did have a vivid imagination," Damien said.

Rafe laughed. "Come on. Let's take this lady for a ride."

Out to sea they went. Damien made sure Emma sat in a perfect chair so she could enjoy the sun sparkling on the turquoise waters. A waiter or staff member, she wasn't sure which, made sure she was never without a drink. Damien sat with her for a while, then excused himself to chat with Rafe.

Suffering from a lack of sleep from her previous active night, Emma dozed. When she woke up, she immediately looked for Damien, but he wasn't close by. Rising from her lounge chair, she went in search of Damien and overheard him talking with his brother.

"How did you wind up with an assistant who looks like that?" Rafe asked.

"I don't know. Maybe De Luca was hoping to distract me."

"The man obviously doesn't know you," Rafe said.

"She's different," Damien admitted.

"I haven't heard you say that about a woman before," Rafe said.

"It doesn't matter," Damien said. "Her first loyalty is to MD."

"And her loyalty should be to you instead?" Rafe asked. "When you're not paying her salary and her entire future is tied up with MD."

"When you put it that way…"

"Yeah?"

"When you put it that way, it seems difficult for her to possibly choose to be loyal to me."

"Do you think De Luca has any idea who you are?" Rafe asked.

"He's too busy covering his own interests to see me as anything other than the person who is taking some control of his company away from him."

Emma's mind whirled from the exchange between the brothers. So Damien *knew* she was loyal to Max.

Yet, he'd made love to her. He'd held her on the balcony and she still thought he may have somehow been behind that Tesla Roadster. Yet, he'd been determined that she didn't know it was him. Confusion twisted through her. Why?

Damien glanced up and caught her gaze. "Emma, too much sun? Or did you get bored?"

She hesitated a second, unable to read his expression hidden by his dark sunglasses. "It's too beautiful to be bored."

"No seasickness?" Rafe asked.

She shook her head.

He smiled and the sun glinted on his wavy hair and white teeth, making him look like a movie star. She wasn't affected in the least.

"Good sailor. Good sign," he said.

"In what way?" she asked.

"A woman who can handle rough waters is a keeper," he said. "Are you sure I can't talk you into working for me?"

"Rafe," Damien said in a warning tone.

Rafe lifted his hands. "Can't blame a guy for trying."

"Once," Damien said. "That makes twice. More than enough."

"Cranky SOB," Rafe muttered and headed down below.

"You're a little hard on him," Emma said.

Damien slid his arm around her back and led her to the railing. "Rafe is one of those people that pushes as far as you let him."

"Even as a kid?" she asked, enjoying the warmth and weight of his arm around her.

"Even as a kid," he said, a smile playing on his lips. "He told wild stories to get out of trouble. He was the charmer, so he did okay with his foster parents. He only went through two before they stuck with him. They weren't wealthy, but they helped him through college. He wheeled and dealed and got into this business. Not too shabby," he said.

"No. He likes having you around, though, doesn't he?"

Damien nodded. "Yeah. For all his charm, he feels things more deeply than you'd expect. When my father died and my mother put us up for foster care, we were all just a little too old to blend in. We couldn't help wanting to go back."

"What about your brother in Georgia?"

"He's an overachiever, too," Damien said. "He feels guilty because he was the one who was supposed to have been riding that train with my dad. Survivor's guilt. Sucks. He drowns it in work."

"I see a common thread," she said.

Damien shot her a sideways glance. "I'm taking time off," he said. "I'm here, not doing the report, not doing assessments, with you."

His gaze shook her down to her bones. "Rough assignment, isn't it?"

His mouth slid into a sexy grin and he cupped her jaw, drawing her toward him. He slid his mouth over hers in a kiss that made her feel far dizzier than the motion of the ocean ever had. "When did you get to be so ornery?"

Good question, she thought, as she felt her knees turn to water and her mind to mud.

Emma gave into temptation and shared the rest of the time in South Beach with Damien in his suite. Every minute seemed to sparkle, so how could she possibly have any complaints about the resort?

She reviewed the resort with Damien on the return flight. "I'm trying to find something to criticize," she said. "Was it just me or was everything perfect?"

He met her gaze. "We're expected to prepare a report despite the fact that someone was obviously told that we were coming."

Emma felt a sliver of guilt. "Were the beds too soft? Too hard?"

"You sound like Goldilocks," he said with a chuckle.

"Okay, the food," she said. "What was wrong with the food?"

"Nothing," he said. "Breakfast was served promptly. Food was hot and prepared to order."

"Beach service?" she asked.

"Fine. Not too intrusive," he said, his gaze falling over her and making her warm.

Emma cleared her throat. "So, our recommendation is to buy."

He shook his head. "Our report is that the resort is extremely well-run under current management."

"Any recommendations?" she asked.

"Unfortunately, since the staff was obviously alerted to our presence, I can't offer any. Can you?"

Emma felt another stab of guilt at his question. "I guess you're right."

"I usually am," he said in a low voice that was far more resigned than cynical.

After they returned to the office, Emma struggled with her feelings for Damien. Behind their locked and closed doors, it was easy for him to come up beside her and stroke her hair. Sometimes he would call her into his office and would simply kiss her. This morning a dozen blush roses mixed with blue forget-me-not flowers arrived for her. No card, but she knew he'd sent them.

"Let me take you to dinner tonight. You've worked hard. I'd like to reward you. I need another hour to wrap things up. Does that work for you?"

The way he looked at her made her heart skip over itself. "I'm not sure it's a good idea for us to be seen in public. We don't want to give people the wrong idea," she said.

"Tell me. What's the wrong idea?" he asked, lifting her hand and sliding his mouth over the inside of her wrist.

It was all she could do not to press herself against him. "What's happened between us," she said.

"Happening," he corrected. "It's not over."

"It's temporary," she said. "I'll be here after you leave."

"And you don't want people to know you've been

fraternizing with the hatchet man," he said, his gaze never leaving her face.

She pulled her hand away. "If you're asking if I'm concerned about my reputation, the answer is yes. Like I said, you won't be staying. I will."

"I could offer you another option," he said.

"What?"

"You could come to work for me. I take care of my people. Ask my employees."

"The same way you've taken care of me?" she asked.

His jaw hardened. "No. I already told you there's something between you and me neither of us wants to pass up. I don't know why you continue to fight our relationship."

"It's just so complicated."

"It doesn't need to be. I want you, and I believe you want me."

She couldn't deny it, but she said nothing.

"I'm ordering dinner for two from Allister's and having it delivered to the office."

She gasped. Allister's was one of the finest restaurants in town. "That's ridiculous. Delivery alone will cost the earth."

"Hope you like champagne," he said with an infuriating hint of a grin just before he entered his office and closed the door behind him.

Eleven

Emma's moan of satisfaction immediately made him hard. Even though the source of her pleasure at the moment was chocolate hazelnut mousse, he could easily recall hearing that same sound when they'd shared his bed. Taking a sip of Dom Pérignon, he watched from below the rim of his flute. The more time he spent with her, the more he wanted from her. He wanted more than her sexual acquiescence; he wanted her affection, her trust, her loyalty. The strength of his desire surprised him.

"Hated the dessert, did you?" he asked, in a mock-serious tone.

She tossed him an accusing look. "How could I possibly turn down a meal from Allister's? With that mousse." She sighed. "I heard all kinds of terrifying things about your reputation, but nothing about how—" She broke off, frowning.

"About how?" he prompted.

"About how seductive you could be."

"That's because this is my first time at seduction. I don't have a lot of practice," he said, but she knew better.

"Right," she said in disbelief. "You clearly have no experience."

"Well," he said, pouring the last of the champagne into her glass. "The truth is I've never seduced a coworker. Too messy. But something about you…"

Her heart turned over. "You flatter me."

"No," he said and clicked his flute of champagne against hers. "I'm just telling the truth. So are you going to put me out of my misery and come over here and kiss me?"

Emma felt a rush of heat. "You don't look at all miserable."

"But I am," he said. "And you can save me from it."

It was such a ridiculous notion that she could save such a powerful man as Damien from anything. But his tie was askew and his gaze said *I want you.* He always invited, and she found his invitations completely irresistible.

Rising from her chair, she went to him and bent over, pressing her mouth against his. He pulled her into his lap and she couldn't muster a protest.

His arms felt wonderful. His mouth made her

forget the rest of the world. She could almost believe that she meant something special to him. Almost...

He took his time kissing her, exploring her mouth, making her feel taken and powerful at the same time. How could that be?

Her temperature rose and she wanted more. She tugged at the buttons of his shirt and pulled at his tie. He made her blouse dissolve and soon enough her breasts were bare. He pulled her over his hard masculinity and thrust inside her.

Emma gasped. He groaned in pleasure and began to coach her to rise and fall in a rhythm that made her sweat with need. Straddling him, she felt her nether regions clench around him.

Sliding his fingers through her hair, he brought her lips to his as he thrust inside her. Her climax began in fits and starts. She didn't think she could stand the sensations, but he kept on thrusting and she flew over the top. Seconds later, he followed, clenching her bottom, taking her mouth at the same time he took the rest of her, mind, body and, heaven help her, soul.

Breaths, minutes, centuries later, he held her against his chest, his heart beating against hers. "You leave first," he whispered. "I don't want people to gossip about you. If we leave together, they will. I'll follow you back to your apartment to make sure you arrive safely."

Still caught in the otherworld of their passion, Emma struggled to absorb his words. "Leave?" she echoed, lifting her head to meet his gaze.

He rubbed his finger over her lips and swore. "I want you again."

What Emma wanted was to stay in his arms all night. Longer if possible. She took a deep breath to gather her wits. "Leave," she said again.

"You first," he said. "I'll follow."

Reluctantly, she stood, separating herself from him. Her knees dipped in protest, but he caught her. "Okay?" he asked.

"Getting there," she said, but her mind was still muddy from passion. She grabbed her clothes and pulled them on. He did the same.

He looked into her eyes. "Do you need me to drive you home?"

She shook her head. "I'll be okay."

He paused a long moment. "I would rather you come back to my condo," he said.

She shook her head again. "Not a good idea."

He pulled her to him and took her mouth in a long, possessive kiss that rocked her world. Pulling away, he rubbed his thumb over her bottom lip. "You look like you've been thoroughly kissed."

She licked her lips, her tongue glancing his finger.

He swore under his breath.

"I have been thoroughly kissed," she whispered. "I should go."

He swore again.

"G'night."

Damien watched her leave, feeling a craving that went far beyond his groin, down to his bones. He couldn't remember wanting a woman this much. He'd thought the weekend in South Beach would ease his ache, but it had only made it worse. He wanted her and was determined to have her.

As she walked out of Megalos-De Luca headquarters, Emma felt like a sexual goddess. And a tramp. This was insane, she thought as she got into her Tesla Roadster and started the engine. It couldn't continue.

She took a deep breath and checked her rearview mirror, catching sight of her disheveled hair and swollen mouth. She had that just-got-out-of-bed look. Covering her eyes for a few seconds, she tried to gather her wits. She had gone totally over the edge with Damien.

Taking a deep breath, she pushed on the accelerator and drove out of the parking lot. Emma had kept herself in check for years. It had been a necessity with her mother's difficulties, but something about Damien had tempted her enough to let down her guard. Now, she needed to put it back in place. After all, she was technically supposed to be spying on Damien for work, not spying on him naked.

Glancing in her rearview mirror, she saw Damien's Ferrari. She needed to get control of this situation. Tomorrow, she told herself. Tomorrow would be the day.

The next morning, Damien arrived early, leaving a fresh bouquet of cream roses and forget-me-not flowers on Emma's desktop. Emma was turning into a constant craving, and he needed to do something about it. He decided she should move in with him. He would hire her away from MD with a higher salary and keep her. Until he got her out of his system. When would that be?

Although he could tell she was inexperienced, he found her completely irresistible. Hearing the door open, he felt his gut knot at her presence. In a matter of seconds, he would see her, hold her, kiss her.

Her footsteps slowed outside his office door. "Damien?" she said.

"Come in," he said, meeting her gaze.

She looked away. He noticed she wore a black dress and her face was pale with pronounced shadows under her eyes. She bit her lip.

His gut knotted again, this time in displeasure.

Taking a deep breath, she finally met his gaze. "I can't keep doing this," she said. "I'm just not cut out for an office affair. From now on, I have to keep our relationship strictly professional," she said, her voice breaking. "Being involved with you personally is too overwhelming. I can't think straight. I'm just not so-phisticated enough to maintain this kind of affair."

The pain in her eyes kept him from sinking into a vat of bitterness. She was afraid, and perhaps rightly so, of the passion that flared between them. She wanted a measure of safety, and to her, he repre-sented a total free fall.

He couldn't help, however, feeling disappointed.

He knew she felt the same way he did. He knew he could make her take back those words right now if he wanted. Her vulnerability stopped him.

He had wanted her to choose him. He wanted her to open herself to him in every possible way. At the same time, he kept himself protected.

"I understand," he finally said, but was determined that he would change her mind.

Twenty-four hours later, a call came in, chilling Emma to the bone. The voice mail had come through when she'd been in a meeting, taking notes for Damien.

"Sweetie," her mother said, her voice breaking. "I'm so sorry, but I've gotten into trouble again."

Within an hour, Emma learned her mother had latched on to Internet gambling and had lost a quarter of a million dollars. Emma was reeling.

The next day she went to work and tried to hide it, but her fear must have shown through her usual calm.

"What's going on?" Damien asked.

"It's personal," she said, unable to meet his gaze.

He wheeled her chair around so that she was facing him and put his hands on the armrests. "You and I have gotten about as personal as a man and woman can get. Tell me what has upset you."

Her stomach clenched and she bit her lip. She felt so ashamed and desperate. Even though she hadn't been the one to gamble, she somehow felt responsible. "I need to sell the roadster."

"Why?" he asked.

"Because I need the money," she whispered.

"For what?"

She still couldn't meet his gaze. "I just have to do it. Can you help me?"

He paused a beat. "Yes. What do you need?"

"A quarter of a million dollars," she said, her throat constricting into a painful knot.

"What the hell would you need—" He broke off. "Your mother," he said.

His correct guess immediately made her feel as if at least half a ton had been lifted from her shoulders. She took a deep breath and exhaled.

"How in the world did she get into gambling again? Didn't you say she'd left Vegas?"

"Online gambling," Emma told him and finally met his gaze. He saw a mixture of confusion and concern.

"Damn," he said, raking his fingers through his hair. "You know the problem with bailing her out is—"

"It could happen again," she said miserably. "But there's no way she could pay this off on her own. And I'm terrified of what those loan shark lenders would do to her. What if they hurt her? What if they—" She couldn't bring herself to say her worst fear.

"It's clear that your mother has an addiction," he said.

"Yes," she agreed.

"I think the best plan would be to pay off her debts and get her into an intense treatment."

"What do you mean?"

"I mean I think she needs to go to a specialized treatment facility and stay until she's truly strong enough to manage her addiction on an outpatient basis."

Emma's head spun at the prospect. "I don't even know if such a facility exists. She's not addicted to drugs."

"I'm sure it exists," Damien said. "We just need to find the most successful one."

"That sounds expensive," she said.

"The alternative isn't cheap," he pointed out.

She nodded in agreement. "I'm just not sure I can afford it."

"I can," he said.

Emma stared at Damien in amazement. "Pardon me?"

"I said I have enough money." Damien gave a wry laugh. "I have money to burn."

"But—"

"You and I can negotiate an arrangement."

Emma frowned, feeling an undercurrent of fear and doubt. "Arrangement?"

"Very simple," he said. "I pay off your mother's debts, you keep your Tesla. You remain my lover and faithful, loyal assistant."

Emma stared at him in disbelief. "You're suggesting that I trade my loyalty in exchange for you paying for my mother's mistakes?"

"I'll compensate you in other ways financially, of course. Seems a fair trade to me," he said.

Emma fought a wave of nausea. "So, I sell myself and my integrity for the sake of my mother."

"That's more harsh than it needs to be. You've been to bed with me. You know we can take care of each other."

Squeezing her forehead, she bit her lip as she thought of the implications. "I would have no future with MD."

"I would take care of you."

"Until you grew tired of me," she said, meeting his gaze. "How long do you propose for this to last?"

Silence swelled between them.

"Until you grow tired of me," she repeated, her stomach twisting violently.

"Actually, I would say indefinitely," he told her, leaning toward her. "I've never met a woman like you. A woman with your combination of qualities. I'm not sure I ever will again."

She saw something in his eyes, want, need, that made his offer feel just a little more palatable. Yet… "I need to think about this," she said.

"How much time do you have?"

"Not much with the people she owes," Emma said. "The problem with bailing her out is that it doesn't give her an opportunity to face her illness."

He nodded. "That's why she may need more than bailout money. Money for treatment. Think about it and let me know."

Emma barely slept at all that night. She tossed and turned. How could she possibly sell her loyalty? Her integrity? The possibility sickened her. She struggled to find an alternative, any alternative, but all the possibilities left her in debt for the rest of her life with the chance that her mother would fall again.

Emma knew that her mother needed to face her creditors for herself and that a bailout was not going to help her mother take responsibility for herself. She just couldn't imagine any other solution. Her mother would never make enough money to pay off her debt. What if her so-called creditors got rough with her? What if they killed her?

Emma wouldn't be able to live with herself if she allowed that to happen. Her mother clearly needed intensive treatment, expensive treatment.

After an endless night, morning finally arrived and Emma applied blush and extra concealer to hide her stress and the dark circles under her eyes. Wearing a cream-colored business dress, she walked into the office, wishing she were wearing sunglasses. A little extra armor would be great. Damien was already in his office. No surprise there. She tapped on his door.

"Yes?" he said.

"It's Emma."

"Come in," he said.

She walked inside, but didn't take a seat. He rose, which forced her to look up to him.

"Good morning," he said.

"The jury's still out on that," she said. "You've made me an offer. I'd like to nail down the terms."

"I thought I made it clear. I'll pay for your

mother's treatment and her debts in exchange for your loyalty as my assistant and my lover."

"I'd like an expiration date on that," she said.

He lifted his eyebrows in surprise. "Really?"

"Really," she said.

"Okay. Two years," he said.

"One," she countered.

He paused. "Okay, but we both may want to re-negotiate."

"I just want the ground rules," she said. "I'll need to take a couple days off."

"Fine. I'll transfer the funds to whatever account you want."

Emma felt another ball of nausea rise to her throat, but she took a deep breath to counter the terrible sensation. This was the best way out of a bad situation. She pulled out a deposit slip from her bank account and gave it to him. "Thank you," she said in a low voice.

"Emma," he said and she felt too much just from the way he said her name.

Shaking her head, she tried to get her emotions in check. "I have a lot of things to do. I'll talk to you later," she said and left his office.

She immediately took the elevator to the executive offices. Hearing the echo of her heels clicking down the hallway, she headed for Alex's office first. She'd always felt Alex was a little more human than Max. It would be easier to tell Alex than Max. Unfortunately, according to his assistant, Alex wouldn't be in today.

Gathering her courage, she walked to Max's office. He, of course, was there, and immediately welcomed her.

"Good to see you, Emma. You're doing a great job," he said, motioning toward a chair in his office suite. "Great warning on the South Beach site. I think we were able to head off any objections from the board."

"I can't do this anymore," she said, remaining standing.

He stared at her for a moment. "Excuse me?"

"I can no longer be a spy against Damien Medici. It's too hard for me to try to be helpful to him at the same time that I'm supposed to be working against him." Sensing Max's extreme disappointment and disapproval, she felt her stomach twist and turn. "I'm sorry, but I just can't do it. I understand if you want to release me."

Silence sat in the room like a heavy, undigested meal. "No," he said. "What we asked you to do would be difficult for most, impossible for many. Damien won't be here forever. You've been a loyal employee. You'll always have a job at Megalos-De Luca Enterprises as long as I have a say."

"Thank you," she said, feeling like a traitor. "That means a lot."

Still sick with worry over her mother, Emma left headquarters and went to her apartment. The famili-arity of her surroundings provided little comfort with her personal and professional life in such upheaval. Pulling out her laptop, she began to research the success rate of facilities designed to help people with gambling addictions. Within days, her mother's debts would be paid, but the larger problem of her mother's illness had to be addressed.

Later that evening as she ate a sandwich and checked flights going to Missouri, a knock sounded at her door. Emma rose and checked the peephole, surprised to see Damien, still dressed in the suit he'd been wearing that morning, on her doorstep. Struggling with an odd sense of combined relief and dread, she opened the door. "Hi."

"Hi," he said in return. "I thought I should check on you to see what your plans are."

"Come in," she said. "I was just looking at flights to Missouri. I've been doing some research on residential treatment facilities."

"I asked my company assistant to do some research, too," he said and pulled an envelope from his coat pocket. "Here's a list of three that are reputable and have high success rates."

Surprised at his thoughtfulness, she accepted the envelope. "Thank you."

"You're welcome. There's no need to fly commercial. You can use my company jet."

Emma shook her head. "That's not necessary. I wouldn't feel right about it."

"I said I would take care of you," he reminded her. "You don't need to do this alone. I can come with you."

Emma bit her lip and fought the strange urge to lean on his strength. She had no doubt that Damien could take care of her. Heaven help her, this situation was complicated. The problem with letting him take care of her was that she dare not get used to it.

"No. It's best if I handle this myself. You're already contributing too much financially," she said.

"Emma, you haven't made a deal with the devil," he told her. "Look at me. You can count on me."

Twelve

Emma made the tough trip to Missouri and confronted her mother about her gambling addiction. She called it that: an addiction. Her mother cried, but confessed her weakness and her need.

Emma required her mother to personally pay off her creditors. Then her mother agreed that she needed help. Emma proposed on-site treatment and to her surprise, her mother leaped at the opportunity. She helped her mother pack and joined her on a flight to the treatment facility she hoped would get her mother on the right track.

Seventy-two hours after she'd first left Las Vegas, her return flight touched down on the runway back home. She was so exhausted she could cry, but she still needed to grab a cab and go home.

She pulled her carry-on bag through the airport, past the slot machines that lured arrival passengers to take a chance and win. The big jackpot was only one pull of the handle away. The thought made her stomach turn. The elusive promise of winning big had continually seduced her mother and made her home life unstable.

Emma didn't believe in the big payoff. In fact, she feared the promise of it, because it never lasted. She walked outside the terminal to catch a cab. Instead of a taxi, however, a low-slung Ferrari pulled alongside the curb and stopped.

Her heart took a dip. It couldn't possibly be Damien. She hadn't been in touch with him since she'd left.

But there he was, stepping out of the driver's side of the car and taking her bag to put it in the trunk. Too weary to be anything but grateful, Emma slid inside the passenger seat and practically melted into the leather.

"How'd it go?" he asked, pulling forward.

"As well as could be expected," she said, leaning back against the headrest. "My mother admitted she has a huge problem and wanted help. All I had to do was mention a treatment facility and she jumped at the opportunity."

"Good. She's lucky to have you as her daughter," he said.

Emma closed her eyes. "It's crazy, but when I was little, I always wondered if she had this problem because of me. Maybe if I hadn't been born or if I was different or—"

"None of that," Damien said with a hint of ruthlessness in his voice. "You're the best thing your mother has. I bet she would say the same thing."

Emma took a deep breath at the same time her heart fluttered. She didn't want to be under Damien's spell. She wanted, no needed, to be in control. "Thank you for picking me up at the airport."

"You're welcome," he said. "Do you need anything to eat?"

Emma shook her head at the same time her stomach growled. "Kids' meal takeout would be great."

"Can do," he said and within minutes placed an order at a drive-thru window.

Emma opened her eyes when Damien paid. The fast food server gawked at the Ferrari.

She smiled. "I guess he doesn't see these every day."

"Guess not," Damien said, sliding a sideways glance at her as she dug into a kids' meal cheeseburger with mustard and pickles. "How is it?"

"Not quite the level of Allister's, but ambrosia at the moment," she said.

"I'm taking you back to my condo tonight. Your place is further from the airport and since tomorrow is Sunday, I thought you could sleep in."

Too weary to argue, she moved her head in a circle. "I'm sure I'll fall asleep the second my head hits the pillow."

In fact, Emma must have fallen asleep as soon as

she finished her burger and a few fries. She awakened to being carried in Damien's arms inside a dimly lit room where she'd never been.

Shaking her head, she glanced around. "What—"

"Shh, you'll wake up the baby," he said.

Emma blinked. *Baby?* Then she realized Damien was referring to her. She couldn't swallow a soft laugh. "Already done. The baby's awake and wants to brush her teeth and wash her face before she goes into a coma again."

He allowed her to slide down his body until her feet touched the floor. "Master bath is to the right. My housekeeper keeps a basket of toiletries underneath the sink."

After a stressful trip and a day of harsh travel, Damien's voice soothed her nerves and his strength felt like a warm blanket. "Thank you for bringing me upstairs."

"No problem," he said. "Do you want a bath?"

"That sounds wonderful," she said. "Tomorrow." Emma padded into the luxurious bathroom and quickly washed her face and brushed her teeth. Realizing she needed her gown, she remembered it was in her bag. She returned to the bedroom. "My ba—" She broke off when she saw Damien standing in nothing but lounge pants. His gleaming broad shoulders and bare chest captured her attention.

"You needed something?" he prompted.

Despite the fact that she should be too tired to keep her eyes open let alone gawk at Damien's body, she couldn't fight a ripple of awareness that ran throughout her body. She cleared her throat. "My bag. I need my gown."

He nodded toward the side of the room where she stood. "There."

She glanced in the same direction he had, sheepish that the bag had been positioned right beside her. Pulling her gown from her carry-on, she scooted back into the bathroom and put it on. Moments later, she returned to find Damien already in bed with the covers folded back.

Feeling a strange twist of nerves, she climbed into bed, hugging the opposite side. Three heart-beats later, she felt his hand wrap around her belly, and he pulled her back against the front of him. "Relax," he said in a low voice against her ear. "Go to sleep."

Seconds later, she did.

The next morning she awakened to the delicious sensation of being in his arms. He nuzzled the back of her neck and she held her breath in anticipation of him making love to her. Instead, he got out of bed. "Be lazy," he instructed her. "I'll be reading the paper outside on the terrace."

Surprised that he hadn't taken sexual advantage of sharing a bed with her, she stared after him for a moment. Then she decided to follow orders and fell back asleep.

After a leisurely bath, she joined him and sunned

on the terrace wearing a pair of his shorts and a cut-off black T-shirt. They snacked on sandwiches prepared by his housekeeper. He touched her frequently, stroking her hair, sliding his hand over the bare skin of her torso.

The intermittent contact put her in a state of perpetual awareness. She felt as if a low hum of arousal buzzed inside her. He almost made her forget that they had made a deal, and she had practically sold herself to him.

He surprised her by preparing dinner. "All the Medici men cook. My father taught us at a young age. His father taught him and so on."

Emma watched him as he prepared a sauce with plum tomatoes, spinach, olive oil, spices. "That smells delicious."

"It will be," he said.

"Did your father ever live in Italy? Or was he raised here?"

Damien's jaw tightened. "He moved to the States when he was seventeen. His family went through a rough time in Italy and his father lost the family home in a business deal where he was cheated. Pretty much ruined them."

"That's terrible," she said.

He nodded. "Yeah. Things were looking up for my father right before he died, and everything fell apart again."

"You miss him," she said, sensing his grief.

"Yes. It was ironic. He and his brothers and sisters

were torn apart and the same thing happened to my brothers and me."

"I bet he would be proud of how well you've done," she said.

"Maybe," he said. "He was from the old school where if someone hurt a member of your family, it was your duty to pay them back."

"He wasn't Mafia, was he?" she asked, his dark tone making her wary.

Damien laughed. "No. Just very Italian. Here, try the sauce." He lifted a spoonful and blew on it before he extended it to her lips.

Emma tasted the spicy sauce and nodded. "Delicious."

"Yes, you are," he said, intently meeting her gaze.

They shared dinner on the terrace. Afterward, he coaxed her into taking a nude dip with him in the Jacuzzi surrounded by a teak lattice privacy screen. She'd thought all her tension from the trip was gone, but the velvet darkness and hot massaging water relaxed her even more.

"This is wonderful. It's a good thing I don't have one of these. I'd never get out," she said, feeling decadent and languid as she sipped the champagne he'd poured for her. "How often do you use it?"

"A couple of times since I arrived," he said, watching her from beneath a hooded gaze as he slid one of his legs between hers. "I've been too busy."

She felt another rush of arousal ooze through her.

She watched his gaze linger on her lips. Taking her hand, he lifted it to his mouth.

He was suddenly too far away and she suddenly couldn't wait a minute longer to be close to him. She moved closer and he immediately pulled her onto his lap. Skimming his hands over her naked, wet body underwater, he lowered his head and took her mouth in a sensual kiss that made her breathless.

He touched the tips of her breasts and kissed her again. "I've been thinking," he said.

"Oh, no," she said, her brain muddled by his effect on her.

"It's not so bad. I've been thinking that you and I should make our arrangement permanent."

Confusion warred with arousal. She frowned. "Permanent," she echoed.

He played with her nipples again, short-circuiting her thought process. "I think we should get married."

Shock raced through her and she gawked at him. "Married? I—I—"

He shot her a half grin before he took her mouth again, his hands distracting her. "Think it over," he murmured against her mouth. "Later."

Awakening the next morning to the sound of Damien in the shower, Emma stretched, feeling the aftereffects of Damien's repeated lovemaking. She covered her face with the sheet when she thought of how uninhibited she'd been.

Shaking off her self-consciousness, she rose from

his bed and pulled on the nightgown she'd never worn last night and went into the kitchen to make coffee. The scent of fresh coffee in a timed maker told her she was too late for that.

She poured herself a cup and added sugar and milk, then gingerly sipped the hot liquid. Hearing the scream of a fax machine, she walked down the hallway and opened the door to an office. A large cherry desk dominated the room lit by three-quarter length windows covered with linen shades.

The fax machine continued to scream and she heard a rustle of paper. Emma rearranged the paper in case it was jammed. Seconds later, several sheets flew onto the floor. Although she wasn't trying to read the fax, her gaze snagged on the name Max De Luca. Quickly scanning the document, she gleaned that it was a report with references to Max's late half brother.

Damien appeared in the doorway, already dressed in black slacks, his shirt not yet buttoned. He lifted a dark eyebrow of inquiry.

"I heard a strange noise from the fax machine. It sounded jammed, so I tried to clear it. What is this about Max De Luca?"

Damien walked toward her and she handed him the papers. "It's a report. I had him investigated. It's not unusual."

"But this mentions his brother. Well, the brother that died. Tony," she said, still confused.

Damien read over the paper. "It appears that Tony briefly worked for MD and stole some money from the company. One of the company attorneys was determined to prosecute. This says Max De Luca not only paid Tony's debt, he also paid the attorney to keep quiet and accept a transfer. Wonder what the board would think of this."

Emma gasped. "You wouldn't tell them, would you? I can't imagine why you would. It doesn't have anything to do with the downsizing."

Damien's jaw tightened. "Always protective of Max and Alex," he said in a velvet voice with an undertone of bitterness. "Don't worry. This is between Max and me."

Confused, she shook her head. "I don't understand."

He thumped the paper with his forefinger. "No. You wouldn't. You remember the story I told you about how my grandfather lost the family home in a business deal where he was cheated?"

"Yes," she said, wondering where this was going.

"Max De Luca's grandfather was the man who cheated my grandfather. My family home is a Megalos-De Luca resort."

"Oh, no," she said, horrified by the connection. Her mind and heart racing, she reached out to him. "That's horrible." She could hardly believe it. "I can't believe Max knows about this. He truly is an honorable man."

"Some might not agree," Damien said, tapping the papers that gave damning evidence.

Her stomach tightened in apprehension. "But you wouldn't use that against him because of something his grandfather did." A long moment of silence passed and she felt a terrible sense of dread. "Would you?"

"Three generations of my family have suffered in some part due to what the De Lucas did to my grandfather," he told her.

His harsh expression made her feel as if she were looking at a different man than the Damien she'd come to know. "How long have you known this?" she asked, trying to make sense of it all. "Why did you accept this assignment if you hated him so—" She broke off, suddenly realizing that Damien had taken the job with revenge in mind.

Emma felt as if her world had been turned upside down. If Damien was so consumed with revenge, where did she fit into the plot? He'd known she was protective of Max and Alex. He'd known…

Realization broke through. Her mind flashed back to that time when she'd told Damien about Max's and Alex's vulnerabilities. He'd used that information to dig deeper into Max's situation with his half brother. She'd given him the clue and he'd run with it.

Nausea swept through her. "You were just using me."

"Just as you were using me. Do you think I didn't know that you went to Alex and Max every time I told you something important?"

Humiliation stung. Overwhelmed, she shook her head. "I was doing my job."

"You tried to spy on me," he said.

The truth hurt, but her heart hurt even more. "I almost thought you cared about me."

"The irony is that I do, and I know you care about me. The situation is unfortunate."

"And you mentioned marriage last night. How could you even begin to think we could have a successful marriage?"

"You thought we could, too," he said. "Admit it."

Never, she thought. "I would never marry you, because I'd only marry for love, and you're not capable of it."

Thirteen

Damien tried to reason with Emma, but she recoiled at his touch. Concerned for her emotional state, he insisted on calling his driver to take her home. She left his condo without a backward glance.

The way she'd looked at him, as if he were a monster, sliced at his gut, but he pushed it aside. He had what he needed to bring down Max De Luca. For the sake of his family, he couldn't stop now.

Damien decided, however, that he wanted an opportunity to talk with Max before he took his final action. Giving his assistant a call, he was immediately put through to Max, and the VP agreed to meet with him.

He carried the report sealed in an envelope in his inner jacket pocket. In a way, he may as well have been carrying a loaded weapon. Max's assistant informed him of Damien's presence and he was ushered inside the VP's richly appointed office.

"Good morning, Damien," Max said. "Sarah, can you get us some coffee please? How do you take yours?"

"Black," Damien said.

Max nodded. "Same. Please have a seat," he said, motioning toward the leather chairs and sofa on the opposite side of the room as the desk. The magnificent view from the floor-to-ceiling windows revealed the mountains in the distance.

"Nice view," Damien said. It occurred to Damien that Max had never spent a day of his life outside the lap of luxury, a life far different than that of his family.

"I prefer the mountains to the strip. More serene."

Sarah delivered the coffee and excused herself.

"I understand employees who are being laid off will receive the news tomorrow?" Max asked, taking a sip of his coffee. "I have to confess I was against you from the beginning. Your reputation precedes you. When I look at the new organizational chart, however, it looks as if you skillfully used a scalpel instead of a hatchet."

Surprised by the praise, he nodded. "There is a right way and a wrong way to reorganize. Sometimes it takes an objective eye to spot redundancies and stay current with changing economies and needs."

"It's a painful process, but I think you made it as humane as possible. So, what do you have going next?"

The conversation felt surreal. Damien was talking

to the man he'd targeted for most of his life. He worked to access his contempt for the man, but for some reason it wasn't as strong as before.

"I may take some time off. I have a brother in Florida who is always bugging me to visit him."

Max lifted his eyebrows. "Time off? You don't strike me as the type. I know I wasn't until I got married. Lilli changed my priorities. Hell," he said. "She changed my life."

"The love of a good woman," Damien said.

Max nodded. "Yeah, although I would have been the last man to believe it was possible. Being a father will turn you around, too."

Silence lingered for a moment. "I'm curious," Damien said. "Did you know your grandfather well?"

"No. I do know that he was very focused on the company. He was determined to expand the empire, so to speak. My father had his own issues. It was left to me to try to rebuild the De Luca name. I had a half brother, but that's another sad story. What makes you ask?"

"Are you familiar with the MD Chateau on the outside of Florence, Italy?" Damien watched Max's face carefully.

Max furrowed his brow in concentration. "It's not in the city? Right?"

"No. It's in the countryside."

"I have a vague recollection, but I don't think I've ever visited it." He lifted his hand and met Damien's gaze. "Why? Is there a problem with it?"

"More the way it was acquired," he said.

"Okay," Max replied, leaning forward, lacing his fingers together. "What do you know about it?"

"I know that Chateau Megalos-De Luca was once Chateau de Medici and it belonged to my grandfather."

Fifteen minutes later, Damien walked out of Max De Luca's office feeling much different than he had going in. He stepped into the elevator thinking that Max De Luca had actually been somewhat reasonable. The damning report about the man felt as if it were burning a hole in his coat pocket.

Damien had spent most of his life fighting one thing or another, the loss of his family, an abusive foster parent, and poverty. He'd always thought that taking down Max De Luca would rid him of one of his biggest demons at the same time it would help right the wrong done to his grandfather.

Now that he had the chance to do it, his appetite for revenge had fled. It wasn't that Max De Luca was Mr. Nice Guy, because he wasn't. During that conversation with Max, though, Damien had seen glimpses of himself in the man he'd been prepared to hate.

Max was a family man. His top priority was taking care of his family. That was why he'd protected his half brother. Max's growing-up situation didn't sound all that rosy, either. His eyes lit up when he mentioned his wife and baby.

Exiting the elevator, Damien couldn't squelch his envy at the man's personal happiness. He couldn't help thinking about Emma and how he felt when he was with her. Just her presence made the world seem better. It was odd as hell, but she made him want to be better.

Swearing under his breath, he walked into his private office and paced the length of it. He pulled the envelope out of his pocket and stared at it. This was the opportunity he'd been waiting for most of his life. He had the gun and the bullet. All he had to do was pull the trigger.

Five minutes later, he'd made his decision and his deed, as far as he was concerned, was done. Hearing the door to the office suite open, he glanced into the outer office, surprised to see Emma.

His heart stuttered in his chest. "I didn't expect you to come in," he said.

She met his gaze, her eyes colder than ice. "I made an agreement. I try very hard to keep my word."

She slid into her chair and turned on her computer. She clearly hated him. The knowledge stabbed at him. The pain he felt took him by surprise. How had she become so important to him? He'd thought he had everything under control.

"I've done some thinking about our agreement," he said.

She shot him a look of suspicion, but said nothing.

"I'm terminating it effective immediately."

Her eyes widened in surprise. "I don't know how long it will take me to pay you back that kind of money, but—"

He lifted his hand. "You fulfilled your part of the agreement. You owe me nothing."

"But—" She lifted her hand to her throat. "But you said a year."

"I changed my mind," he said, giving her a wry smile. "Billionaire's prerogative. I can't buy your loyalty or your trust. I'm not sure I would want to if I could." He shrugged. "I'm cleaning out my office. I've finished this project. You can take off the rest of the day. Except one thing," he said. "I'd like you to make sure the paper in the shredder basket is destroyed."

She looked at him in confusion. "Okay. Would you like me to do that now?"

"Yes, I would," he said and stepped aside so she could go into his office to collect the basket. He caught a draft of her subtle, sweet scent as she passed him and clenched his jaw. He would never hold her again.

"Where do you want me to take it?" she asked.

"Somewhere off-site," he said.

She dipped her head in surprise.

"It's the report on Max De Luca," he said.

Her jaw dropped and she looked at him in surprise, followed by hope, followed by confusion. Clearing her throat, she licked her lips and nodded. "I'll take care of it right away," she said softly.

"Thank you," he said, meeting her gaze for a long moment, his mind replaying the times she'd smiled at him, the times she'd come to him and kissed him, the time they'd talked about wishes, and she'd made him start wishing again.

She looked away. "Thank you," she finally said. "For everything."

"Goodbye," he said, more for himself than for her. She was never going to be his. Never.

Emma considered stopping to throw the shredded report away at a mall, a service station, a fast-food restaurant. None seemed right, so she drove all the way to her apartment.

She was in shock, numb. She'd been so furious earlier this morning when she'd realized he'd used her. Furious with him for pointing out her deception with him. She considered her so-called spying assignment with Damien to be the lowest thing she'd ever done.

Then when she'd learned he had information he planned to use against Max, information she'd helped him find, she hadn't known who she detested more, Damien or herself.

It had taken everything in her to show up for work. She had to stick to the agreement for her mother's sake. She was fully prepared to despise him and resent him for the rest of her life.

But then he'd let her off the hook. No reprisals, no you-owe-me, nothing. On top of that, telling her to destroy the remnants of the report about Max totally boggled her mind. She didn't know what to think or feel.

Parking her car in the paved parking lot, she walked inside her apartment to get some matches and a pitcher of water. She returned to the parking lot, dumped the contents of the bin onto the pavement and burned them. Staring into the fire, she wondered what had made Damien decide not to go after Max. She wondered what had changed his mind.

As Damien had instructed, she took off the rest of the day. She caught up on cleaning her apartment and doing laundry, turned on the television for a while, then turned it off. Fighting a bone-deep restlessness, she escaped her apartment and visited a park.

She saw a couple and thought of Damien. She saw a golden retriever and thought of Damien. Frustrated with herself, she went to a movie by herself, a foreign film, French. Surely that would distract her. Except midway through the movie, an Italian character was introduced. She began to feel haunted.

Bedtime finally arrived and Emma crawled into bed, craving escape from Damien. Instead, she dreamed of him. She dreamed he died and she woke up in a cold sweat, screaming.

Hugging her knees to her chest, she gasped for breath. Something had changed, she realized. Without really knowing it, some part of her had begun to count on him. She'd been so busy doubting him, but something inside her had made another determination about him.

Her heart? Somehow, someway, she had begun to love him.

Her stomach twisted with the realization and she laughed, the harsh, bitter sound breaking the silence of the night. How futile was that? she thought. If ever a man was incapable of love, it was Damien.

Damien missed his next shot. He was winning against his brother, but not by much.

Rafe downed a shot of tequila and made a hissing sound. "You're off your game, bro," he said and chalked the cue.

"I'm doing okay," Damien said, taking a sip of scotch.

"Got something on your mind?" Rafe asked, banking a shot that just missed the pocket. "Damn," he muttered and raked his hand through his hair. "What's up? You've been walking around crabby and distracted since you got here."

Damien shrugged. "This was a big contract. Sometimes it takes awhile to wind down." He took a shot against another ball. And missed. He swore under his breath.

"Sounds like BS to me," Rafe said. He took a shot and sank it into the pocket. "Score," he said, then missed the next one.

Damien gritted his teeth and lined up his next shot.

"This wouldn't have anything to do with that pretty assistant you brought onboard when you visited South Beach a few weeks ago, would it?"

Damien scratched the table with his cue and glared at his brother for his bad timing. "I wouldn't go there if I were you."

"Why not?" Rafe asked. "If I keep pushing on that

raw place, I may win. Then I can hold it over your head for years."

"In your dreams," Damien said.

Rafe chuckled but missed his next shot.

Damien swallowed a growl and chalked his cue.

"She must not have liked you. Did she dump you?" Rafe taunted.

Damien clenched his jaw, then forced himself to relax.

"Did she decide she wanted a man with a heart *and* brains?"

Rafe's words cut close, but Damien ruthlessly turned him off. He focused on his shot and sank the last ball into the pocket. Taking a deep breath, he heard Rafe swear and lifted his glass of scotch in salute.

"How do you do that? Even on an off day," Rafe said.

"I'm hungrier than you are," Damien said. He felt not an ounce of satisfaction at beating his brother. "I always have been."

"Hungry enough to go after Miss Emma Weatherfield?" Rafe asked.

Damien met Rafe's gaze. "I've been hungry to survive, to succeed. Women come and go. I'm usually glad when they go."

"But not this time," Rafe said with a knowing glance.

Damien sighed. "You can be a real pain in the butt."

Rafe stretched his lips in a sharklike smile. "Part of my charm." His brother moved toward him and clapped him on the back. "I think you've met your waterloo."

Damien shook his head, not wanting it to be true. But

it was. "She despises me. I—" He paused. "I seduced information out of her. She'll never forgive me."

"If she surrendered to the seduction, then she can't totally despise you," Rafe said.

Damien threw him a sideways glance.

"Unless you blew it in some other way."

Damien shifted from one foot to the other.

"Like omitting the four-letter word that starts with *L*," Rafe said.

"What makes you an expert?" Damien asked, feeling as if he was being fried alive.

Rafe lifted his hand. "Nothing. I've just heard that women really want to hear the L word. For some of them, it's a requirement. But if she's not a keeper, then—"

"She's a keeper," Damien retorted.

Silence followed and he met Rafe's gaze again.

Rafe lifted his eyebrows. "I think you just answered your question."

Damien sank into a leather chair and exhaled. "It's not that easy. I screwed it up."

"That hasn't stopped you from succeeding with your business or anything else you've wanted. Why would it stop you now?"

Damien raked his fingers through his hair. "You don't know."

"I don't have to," Rafe said. "I just know that if this woman makes you feel like you found home, then you better find a way to keep her or you'll spend the rest of your life regretting it."

* * *

Emma pulled her Tesla Roadster into a parking spot just outside her condominium and cut the engine. Sitting for a moment, she leaned against the steering wheel and stared out the window.

A familiar restlessness rippled through her. Maybe it was time for her to leave Las Vegas. Maybe it was time for her to leave Megalos-De Luca.

The mere notion was shocking. She'd thought she would stay at MD forever, but lately she'd felt dissatisfied and unhappy. She felt like Goldilocks, except there was no "just right."

Sighing, she dismissed her ongoing dissatisfaction and rose from her car. She had a great job with excellent pay, a fabulous car and nice friends. She had no reason to whine.

Since Damien had completed his contract with MD, she'd been reassigned to a new VP, a nice older gentleman planning to retire in two years. Her stomach no longer knotted in apprehension as she arrived at the headquarters. Her heart didn't race. Everything was back to normal.

Emma had never thought she'd want anything but a normal, stable life until now. She missed Damien. She missed his passion. She missed his strength. She even missed his flaws.

"You can't have him," she whispered to herself. "So stop thinking about him."

Stepping inside her apartment, she closed the door behind her. She heard a scratching sound and— A bark? Seconds later, a small mass of fur with long floppy ears ran toward her barking and wagging its tail.

Emma gaped at the puppy and immediately kneeled to the floor. "Who are you? And how did you get in here?"

The white-and-caramel colored spaniel jumped into her lap. How had the dog gotten into her apartment? Emma laughed as the puppy licked her chin.

"Lucky dog," said a low, familiar voice from the doorway.

Emma's heart stuttered. She jerked her head upward and stared at Damien as he leaned against the doorjamb. She blinked to make sure she wasn't hallucinating.

"What are you—" Her chest squeezed so tightly that she couldn't finish her question.

"Doing here?" he finished for her and pushed away from the doorjamb, walking toward her. "Some people would say I'm a glutton for punishment, but when I find something I want, I don't like to quit."

Emma bit the inside of her lip. "Something?" she said.

"Someone," he said and extended his hand.

She slid her hand in his strong, warm palm and allowed him to help her stand.

"You like your new dog?" he asked, his lips lifting in a faint smile as the puppy danced at their feet.

"Mine?" she echoed. "I work all day. I shouldn't

have a dog. It's not fair to him." But how could she possibly resist those eyes? she thought.

"What if you didn't need to work all day? Or what if you could bring your dog to work?"

"MD would never go for that," she said, giving a short laugh at the idea.

"I would," he said. "You could come to work for me. I'd double your salary."

Emma dropped her jaw.

"Or," he said, carefully watching her. "You could put me out of my misery and marry me."

Emma's head was spinning. It took her a full moment to find her voice. "Misery?" she said.

He stepped closer and slid his fingers through her hair, tilting her head so that she could see his face, the ruthless scar and dark gaze full of passion and something far deeper. "I've been missing a home most of my life. Being with you makes me feel like I finally found where I belong."

Emma's knees weakened and she felt her eyes well with tears. "Oh, Damien," she whispered. "I never thought this was possible. I never thought you would let me into your heart."

"Trust me, woman. You're in," he said in a rough voice.

Emma saw the love shining in his eyes and felt as if she needed to pinch herself.

"You think you can go the distance with me? You turned me away before."

Emma shook her head. "I was afraid of how much I felt for you. And then you told me to leave."

"That was pure hell. I didn't want you to stay because I was forcing you."

She studied his face. "And part of the reason you decided not to go after Max—"

"Was you," he finished for her. "It just didn't seem as important anymore."

Emma shook her head. "We've both made mistakes."

He took a deep breath and expelled it, looking away from her. "I thought you hated me."

"I thought I should," she said, feeling a deep stab of pain even as she said the words. "I hated myself for trying to deceive you."

"I understood."

Emma felt her throat knot and her eyes sting with unshed tears. If he'd come back after she'd turned him away, then she needed to bare her heart to him. It was only fair. "You're an amazing man. I don't know when it happened, but somewhere along the line, you became my soulmate, my rescuer. Somewhere along the line you made me belong to you."

His nostrils flared as he drew in another breath. "Amazing, huh. Amazing enough for you to marry?"

Her heart stopped. "Do you love me?"

He closed his eyes for a moment and her heart seemed to sink into the floor.

"I don't know much about love, but I know I

love you. More than my life. More than I ever thought possible."

Emma couldn't hold back the tears any longer. "Oh, Damien." She slid her arms around the back of his neck, craving his closeness. "We could have given up on each other. The thought of it terrifies me."

"It wouldn't have happened. If I couldn't convince you, then I hoped the dog would." His gaze turned serious. "More than anything, I wanted to hear you say you believe in me."

"I do," she said, lifting her hand to his cheek. "I'll believe in you for the rest of our lives."

Damien pulled her off her feet against him. "And I love you. Lord, you feel good. How do you feel about getting married in Vegas?"

She smiled, feeling giddy. "Anywhere is good."

"And how do you feel about a honeymoon in Italy?"

She drew back slightly to look into his face. His lips turned up at the edges and his eyes glinted with happiness. "I talked with Max. He did some research into the dirty deal his grandfather did with mine and he has set aside a cottage for the Medici family forever."

Stunned, she stared at him. "You're kidding."

He shook his head. "He's a stand-up guy just like you said."

"You're the most stand-up guy I've ever met," she said, thinking of how many times he had already come through for her. She was the luckiest woman in the world.

"I love you," he said simply. "And I'll spend the rest of my life making your wishes come true."

"I love you, too." She knew, with all her heart, that he was telling the truth. She also knew, with all her heart, that her biggest wish had just come true.

* * * * *

A sneaky peek at next month…

By Request

RELIVE THE ROMANCE WITH THE BEST OF THE BEST

My wish list for next month's titles…

In stores from 17th May 2013:

❏ The Hudsons: Luc, Jack and Charlotte –
  Leanne Banks, Emily McKay & Barbara Dunlop

❏ Bella Rosa Proposals – Jackie Braun,
  Barbara McMahon & Barbara Hannay

3 stories in each book - only £5.99!

In stores from 7th June 2013:

❏ The Spaniard's Summer Seduction
  – Kim Lawrence, Cathy Williams, Maggie Cox

Available at WHSmith, Tesco, Asda, Eason, Amazon and Apple

Just can't wait?

0513/05